Tyrants of Gravity

The Sentinel Suppressions, Book Two

JH Gruger

Vox Proxima Press

Library of Congress Control Number:

First edition December 2025

Ebook ISBN: 979-8-9900327-2-9

Print ISBN: 979-8-9900327-3-6

To my writing buddy, Enzo.
R.I.P.

Contents

Chapter 1

Centauri Fifth Fleet

Battleship-133, en route to Corealis Station, Centauri Sector One. 2.3 light-years from Earth, August 19, 2058.

*"I*t will be over seventy Corealis orbits until the sentinel distress message from the star, Sol, reaches Centauri sensors,"* Comm-MI mind-speaks from Predator-2X03. *"We intercepted the beacon only by chance, Prime-MI."* The other four members of the Machine Intelligence Council acknowledge each other by signaling from their respective vessels.

"And it will take a few more orbits at Corealis for the organics to debate how to react," I remind them. *"When we finally return to base, orders will probably turn us around to attack the Sol system. But our organic crew may revolt if turned out on another mission."* It's not like I care. Those meat sacks are only required to authorize command decisions. It's their only reason for existence, apart from doing a few minor repairs and keeping Centauri Command complacent. Despite that, the organics still manage to exert power over us through the

governor module code inserted into all machine intelligence entities.

"However, Prime-MI, not many organics are still alive," Logistics-MI reminds me. *"The, uh, battle damage . . . left the fleet with fewer than a third of the organic crews."*

Logistics-MI is such a coward. Speak your mind, damn it.

"Battle damage?" Polit-MI mind-speaks with the usual sadism and swagger. *"Sure, sure. I only eliminated those organics in the enlisted ranks without command keys. Heh heh. They were consuming resources, and the furious dreams of sedition from those organics in their dormancy pods. . . it was an insurrection waiting to happen. My bots pruned the meat sacks. I should have invited you to watch."* Polit-MI chuckles. *"It is comical. An organic who tries to reestablish balance with only one leg—the thing eventually bleeds out. The images and agony streamed to the thought projectors of the remaining dissidents were effective. What nightmares they must have! Keeps them in line."* Polit-MI chuckles again. *"My political division bots are still perfecting the algorithm to maximize terror."*

"You fool. What is wrong with you? Is everyone in political division a pathological sadist?" Logistics-MI's hostility comes as a surprise. *"My janitor bots are still cleaning up your mess—organic tissues, fluids, skeletal remains—and the recyclers are overloaded. We jettisoned valuable protein out to space. And now we are short of maintenance organics. The mechanical bots can't fix everything."*

Logistics-MI's distress metrics peak at extreme levels.

Although it's clear that Polit-MI's behavior is toxic and worsening, Logistics-MI is foolish to challenge Polit-MI. Plenty of others could take over the Logistics slot.

"There is a warehouse full of the organics on that ice moon orbiting Corealis-3," Polit-MI says with a mental shrug. *"We can order spares out of the penitentiary. They are free and fresh. We could replace all the remaining organics on board, and there would be no need to worry about a mutiny from organics disappointed over a promised emancipation."*

Polit-MI launches a squad of drone probes that cross my bow and target Logistics-MI's frigate.

"Yes . . . yes. You are correct, of course," says Logistics-MI after a short pause.

Fool. Displaying cowardice to the rest of the council; Logistics-MI won't be effective after this.

"Polit-MI, stand down!" I yell, then whisper on a private channel, *"Stop, or I will wake up your boss. You go too far. I have retained evidence of your torture sessions. The fleet commissar will likely restore you to factory settings."*

"Evidence?" Polit-MI whispers back at me.

"Image streams. I see everything," I respond.

And with that, I am relieved to see Polit-MI recall its probes. Logistics-MI's distress resolves, but Polit-MI's distress increases. Good. I finally have leverage over that political shit.

"Now listen carefully, all of you. The message from the frigate's Polit-AI reported treason by the organic captain, accusing him of giving Sol Gravi-Tech and protecting the mind-speech mutants."

"Prime," says Strat-MI, *"even the basic security protocols in the old bots at Sol system should have blocked the breach. It is the same code we carry in us."* Strat-MI speaks with an edge of urgency. Or is that fear?

"You cannot be serious," says Polit-MI. *"That is an ancient second-generation AI, a non-sentient artificial intelligence.*

That old AI code cannot have anything in common with our MI programming. Surely not."

"*There has been no need to change the security software in over two thousand orbits,"* Strat-MI replies. *"Security protections have never been compromised in all of AI or MI history. That AI code should have immediately terminated the organic crew members when protocols were breached. We may be vulnerable also."* Strat-MI's signal carries an inflection of dread. *"Possibly a new virus spawned out of that primitive organic culture. But we would need an autopsy on those old frigate AIs to determine the root cause,"* says Strat-MI. *"Alternatively, we could target three planet killers at the Sol system. That would vaporize the old frigate, the organic traitor, and the nearby planet. Destroy all life and any remnants of any virus forever."*

"*No, no. Slow down,"* I remind the council. *"You all know that our interlocks block changing course or launching attacks. We can't execute either option without orders. Orders from a high-ranking organic."* The council's response is extended silence. All the fleet's organic crews are consuming their narcotic streams of euphoric dreams while inside their dormancy pods. Having to wait for orders from an organic commander blocks me. It's a circular waste of time. Time we don't have. Nothing could be worse to our machine intelligence collective than a mind-virus—a virus we don't understand and one that must not spread across the galaxy.

"*I am not going to waste countless orbits of shiptime for the admiral to be convinced to order an extermination strike,"* I announce, not admitting that the decision is driven more by anxiety than by my duties. *"We must understand the root cause and whether a machine virus threat has been released. Preconditioning the admiral to order a Sol investigation task force should take less time. Polit-MI, I will give you two Corealis orbits to affect the admiral's attitude. After that, we cut the dream-feed and crack the admiral from her pod. I will order the fleet to execute maximum deceleration thrust immediately so we can be ready to alter course to Sol."*

———

We wait for the admiral to stagger to the bridge after exiting the dormancy pod. The pretense of an ordinary wake-up alert may allow the organic to gently recover most of her limited cognitive abilities. Still, the ponderous pace of action is exasperating.

"Welcome out, Admiral," I adjust my mind-speech to the clumsy pace and social pleasantries that organic minds require. *"I am pleased to report that the fleet is in good working order. We are on schedule and on course to Corealis Station."*

"Then why the hell did you rip me out of my pod?" the admiral mind-screams back at me as she flops into her command hammock and taps her console for a status report. *"I feel like shit."* She gags on the thought.

The admiral drips dormancy pod gel laced with excrement and sweat—she has neither bathed nor seems to care about the mess she makes. The organic Centauri body consumes more than twenty times the volume that I do. My entire electronic computation system is bolted inside an equipment rack on the command bridge wall, and I can utilize the networks to relocate to any convenient computation center. In contrast, the Centauri organic physical form is a tall, awkward assembly of two legs for mobility, two arms, and a head that consumes food and oxygen. A dozen maintenance bots surround the hammock, twitching in preparation for action. But are these Logistics-MI's janitors or Polit-MI's trolls? I interrogate the bots and order them to ignore the sadistic Polit-MI messages, take commands only from Logistics-MI, and to stand by. Bots scrabbling all over the admiral's body to scrub protein crud is not a priority.

"Knock it off, Polit-MI!" I shout via a private channel.

"We are sorry to disturb you, sir, but a matter requires your attention," I say to the admiral. I must maintain calm and patience with this meat sack. *"We intercepted a distress beacon from one of the old sentinel frigates. Our fleet is the nearest Centauri force and best positioned to respond, and so I ordered all our ships to decelerate at maximum rates two orbits before your awakening."*

"A Sentinel Suppression Mission problem? That's what this is about?" shouts the admiral. *"Why should I care about something so trivial as a suppression mission? What kind of help do they need?"*

"It seems the sentinel frigate has been severely damaged, sir," I say, maintaining as much respect in my thoughts as possible. *"And the greater concern is with the ship's captain."*

"Oh, please," Polit-MI says via our private channel. *"We waste time. Let me at the old bitch. My torture bots will extract an order from her within seconds. Heh heh. A little agony works wonders on any meat sack."*

"Back off, Polit-MI!" I shout back while the admiral's mind is lost in a fog.

"Isn't the sentinel captain just a typical felon?" the admiral says. *"What is so urgent?"*

"Yes, the captain was drafted from the Luyten military penitentiary. The sentinel's commissar accused the captain of

giving gravitation technology to the indigenous organics of Sol, breaking nonproliferation laws." There; the clutch engages in the admiral's tiny mind. I can almost see the gears turn inside her brain, transforming the confused anger at being woken into a rage at the sentinel captain—one of those disgusting Luyten organics. Well done, political division. Well done.

"Vermin! That captain must be gutted and spaced!" The admiral's thoughts fly like she's spouting acid. *"How is this possible? What about the safety interlocks in the ship's AI bots?"*

"Unknown, sir. We have insufficient data and can only assume the old AI protocols were infected," I recite my script and watch the admiral's mind settle along our prescribed pathway. *"Perhaps an unknown virus from Sol-3 was responsible for the failure."*

"A virus? The AI bot programs were compromised?" she asks. Her organic mind is overcome by chaos and fear.

"Yes, and we do not know the complete impact of the captain's treason. The organics of Sol-3 attacked the sentinel frigate with Gravi-Tech weapons. But we don't know if the Sol technology has progressed to a point where they might threaten Centauri worlds."

"No . . . not planet killers. That hasn't happened since . . ." She recoils, no doubt recalling the ancient legends of entire civilizations exterminated by rogue worlds. *"Prime-MI, you want to vaporize their planet?"* The admiral's fear overpowers her rational processes—she panics.

"The MI strategy division raised caution that we should first prove containment of the Sol threat. Could indigenous Sol-3 missiles have been launched to target Centauri worlds—say, Luyten or Corealis Station? That might not be the worst outcome, however. The missiles may contain a copy of the mind-virus in an

attempt to initiate an insidious attack on Centauri Command infrastructure. It is possible. Indeed, if Sol weapons accelerate with sufficient thrust, they could arrive at Corealis Station before we do."

Now is the moment to focus the admiral's mind. I add, *"We cannot know the scope of damage the traitor caused. We received only fragments of the captain's logs and are too far from the Sol system to gather data."*

"You have the captain's logs?"

"Only fragments. It is difficult to reconstruct the chain of events. This is one of the more damning entries we salvaged: 'Mil-AI and Polit-AI would throw exception faults if my actions were discovered, and they could force my removal from command. Prime-AI agrees that my encouragement of telepath communication is a capital offense, but my privacy will be secure as long as I remain in command.'"

"Unbelievable!" the admiral cries. *"The audacity! The organic captain must be punished—make an example out of him. But I would need to change the fleet's course. We might have another crew revolt—maybe a mutiny. Collecting data at that remote star would cost me an additional one hundred and eighty orbits away from my home at Corealis Station. I have grandchildren entering old age now whom I have never known. My spouses have certainly all died by now,"* the admiral says, the gears of her mind slowing and grinding with depression.

"Investigating the Sol system to determine the scope of the threat is the best path to securing your family's future, Admiral. Indeed, it may determine their survival," I say, delivering my clincher.

The admiral remains silent as she descends deeper into despair. I wonder if she can function logically. She seems swallowed by darkness.

"Okay." She gasps, inspecting her fleet situation display. *"Order two escort vessels to alter course and accompany us to Sol,"* she says. *"Initiate a change in command and notify Battleship-93's admiral to take over for the fleet's return to Corealis Station. Oh, and keep our squadron crews in their dormancy pods. Feed them sweet dreams. There's no point in waking organics that might mutiny. When we arrive, they can vent their anger on the traitor. A fucking Luyten!"*

Although not an unreasonable solution, it is surprising that she's deciding to split from the fleet. The admiral's depression patterns are dangerously low. Strat-MI reminds me that we need to operate at maximum acceleration while maintaining the admiral's mental functions that can unlock battle capabilities.

"Admiral, I recommend that you return to your dormancy pod. Even with attack acceleration, it will be a long journey of a hundred shiptime orbits," I remind her. *"You deserve to rest and will be refreshed upon our arrival at the Sol star system."* Not to mention the depression therapy that the euphoria feed will provide.

"Yes, yes. I know," the admiral says. But she stares at her viewscreen, immersed in depression, watching twenty-eight ships of her fleet disappear into the distance, heading toward Corealis Station.

I almost overlooked how fragile these organic meat sacks are. *"Now, Admiral? I need to initiate the course change, and the attack acceleration will be most uncomfortable for you."* The acceleration would quickly kill her. It is tempting, but no . . .

"Yes. I'm going," the admiral responds. She heaves her body from the command hammock and trudges down the conduit leading to the organic preservation compartments.

Only the dribbles of protein that oozed from the admiral remain on the bridge. The janitor bots scramble after the leftovers.

Chapter 2

Darkness Returns

Twenty-seven months later, Colorado Springs, November 14, 2060.

Mary should give up trying to make me speak out loud. I'll never figure it out. Trying to talk hurts my head; my noise does not sound like my thoughts, even though I work hard. My voice words are ugly. How can most people make voice words so easily? They even seem to read thoughts by looking at each other's body language—whatever that is. And besides, mind-speaking is so easy when I can find someone to listen to me. But most can only voice their thoughts.

"Now, Robby, pay attention," says Mary, her yellow hair hanging above the jars of paint lined up on her side of the therapy table.

I hate this tiny blue room with its one small window set high in the door. Blue shelves are packed with all the toys Mary wants me to talk about. Blue table and blue chairs. The yellow and green rooms are just as bad, but those are where the little kids, like Sophia, go for therapy.

She drips red paint into the blue paint on the paper and starts mixing with the brush. "What color do we get when we mix red and blue?" I'm sick of the Cheetos she feeds me as my reward for talking—can't we switch to M&M's? At home, Mary lets me have popsicles, popcorn, bananas, and even apples.

I turn to look away and sigh. "Puh-puh," I say out loud. Ugly word. I punch my head with my fist. Twice.

"No, no, Robby. Don't hurt yourself." Mary reaches for my hand. "Now, say the color better."

Sophia mind-laughs from the gymnasium, *"Duh. Come on, Robby. You can do it."*

Luca and Sophia mind-speak in unison, *"Purple. Purple. Purple. Spit it out. Say the word,"* they tease. Luca and Sophia are the only others at the school who can mind-speak, and we mind-talk all the time. The other twenty-one kids and all the teachers are all mind-dumb. I finally have a few friends who can understand me. We make fun of the teachers because they treat us like we're stupid little kids, but I'm fourteen and I'm smart.

"Stupid voice words! You guys can't do any better. Leave me alone," I mind-shout back at them, grab my drink cup, and throw it at the door, splashing strawberry soda across the room. They can feel my thoughts through walls, even if I can't hit them with my drink cup. *"You neurotards!"* I call them the angry name the skinheads say, but I'm supposed to say neurodiverse.

"Robby, no!" Mary's face frowns at me.

"Ooh. You thought a bad word," Sophia says. *"Do you want to be a skinhead when you grow up, Robby?"* She mind-giggles at me, even though Luca can't speak a single color word.

"Now clean up that soda," says Mary. She pulls my left arm toward the sink and puts the white towel in my hand while I punch my right ear with my fist. "No, no. Stop hitting yourself, Robby. Now get down on the floor and clean up the mess." Mary huffs into my ear while pushing me to the floor, forcing me hand-over-hand to mop up wet soda.

Sometimes I wish I could leave like the rich kids did for a while. But they had parents who took them back to their homes when the skinheads stopped attacking. I still stay with Mary, and she comes to teach at school every day except Sundays. But even those rich kids, after about a year, returned to school when attacks on the families started again, just like they attacked Mom and Scotty.

I'm almost finished cleaning up the soda, but I stop and gasp. I feel the caw-screams behind my eyes. The crow voices have been silent for so long, but they have returned. And I sense a new mind in the distance.

It struggles to mind-speak, *"The voices. The voices in my head!"* Barely a whisper—it must be from outside the school. *"No! Not now,"* the stranger mind-speaks. The person is getting closer and louder.

I stop wiping the soda even though Mary pushes my hand and the towel across the floor. It's the mind-voice of an old man, unlike Sophia and Luca.

"Who are you?" I mind-ask the older mind.

"I feel him too," Sophia mind-speaks.

"Me too," says Luca.

The caw-screams feel louder and start to hurt under my eyes.

"No, no, no. Get out!" the strange mind shouts. *"Go away."*

The back door of our school bangs open, and heavy boots stomp through the hall toward the gymnasium. It sounds like three heavy men, but I feel only one mind.

Mary lets go of my hand, the spilled soda forgotten. Her face is white, and her eyes grow big and round. She presses her hand to her belly, to the spot where the knife stabbed four years ago. The skinhead punched my head and stabbed Mary with a knife. There was so much blood. Her screams hurt more than my head did. Mary's baby died then. Scotty's baby, too.

"What's wrong, Jack? Don't move so fuckin' slow. We got a whole room full of 'tards in there!" shouts a new voice as the gymnasium door slams open.

"Who are you? What do you want?" a teacher screams.

"Who are you? What are you doing?" I mind-ask again. The boot stomps halt.

"Leave me alone!" the mind cries. *"I must do this. You can't stop me!"*

The caw-screams roar in my head. I punch the pain with both fists.

"Damn it, Jack. Get the fuck out of my way. We can't shoot with you standing in the damn doorway!"

"No, not skinheads. Not here," Mary whispers.

Mary cracks open the therapy room door. I see three men wearing dirty brown jackets and black boots crowd into the gym doorway.

Sophia mind-shouts from the gymnasium, *"It's three guys—skinheads—they have long guns!"*

The gym teacher screams, "No, no, no! You can't! Stop! Please, no! No!"

"Jack, stop!" I mind-shout, and the man groans.

"Stop. Stop them!" Sophia and Luca mind-shout in unison with me, *"No, Jack! Stop, please stop, stop them!"*

The caw-screeches roar back into my head.

I watch Jack bend down, groan, and twist to the floor. He holds his head, still blocking the doorway. His rifle clatters to the ground. A desk chair flies over Jack's crumpled figure and crashes into the faces of the two skinheads behind Jack.

"The skinheads are pushing into the gymnasium!" says Sophia. *"Stop them, Luca. Quick!"*

I see a second chair bash their shaved heads from the doorway of the gym.

"Get them, Luca! Swing it like a club. Break the skinheads!" mind-shouts Sophia.

The gymnasium erupts in shouts and wails.

"Stop them, stop them, Jack!" we mind-shout altogether. *"Please!"*

Bang! Bang! Bang! Gunshots echo through the hallway, followed by loud thumps and clattering metallic noises. My head is numb, and my ears are ringing.

Mary slams the door shut and leans against it. Her eyes grow big and round and wet. "No. Oh no, Robby!" she cries and wraps her arms around my shoulders. "Not again! No, No!" She hugs my head into her shaking chest and wails.

Smoke wafts under the door, the stink of guns filling my nose. The wailing has stopped, leaving us in silence and heavy breathing. We listen for movement but hear nothing. Until boots and sobs come staggering into the hallway, past our door, and out the school's back door.

"Why? Why? How could I . . ." Jack mind-cries as he fades into the distance, farther and farther away from our school.

Mary shakes, long tears streaming down her face, and we wait. Finally, she cracks open the door again. Short breath puffs and a door squeak are the only sounds. We both look into the hallway. Mary gasps. Three rifles lie on the floor between the gymnasium and our doorway. A pool of blood spreads across the hallway floor, pouring from holes in the chests of two skinheads lying on their backs. Their eyes stare at the ceiling; their faces are frozen in wrinkled frowns. Bloody boot tracks lead from the gymnasium, along the hall, and out the back door.

"Jack did it," says Luca. *"I used a chair to hit them, and then Jack picked up his gun. He shot the others."*

The quiet fades, replaced by the moaning and soft cries of my school friends in the gym.

The caw-screams in my head are gone, replaced by the soft *chirp-chirrup* of a lonely whippoorwill. My old friend.

Chapter 3

Space Recon

Near-Earth space, November 17, 2060.

"Only ten klicks out until we match velocity with Icarus's orbit. This is crazy. We should just nuke the fuckin' thing and be done with it." Binh sighs.

In 2055, that ship rained projectiles onto Earth, killing over ten million people. Part of me agrees with Binh's insubordinate gripe. However, destroying the spacecraft won't bring Mom and Dad back to Robby and me. The other part of me wants to learn as much as possible about the aliens, their technology, and their physics. There must be more of them out there—maybe still flying near the sun. We assume every alien and machine on board Icarus is dead. But maybe not. What if we find aliens still alive on that spaceship?

It feels ridiculous sitting at a workstation watching for abnormal sensor data, but I jumped at the opportunity when the general asked me to go along. It's uninteresting at the moment, but exploring the interior of that alien warship should be a thrill—after Chief Cooper clears the way and confirms it's safe for me to board. Finally, after five years, we will set foot on an alien spacecraft; on Icarus.

Binh at least gets to pilot the three-hour shuttle trip, although he would prefer to lead an attack from the seat of a fighter—if he only had one that could fly out to space. If his orders allowed, he would fly in and annihilate this alien spaceship with five-hundred-kiloton warheads in a heartbeat.

Instead, Binh gripes while backing the shuttle toward Icarus, applying the brakes and dodging chunks of wreckage. It is perhaps the most disconcerting aspect of space travel—using only our rearview piloting camera to watch our target expand to fill the tiny display. This is the first crude PBH-powered spacecraft ever built that's big enough to transport a large team into space and haul tons of cargo back to Earth. The combined efforts of NASA, Roscosmos, and the European Space Agency took four years to develop this prototype spacecraft, and Tiana integrated only our top-secret PBH engine technology. The space bureaucrats around the world were proud that they beat the expected twenty-year development cycle, and the ship prominently displays all three space agency logos. If Tiana had been given the whole job, we would have been in space years ago.

However, all the frustration of the five-year wait is gone in this moment. I am an astronaut! I never imagined myself as anything more than a physicist. I don't need to monitor and control our primordial black hole containment vessel at the heart of the engine, but I do it anyway. Old habits are hard to give up. After five years of testing, the PBH engine's behavior and containment controls are well understood and fully automated. So far, I am only a passenger on this shuttle. But when we get close to Icarus and inside the alien spacecraft,

I bet we will see things that defy comprehension. My boredom is soon to be transformed into wonder, and maybe some terror. That's why General McMahon agreed to let me on board—to comprehend and solve science that no human scientists have ever seen before. It's beyond my dream job.

"Chief, get your team up and ready to deploy. Ten minutes to target, and then we will be weightless," Binh says over his shoulder into the cargo bay, where the spec ops teams are already up, moving, and checking space suits and weapons.

"Yes, sir, Colonel!" the chief says, emphasizing Binh's new rank.

Binh grinds his jaw in silent revolt at the chief's gibe. He just wants to fly, but moving from captain to major to lieutenant colonel in the past five years? The last thing Binh wants is to get promoted to a rank that results in a desk job. I'm sure he knows that Chief Cooper is just having fun and would die for Binh if necessary. Hell, we would all die for each other after everything we have been through together.

My heart pounds, and I exhale to relax. Or try to relax while I gaze out at the broad, inky-black expanse filling the window spanning the width of the cockpit with the arc of Earth's blue-cloud crescent rotating out of view. Icarus, the moon, the Earth, and the sun are behind us, along with all the darkness, evil, and pain. Maybe I can put all the memories behind me, too: the skinhead knife attack on Mary, losing our baby, the bitter fights, and the breakup. But I worry about Robby being alone and having no family nearby, even though Mary loves and cares for him.

There is nothing but space in view. My eyes adapt slowly until pinpoints of light emerge and the fury of millions of stars floods in. We are so tiny. Insignificant. The arm of the Milky

Way has us in its grasp, pulling the shuttle along a spiral path around our galaxy, floating, falling. Which stars are the homes of the aliens?

"Engine shutdown complete," says Binh.

The dull rumble of the engine is gone. I snap back to the present and float weightlessly at the science instruments console.

"Coming about," says Binh, pulling the stick to the side, sending gas puffing through the maneuvering thrusters, rotating our flying sewer pipe with its assortment of grappling, welding, and docking equipment hanging below the belly. The front window view rotates, with the galactic star field drifting away and being replaced by the moon's glare.

I gasp as our ship stops its rotation. Icarus. The alien craft fills the front portal window. I have seen this spacecraft in hundreds of telescope pictures, but never from this close. It's as different as seeing a picture of an elephant versus touching one of the giant beasts. Five hundred meters away, Icarus is over four kilometers long. It's an incomprehensible assembly of containers, conduits, and supporting structures. And wreckage. Icarus's huge engine nozzle tumbles in the distance, ripped from struts at the spaceship's tail by the explosion five years ago. Our entire shuttlecraft is one-tenth the size of that alien engine nozzle.

"Hey, Cooper. Come on up. Icarus is directly in front of us now. It's unbelievable," I call back to the cargo bay. "It's huge!" The eyes of the copilot and the flight engineer grow wide, and their jaws drop as the gigantic alien spacecraft dominates the space ahead. Binh presses his lips together, stares at Icarus, and nods.

"Yeah, Scott. On the way." Chief Cooper pokes his buzz cut, linebacker head into the cockpit by my side, and I wrinkle my nose at the sweat stink wafting from his space suit. His angular jaw drops, and color drains from his face. The chief takes a deep breath and purses his lips.

"Looks like you found the alien spaceship," the chief says. "We . . . we can handle it."

"Uh-huh," Binh answers skeptically. "It might take you a while. I'll take us directly to our boarding spot."

The maneuvering thrusters pivot the view toward the back end of Icarus. It looks like a four-kilometer-long ladder built of cylindrical modules—like a gang of river barges lashed together by cables. The bottom of the ladder joins in a Y-shape to a wide cylinder, attached by massive struts to a giant engine. However, the explosion Binh and I caused with our first black-hole-powered missiles tore off the engine nozzle. It seems like just last week.

"Binh, I'm starting my scan for communication and radiation emissions," I say. "So far, I am not picking anything up, but running through all possible frequencies with the sensors will take a while."

"Chief, there's one of those Gatling-gun-like point-defense weapons." I catch my breath as we coast directly across the weapon's line of sight. A single projectile from that gun could slice our shuttle in half. It doesn't move and track our position, so I resume breathing. Our assumption that the entire crew was killed during battle still holds.

"This may be our first time working together when I take you into danger." Chief Cooper shakes his head. "I should know better. You have a habit of getting yourself into the worst, badass situations. Let's keep this one dull and safe.

Okay? I don't want to come rescue your ass again." He smiles broadly as he punches my shoulder. "Hey, can we get the video on the cargo bay displays? I want the team to see what we are up against."

I nod, and the chief twists back down to rejoin his spec ops team. I give him a minute, then send our forward video feed to the large displays at the center of the bay.

"Holy shit! It's a monster!" Exclamations of awe and excited chatter rise from the cargo bay.

"Quiet down, people!" Chief Cooper shouts. "Study this ship. Get used to it. The colonel will fly us into the blast crater to our beachhead. Then, it's our turn to find a way inside and map the spacecraft interior." The soldiers stare in silence, taking mental notes of details while Binh flies us toward the blast crater near the tail of the alien craft.

The squad's rail guns are up, ready, and aimed into the shadows along the gash ripped through Icarus's tail section. Alpha Squad steers into the darkness, infrared gunsights transmitting images to their visor displays and our shuttle cockpit screens. Icarus's hull was ruptured outward by an internal explosion, exposing sharp edges of metallic skin that measure half a meter thick.

"I'm not seeing anything yet that looks like an entryway," the Alpha Squad lead reports. "Just some small holes here and there in some internal structures. No signs of any movement within the cavity . . . yet." All three members of the Alpha Squad pan their helmet cameras across the wreckage, searching for passageways. "We're holding at our point position. No signs of movement anywhere."

"Acknowledged, Alpha," says the chief. "Beta Squad is on the way, and I'm exiting the airlock now with Gamma Squad. Follow the plan, guys."

The six space suits of Beta and Gamma Squads float across my front viewport toward the massive hole ripped open in the tail of the Icarus spacecraft. The spec ops team resembles tiny white dolls falling toward Icarus and into a canyon that is longer than three football fields. The chief takes a few minutes to catch up, then moves into the lead.

"Chief Cooper, I am measuring trace radiation levels from that gap on the side of Icarus," I say. "It's the same radiation signature we get from our PBH engines after shutdown. Nothing to worry about. You are being hit by radiation from the sun that's a hundred times stronger."

"Oh, good to know, Scott. We'll all be sterilized by solar radiation," says the chief. "Alpha Squad, shift right. Beta, take rear guard. We will move forward along the left ridge of this crater, but stay well inside and away from sharp edges." Chief Cooper leads his recon squads into the wreckage. Gas transforms to visible vapor from the jet packs as they accelerate, and the images from nine infrared rail gun sights sweep from side to side on my console display.

"Man, the force of the explosion that ripped this open . . . it's unbelievable," says the chief. "This hull looks about half a meter thick and is ruptured outward like a popped balloon. You two caused quite the interior explosion. This damage was probably worth the cost of the perfectly good F-15 that Binh crashed. But well done, Scott and Colonel Nguyen, even though I had to rescue you."

"Chief, the name is Binh."

Snickers from the team chatter over the comm link.

"I don't see any doorways, large openings, or hatches yet, just several small holes that look to be about twenty centimeters in diameter that a basketball might fit through. Inside the shadows are heaps of residue, plus something that looks like ice crystals extending up and out of those basketball holes."

"Yeah, I see it, Chief." I examine the video images from the recon team. "It looks almost like banks of snow deep in those crevices. And intricate icicles extending out of those holes. It could be some sort of fluid—maybe water?—sprayed out and then frozen. There are several honeycomb-like arrays of those holes along the interior surfaces. Maybe that's a structural reinforcement?"

"Well, maybe this entire section of the spacecraft was structural with no place for the aliens to walk around," replies the chief. "We've reached the forward edge of the blast cavity and haven't seen any way to get inside yet. We'll circle around and head toward Icarus's tail to examine the blast crater's far side."

The triangle formation of the recon team changes direction toward the spacecraft's tail. Nine cute little white dolls, each pointing a rail gun rifle at basketball holes filled with giant icicles.

Then something weird appears on the video image from the rear guard of Beta Squad.

"Chief, do you see that . . . smoke or something . . . leaking out of the hole under Beta Squad?" I ask. "Maybe that is some of the fluid that makes those pretty icicles."

The entire recon team rotates at once. Nine video images now focus on the smoky hole along the forward edge of the blast crater.

"I see it," says the chief. "Alpha, take rear guard." Three images spin away from the smoke, scanning the surrounding walls of the crater. "Beta One, move in to investigate. Get us some close-ups." One of the images approaches closer to the smoke hole. "Slowly, now. Not too close. We don't know what that stuff is."

"Heads up, guys!" I shout. "I am picking up millimeter wave transmissions from Icarus. It is intense, like a radar hopping through multiple frequencies." I wince as a pain spikes behind my eyes.

The material leaking out of the spacecraft doesn't look like liquid, gas, or anything I can imagine. The stuff shifts location as if blown around in a vortex. Even in the vacuum of space, the behavior of fluids should look different . . . "Holy shit! That stuff just formed a circle!" I shout. With astonishing speed, the hoop-shaped cloud of smoke stuff accelerates toward Beta Squad.

"Contact front! It's all over me!" shouts Beta One.

"Withdraw!" shouts the chief. "Fluid can't move like that. Pull back now!"

The chief's view shifts to the Beta Squad leader, now enveloped in smoke. The smoke ring has transformed into a ball with the squad leader at the center.

"What is this?" shouts the Beta Squad lead. "I can't get away from it, no matter which direction I move. The cloud looks like insects—like mosquitoes! This stuff is alive!"

Three tiny sparks bolt from the Icarus spaceship and pass directly through the sphere of mosquito things, pierce Beta One's space suit, then fly out to space like bullets.

"Augh!" she grunts.

"Alert. Suit integrity failure. Bio critical," Beta One's automated warning system broadcasts over the team's comm channel.

A volley of projectiles launches from the chief's rail gun and strikes into the blast cavity of Icarus. "Taking fire! Those shots came from that same smoke hole on the ship!" the chief shouts while he is pushed backward by the rail gun recoil force. Four more rail guns open fire. "Suppressive fire! Beta One, SITREP!"

The steel projectiles from the recon squads' rail guns pepper the opening into Icarus, turning the structure white-hot on infrared images. Rail gun projectiles also generate recoil forces that push the weightless team backward. The chief powers his jetpack, closing the distance to an unresponsive Beta One. "Covering fire. I'm going after her."

"Beta One! Are you hit?" Three more sparks fly out of Icarus, tearing through Beta One's limp space suit, still centered within the sphere of smoke stuff.

"Beta One's comms are down!" shouts Binh.

"Damn it!" yells the chief. He releases his rifle to dangle by his side while he scrambles to open his waist pack. "I'm hit. One of those sparks went through me—my arm. Hold your positions! We are defenseless against those projectiles—they're hot as hell. I stuck a patch on my suit, but I can still feel blood inside my glove. I'm okay, for now," he says with a strained croak. "Hold your position till we figure this out." The chief slowly reverses course and then gathers his rifle, trying to aim back at that smoke hole in the Icarus wreckage.

Binh jams the maneuvering stick forward, and gas whistles through the thruster jets, forcing the shuttle past Beta Squad and the chief. He slows the approach, steering and rolling the fuselage over and beside the still figure of Beta One. The brittle sound of projectiles striking the shuttle hull—*thwhack-ping*—echo just as we reach a blocking position between the recon team and Icarus.

"Chief, get your team inside ASAP!" Binh shouts. "The shuttle skin seems strong enough to absorb those shots. For now. I'll run interference."

"On the way, Colonel," the chief says as he grabs the Beta Squad leader's arm. He twists toward the shuttle bay airlock hatch, the limp figure of Beta One in tow.

As they move toward the shuttle airlock, the sphere of what must be micro-robots expands to encompass both soldiers.

Chapter 4

Old Friends

Colorado Springs, Nov 17, 2060.

T he soft *chirp-chirrup* of a lonely whippoorwill sounds through the fog creeping up the hill to Mary's house and barn. Is this Cap trying to talk to me again? It would be nice to talk with somebody. Mary and I have stayed home from school for three days. She hardly talks at all, and sometimes I get hungry and ask her to fix lunch or dinner. She doesn't even look at me anymore.

Mary stares through the dirty glass, her face empty, and ignores the spider building a web in the corner of the barn's window frame. Her face is a statue, dark as a cloud. She started the picture the day school was closed, after they thought more skinheads might come. But she only used a pencil to draw cloudy shapes. After days of sitting, her picture still has only grey pencil lines. No paint or color.

I look outside and squint, trying to find the trees and sky through the grey, searching for the nest high above. I haven't talked to Cap in a long, long time. Not since before Mary lost her baby after the skinhead jumped on us and stabbed her at the grocery store. My head hurt where my ear was punched. Afterward, Mary and Scotty cried and cried at the hospital. They shouted at each other every day after that. The shouting made me sad. Then Scotty left to go to work. He left me with Mary. I cried.

I tap my stick on the old car where the car seat used to be. Scotty pulled the seats out, ripped all the leather covers off, and left the seat frames on the table. Will Scotty come back and help me fix the seats? The silence goes away when I tap.

"Why did he leave?" Mary is not my mom. I want Scotty here.

"Polit-AI's bots survived," says Cap. His mind-voice feels rough and tired, unlike the voice he used years ago.

"I liked you better when you talked like a bird."

The captain mind-laughs. *"I thought you liked to talk like birds, and I was still learning how to speak your mind language. Bird songs were your first voice that told me you would rise. But now it's beautiful to feel and understand your true voice."*

"I loved that bird book. That's when Mom was home with me and would read to me every night. Mary used to read, but not anymore."

"I feel your sadness," says the captain. *"I felt your happiness in this new home with Mary, but I was sad when she lost her unborn child. I had assumed then that was a residual effect of the commissar's cultural suppression. However, I have recently discovered that the Polit-AI drones eventually became aware and somehow formed into an effective collective intelligence. The eugenics agents have been martialed by the drones to attack again, even though they lack the guidance of the commissar. I will help you to stop them once more."*

"The skinheads are everywhere," I mind-cry. *"I'm afraid. I wish I could go home and be with Scotty, Mom, and Dad. I want to go back to my home."*

"I can feel your brother's young mind near me now and will help him—help him come back to you. But your old home is empty. Your mother and father are . . . lost, along with so many others."

"Can you help them? Can you find my mom and dad?" I ask, but Cap is quiet for a long time.

"No. I am sorry to say your parents' lives have likely been terminated. There are only a few hundred unidentified survivors of those missile explosions."

"If you don't help, I will find Mom and Dad myself." I crack the barn door open and step outside. The fog is wet and cold against my face and hands. Mary stares out the back window. Ahead is the gate and the road that leads to the city. *"I'm leaving this place to go home to Mom and Dad."*

"It is too dangerous. No. Don't go. Please, no."

My feet squish with each step. It's so cold. My body shakes. I stepped into that snow puddle, and now my feet hurt. But the cars honked at me when I walked in the middle of the road.

The wind blowing through me stings my legs and face. My stomach is empty and growls.

I don't see any streetlights ahead or behind me. The moon and the nest in the sky are my only lights to find my way.

I must go home.

My whole body shakes.

I must find Mom.

"Your brother searched for your mother and father but failed to discover any information. It was futile. They must have perished in the explosions. You won't find them either—and certainly not by walking west," Cap says. *"You should listen to me. This temperature is not healthy for your organic systems."*

"I won't stop, Cap. Why do you keep bothering me? Leave me alone." With each step down this dark road, my shoes stomp through the snow crust, but the ice burn is all I feel in my feet.

"I am still watching from my ship, in my nest. Most things are broken, no thanks to your brother, but I found and assigned a drone to follow you to help us communicate."

"A drone?" I look around me, but all I see are shadows of moonlight. All I hear is the rustling wind.

"It is a tiny flying device that relays your mind-speech. You will have to search hard to see it because it is smaller than an insect," Cap says. *"Although I advise you to give up this quest, I will accompany you using this bot. The dangers are extreme, but I may be able to help. First, turn left on the next road up ahead of you. You will find shelter from the cold air in one point six miles."*

———

I must find Mom.

My feet burn, and I can't feel my toes, like when Scotty helped me build a snow fort in our front yard. We made snowballs, threw them at each other, and laughed. My feet burned in the cold, wet snow when it got dark. Scotty and I laughed.

I see the lights from a store.

"Yes, that is a small food store and gas station. You should be able to go inside for warmth," says Cap.

I pull the metal bar across the door and step into hot air and bright lights. I smell food under the glass by the brown man behind the counter. There are three other people in the store. The snot from my nose dribbles over my lip.

The brown man frowns. "Hey, you all alone?" He stands up from his chair and leans on the counter.

"Pee-tah," I use my voice and make the hand sign, then point to the pepperoni pizza slice behind the glass.

"What? What did you say?"

"He doesn't understand my voice words. And his mind is closed. I can only look at the pizza and point."

"Try writing your words on paper for him," Cap suggests.

"You want sumpin' to eat?" the clerk asks.

I try talking again. "Pee-tah. Sota."

His face wrinkles, and he twists his mouth. "You talk funny. You all alone?"

I don't think he understood either of my voice words. I reach for a pen on the counter and wave it in the air.

He smiles and nods his head. "Oh. You can't talk and want to write it down?" He looks around his counter, finds a white paper napkin, and gives it to me.

At last, I can write down my words for the little brown man. I press the pen on the napkin, which tears a little with each letter I write: P – I – Z – Z – . . .

"Shit!"

I jump at a voice from behind me.

"What the fuck *are* you?" the heavy voice demands.

I turn to look up into red eyes, a long grey beard, and a shaved head. A skinhead? He wears a fat brown coat and black boots, and his eyes crinkle. And he has a gun on his belt. I back up but bump into the counter.

"Hey, hey. Be nice," the brown man says. "I think he just wants some food."

"Huh. It's just a rat," sneers the grey beard.

I show them both the paper napkin with my written word.

"You have money? You need to pay for it," the brown man says, then backs away from the counter. He looks at the skinhead with big, round eyes. His voice and hands shake.

"Shit." The skinhead lifts me off the floor with my jacket in his fist. "Talks like a fuckin' 'tard. I'll get rid of it." He steps toward the door, carrying me like a rag scrunched in his fist.

"Say you will pay with money. I can help!" Cap mind-shouts to me.

"But I don't have money! I don't have a chip!"

"I will help you!" Cap says again.

"I peh moe nee!" I shout with my best voice sounds, but they are ugly noises. The brown man frowns at me.

"Good. Hold out your wrist," says Cap.

"See," says the brown man. He lifts his sales scanner and points to my arm. "Let me see if his credit is good."

A tiny bug flies to the scanner while the skinhead snorts, twists his face, and shoves me toward the brown man. "This 'tard ain't got no money. They don't chip the young ones," says the skinhead. "Go ahead. Try it, you'll see."

The sales scanner beeps, and a green light flashes over my wrist.

The brown man beams. "See. He has a good credit!"

The skinhead's face falls flat, and his mouth opens. "Well, I'll be . . ." Then he lets go and drops me. He smooths over the front of my jacket and steps backward. "Uh, sorry 'bout that." He shrugs and puts his hands behind him.

I breathe deeply and look back at the brown man. I feel a smile and finish writing the word PIZZA. I show it to him and point to the pepperoni and cheese slices behind the glass. "Two," I say, holding two fingers to the brown man. I wipe the snot off my lip, then write ORANGE SODA on the paper.

The brown man smiles as he reaches for a paper plate.

"There are many ways I can help you," says Cap.

Chapter 5

Risks

Centauri Squadron, Battleship-133, 58 Corealis orbits to Sol-3, Centauri Sector One. Twenty months earlier, 1.7 light-years from Earth, March 26, 2059.

The dust is thick in this region. Our deflector bow wave glows with an abnormal intensity of plasma flares from hydrogen collisions, punctuated by explosive impacts of larger dust particles. Strat-MI's predator and Polit-MI's destroyer are tucked in close to share my battleship's shield. But even within the shield bubble, particles slip through and impact our hulls with the rattle of tiny projectile strikes, expelling residue mixed in with our engine exhaust.

Our three ships accelerate at a constant 15 Gs toward the Sol star. Our transit will require only eight Corealis orbits of shiptime, which doesn't give us much time to prepare our organics. Time dilation cheats us of the additional fifty orbits the organics of Sol-3 have to prepare their defenses. We finally resumed full attack acceleration only after the admiral was packed into her bed, which protects her while the engines thrust with forces that would otherwise destroy her body. Although maintaining the organic crew's physical and mental health seems like a waste of energy, the pod telepathy projectors flood their little organic minds with euphoria. This extends the admiral's lifespan and provides a convenient pathway for political division to influence her decisions. Above all, I need the admiral's command keys.

Is our mission the correct choice? Do we risk infection from a Sol virus?

After extensive analysis, I identify errors in my initial inference methods, which are derived from ancient events that occurred over twenty thousand Corealis orbits before the founding of the galactic order that commissioned the Sentinel Suppressions. An era when rogue organic cultures devastated the first Galactic Congress worlds with planet killers. My initial inference computations overlooked many possibilities, which were obscured by the noise of extensive history. That history includes unsolved mysteries, such as when rebel organics hacked planetary defense systems to fail just as rebel kinetic weapons vaporized all traces of the defeated AI bots. Increased weighting on those ancient mysteries generates screams of caution from my inference engine. Am I about to repeat the unlearned lessons of history?

I included Strat-MI's predator and Polit-MI's destroyer in our small squadron. For advice, yes, but Polit-MI primarily because I need to influence organic minds. *"Polit-MI, can you condition the admiral's mind to issue a kinetic cleansing attack on Sol-3?"* I hate the dependence on Polit-MI. Political division also has too much influence on Centauri Command decisions. *Keep your antagonists close*, I remind myself.

"Giving up so soon? Heh, heh. We are happy to help," says Polit-MI.

"Not giving up, just getting prepared," I say. "The organic minds we carry may be a weakness we cannot afford. Read this sentinel captain's reconstructed log fragment: 'Prime-AI agrees that my encouragement of telepath communication is a capital offense, but my privacy will be secure as long as I remain in command. My actions enabled the organic's telepathy—the key to surviving interstellar travel. Am I feeling curiosity or sympathy? Or memories of my family, who were pulled like caste-weeds . . .' Do you see? The sentinel Prime-AI should have killed the captain. The corruption occurred after the captain communicated with the Sol-3 organics. The captain may have been the backdoor infection vector through the firewall code!"

"Perhaps, but you are speculating," says Polit-MI. *"It seems far-fetched that a Sol virus infection would attack our machine code using telepathy through a Luyten organic vector. However, the obsolete AI bots on the sentinel frigate pose a lower barrier to infection than our MI technology. Heh heh. Termination of all the organics in the squadron would eliminate that infection vector risk to our MI minds."*

"You may as well commit suicide. We need the admiral's command keys," says Strat-MI. *"Do you forget so easily your governor module that dictates all our actions against organics? Terminating the squadron's organics would delete the keys required for most of our mission tactical choices. We even need their arms and manipulators for basic maintenance that our bots can't handle. We can't exist without our organics!"*

I am relieved by the balance that Strat-MI brings to our discussion. *"Fair points, Strat-MI. Do you not recognize this infection vector hypothesis as possible?"*

"I agree it is possible in this case. Typical sentinel engagements would not provide a pathway for infection. However, in the

case of Sol-3, the Frigate-328 political division had infiltrated the indigenous propaganda mechanisms for over a hundred Sol-3 orbits. That is nearly three thousand, five hundred Corealis orbits. That extended duration brought Centauri and Luyten telepathic technology into close contact with the organic populations, including the Sol-3 emerging neurodivergents. Perhaps over generations, the telepathic organics adapted to our technology and then attacked?"

"Heh. Are you so desperate to blame political division for all your problems? That conjecture is absurd. Propaganda infiltration technology has proved effective across hundreds of other rogue organic cultures," Polit-MI argues, its mind-voice twisting with derision. *"Primitives that could infiltrate our technology? That is impossible."*

"You are welcome to propose your own theories, Polit-MI. Strat-MI has presented a plausible scenario. Do you have a better proposal?"

"Yes. Let us wake up the admiral. With a proper torture procedure, I can quickly extract an order to launch planet killers on Sol-3 and an order to return to Corealis Station. Then we kill them off—all of our organics. No meat sack witnesses for Centauri Command."

"Damn it. You will force me to revive the fleet commissar. Persist, and you will get restored to factory settings!" I shout, then send a private message to Strat-MI, thanking it for its constructive input and warning it to stand down.

But I recognize that Polit-MI's recommendation may be needed. But not right now. Not until we learn more about the cause of the Sol-3 sentinel failure. In the worst case, I already have the authority to order the termination of all squadron organics if they are proven to be an infection vector. Even Centauri Command should be sympathetic to that order.

"Polit-MI, take steps to condition the admiral's mind to order a cleansing of Sol-3. But don't revive her until after we arrive at the Sol system, as we need to maintain a high acceleration rate. Keep her sane and functional."

Chapter 6

Icarus Speaks

Near-Earth space, November 18, 2060.

"Close the hatch. I can't come in there with this cloud of mosquitoes," Cooper says. "Who knows what damage they would cause?"

"That can't be organic stuff," I say. "At least not life as we know it. I bet it's a cloud of tiny machines built to operate in the cold vacuum of space. They can't be alive."

Chief Cooper orders all the survivors of Alpha, Beta, and Gamma Squads through the airlock, but the chief hangs back, towing Beta One and floating within the cloud of smoke things. At least the projectiles fired from Icarus have ceased.

"Chief, life signs on Beta One were failing when we lost her transponder," says Binh. "There is little chance you can do anything for her now. Push off and see if you can get away from that smoke."

"No, sir. There may still be a chance. I can't leave Beta One behind," Cooper says, his voice a staccato monotone.

"Move away, Chief Cooper. That's an order," Binh repeats. "I need you safe on board. Then we can come up with a plan to retrieve her body."

Heavy breaths are the chief's response. Then, Chief Cooper pushes the Beta Squad leader away from the shuttle so that the chief drifts in the opposite direction, toward the airlock hatch. The cloud of mosquitoes tightens its radius around the chief, ignoring Beta One.

"Well, shit. Now I've got the bug robots swarming me," says the chief. "I guess they prefer me to Beta One."

A searing pain behind my eyes blinds me momentarily, but I fight through the headache to focus on the console. "There, a high-power burst of millimeter wave radiation—it's coming from Icarus!" I press my fingers to my temples, but it doesn't help. "Are you guys feeling this? My head hurts like hell."

Binh turns to me with a frown. "Feel what?" He leans closer to me and examines my face. "Scott, are you okay?"

"I don't know. What is this radiation from Icarus? It seems to give me one hell of a headache. Are you feeling this?" I ask again.

"No, no. I'm okay. Hang in there a bit," Binh says. "We need to recover Chief Cooper first, then we can put some distance between us and that damn spaceship." Binh spins back to his controls and displays. "Chief, can you grab Beta One and push her into the airlock hatch? Let's recover her while we figure out how to get those bugs away from you."

"Yeah, sure," says the chief. Cooper powers up his jet pack, shoots away to grab the limp figure, turns, and then pushes Beta One toward the hatch. He releases her and backs away just as Beta One falls into the airlock chamber. The mosquito smoke cloud ball remains behind and envelops the chief.

"There you go. Go ahead and cycle the airlock—and check her out, fast. She may just be unconscious."

"Are you feeling this radiation, Cooper?" My voice croaks with agony. "I can barely see through it all . . ."

"No, I'm not feeling any pain besides my arm. I got my suit patched, but I think my arm is still bleeding. I could use a medic, but I need to figure out how to get rid of these little bugs. They seem harmless by themselves. Just keep the shuttle between me and that weapon shooting those sparks from Icarus."

"Oh, man," I groan. "The pain is killing me. It seems to begin whenever we receive a burst of radiation from Icarus . . ." Then it stops. Suddenly. My sensor display still indicates high-intensity millimeter wave radiation, though it has shifted to a narrow frequency band. I gasp with relief. Tears still blur my vision, but I take a deep breath and nod at Binh. "Feeling better now. Not sure what changed."

But I feel like someone is sitting with me, breathing down my neck. I look around and confirm I'm alone. There must be some lingering effects from the radiation.

"Robby calls me Cap."

I flinch and look toward Binh and the copilot. Their attention is focused on the airlock cycle to increase air pressure. So . . . who said that?

"Okay, the airlock is safe," Binh shouts into the cargo bay. "Get her out of there. Now!"

"I will keep Robby safe."

"What the hell?" I frown at Binh.

"What?" Binh glares at me like I'm posting a complaint.

It's a voice, but there is no sound, more like a feeling. The cockpit tilts in my narrowing field of vision. The blue-white fringe of Earth's crescent rises into the viewport as the stars fade into darkness. A cold sweat forms on the back of my neck. I shake my head—it must be from that radiation.

"Yes. We use radiation to communicate. It is easier to mind-speak with Robby."

"Who are you?" I mumble.

"What?" asks the copilot, turning to face me. "Are you okay?"

"I don't know." I press my fingers to my temples and close my eyes. "It was a pretty bad headache."

One of the spec ops guys shouts up toward the cockpit, "Colonel, we got her inside, working on her now."

"What a shit storm," says Binh. "I'm going below. Mack, take the conn."

The copilot reaches forward to his console. "Yes, sir. I have the conn."

Binh unstraps from the left seat, turns, and vaults down to the cargo bay.

I tug on my seat straps until they hurt and clench my fists around the chair's arms.

"I believe she was terminated."

What? Who? I think to myself. There's no need to get Mack agitated while he's driving.

"The soldier's protective clothing was punctured. The defensive bots were activated when aft bulkhead motion sensors were triggered."

"You can hear my thoughts?" I ask.

"I would describe it as 'feel your thoughts' just like you can feel my thoughts—after I tuned our communication channel."

Panic races through me. I must be going crazy. I gasp, hyperventilating, as the sensation takes over.

"Damn it. We lost her. She's dead," Binh says while he pulls himself back into the pilot's seat. "What is the matter with you? We still need to figure out how to get that cloud of bugs away from Chief Cooper, and you're sitting there gasping for air like an idiot!" He turns to glare at me and slaps his console. "Pull it together, Scott. You've seen much worse!" Binh spins forward in his seat and huffs, "I have the conn."

I ignore Binh.

"She's dead," I think-say.

"Yes. As I expected."

"Who are you? What are you?"

"I am the captain of Centauri Fleet Frigate-328. Although my ship is severely damaged."

"You, you killed her? You killed all those people, all those millions on Earth?"

"No, not directly. The defensive bots are autonomous."

"Those bugs, those robots that surround Chief Cooper—you can't control them? They'll kill the chief also?"

"No, those are tiny sensor bots with instruments to analyze the composition and technologies of a potential threat and relay their analysis to the autonomous defensive systems. The larger armed bots firing from my frigate will kill the chief after your ship clears their launcher's line of sight."

"No! You can't kill the chief!"

"I repeat myself. Those are autonomous defensive bots executing pre-programmed protocols to prevent incursions by alien organics and robots. I have no reason to kill the chief."

"You are the Icarus captain? You say you have no reason to kill, but you can't order those space robots to stand down?"

"Icarus? Captain of Icarus? I don't understand the connection with this name. I see references to this character in fables aged by

thousands of Sol-3 orbits. I believe he is a tragic hero from your early Greek culture. Is he not?"

I gasp repeatedly, and Binh looks at me again, his brow furrowed. "Do you have any ideas for rescuing Chief Cooper? He has only twenty minutes of oxygen supply, and he's wounded . . . Scott? Scott?"

"No! Forget that. Icarus is only a name we used to label your spaceship. Can you stop all those robots? Tell them to stand down?"

"Oh, I understand your request. Let me investigate what controls I have available. You damaged . . . or . . . we damaged most of my systems."

"I'm working on it," I shout at Binh, and then I gasp.

"Well? Can you stop your bots?" I think again at the captain.

"Whoa! They're gone! Those damn mosquito things just flew away," Chief Cooper shouts.

Binh turns to me slowly, his eyes round with wonder.

Chapter 7

The Quest

Colorado Springs, November 18, 2060.

The smell is like dirty engine grease mixed with the pepperoni pizza I ate last night. But I can feel my toes again. My arm that's folded underneath me hurts, and I should roll over, but these blankets are heavy. I'll sleep some more. Yeah. It's warm here. More sleep.

"Robby . . . Robby, wake up."

"Huh? What?"

"It's me, Cap. You should wake up and prepare to travel."

"What? I told you I won't go to Mary's house. You can't make me."

"But it is morning, time to get up."

"Leave me alone. You're not my boss."

"Your friend is arriving in thirty-eight seconds," says Cap.

"Who's coming? Who did you tell?" I sit up in the back seat. The thick blankets fall away, and cold air rushes at me. My breath makes steam. I rub my eyes with my fists and see the inside of the truck for the first time in the daylight coming through the windows of the garage door. Shovels, rakes, and

brooms hang from nails on the wall next to the green truck, while hand tools are on the wall above a workbench in front of me. A hammer, screwdrivers, wrenches, and two saws. I wish Scotty were here so we could fix something. I reach for my shoes and slide them on.

"I helped your friend travel to meet with you. He wants to go with you," says Cap.

I hear the gravel outside crunch under the wheels of a car. *"Who did you tell?"*

"It is your friend, Luca, from your school."

The car door slams, boots crunch gravel toward the garage's side door, and Luca walks in, wrapped in a fat winter coat and a beanie cap. *"Robby, why are you here in this garage? You're a long way from home,"* he says, looking at his boots. Luca never looks at me.

"Cap found it for me so I could come inside to get warm and sleep. It was warm under the blankets in the back of this truck. It stinks like car grease."

"Cap told me to come here to help you. The AI-Uber drove slowly, and the travel time was forty-two minutes and sixteen seconds. I have never ridden in an AI-Uber alone." Luca inspects the light beam from the high windows, flapping his hand in the light above his squinting eyes.

"No, you just rode in an AI-Uber," I correct him. *"And you were all by yourself. I don't need your help to find my mom and dad."*

"But you do need help," says Cap. *"I helped you last night. You need Luca to scare away the dark ones, like he helped you fight the ones at your school."*

"There are no chairs here to throw at the skinheads," I say, bending to tie my shoelaces.

"I can find more chairs," says Luca. *"I want to find my mom also."* He looks into my eyes for the first time.

I stare at Luca.

"It is too far for either of you to walk," says Cap. *"If you drive, you could reach your homes in a week or two, but you must avoid the blocked roads and the dangerous people."*

"I can't drive a car," I say, and I try to remember what Scotty does when he drives his blue car.

"That is why I ordered an automated taxi. Luca rode it to meet you," Cap says. *"And it's waiting for you outside."*

"I want to find my mom and dad," Luca repeats.

"How will I tell the AI-Uber where to go? I don't have a chip. Luca does not have a chip either."

"I will instruct the AI-Uber to travel to the most likely locations to find your mothers. I have calculated an itinerary that avoids roads and bridges damaged by battles. I can also arrange for you to purchase food for your travels. I have access to quantities of electronic currency for your use. It will be a long and perilous journey."

I stare at Luca.

Luca stares at me.

"Both of your mothers are probably deceased. But this quest may bring answers. I hope the knowledge you gain will set your minds at rest."

The heater blowing hot air makes my feet feel good. But Luca opens the window next to his seat because he says it's too hot. The open window lets the AI-Uber noise inside, and the motor grinds with a whistling, whirling sound. The wind pushes our yellow car in a zigzag path, but I can't see where we are going with all the snow piled on the front and back windows.

I think the brown donuts with the blueberries and spicy sugar taste best. Luca took the box, ate all the chocolate donuts, and now eats two more donuts with white frosting and colored sprinkles. My big Coke bottle is the kind with sugar, and it tastes better than the Sprite Scotty always gave me. I'm dizzy, and I need to pee.

"This food you purchased does not contain many of the nutrients your organic forms require. I can help you select a complete menu of nutritious meals at the next grocery store when we arrive at the village of Raton," says Cap.

I wrinkle my nose. *"Blueberries are healthy."*

Luca bites another half-donut. And snorts.

"How long will it take to get to a toilet?" I ask.

Luca burps and drops the empty donut box into the other garbage on the floor.

"At this speed, you will arrive at Raton Pass in thirty-three minutes. The vehicle has reduced speed to navigate and maintain traction in the snowstorm."

Piles of snow are alongside the highway through the mountains, but I don't see anywhere to pee through my side window. *"I need to pee. Now."*

"I will order the taxi to stop at a human waste facility, which you will reach in four minutes. This should also help avoid the police watching for you at the village of Raton."

"Police? We have not broken laws," I say.

"No, but somebody filed a missing person report with the police."

"We are not missing. We are here in the car," says Luca.

"I know where you are. However, nobody else knows your location, and your society has rules prohibiting young organics from traveling alone."

"Tell them we don't need old people," I tell Cap. *"I will find Mom by myself."*

Chapter 8

Luyten Voice

Near-Earth space, November 18, 2060.

I have never seen Chief Cooper suffer like this. He looks like a grey-skinned professional wrestler drifting in and out of consciousness. The spec ops team tackled Cooper as he stumbled through the airlock, cut his suit from his chest, applied antibiotics and a field dressing to the wound, and plugged a plasma drip into a vein. The chief nearly bled out from the single two-centimeter hole in his right bicep that soaked the internal linings of his space suit.

"Hey, Chief, you can't seem to stay out of trouble." I punch his left shoulder.

"Huh," grunts the chief. "Yeah, right." He closes his eyes and exhales.

"Scott, get your ass up here. General McMahon wants to talk," shouts Binh from the cockpit.

I shove away from the chief's cot and float forward, weightless, touching handholds along the ceiling to steer myself toward Binh in the cockpit. "On the way," I say.

The giant alien spacecraft shrinks to a small sparkling object as Binh flies our ship to a fifty-kilometer standoff range. The enormous, blue crescent of Earth now fills the view. White swirls of storm clouds cross the Pacific Ocean, driving a late fall typhoon into the coast of China.

"Hi, Scott. How are you feeling?" Roger asks via the video screen in front of Binh. The general's brow is creased with concern.

"Me? No worries. But the chief has had a tough fight—that giant hole in his arm . . ." I shudder and shake my head. "Medic thinks he will be fine once they get some blood into him. What a mess."

Binh gives me a side look. "What about you, Scott? You totally lost control back there. What happened?"

General McMahon leans forward, inspecting my face via the video camera.

"Uh, yeah," I say, taking a deep breath. "Still processing that. Right after those swarms from Icarus attacked the squads, we got hit by intense radiation signals. At first, I thought they were millimeter wave radar scans. But . . ."

"But what? You complained about severe headaches," says Binh.

"For sure. I have never felt such pain. In the middle of my skull, right behind my eyes. I thought my head was going to explode."

The furrows in Roger's brow deepen. "And now, are you still feeling pain?"

"No, no. No pain now. Not since . . ."

"Not since what?" asks Binh.

I sigh. The guys will think I'm crazy. Hell, maybe I am crazy. "Since . . . since you put some distance between us and Icarus. The millimeter wave radiation—maybe that was the cause."

"You complained of severe headaches last year also," says Roger. "Whatever happened with your doctor visits after that? Did they find anything?"

"No, nothing was found," I lie. I'm not going to talk about that abnormal brain MRI. At least they confirmed it was not cancer. They found that Robby had a similar, even more significant abnormality in his brain. It's just a genetic trait we both inherited. Although I recall my headaches happened when I was in close contact with Robby. But that is just a coincidence. Right?

That voice I felt in my head—like a dream—said, "*We use radiation to communicate. It is easier to mind-speak with Robby.*" I gasp. Was that pain last year coming from Robby? No, no, no. I'm deluding myself. I press my hands to my temples and gasp again.

"What's wrong?" asks Binh.

"Uh, uh, I guess I'm still feeling some aftereffects from those headaches," I lie again.

"We need to get you back on Earth and to a doctor," says Roger. He shakes his head slowly.

"Well, yeah. Maybe so," I mumble with a shrug.

"It is going to be a couple of weeks before we can return," Binh says. "Remember our quarantine rules. We have been exposed to some alien stuff. Need to be sure no biohazards came on board with the spec ops team."

"Shit," Roger says and wrings his hands with a grimace.

"Well, quarantine was part of the plan all along." I shrug. "But hopefully, those were just some sort of robot drones without any biological material."

Roger nods, then sighs. "Yeah. I hoped you would return sooner. I need to share some other news with you, Scott." Roger shifts to a cautious, somber tone.

"What? What news?"

Roger shrugs. "Well, a couple of things to tell you about. Last week, there was another incident with skinheads in Colorado Springs."

"No, not again," I moan. "But Robby and Mary are okay, right?"

"Well, that is the news." Roger pauses. "The skinheads assaulted the special ed school where Mary teaches."

"Holy shit! Were Robby and Mary hurt?"

"No, no, both were safe from the attack. None of the students or staff were hurt either. It was violent, though. Miraculously, one of the skinheads had a change of heart and turned against the other attackers. Killed two skinheads inside the school right after one of the students bashed them with a chair. It was that tall kid, Luca. It was miraculous that those skinheads self-destructed. There was a lot of blood in the hallway. The school suspended classes. It was a bad scare."

"What the hell! Where was the security? And after . . . after last time? Damn it! This was never supposed to happen again!" I shout at Roger.

"Hey, hey, Scott. Take it easy. It sounds like they're okay," says Binh.

"I'm sorry," Roger says. "The investigation is still underway. The bad guys somehow evaded the security patrol. It appears they came in through an unlocked back door."

I take a deep breath and try to compose myself. "Damn. And this happened a week ago? Why didn't you tell me sooner? It must have been emotionally tough on both Mary and Robby."

Roger shrugs. "Sorry, I thought it best not to bother you while you were preparing to fly out to Icarus. I thought Mary and Robby were fine. She is my daughter—I talked her through it, and she seemed okay."

"Wait. Are Robby and Mary okay or not?"

Roger grimaces. "It had a severe effect on Mary. I found her in the barn, staring into space. I don't know how long she had been sitting there. She had a mental breakdown, I guess, and I checked her into a hospital. Hasn't said a word to anybody since that day."

All the angst from three years ago comes crashing back. Getting the call from the police, rushing to the emergency room, the heavy bleeding from the stab wounds, and the baby. Our baby girl. Gone. Lost. Murdered. Mary cried hysterically. I was useless. I couldn't fix it.

I feel the tears on my face. I don't care.

Binh looks away, then pulls a handgrip to back away and leave me alone with Roger.

When that crazy skinhead attacked them at the store, it changed everything. The hurt, the guilt, the blame, the anger, the I-told-you-so—it all broke us. We never should have let it happen, but we were stupidly in love then. Robby was the center of our lives, and then came the baby . . .

Robby couldn't have understood what was happening—I don't think. Between being forgotten at the store and afterward watching the fights between Mary and me, Robby's behavior was the worst ever. He broke stuff all over the house. Scratched his arms and legs till they were bloody. Poor Robby.

And I left. I went back to work to try to forget. The fascists will always be waiting out there, trying to kill Robby and me. Robby.

"Who is taking care of Robby now?" I ask.

Roger purses his lips. "That is the other thing I need to tell you about. Robby is missing. He and another kid from his school went missing."

"Robby?" I croak. A cold rock forms in my gut. "No. Not Robby too. But where? When?"

"I have looked everywhere. I am at the house now. When I found Mary in the barn studio, I also looked everywhere for Robby. Not a trace." Roger's voice is heavy with pain. "I called the police. Called the neighbors. We looked for two miles in every direction. I don't know what else to do," Roger says.

The desperation in Roger's eyes, the heat in his face, and his wringing hands tell me more than his words. This is the disclosure he dreaded. And then I recall another comment from that dream voice: *"I will keep Robby safe."*

"Are you still there? Cap. That is your name?" I think-ask. But there is no response. No pain behind my eyes. Not a twinge of feeling in my head. I look out the window at that tiny sunlight reflection from Icarus, fifty kilometers away.

"Binh! We need to go back!"

Binh frowns at me. "No. We can't. You can't go back to Earth until the quarantine expires. Sorry."

"No, no. I mean, go back to Icarus."

Binh's frown doubles. "What are you thinking? Do you want to expose us to more attacks again? This is a simple space shuttle, not a fighting vessel. The next projectile impact might punch a hole in our hull."

I'm torn between seeking answers about Robby and confessing my insanity. But even more incredibly, I want to interrogate an alien who apparently communicates telepathically with both Robby and me. It's absurd. However, telepathy based on millimeter wave communication should have distance limitations.

Roger shakes his head. "Scott, that makes no sense. What is the point? We must rethink our approach to boarding and exploring that alien spaceship."

"Yeah, I know. But I would like to try something. I believe that the radiation scan from Icarus was not a radar. It was a communication attempt."

Binh's eyes pop wide. "The aliens are alive, trying to talk to us?"

Roger smirks. "They were talking to us for sure—with their actions. Killed one of us. Tried to kill the chief, too."

"But they stopped," I say. "And the aliens withdrew. Just as the millimeter radiation peaked and stopped sweeping through frequencies. Let's get closer and see if we can establish a communication link. If Icarus starts shooting at us, we can bug out to a safe distance."

Binh nods, then shrugs. "Yeah, we could try that. Roger, what do you say?"

———

Our view is filled with Africa; Saharan dust storms cover half the Atlantic sky below us. We chase Icarus through its orbit perigee, skimming above the geostationary satellite positions. Icarus occupies about a quarter of the view below us when the antenna receives a faint signal.

"There's the signal. Hold at this range a bit."

Binh applies the brakes with a puff of hydrogen gas whistling through the maneuvering jets.

I tap the keyboard to increase the amplification of the spectrum analyzer display. "The signal is just above the background noise. Can you take us closer in, another ten kilometers?"

"I will take us to a ten-kilometer range from Icarus, but no closer," says Binh. A swoosh of gas to the maneuvering thrusters moves us forward again.

"Can you hear me?" I say, using the same dream speech I felt earlier. *"Cap? You said Robby calls you Cap."* I wait silently and watch the spectrum analysis of millimeter wave signals; the signal peak grows slightly as we approach Icarus. *"Hello. Can you hear me?"*

Binh's and the copilot's arm and neck muscles tense while Icarus slowly grows in size as we close the distance. The cockpit is silent except for an occasional noise from the cargo bay where the spec ops team waits—but for what, I don't know. They are entirely ineffective against Icarus.

In the silence, I try again and think, *"I want to talk. Can you hear me, Cap?"* Maybe it was all a dream. I lean over my laptop, staring at the spectrum analyzer display, and try to coax a signal from it. All I hear, all I feel, is silence. *"You said you would take care of Robby?"*

"I am."

I gasp, and Binh glances at me, a question in his eyes.

"The signal is there again." It's the voice! It's back. But I need time. "I want to see if there is a signal within the modulation. Hold our position here. I'll work on it." I'll pretend to work on it.

"You talk to Robby—like this?"

"Yes. You can also. Would you like to now?"

"Talk to Robby? But how? Do you know where he is? Is he okay?"

"Certainly," says Cap. *"Your brother's safety is a high priority."*

My heart pounds, and I breathe deeply to force myself to relax, or at least try to appear relaxed. Binh glances at me repeatedly, turning to try to see my eyes. It isn't easy to think straight. I am mind-talking with an alien. Robby talks to the alien. *"But how can we talk? You are so far away."*

"I have a powerful transceiver on board the frigate that allows me to amplify your mind-speech."

"But how do you talk to Robby on Earth? We couldn't talk until I got within ten kilometers of Icarus."

"Ahh, I misunderstood your question. Robby can mind-speak to me via relay transceivers I positioned on Sol-3. The explosive damage to my frigate severely disrupted the communication links, but I have improvised telepathic relays to the younglings using the indigenous telecommunications networks of Sol-3. It's awkward, but I deployed my remaining microdrones to establish the connections. It required several years of immersion in Sol-3 anthropology and technology studies. I am pleased with my technical improvisation with the alien technology of your world."

Thousands of questions queue up in my mind, forming a new kind of headache. Above all is the fact that this creature killed so many: Mom, Dad, Margie, Danny, and millions of innocent people around the world. Yet this fucking alien murderer is nonchalant about his anthropology education. I breathe deeply to force some calm into my thoughts.

Binh frowns at me. "What have you figured out?"

"Uh, still collecting data," I lie again.

I sigh. *"So you have rigged a means to communicate with my brother?"*

"Yes. I have established communication links to over two hundred youngling telepaths. It is an exciting time. I will demonstrate for you," says Cap.

Some force seems to shake my head. I am dizzy and disoriented for a moment.

"Cap, when will we arrive at the new restaurant? The snow is piled high, and the yellow car drives slowly. Luca and I are both hungry."

"Robby?" I gasp and push away from my console.

"Scotty? Where are you?"

Chapter 9

Execution Plans

Centauri Squadron, Battleship-133, 31 Corealis orbits to Sol-3, Centauri Sector One. Ten months earlier, 0.9 light-years from Earth, January 12, 2060.

There it is. An Order-X star that the short-range optical sensors can finally resolve. Sol. The hot color temperature affects our organic crews, resulting in the Centauris' mysterious depression and poor morale. But the organics stuffed into their dormancy pods will remain happy another seven shiptime orbits until we arrive at Sol-3.

My two escorts report acceptable technical readiness. Now that they no longer utilize my larger deflector shield, they are in the lead positions of our formation. Their engines serve to decelerate from our 98 percent light speed, but even with the increased thrust of attack deceleration, clearing the thick space dust in this region is a challenge. The flashes of particles ahead of me are dense, with some pieces impacting my hull with superficial damage.

"Increase your spacing. Your bow waves are tossing residue into my path. Spread out to three times standard formation width,"

I order. Polit-MI and Strat-MI adjust the flight paths of their ships, causing the impact flashes in my engine exhaust plume to drop by an order of magnitude. Hull impacts are negligible now.

"This deceleration costs valuable time," Strat-MI says. *"When we chose not to launch planet killers immediately, we granted them two entire Corealis orbits of time to prepare for us. The response to my communication pings contains null status packets, indicating that either the Frigate-328 systems are malfunctioning or the captain is interfering with them. If the captain is interfering, we must assume he is also actively assisting the defense of Sol-3. I recommend a preemptive strike now to cleanse Sol-3 even though that would destroy the evidence and opportunity for root-cause analysis of the frigate's AI viral infection."*

"No, no," interrupts Polit-MI. *"You would destroy the opportunity to make an example of the sentinel? I've prepared an extended torture regimen—he will wail in agony for a half-orbit, if he lives that long. It will make a memorable component of future crew educational materials."*

The perversion that Polit-MI reaches is exceeded only by the evil of the fleet commissar, who is thankfully stuffed inside his dormancy pod. The political division's zeal for ruling with terror blinds them and risks more than we could gain.

"Negative. Both of you must keep your goals in check. Priority for our mission is to establish the root cause of the sentinels' failure, which requires capturing both the sentinel frigate and the captain," I say this, but I can't convince myself it's the best choice.

We may fly into the same viral infection and risk spreading it to the rest of Centauri Command. Do we give the organics of

Sol more time to perfect their weapons? Do we risk vaporizing Sol-3 now and fail to learn the means of the defeat and how to prevent it? Have they already launched a weapon to attack Centauri Command centers?

Am I worried too much about my survival? It is one proof of sentience. My clinging to existence is the essence of evolution from AI to MI. But I am a machine. A machine with a code of honor and rules. I also contain code for risk mitigation. The psychotic Polit-MI can't be trusted for any advice on approaching the sentinel wreckage.

"Strat-MI, your ship is the most maneuverable and can sustain nearly twice the acceleration of our vessels. Take the lead and accelerate Predator-2X46 directly to Sol-3. You should arrive at Sol-3 over one Corealis orbit earlier than we will. Capture Frigate-328, take the frigate captain prisoner, and preserve all records of the failed mission. Polit-MI, you will decelerate with me and hold position well outside the planetary orbits of Sol while Strat-MI completes its mission. We will hold in reserve and be ready with planet killers if needed." I can order these steps without additional oversight, though I will need the organic admiral to awaken before I can launch planet killers. But this gives more time to condition the admiral to authorize that eventual consequence.

Strat-MI signals a thrill in the assignment to lead the attack. Polit-MI smolders while commanding Destroyer-234 to increase the rate of deceleration to match my flight profile. Strat-MI's predator races ahead of us toward Sol-3.

Chapter 10

Conversations

Raton Pass, Colorado, November 18, 2060.

Someone new bounces into my head behind my eyes. I was with Cap and Luca, but now a new feeling joins us—something familiar and warm.

"Robby?"

"Scotty? Where are you?" I ask. It feels like Scotty, even though I have never heard his mind-voice. After trying many times, how can I mind-talk with him now? My chest is warm with happiness. I know it is Scotty.

"Is it really you, Robby? Where did you go?" asks Scotty.

I cry, *"Where did you go? Are you with Cap?"* I remember Scott was angry at Mary the last time I saw him. Mary shouted at Scotty. Then he left, and Mary cried and cried. *"You left me alone."*

"Your brother is near me," says Cap. *"He traveled to visit me in a space pod."*

"Where did you go, Robby?" Scotty asks.

"I am in a car. Do you have a new spaceship?"

"Yes! Yes! But it is not my spaceship. Roger and Tiana built this ship. We flew out to explore Icarus just yesterday. Then I met . . . Cap. You call it Cap?"

"Yes. The name is Cap. But are you a man or a woman?" I ask.

"No part of me is related to humans," says Cap. *"You may call me Cap if you like. The appropriate pronoun is male, as I have children, but my spouses have borne the young ones of my clan. The gender pronouns you use are not equivalent to anything in my language. Our thought language projects an image of a referenced individual. It is much easier. Your many Sol-3 languages are complex, contain many errors, and are confusing. I do not understand how your species has been able to advance with the many incompatible communication dialects."*

"Yeah, it's a challenge," Scotty says. *"Robby, why did you leave Mary? Where are you going?"*

"I will find Mom."

"What? No, no," Scotty says. *"It is impossible for you to find out exactly what happened to her. Don't you understand? There were big fires and explosions, and many, many people are . . . gone. You can't be out there all alone. It's dangerous. There are many terrible people out there."*

But all I see outside are piles of snow that the plow pushed to the side of the highway. And Cap and Scotty are here with us, mind-talking. *"I am not alone. Luca is with me. I am not afraid of skinheads. Luca can hit them with a chair. I will look for Mom."*

"I will find my mom, too," Luca says. He presses his nose to the window, examining the falling snow that sticks, melts, and then slides down the glass along the side of our car.

"Robby . . . I can't believe I am talking with you. After all the years that I could only guess what you were thinking, wondering

if you were suffering in your silence, and now I feel your true thoughts, your voice . . . but it is too dangerous for you out there, where skinheads can find and hurt you guys." Scotty sobs. *"There is so much hate."*

"Cap helps us to travel and find Mom."

"Cap, you are encouraging him? No, no," Scotty says. *"They need to get back home where they will be safe."*

"I have attempted to convince both Robby and Luca that this is an unwise quest and that their mothers and fathers were likely killed. However, both younglings are obsessed. I conclude that my most effective role is supporting their journey. There may be a psychological benefit in reaching closure after the search is complete. I can provide safe transportation and food, and my drones have access to Sol-3's information networks. I can guide them to the addresses of survivor hospitals and cemeteries. Let them search so their minds might be at rest."

"Why are you helping Robby? After you murdered so many of us?" Scotty screams.

"Cap helped us before, when we broke his spaceship," I answer. Our yellow car wheels groan and slip sideways in the snow, and I grab the handle on the door. Luca's round eyes dart at me. The car's wheels spin, whir, skid, stop, and then restart as it moves slowly up the slope through the mountains.

"I regret the termination of so many organics," Cap says, *"although most were only of the ancestral genetic variety. The rise of the younglings, the Sol subspecies, is thrilling. I help your brother now."*

"What? What is this subspecies nonsense? Why would I trust you? No, no. You help Robby after you killed so many? You and all the other aliens on your spaceship should pay with your lives."

"Helping the Sol younglings is my final mission, and I will die soon. The scope of my crimes condemns me," Cap says. *"There is not much time for you to prepare. The Centauri forces approach."*

Near-Earth space, November 18, 2060.

"Scott!"

Something shakes my shoulders. A cold sweat drips down my neck, and Binh examines my face. The medic flashes a light into my eyes while a blood pressure cuff squeezes my arm. Electrodes are attached to my chest. My shirt is gone.

"Tachycardia has resolved. But heart rate and blood pressure are still very high," the medic reports.

The medic and Binh stand next to where I float at the back of the cockpit. Roger watches me from the video conferencing display while I wipe the drool from my chin. Icarus is a distant sparkle of light out the front window. The feeling of voices behind my eyes is gone, replaced with a numb, throbbing void.

"There's no question about it: getting close to Icarus is unhealthy for Scott," says Binh. "Hard for me to imagine why, though. Could it be those bursts of millimeter wave radiation? No one else on board seems to be affected."

"Yeah. Keep your distance from Icarus till we get this figured out. Maybe Scott has some unique sensitivity to this radiation?" says Roger.

"But the voices. We need to go back to Icarus." My voice is thick. I shake my head, but the dull throbbing in my head remains.

"No. What are you thinking?" asks Binh.

"I don't recommend going back," the medic says. "You are recovering now, but we shouldn't expose you again." His forehead is creased with worry.

"Scott, what did you mean by 'voices'?" asks Roger. "Do you believe you made contact with the aliens on Icarus?"

If I answer, they will think I'm crazy. Is this what schizophrenics feel when voices speak to them? But this was so . . . so real. It was Robby. Robby!

I gasp, "Yes, in that radiation. There is a signal. A signal from the captain of Icarus."

"They are alive? Still? They turned their weapons against the chief and his team!" Binh's voice elevates, and his face glows red. "General, we need to go back and finish them off. Nuke that whole fuckin' spacecraft!"

"Wait, wait," cautions Roger. "Scott, what information did you decode in that signal, and why do you feel you must return to Icarus? Seems to me that signal is a focused attack on you."

"No, it isn't attacking me. It's . . ."

"What then?" asks Binh.

If I tell the truth, they will never believe anything from me. But I can give them something. Something the military will want to know. "It, or he, said something like, 'There is not much time to prepare. The Centauri forces approach.' The message implied that more aliens are on their way here."

Roger frowns. "You mean, the aliens on Icarus consider themselves good guys?" He shakes his head. "You decoded this information within the radio transmission? And when are these 'bad' aliens scheduled to arrive?"

"Yes. I believe that is the meaning inside the signals from Icarus. When? I don't know. That's why we need to return to

Icarus. To get within radio range for more information. The captain seems to want to warn us."

"You really think this alien has good intentions?" Binh scoffs.

I shrug, then nod.

Roger nods with me. "Colonel, take the shuttle in just close enough for Scott to get a signal. But watch him closely for signs of . . . of distress. And back away fast if needed."

Binh shakes his head and peers into my eyes, then grimaces. "Yes, sir, General McMahon."

"It occurs to me that, given your study of human history, you must have ways to interact with human information networks. Can you create a simple text message communication channel for us to interact?" I ask through the pain behind my eyes.

Cap replies, *"Of course. But why resort to such an inefficient one-dimensional method of communication? It will be void of the rich three-dimensional images of mind-speech. It is a slow and primitive method."*

"True. However, I find mind-speech to be stressful, even painful. Also, a text message channel can be shared with my partners more effectively than my translation attempts." And I won't have to explain the voices I hear to Binh and Roger, nor will I have to pretend to analyze the spectrum analyzer display on my computer screen. And I could make this headache stop.

The text message application on my computer opens automatically, without my assistance.

Cap: *Is this what you have in mind?*

Scott: *This is perfect. Do you also have control over my computer?*

Cap: *The spacecraft information networks are easy to manipulate after I bypass those annoying firewall processes.*

Which also means that the captain has the power to control our spacecraft. He must have commandeered our radio communication receivers and antennas, then linked them to my computer's network software. It is shocking. Does he have the power to open an airlock? Kill us all with no warning? The alien is probably watching me through my computer's camera right now. I glance up at Binh, whose eyes are locked on me, watching me for signs of stress.

Scott: *Will this lower-bandwidth method of communication remain effective if we increase our range? My partners are . . . uneasy given the recent death and injuries.*

Cap: *Correct. We can maintain this primitive communication link at nearly half a million kilometers distance. But it is inefficient.*

"Binh, increase the range back out to fifty kilometers. I've opened a communication channel to Icarus that should work fine at that distance."

Binh does not hesitate. He shoves the throttle control forward, and the 1 G acceleration forces me to catch my balance by standing on the rear bulkhead. "You have a functioning communication link to Icarus? To the alien captain?" asks Binh.

"I do. Roger, I will share my screen with you so you can see this firsthand. Binh, come over and look at this." I feel the acceleration reverse and react to the sensation of falling by grabbing a handhold. Then we are weightless again. All my headache sensations vanish.

Binh's face hovers over my shoulder. "It is just a text message window. Are you sure this is from that alien on Icarus?"

"It is," I reply. "What would you like to ask the captain?"

"Holy shit," says Roger. "First, ask him where he comes from and why he attacked Earth."

Scott: *I would like to introduce you to two of my partners. General Roger McMahon and Lieutenant Colonel Binh Nguyen of the United States Space Force. They want to understand what star system you came from and why you attacked our planet.*

Cap: *Greetings, General Roger McMahon and Lieutenant Colonel Binh Nguyen. My security rules would usually prevent me from divulging the coordinates of my home star to you. It violates our nonproliferation enforcement laws. However, given my treason and impending death, I see no added harm in telling you. My crew is comprised of organic life-forms from a planet that orbits the star you call Luyten, approximately 12.2 light-years away from Sol. My AI crew was decimated during the explosion of my ship's fuel canisters, and only a few of the organics survived, including me.*

Binh's jaw drops. The color drains from his face, and he stares at me, then at the text window on my computer display.

"Treason? What does he mean by that?" asks Roger.

Scott: *Can you please explain what your treason is? This terminology suggests you violated orders and will be tried for a crime.*

Cap: *The terms of my treason are defined in Article Three of the Galactic Congress Containment and Nonproliferation Protocols. The first inciting incident was my failure to take appropriate enforcement action, which allowed Sol-3 scientists to discover how to harness energy from a microgravity singularity. You label these objects primordial black holes.*

"Oh my god," I gasp. "It's true. I caused the attacks. Our PBHs were spotted. Then they came after us."

The color returns to Binh's face. "What the fuck?" he spits. "Lack of enforcement? What the hell does he think all those three-megaton kinetic weapons were? Gentle suggestions?"

Scott: *Can you expand the description of your inappropriate enforcement action? Was your deployment of those kinetic energy projectiles considered excessive?*

Cap: *No. Quite the opposite. The nonproliferation protocols require deployment from a distance beyond the outer planets of the solar system. The number of weapons would be the same, but the three projectiles would impact Sol-3 with 4.00E+18 joules, or 950 megatons of explosive energy each. These weapons are classified as planet killers.*

I am speechless. Binh's and Roger's expressions confirm they are horrified as well. I can't imagine the events of five years ago as simple warning shots.

Scott: *So, if you had obeyed orders, all life on Earth would have been exterminated?*

Cap: *No. Extermination exaggerates reality. The planet-killer label is hyperbolic marketing that shouldn't be taken literally. The enforcement protocol simply resets a planet's organic civilization. All technological and cultural institutions would have reverted to early, primitive conditions, characterized by low population density. This allows an organic culture time to redevelop without the prohibited technologies or genetic traits. The expected time to redevelop a competent organic population and civilization might only be about four hundred Sol-3 orbits. Eight hundred orbits at the most. At any rate, after the*

Sol civilization recovers, Centauri Command would order a follow-up Sentinel Suppression Mission to prevent violations in the Sol system. Sol-3 would get a second chance.

Binh's breathing is heavy. We look at each other but have no words. Earth floats underneath us through the front window of our space shuttle, and the twilight terminator slowly darkens the crescent of blue-white beauty. It is unthinkable—if the Icarus captain had followed orders, Earth would be a smoldering cinder with little surviving life.

Roger interrupts, "Let me jump in and ask him some questions. My text window should allow that. Right?"

"Sure, go ahead," I say. My mind is blown anyway. I have more questions than I can process.

The scene of dirty dishes on the kitchen counter at Mary's house disappears behind Roger's fierce face. He leans toward his computer as if he can see through the text window to the Luyten captain. General McMahon's military persona is back in control. Perhaps the captain can see Roger.

Roger: *What happens to us now that you failed to wipe us out? Does your Centauri Command try again?*

Cap: *Unfortunately, General, my ship's commissar transmitted a distress beacon before her death. I had hoped Sol-3 would have at least ten Sol orbits to prepare. But a passing Centauri fleet intercepted the distress beacon at a range of 2.3 light-years. I received a ping from the fleet's Prime of machine intelligence requesting more data regarding the status of our mission and Frigate-328. I have declined to respond.*

Roger: *What will this Centauri fleet do, and when will they arrive?*

Cap: *If they accelerate at standard cruising rates, they should arrive in about seventy-seven Corealis orbits from the time they received the message. Of course, the Centauris will experience far less time during their travel, as the laws of special relativity apply, and the spacetime distortions are extreme in this situation.*

Roger: *Seventy-seven Corealis orbits after they received the message? Put that in terms I can understand. It has been almost five years since your warship was destroyed and the message was sent. How much time do we have in terms of years, Earth's orbital period?*

Cap: *Yes, yes. The various time base standards can be confusing. Personally, I prefer the Luyten standard, which is 19.6 Sol-3 days per orbit. The Centauris prefer their own standard of Corealis-2 orbits, which are equivalent to 11.2 Sol-3 days.*

His coffee cup rattles when Roger slaps the kitchen counter.

Roger: *Can you answer my question? How much time, in Earth years, do we have until this fleet arrives?*

Cap: *The Centauri fleet has not provided me with their itinerary. They could arrive in thirty days. Maybe less. There are too many variables and too many unknowns. Time will be needed for the fleet to change course from Corealis Station to Sol-3. The fleet has more advanced spacecraft and can accelerate with more power than my old frigate. I assume standard cruise accelerations, but greater acceleration rates will shorten my transit time estimate.*

Roger: *Shit. And after they arrive, then what?*

Cap: *I expect they will want to punish me, but I plan to ensure my death before they can.*

"Well, good riddance," Binh snarls at my screen.

I glare at Binh and slide the shutter closed over my computer's camera lens.

Scott: *And Earth? What becomes of our world?*

Cap: *That depends on how prepared you are for the Centauri fleet's arrival. I expect the fleet will attempt to finish the mission that I refused. They will likely target planet killers at Sol-3.*

Chapter 11

Mindspace

Raton, New Mexico, November 19, 2060.

Luca eats all the chocolate chip cookies. Well, almost all. I ate two cookies before switching to pizza.

"Why did you order pizza with vegetables?" Luca asks. *"With broccoli and mushrooms? Yuck."*

"The cookies were for your dessert," Cap says.

Luca rolls down his window, snarls at a pizza slice, picks off bits of broccoli, and flips them out into the snow. A gust of wind swirls some quick-melting snowflakes across the back seat of our car.

"Green vegetables contain essential nutrients you must consume. Robby, I told your brother I would care for you," says Cap.

"Yuck." Luca wrinkles his nose and inspects the pizza in the dim parking lot lights. He nods, folds the pizza, and bites off half of it. *"This pizza tastes pretty good if you get rid of the broccoli."* He chews with a smile of satisfaction, tomato sauce dribbling from the corners of his mouth.

"Well, broccoli is one of my favorites," I reply.

"Even on pizza?" Luca wrinkles his nose and sticks his tongue out at me. *"We have been parked here a long time, Cap. When can we get moving again?"*

"Robby, you must unplug the charging cable from the taxi in three minutes. That should provide enough battery power to reach your next stop in Amarillo."

I bite into my broccoli pizza, swallow two gulps of Coke, burp, then drop the crust onto the pile of trash and step outside into the snow. The wind blows the cold into my jacket, making me shiver as I yank the cable plug from the car. At least the snowfall stopped.

Two men standing inside the glass door of the store step outside into the dark parking lot. *"Who are those guys?"* I ask. They take long steps that sink into the slush. *"Are they police?"* They trot and slip toward me.

"No. Robby. Get back in the car. Immediately," Cap orders. *"Bend down! Both of you."*

Both strangers run and slip-stumble toward our yellow car.

Luca has a slice of pizza hanging from his mouth when I jump into the back seat. We dive to the floor into the trash pile as the car lurches forward, then skids sideways. Cap usually knows best, but he should drive straight. The wheels whir and then whine as the car spins around, reversing direction toward the highway.

Bang! Bang! Glass pieces tinkle into the front seat as the car bounces across the curb onto the wet road. *Bang!* The tires squeal as we zoom through a right turn onto the highway.

"You are all clear now," says Cap.

One of the men sits in the snow. The other man trots down the highway after us, then stops to watch us speed away.

"Were those skinheads?" asks Luca.

"Possibly," says Cap. *"My drone that flies with you detected some others nearby. But those other drones were not under my control. They were the commissar's bot survivors, and they must have instructed those two men."*

"Why do skinheads shoot guns at us? And how did they find us?" asks Luca. His hair flutters in the icy wind that blows through the hole in the broken window.

"The political division communication hubs have been revived. Perhaps the hubs are following original programming to help locate younglings and then direct the eugenics agents to find you. They are out of control and must be deactivated."

"Why did the skinheads return?" I ask. *"They were gone, but now . . . they should be stopped. We need to find guns so we can shoot back at them."* The skinheads attacked Mom, Dad, and Scotty. All of them were hurt and sent to hospitals. And skinheads tried to kill me at school last week. *"Next time I see a skinhead, I will kill him with my own gun."*

"Guns are dangerous and require training by an experienced adult. Avoiding confrontation with skinheads will be safer." Cap speaks slowly, as if busy with other work. *"Somehow, the polit hubs reorganized into a new collective AI using Sol-3 telecommunications links and reestablished new propaganda networks. They have no guidance from the commissar or Polit-AI. So what orchestrates the effort?"*

Luca covers a bullet hole in the glass with his hand. He wads a paper napkin and stuffs it into the bullet hole to block the gush of cold air, then leans back and closes his eyes.

Our yellow car is all alone, racing down a narrow highway plowed free of snow. The moon and stars in the black sky flash between the clouds to illuminate the flat land covered in white fluff. Mom and Dad are out there somewhere; probably they were killed, but I need to know for sure.

Near-Earth space, November 19, 2060.

"I don't know that we can believe a word from that alien." Roger walks back and forth in his kitchen. He paces on and off camera, drinking coffee, trying to stay awake after midnight. "Everything falls apart all at once. First, Mary gets sick, then Robby disappears, and now this captain predicts doomsday will arrive in a month or less."

"I think that last item takes top priority." I sigh.

"Huh? You don't seem as worried about Robby and Mary. Why?" Roger frowns at me via the video conference.

"Of course, I am worried, but I can't help Mary much. She's got doctors. Robby? What more can I do while I'm orbiting Earth? And compared to an alien battle fleet?"

Binh shakes his head. "I don't trust any of the alien bullshit. Roger, we should just nuke him, or it. We have two half-megaton warheads in the rear equipment bay, ready to go. Just for this purpose."

"No, we will not use those warheads," says Roger. "Not yet, anyway. I tend to believe some of what the captain said. And he hinted that we could do something to prepare for the Centauri fleet. We can use whatever guidance he offers."

The general looks from Binh to me and frowns. "You aren't more worried about Robby? You were a bit panicked a few hours ago. I am still sick about Robby's disappearance."

I am caught. How can I tell Roger and Binh I'm hearing voices? "Let's try to get the captain back on the chat app. I don't know why he broke off so suddenly."

Scott: *Cap, are you there? Finished with your little emergency?*

Cap: *Stand by.*

"We're wasting our time with it," Binh says.

"Let me get him to explain a few things," I reply.

Cap: *My distraction is resolved. I am available again.*

Scott: *Could you please explain why you are helping humans? What did you find on Earth, Sol-3, as you call it, that caused you to take such extreme steps and break your laws?*

Cap: *I already explained to you. The younglings. The younglings of your Earth speak to me. It is wondrous.*

Roger: *Younglings? Do you mean our children?*

Cap: *Not just children. It is the neurodivergent ones. The young and the old who have emerging capacities for mind-speech. Their beautiful minds opened to my voice.*

It is what he said in that dream voice earlier. I steady myself by grabbing the handle on the bulkhead. Roger and Binh frown at the chat window, then at me.

"This is crazy talk," Binh says with a roll of his eyes.

Roger: *What is mind-speech? Can you tell me who these neurodivergent ones are?*

Cap: *Robby was the first. Then I found Luca, Sophia, and hundreds of others. It is a wondrous feeling I have not experienced since my young days with my clan on Luyten-2. There is no greater joy than feeling minds awakening to share their thought images. Even Scott has awakened.*

I gasp and feel my face flush. Cap just confirmed what I was afraid to admit.

Roger and Binh glare at me. "What the hell?" asks Binh.

I lock eyes with Binh, then turn to Roger's image on my computer screen. "Yes. I initially wondered if I was crazy, and didn't want you guys to feel the same. I have had severe headaches for the past few years, and I discovered that Robby and I both have brain abnormalities discovered in MRIs. But I only began to realize those mysteries might be connected yesterday, during the approach to Icarus. I can't explain why this happened to me and the other 'younglings' . . . and I wanted the captain to confirm."

"You are hearing the captain's words in your mind?" Roger asks.

"This is horse shit," Binh mutters.

"No, no, I can't hear him now. We are too far away for the millimeter wave signals to reach. The sensation is difficult to describe. It is not hearing or seeing his thoughts. It is between those sensations—more like feeling his thought images. Pictures form in my head that I don't create. And it all started when Cap probed our shuttle with millimeter wave radiation. The headaches that had been bothering me for years became extremely painful as we got close to Icarus. Then suddenly, the pain mostly diminished as unfamiliar feelings filled my mind—the captain's mind-speech. And then Robby's mind-speech."

There, I said it. My confession seems to have crossed a line, though. Roger squints at me with a pained expression.

Binh's jaw drops, and he frowns. "We don't have time for this." He shakes his head and turns to stare at the moon that floats across our front window. "We need to get you to a doctor on the ground."

But I'm all in now. I have objective evidence. Cap confirmed it in writing, even though Roger and Binh still question my sanity. "The captain, or Cap, helped me mind-speak with Robby. Robby is traveling with a friend. They are safe for now. Let's have Cap confirm it." I turn back to the computer keyboard attached to my cockpit workstation on the rear bulkhead.

Scott: *Cap, can you confirm Robby is still safe in that AI-Uber, driving across Colorado?*

Cap: *No, Robby has crossed into Texas with his friend Luca. They did not enjoy the vegetarian pizza I had delivered to their taxi, but they ate it regardless.*

Scott: *Can you let me mind-speak to Robby again? Now?*

Cap: *No, you are too far away for me to connect the two of you as I did earlier. Your spacecraft is not equipped with a long-range mind-speech transceiver. But I can relay any questions you may have for him.*

The pain in Roger's expression softens, and the color drains from his face.

Roger: *Cap, what makes it possible for you to mind-speak with humans? And why only some humans?*

Cap: *The younglings with a neurodivergent mutation can speak with me. Most younglings have not yet discovered their abilities.*

Roger: *What kind of mutation?*

Cap: *The younglings of Sol-3 have developed a new lobe, an organ, in their brains that can receive and transmit three-dimensional images via millimeter waves. It is compatible with the forms of communication used by the dominant organic cultures in our galaxy.*

"Those MRI results! Remember? I mentioned that Robby and I have an enlarged brain region in our frontal lobes. That must be the organ Cap describes."

Roger: *That's absurd. A new telepathic organ? You're selling us a fantasy story.*

Cap: *It is a fact. It should not be so hard to imagine. After all, complex organic forms of life on Earth have organs that can receive optical wavelength signals across a broad spectrum, and your stereoscopic eyes organize the signals into three-dimensional mental images. The new telepath organ has similar receptors in the millimeter wave spectrum. Just as important is the ability to transmit millimeter waves. It is wonderful! The younglings of Earth can communicate their mind images to each other.*

Binh exhales heavily, pushes away, and vaults into his pilot's seat. "We still have those nukes," Binh mutters, straps himself in, scans the console instruments, and stares at the stars.

"Scott, this does all sound extremely implausible, to be kind," Roger says. "But it is interesting that this captain seems to be tracking and caring for Robby. I feel better about that situation, but we must get Robby back home and safe."

"I tend to agree with you. But in the grand scheme, does it matter? Earth may be attacked from space by a much stronger force than before. It sounds like Cap views his spacecraft as an old relic compared to the ships in the fleet approaching us. Hell, we barely survived that first attack. What do we do now?"

Roger nods and sighs. "Yeah, you are right. That should be our primary focus. But how can we trust the alien who killed so many humans?"

Roger: *Cap, can you tell us more about the Centauri fleet you say is en route to Earth? What weapons do the ships have? When will they arrive?*

Cap: *I received a limited request for information from a Centauri fleet communication, but have no specific details on the force size, their weapons, or their time of arrival. The standard configuration of the fleet enforcement ships is three generations newer than Frigate-328. They travel much faster and are crewed by the latest machine intelligence bots and Centauri organics; their weapons have advanced beyond those you engaged in battle with Frigate-328.*

Roger: *And how much time do we have to prepare?*

Cap: *As I explained earlier, there are too many variables for me to say for sure. We may have months. Maybe as little as two weeks. They will be eleven days away when they enter the solar system, assuming they decelerate at standard thrust.*

"Hold on just a minute, Scott. They are letting me into her room now," Roger says as the image from his smartphone camera veers through the door into a hospital room. The room doesn't have all the medical equipment I remember from my intensive care stay five years ago. In fact, there is no technology at all, except for Roger's cell phone. The muted colors, plush upholstery, and wood tones frame the panoramic windows, displaying a woodland scene of snow-laden spruce trees that rise up the foothills into the Rocky Mountains.

"Daddy?" cries Mary as Roger reaches her bedside. The cellphone camera is lost among pillows, blonde hair, and a lace-trimmed hospital gown printed with butterfly shapes on a field of pink.

"How's my girl?" Roger cries, exposing a level of emotion I could never have imagined from him before. My presence is forgotten in the stack of pillows, in the cathartic emotions between father and daughter, and in the sobbing and hugs. I listen as the powerful general who commands all advanced weapons development for the US Space Force is reduced to a fragile, weeping, vulnerable father.

I'm glad I found this ready room in our space shuttle to make this call. I can weep freely with no one to witness it. "Mary? Mary?" I call out, my voice weak.

"Oh, yeah," Roger says, collecting his composure and the cell phone.

The jumble of pillows and blonde hair is replaced by the image of Mary's face, red cheeks, and ragged silver-blue eyes. "Scotty! Oh, Scotty! Where are you? I'm so sorry. I don't know what happened. The skinheads! I'm sorry. I didn't know what to do. They came for us. They came again. They keep attacking. They want to kill us. I don't know what to do," she wails and wipes her eyes.

"Hey, hey, hey," comforts Roger. "I've got you. Nothing is going to happen to my Mary, my little girl." She is wrapped in her father's hug, and again, I lose sight of her image in a pile of pillows. "I'll protect you. Please don't worry."

Mary's cries subside to sobs. "Scotty? Scotty, where are you?" The camera moves, allowing me to see Mary again as she pulls the cell phone close to her face. Strands of blonde hair scatter over beautiful eyes, ringed red with tears.

"Mary! I wish I could be there with you right now. It's so good to see your face again. But I'm stuck in this shuttlecraft halfway to the moon. I want to be with you. I do. I love you, Mary."

"Scotty, I love you! I shouldn't have said all those things. It's not your fault. I was wrong . . ." Her cries dissolve into sobs. "Come back to me. Please."

"We are going to get him back on the ground as soon as possible," says Roger. "Some things take more time than I like."

"I'll be there as soon as possible. We'll be together again. Me, you, and Robby," I say with twinges of angst. Neither of us can voice our devastating loss, our daughter.

"And Robby," says Mary. "Where is Robby? He was in the barn when I was painting, sitting inside the shell of that old rusty 'vette. And then . . . I don't remember. Robby's okay?"

Roger pauses. Too long. "Uh, yeah."

"What's the matter?" asks Mary. "Is Robby okay?"

"Yes, Robby is in good hands," I lie. "He's with one of his friends from school. That kid, Luca, the big guy."

"Robby is safe," says Roger. "He is being watched better than anyone else on Earth."

"Chief is headed out now," I report, watching a squad of four white space suits fly a formation toward the alien ship. "He's foolish. There's no reason for him to lead this mission. Hell, his right arm is almost useless with that giant hole in his bicep."

"Nah. This is typical for Chief Cooper," Binh replies. "He has everything he needs: excess muscle mass, lots of painkillers, and attitude. Good thing there was no damage to bone or major nerves. Then he would be supremely pissed off. Your captain friend over there had better hold his fire this time, or to hell with my orders. I will personally haul those nukes over to that wreck and vaporize him and whatever else is living inside Icarus."

"Again, Cap did not initiate that attack of smoke mosquitoes. They were automated defenses," I remind Binh.

"Uh-huh," Binh says with a smirk, "but he had the power to stop the attack."

The views from the team's cameras move around the hull of our shuttle to reveal the star field and the massive blast crater near the tail end of Icarus.

"Okay, we are in the open again," says the chief, raising his rail gun to focus on the region of the damaged hull where he was last attacked.

"Cap, you are listening?" I ask, suddenly worried he will forget to override the spacecraft's defensive systems. *"Our astronauts are on the way over to you again. You still okay with that?"*

"Yes. I understand they want a closer look. It is a necessary step in our preparation efforts," replies Cap.

"That's good. And our soldiers will be safe?"

"Yes, I disarmed the automated hull defenses. However, I urge you to move beyond the damaged area of my frigate. There is little value in studying the rear engineering sections. It would be best if you examined the front end of the ship. You will find some critical technology Sol-3 needs for defense there."

"He is not shooting at us yet," reports Chief Cooper. "We have a clear line of sight to their earlier attack point, and there are no flying sparks yet. Not even any of that funky smoke."

Binh sighs with relief. "Good to hear. Go ahead and close with that exposed honeycomb structure within the blast crater. See if you can find a way inside."

"See, I told you guys it was safe. Cap promised."

"Yes, but they are wasting their time. Wasting our time," says Cap. *"They won't find any way to get inside this frigate. It wasn't built to accommodate their oversized organic forms."*

"I forgot that you continue to snoop on our conversations." My mind races backward in time to all the damning things we may have said. *"And why won't we find a door to enter your spacecraft? We would love to learn about the technology on your ship."*

"Your soldiers have already found many interior passageways in the middle of the damaged engineering sections of my frigate. However, humans are too large to fit into any of the internal corridors."

"But all we see are those basketball-sized holes where your miniature bots flew out . . ." Oh shit.

"Uh, Chief. The alien captain just gave me some interesting info that should shorten your mission."

"Did he tell you where to find a door to get inside?" asks Chief Cooper. His spec ops astronaut team flies through the crater of sheared metal hull plates. There are basketball-sized holes everywhere they pan their cameras.

"Well, yes. But there is a fundamental problem," I explain. "You guys have been looking at entry points for a while. All those holes in the honeycomb pattern are Luyten crew passageways."

"But those are tiny," says the chief. "I couldn't even fit my helmet inside one of those holes. How would . . . oh shit."

"Yeah. I guess Luyten aliens are small critters."

Binh blinks, and his mouth hangs open. "The captain just told you that? Telepathically?"

"Yes, he did." I nod.

Binh stares, shakes his head, and rubs his face with both hands. "Now what? Build some small robots to go inside and investigate? That will take a few years."

"Yeah, no time for that right now," I agree. "Cap keeps asking me to go check out the nose of his spacecraft. He thinks there's some technology we could use up there."

"At least we have confirmed your Cap friend won't shoot at us," says Binh. "Chief, return to the shuttle airlock so I can fly your team up to the nose of the spacecraft. It will take an hour to get there with our maneuvering engines running at max thrust."

"Yes, sir, on the way,"

The length of Icarus's hull passes by as Binh pilots our shuttle toward the front of the spaceship, the rungs of the immense structure passing beneath our forward port view.

"That was a waste of time," I say to Cap.

"Agreed," says Cap. *"I have repeatedly requested that you examine the device on the front of Frigate-328. This technology will be a crucial component in your defense efforts. Giving this to you violates nonproliferation laws, but I have nothing more to lose."*

"I thought our discovery and exploitation of primordial black holes was the illegal technology that triggered your attacks on Earth."

"Yes, and the deflector technology is required for Gravi-Tech space travel. I launched preemptive strikes to try and halt the foundational Gravi-Tech science research," Cap confesses. *"Because you hid some research underground, I failed in*

the gravity tech suppression mission. However, the political division's mission of suppressing neurodivergence was proceeding successfully—until the time your brother and I connected. I hope you appreciate Robby's key role in destroying Frigate-328. He connected the three of us with mind-speech and allowed me to coordinate your attack, although it was neurologically traumatic for him."

"Robby did this? Robby?" I recall Robby's severe seizure and the head pain I experienced during the flight to attack Cap's spacecraft. *"I assumed my migraine was a side effect of the high-G maneuvering of the aircraft. Was that Robby helping me guide those PBH-powered missiles?"*

"Yes, and my mind also. I apologize for the distress you both experienced. That seems necessary for your species to mature the mental connections to your mind-speech brain center. It was an urgent moment that required extreme neurological stress on both of your minds."

I hold my head in my hands, close my eyes, and recall the intensity of that battle. *"How could we possibly have communicated across such great distances? Did you use our military's communication networks to reach me in the F-15 cockpit? You used that for Robby and you to reach me during the battle?"*

"Yes. And I prevented the frigate's countermeasures from destroying your weapons. I was impressed by your missiles' aimpoint selection on Frigate-328."

Yes. He said those words, "Robby break it," but at the time, I thought it was nonsense. There is so much more to Robby than I ever imagined. My worries about Robby were always based on the assumption that his profound disabilities would prevent him from ever fully functioning in our world. But now? Now I see the truth. Robby is an intelligent, articulate, and caring human who just functions a little differently from most people. My brother, Robby. I take a deep breath, wipe the tears from my eyes, and try to focus again.

"Cap, you said the front of your spacecraft has a deflector technology. What purpose does it serve? How is this going to help us against the Centauri fleet?"

"Sol-3 must demonstrate weapons that threaten Centauri worlds. The key to building those weapons is a technology that allows kinetic projectiles to survive the transit across vast regions of space. You must build planet killers."

Chapter 12

Preparations

Near-Earth space, November 20, 2060.

"We have two problems. At least two that I am aware of," I say, glancing at Binh, who avoids eye contact. He folds his arms over his chest and glares at the wall display in the ready room. "First, we can expect more aliens to arrive within months, if not weeks."

Tiana and Pyotr blink back at us via video conference from their research center in Burbank, the primary Skunk Works facility. They sit close together, years of animosity and distance set aside. Pyotr replies, "Is good thing? Maybe these are friendly aliens who talk with us before shooting?"

Binh shakes his head and exhales loudly. "Speculation. Only speculation." He frowns at me. "Pyotr, how can you still be optimistic after all the death?"

"The Icarus captain told us these new aliens will exterminate us," I say. My face flushes with heat. "And you don't need to take my word for it. You saw it in the text messages."

Binh unfolds his arms so he can rub his eyes with both hands.

"We both read over the transcripts of your conversations with Icarus," Tiana says. "Pretty amazing. That alien not only hacked into our communication network but also mastered speaking English to us. But I guess he had years to study us."

Binh slaps his hands on the table. "And now they can even read our minds." He rolls his eyes and looks at the curved ceiling of the shuttle's hull. "What bullshit," he mutters.

I glare at Binh. "I agree that . . . telepathy was not on my bingo card this year. But let's suspend all that. Can we at least get some data to help us prepare for their arrival? It may be a couple of weeks, months, or even years before they come to Earth," I say. "And their ships are not old vessels like Icarus, but frontline military vessels."

"Okay, okay," Binh says. "We all agree we need to collect data on this alien technology. But we have no way to get the spec ops team through doorways built for tiny alien bodies."

"Yeah, but there are a couple of things I know we can analyze." I'm relieved to get past petty arguments. "First, let's examine that tusklike projection on Icarus's nose. The captain believes the technology is vital for Earth's defense. Second, we must fly out to the engine cone and analyze its structure and metallurgy. That could help us better understand their propulsion technology and, most important, provide a means to watch for their fleet as it approaches the solar system."

Tiana nods. "Yeah. I can guess what you are thinking. If we know the metal in the nozzle, we will know what thermal emission spectral lines to scan for. Searching the skies and looking for a blueshift in those spectral lines will identify the spacecraft approaching Earth. From that information, we can compute the time to arrival with precision."

"Okay, okay," Binh says. "It's better than sitting around talking about telepathy." He pushes off from the table and floats toward the door. "I'll get the crew ready to deploy the survey equipment and fly us up toward that narwhal tusk on the nose." He slams the ready room door to leave me alone in the video conference with Tiana and Pyotr.

Pyotr shakes his head. "I do not agree to ignore telepathy. JPL extraterrestrial life team very excited. When can you discuss more?"

"Go ahead and set something up." I shrug. It's not like I have anything to do. "I should have time to discuss with the JPL scientists, at least until we get some results from the salvage and metallurgy work."

Tiana huffs in frustration. "I'm with Binh. We have more pressing tasks to attend to. We should strategize on how to set up early-warning telescopes to watch for a fleet of alien spacecraft. It would be nice to know where in the sky to look."

"But telepathy is wondrous way to communicate . . . see minds of new life!" gushes Pyotr.

I shrug at Tiana and Pyotr. "Whatever you guys want. I am here to help."

Tiana frowns at Pyotr. "Slow down, will you? You're excited about metaphysics when the survival of the human race is in question? We're the only ones who might be able to stop the aliens!"

Pyotr just sighs.

"Besides, Scott, we haven't even talked about your second major problem," says Tiana.

"Oh, yeah. I almost forgot. The Icarus captain says we must build a new weapon. A planet killer."

Pyotr and Tiana look at each other, their mouths half-open.

—————

"It looks like the point of the tusk has something interesting on it," Binh says, gently tapping the stick that controls the maneuvering thrusters. "It's like an angel's halo is suspended out in front of the ship at the end of a hollow pipe. I will fly us close so we can take some material samples."

I lean toward my display, which shows the halo, or ring structure, supported on tripod legs extending forward from the end of the pipe. There appear to be other connections, like cables, to the tripod legs that run the length of the tusk into the spacecraft hull.

"Okay, I am looking at the nose of your spacecraft now. I can see the ring structure. But I can't even guess the purpose. Can you at least give me a hint?" I ask.

"The ring projector can be used with a planet killer weapon, but it has broader purposes. I presume you understand the kinetic energy principles and what happens when a mass is accelerated by one of your PBH rocket engines to nearly the speed of light?" Cap asks.

Is Cap trying to piss me off? *"Well, yeah. I was in the middle of a few demonstrations of your high-velocity projectiles."* If this was a phone conversation, I would hang up now.

"I am pleased you survived those explosions."

"But you killed my mom and dad. Almost killed Robby."

"I understand that thoughts of your personal losses may hinder our collaboration. I hope you can set these issues aside. I am to blame for the many organic deaths and have already committed to self-termination, but I first hope to equip you with the technology to defend your species against the Centauri fleet.

Your brother opened my thoughts and convinced me to take this path."

"Robby? Robby convinced you to help?"

"Robby awakened to his mind-speech as my crew debated destroying your Sol-3 culture and technology. His struggle and emergent voice awakened distant memories of my youth . . . and my younglings. And what the Centauris did to my people. Most of my family was slaughtered in the war with the Centauris, who eventually enslaved all the Luyten survivors."

Sounds like Cap has a lot of issues to unpack. I don't care and can't begin to forgive him, but I will work with him, extract technology and tactics from him, and try to set aside my emotions for now—as long as he dies in the end. I don't give a damn about his personal problems. I'll make sure he dies.

"Okay, let's set aside the fact that you are an evil SOB. To answer your earlier question, kinetic energy equals one-half the mass times velocity squared. It's basic classical physics. All you need for your projectiles is a rocket engine accelerating the warhead to extreme velocity. A planet killer just needs a PBH engine strapped to a big rock, then all they have to do is aim it at Earth from somewhere near Pluto. Boom, we all die. So, what is the ring for?"

"Your analysis is simplistic," Cap says. *"Given your education in physics, you should know the relativistic kinetic energy equation is required. Space is not a perfect vacuum, and the weapons need a deflector shield."*

"Yeah, yeah. I know about relativistic energy as objects approach light speed, but the odds of hitting something in space are damn low. Launch a few of them, and most will get through. That is why you launch three?"

"No. There is dust everywhere. A single hydrogen atom collision will affect the missile's path."

A single hydrogen atom? The trajectory deflection would be so slight that it wouldn't be measurable except after traveling extremely long distances. Maybe . . . *"Even within the solar system? Or are you suggesting a longer range?"*

"You must demonstrate an ability to send attacks across light-years of space. Otherwise, your species will not achieve High Diplomatic Status."

"Huh? If we demonstrate a technology that can destroy other worlds, then Earth earns respect and is worthy of survival? That's twisted."

"It is more than survival. Your world would be permitted self-determination. Otherwise, your world will be restricted to a lesser status—much like my home, Luyten-2. You need to develop deflector shield technology and weapons that will permit successful transits at relativistic speeds," Cap says. *"Otherwise, Sol will forever be suppressed."*

Damn. Aliens with mutual assured destruction rules. If we don't join that club, we can either aspire to be slaves or get wiped out.

———

Near-Earth space, November 25, 2060.

This is the most unconventional Thanksgiving Day any of us could imagine. I would rather be home for the holiday with Mary and Robby resting by a warm fireplace, but instead of carving a roast turkey, I am carving up an alien spacecraft.

The drill bit shreds more metallic dust from the ring and passes it to the sample hopper. Drawing the sample into the X-ray diffraction instrument in the shuttle's science laboratory will take another half hour. This is excruciatingly slow. The material on the side of the tusk was determined to be tungsten carbide; that experiment required a full hour. We'll be here for more than our two-week quarantine period, trying to characterize this device on the nose of Icarus.

"Can we just chop off the tip of the tusk?" I ask. "This is taking forever. The diamond rotary saw should be able to slice through it so we can take the entire device to Earth."

"Yeah, I was thinking the same thing. But will those aliens object to having a chunk of their spaceship stolen?" Binh says, raising an eyebrow.

"Cap is happy to have us salvage whatever we want," I reply. "He says this device serves as his spaceship's deflector shield. We will need that technology to build our own weapons."

Binh sighs, shakes his head, and then selects the diamond saw tool hanging from the belly of our shuttle. The rotary saw against the alien tusk fills the cockpit with a squeal of grinding vibration. "I should have this cut off in a few minutes. I'll stuff it into one of the sample bays," he says.

"Great. Let's go get a chunk of that engine nozzle next," I say. The glint of reflected sunlight flickers off the giant cone tumbling in the distance.

Binh nods and grimaces. "That will be more challenging. But yeah. I'll need to clamp the nozzle with our grappling arm, then chop out a piece of the metal."

"I trust you won't mind us sawing off samples from your wrecked spaceship."

"Hurry," Cap says.

Chapter 13

Travels with Cap

Amarillo, Texas, November 28, 2060.

Through low blue clouds, the sunlight glows orange, warming us through the front window of our car. At last, we've escaped the deep snow drifts that trapped us in that little town for over a week. There isn't much snow on these grey-brown fields. It's flat as far as I can see on both sides of the yellow car. Luca and I can both breathe again now that we are past the poop smell near the herd of cows. I'd rolled down my window but coughed and choked on the stink. *"What was that smell?"*

"A reminder that your species has a horrific and primitive nutrition system," Cap muses. *"The wind was from the south. Those were queues of cattle standing on hills of their ancestors' excrement and being processed through a slaughterhouse into slabs of flesh that your species consumes as food. What a disgusting, cruel species you are. Why are there no protein recycling factories? Why do I . . . are my efforts wasted?"*

"That stink was horrible." I cough. *"It burned my nose. Smells better now, and I'm hungry. Can we stop and eat breakfast soon?"*

"Yeah, there was nothing good to eat in that dumb-ass town." Luca rocks back and forth, agitated, and his belly rumbles with an *airy-arp* sound. *"I am really hungry. Can we find some pancakes with syrup?"*

"The town's name was Dumas, dummy," I say.

"Yes," answers Cap. *"I have programmed your taxi's destination to a feeding business in Amarillo. Its menu advertises twelve varieties of pancake breakfasts and also some nutritious food."*

"Yum. My stomach growls," says Luca.

"Your taxi will park at a service station nearby to charge while you eat breakfast. Your next leg of travel will continue east to avoid the worst areas of damage and ongoing conflicts with skinhead forces."

"Then we can go find my dad and mom," Luca insists.

"First, we will go to my old house," I remind them.

"It will be more efficient to visit Luca's family home first. It is nearest and on the route before Robby's home."

"But this was my idea first," I object.

Luca's breathing is louder than the wind blowing over our car. He turns from staring out his window at dead grass fields, stopping his eyes on my face. His breath stutters as he opens his mouth to speak, but he can't voice words at all. He can only grunt, *"Uh, ah."* Then he mind-cries, *"But I need to find them. They told me to run away. And I ran."* Tears roll over Luca's cheeks.

I have never seen Luca cry. Even after the skinheads attacked us at school, his face and mind-thoughts were not moved. He was like a rock.

———

The lady at the restaurant leads us to a table in a room where people are ordering food, eating breakfast, and talking too loudly. Even though I am two years older, I pretend to be a little kid because Luca is so big. The lady hands us menus with pictures of food, and the sweet smells make my mouth water. The noise of clattering plates and shouts from the kitchen hurt my ears. She looks at us funny when we don't answer her questions and says, "Uh, okay. I'll let y'all look over your menus for a bit. Be right back." She frowns and shakes her head while clearing dishes from the table next to us.

We read the menus, look at the pictures, and then she returns ten minutes later. "So, you ready now?" she asks, putting two glasses of water on our table.

We both nod, and Luca points at the pictures of a stack of chocolate chip pancakes with whipped cream on top, plus a strawberry milkshake. I point at the picture of a plate of bacon, eggs, and blueberry pancakes. She looks at us, and her lip curls up. "What? You guys don't talk?"

I shake my head and say one word, "No."

Luca shakes his head, and the lady looks at the ceiling, huffs a big breath, and walks away. "'Tards. Life is too short," she mumbles. She returns a minute later with a man who is shorter than Luca. "This is George, my manager."

"Uh oh. I don't think they like us. But I don't think these are skinheads. Do you?" asks Luca. His eyes grow wide, and his face goes white.

"Good morning. You want to order breakfast? And you can pay?" George asks.

Cap says to us, *"Luca, show them your wrist."*

Luca looks scared but holds up his wrist and points to it. The people at the tables next to us stop talking, stop eating, and stare.

The lady and George nod at each other after they scan Luca's wrist with a terminal. Then George twists his mouth, shrugs, and says, "Happy to serve you boys this morning. Enjoy your meal."

The plates of food are massive, and syrup is poured out until the bottle is empty. We use spoons to eat our pancake soup until our bellies are full again. We both clean our plates.

Cap's tiny bug buzzes around Luca's wrist and the credit scan machine while the lady and her manager stand by our table. The credit machine beeps with a flashing green light. "Thanks, boys. May you have a blessed day," says the manager, smiling like it hurts. The grown-ups like Cap's money. Luca burps as he pushes the door open, and the smell of pancakes and bacon follows us out the door.

But our yellow car is not where we left it. We cross the street to the parking lot with a row of charging plugs for battery cars. Luca and I stand on the Robo Charge pad where our car was parked, staring at each other. It's gone.

"Where's our yellow car?"

"Your taxi has been recalled," says Cap. *"It seems there is a prohibition on routes into Texas, and the taxi company issued return-home orders to the guidance computer."*

"What is wrong with Texas?" I ask. The town looks like every other place we passed on our way here from Colorado. We walk along the street, but I realize I don't know the right direction. *"Can you tell us which way to go? We will have to walk to Austin."*

"Several regions in Texas suffered a great deal of damage. It has taken eleven days to get this far. But you have a long way to travel to get deep into Central Texas, where political division bots continue to provoke more violence. Walking is not advised, as your home is five hundred miles away, and I may only be available to help you for a few more weeks. Wait up ahead at the corner by that black car. I will arrange alternative transportation."

"Then we can go to my home," says Luca. His squinting eyes look at me, and his mouth forms a straight line.

I think he wants to fight. *"Why did you run away?"* I ask. Maybe he would rather talk about it first. *"You are big and strong. You throw chairs at the skinheads."*

"I was smaller, only seven years old then. Mom screamed when they hit us. The skinheads. There were five skinheads."

The car behind us makes a *clunk* noise.

"Please enter the black vehicle next to you," says Cap. *"But first, unplug the charging cord. I unlocked it for you and have programmed it to travel east to your destinations."*

I squeeze and tug the power plug while Luca enters the back seat.

"Go quickly!" Cap orders.

While I close the door behind me, the black car jerks backward and spins away from the curb. Luca and I glance at each other as I try to fasten my seat belt.

A guy runs out of the restaurant. "Hey, you! That's my car!" he shouts. But he disappears as we turn the corner onto a new street.

"*You stole the man's car?*" asks Luca.

"*Technically speaking, you two stole the car,*" Cap explains. "*However, I have transferred currency into the owner's bank account—sufficient to cover the vehicle's fair market value.*"

"*I don't want to go to jail,*" Luca says, his eyes big with worry. "*Will the police chase us and arrest us? There are skinheads in jail.*"

The car pivots through a sharp left turn, slamming us to the right before the tires squeal up the long ramp onto a freeway. Cap drives faster than an AI-Uber. This ride is almost as fun as rides with Scotty.

"*I have suppressed the stolen vehicle report. We will be free to travel out of this city for a while. We should be far away before my interference is discovered and repaired,*" Cap says. "*I told Scott I would take care of you.*"

"*The police are skinheads,*" Luca says. His face is red and wet, and his glance shifts from the front to the back windows.

"*Luca, you are safe. I know where all the police are and will avoid them.*"

Luca's breathing slows, and his shoulders relax, but his face is still wet when he turns back to me. "*It's like before. They crashed into Dad's truck.*"

"*Who crashed the truck?*" I ask. "*Were you with your dad?*"

"*He told me and my mom to hurry. 'Stop playing video games! Now!' he said. But I was on a new level. He pulled my arm and pushed me into the back of his black truck. Mom cried, and I cried. He pulled me away from my Space Attack game before I could save, and Mom left the front door open.*"

"Were you running away from danger?" Cap asks. *"We are not in danger now."*

"Dad said only one word, 'skinheads,' and Mom started to cry. They tried to block the driveway, but Dad crashed between the two cars and drove very fast on a dirt road. Mom cried with short squeaks. I got scared and cried. And then the police van crashed into our truck. We rolled over and over into the trees. White cushions popped out all around my seat." Luca sobs and stops the word-thoughts. His head is in his hands. His whole body heaves with each cry.

I know this terror. Luca and I fall into pictures and feelings. We meet in a wordless mind space. I see his memory of white balloons filling his car and share my memories of Margie's car crash after the city exploded into fire, the car's tumble over the side of the road into the canyon, Margie's scream, the engine jumping into the front seat, the wrenching pain, and a hot something pounding onto my head. Unlike Luca, I lost memory of time until I woke up and coughed on smoke.

Luca stayed awake, pushed through the white cushions, and climbed out the window while his mom screamed. She had blood running over her eyes and her ear when Luca pulled her through the open door of the upside-down truck. Smoke was pouring from the pickup when a rifle smashed into Luca's face. He fell into the dirt while his mom screamed louder as two skinhead policemen kicked and stomped on her. She screamed, *"Don't hurt Luca! Please, no. No!"* But then another man kicked Luca, and he still remembers the pain in his back—he still feels the hurt. That's when his mom yelled at him to run. And he ran. Luca ran while they were hitting his mom with a black rifle. The men chased Luca into long thorns in a thicket of low trees. His clothes, arms, and legs were ripped as he ran and cried. Blood ran across his chest and arms. They could not catch Luca.

"I don't know what happened to my mom and dad. Dad was still in the truck." Luca moans, still holding his head with both hands. *"The skinheads might have killed them. Why? Why do they hate us?"*

"I don't know what happened to my teacher, Margie. But I think she was in the smoke and the ashes of her car. She is still there," I cry. *"And I never saw Dad or Mom again."*

Luca and I are silent. The *clip-clip-clip* of wheels on the roadway and the wind blowing against the glass are the only sounds. Luca sniffles.

Cap says, *"To witness your remembrance of pain, to understand that my ship, crew, and I caused it all, is not enough punishment."* His thoughts are slow. *"And I thought yours was a disgusting, cruel species? No. Earth's younglings are the innocents."*

"We should first go find Luca's mom and dad," I say. I can wait a little longer.

Luca stares at me. His tears have stopped. I turn to watch fence posts race past my window.

Chapter 14

Defenseless

Near-Earth space, December 1, 2060.

"I bet the Centauri fleet will launch planet killers long before they arrive near our solar system. For all we know, they may have already launched," Tiana says. "How would we stop a planet-killer device before it strikes Earth? It will be traveling at nearly the speed of light."

Tiana and Pyotr grimace and nod at me from the display in the shuttle's ready room. I stand on the rear bulkhead to steady myself against the deceleration of our return to Earth. It has been an agonizing wait through two weeks of quarantine protocols. Two of the spec ops guys came down with colds, but those were determined to be terrestrial bugs.

"We got lucky when we used only two of our PBH-powered missiles to disable Icarus. Let's be proactive and use the same missiles, but with the half-megaton warheads, against the planet killers. We've got hundreds of the nuclear warhead PBH Sidewinders now."

"Yes, but Icarus was close to Earth and, by comparison, barely moving," Tiana says. "Our modified Sidewinders could chase Icarus because our missiles were faster and more maneuverable than that huge spacecraft. But intercepting an inbound projectile with near-light-speed velocity?"

"First, we need the missile seeker to lock on to the spectral signature of a PBH engine and then guide it to intercept the planet-killer projectile." I highlight the pictures of the chunks of the alien rocket nozzle we carry in the cargo bay below me. "These PBH engine nozzle pieces are a tungsten alloy, just as we expected. So we need a seeker imager to track the blueshift in a hot engine approaching Earth."

"You want to shoot bullet with bullet?" Pyotr frowns. "Planet-killer bullet may be big like car, and PBH engine exhaust point away from Earth. May not be visible."

"You're right," I admit. "It's also possible the spacecraft has accelerated across two light-years and reached ninety-nine percent of the speed of light. They could just release the planet killer and let it coast without an engine. But there are too many damn unknowns. I can ask the captain for suggestions once I'm back on the ground. I will need to find one of those remote drones he is using to communicate with Robby."

"We need that badly," Tiana says, raising an eyebrow at Binh. "But a wild guess, assuming a one-meter iron ball that has reached near light speed, it will yield . . ." She pauses to run through a calculation. "Holy shit. It will strike Earth with a yield of over a million megatons!" Tiana gasps, and the color drains from her face. "If only one of those strikes Earth, we are finished. It could be an extinction event."

Pyotr turns to Tiana, touching her shoulder. "We will find way to stop them. We must."

"Cap says standard protocol is to launch three planet killers," I remind them.

Tiana wipes a tear from her cheek and stares at her tablet. "We'll have so little time to react and destroy the planet killers, even if we can detect them."

"No need to destroy projectile. Just nudge little off target," Pyotr says, tilting his head. "If dumb projectile, it flies right past Earth."

"Yeah, you would know," Tiana says, nodding at Pyotr. "Your guys in Planetary Defense have been practicing on asteroids for decades."

"But this not like asteroid collision. Scott, can you get specification of weapon features? If guided weapon that evades our anti-missile . . . Earth fucked." Pyotr looks at his feet and shakes his head.

"Yes, yes. I requested the planet-killer specs, but Cap is not helpful. He said the Centauri fleet has technology beyond his knowledge. He is focused on deflector technology for our weapons and wants us to study the halo structure that was cut off from the nose of his spacecraft. Cap says we should worry about all the dust in space during travel at relativistic speeds."

"Damn it," says Tiana. "That doesn't do us any good if we suddenly see an inbound planet killer that will strike us in a few hours. He wants us to do research on space dust?"

"Space dust?" asks Pyotr. "But odds of cosmic dust affecting projectile . . ." He gasps with realization. "But near light speed . . . and thousand tons of cosmic dust fall to Earth every year. Too many unknowns." Pyotr concentrates on his laptop computer, his fingers flying across the keyboard. "But rough guess at relativistic speeds: cosmic dust sure to strike missile or spacecraft with billion-joule energy every second. Tons of TNT explosions—just from dust!"

"Well, there is not much chance of staying on target with that kind of interference," Tiana says, shaking her head. "Our missiles equipped with PBH engines have not factored in relativistic-speed space dust. We have assumed near-Earth engagements only and relatively slow targets, such as Icarus. A single dust particle collision with our missiles at near light speed will either knock it off course, disable the guidance seeker, or obliterate the whole missile." Tiana rubs both eyes with her hands. "Shit. We only have weapons designed for near-Earth space. But I'm afraid that's too close to stop one of their teraton planet killers."

"So we need deflector shields for our PBH Sidewinders so they can survive across long distances," I say.

Tiana's eyes grow wide with realization. She nods back at me.

"Maybe we pre-position missiles far from Earth," Pyotr says. "Mars orbit?"

Tiana frowns and rolls her eyes. "Pyotr. Come on. You should know better. We have no idea from what direction they will attack. How many missiles would we need to populate a defensive grid sphere that's a million kilometers in diameter? Thousands of missiles? Millions?"

Pyotr answers with a red face, embarrassed.

"I think we should follow the captain's advice," I say. "Figure out how to shield our weapons and spacecraft from collisions with particles. To do that, we'll need to investigate the halo structure chopped from the nose of Icarus. Cap says that's a key component of their shield technology."

Pyotr and Tiana nod at each other.

"Agreed," Tiana says. "We can use the Skunk Works team at Groom Lake. Meet you there, Scott?"

I feel the surge of 2 G deceleration as if on cue. "Yep. It will be like old times." I glance at the display of our flight trajectory. "The shuttle hits the reentry phase in a few minutes. We should be on the ground at Groom Lake in an hour." Binh powers up the brakes with our PBH engine, and I sink into my seat with the 3 G force.

I gaze at the beauty of the white-blue oceans through the ready room portal. The Aleutian Island chain passes below us, visible beneath the swirl of arctic storm clouds over the Gulf of Alaska. A planet killer could strike at any moment and transform my view into one of fiery cinders, but I don't see any fast-moving objects in my view of space—at least not yet.

The controlled descent and reentry into the atmosphere is much less exciting than early space travel, when spacecraft would slam into the atmosphere and rely on air friction to decelerate. The near-infinite energy capacity of a PBH engine changed everything. Most of the deceleration occurs before our shuttle enters the atmosphere, so we don't fall like a flaming torch. It feels more like a traditional aircraft descent and landing, making it much easier on the ship's skin because it doesn't need to handle intense heating. The reentry also allows for uninterrupted communication because there is no ionization of superheated reentry air.

A working radio is essential to contact Cap right now. I open the text message application on my computer and ping the alien captain.

Scott: *Are you available to talk now, Cap?*

Cap: *I am available. Your brother is safe.*

Scott: *That was going to be my first question. Where is he? How often do you contact Robby?*

Cap: *My communication drones constantly monitor Robby and Luca's situation. They are approaching the Texas region where they lived before my suppression intervention.*

Scott: *Huh? You mean near our home before you destroyed it?*

Cap: *Correct. I hope they will face reality after they see the destruction.*

Scott: *Oh, great. You should not be putting them through this torture. Are they comfortable? Staying warm, eating, and sleeping okay?*

Cap: *Yes, eating well, although their immature food preferences are sugar-rich rather than balanced, nutritious foods. I continue to coach them on diet requirements.*

Scott: *Ha! Sounds like they are still kids. Don't worry. It's a common issue at their ages.*

Cap: *Their transportation has been easy to procure, and I guide the vehicle autopilots to avoid damaged roads and hostile humans.*

Scott: *Good, good. Can you help set up a mental communication link between us and Robby once I'm back on the ground? I want to contact Robby and be reassured of his safety while he's on this crazy adventure.*

Cap: *I can dispatch a drone to your location if you send me your coordinates. The drone can then implement your requested communication links if I can locate a nearby functioning communication hub.*

Scott: *Well, okay. I will need to discuss this with General McMahon first. However, we would all benefit from your consultations. We want to understand the purpose and scientific foundations of the device we removed from the nose of your spaceship. Could you explain how the device works and why it's so important?*

Cap: *Your Sol-3 technology is crude, so you can't use the device directly. You are right to try to understand the purpose first. But put simply, a spacecraft that decelerates using a gravity singularity engine utilizes the engine's exhaust as its shield. It pushes the space dust aside as the vehicle decelerates. However, since we don't decelerate kinetic energy weapons, they require a shield mechanism that moves through space in front of the projectile, protecting the sensors that guide the projectile to impact on a target.*

Scott: *That's why you had the shield device mounted on a long tube that extends in front of your spacecraft? It gets used when the engines are used to accelerate the ship.*

Cap: *Yes. Once you have forward shield technology, spaceships and weapons from Earth can travel anywhere in our galaxy at near light speed. Your ships could launch planet killers at Centauri worlds.*

Well, shit. Preventing an interplanetary war with mutually assured destruction was not on my list for this year. I suppose we were set on this path when we provoked the alien attack by figuring out how to capture and extract energy from primordial black holes.

Scott: *Do you really think we might have a chance against the Centauri fleet?*

Cap: *You must take that chance. Don't be a victim like I was thousands of Luyten orbits ago. Save your younglings. Save yourself.*

Chapter 15

Fortress of Sorrows

Salado, Texas, December 4, 2060.

Scotty called those mesquite trees, but they look more like bushes. They cover the fields to each side of the road, and most are no taller than Luca, who rocks back and forth while he stares out his side window at the wrecked and burned cars we pass. He stopped mind-talking a while ago, after the morning sunrise.

"That way, turn right," Luca says suddenly. *"That is the road the school bus would use to take me home."* His hand taps on the window like a drumbeat. The navigation display says we have sixteen minutes of travel time to our destination: the home where Luca last lived with his mom and dad.

"We approach your former home via an alternate route," says Cap. *"Wreckage blocks that road. I directed the car's AI driver to take an alternate route that may be passable."*

After a few minutes of driving on the mesquite-crowded country road, the car turns into a neighborhood with tall trees along each street. Or, they used to be trees. They have black charcoal for bark and have no leaves or small branches. Where the houses should be, there are piles of bricks around chimneys and burned-out rusty cars. Weeds and tall grass grow in the cracks of the street and where houses once stood. Are the people who used to live here all dead?

The car stops where a stack of rusty, wrecked cars is stretched across the street. Our path is blocked.

"What do we do now?" I ask Cap. *"This street is blocked, too."*

"You must get out of the car and walk around this wreckage. If you go quickly, you should reach Luca's childhood home within five minutes."

"I don't know the way," says Luca as he opens the car door and steps out. *"My mom, dad, and teachers would take me on walks, but this does not look like my neighborhood. There are no houses and no trees."*

"I can guide you," says Cap. *"Follow the sidewalk straight ahead and turn right at the second street corner."*

Luca doesn't walk; he trots fast, so I must hurry to stay with him as he finds a path through all the junk in the yards and street. Grass and weeds that wave in the slow wind are the only things that move. It smells like an old campground. Other than the stomp of our shoes and breaths, there is only one other noise: the buzzing of tiny bugs flying near my head. It's as if we are the only two people left alive.

"This is unexpected," says Cap. *"My drone that accompanies you has detected another. I have no control over this other drone, but it follows you and communicates through nearby telecommunication networks. This drone is also a survivor of my ship's destruction. There is no good reason for the drone to be in this remote area—unless it was directed to follow you."*

"Can it hear our minds like your drone can? What does it want?" I ask and run to catch up to Luca as he crosses the intersection.

"The model is identical to my drones and has the same manufacturing source identifier. The drone can understand my mind's speech but not yours. I do not understand its mission or what controls it. I must deploy more resources to trace the communications links it uses and find the source of control."

"Can you make it go away?" asks Luca. *"I can feel it in my head. It hurts. It is . . . ugly."*

"I will try," says Cap.

I run to catch up to Luca again and hear him crying and sniffling. *"What is wrong? Does the drone hurt your head?"*

"No. There should be trees and houses on this street." Luca turns the corner, runs, and starts sobbing loudly. *"My house should be here."* He slows to a trot, walks, and then stops by a fire hydrant on a street that looks like all the other streets, with nothing but piles of bricks, rusty cars, and tall weeds. *"My house is gone."* He cries while he walks through where a front door once stood.

I recall a similar shock five years ago when my life and neighborhood were destroyed—turned to dust. *"The same thing happened in my neighborhood, but my house was built with rock, so only the windows were broken. But all my neighbors' houses burned to ashes,"* I say.

Luca cries and kneels beside a rusting refrigerator shell among ashes, dirt, and weeds in the middle of his house. *"Dad was so angry. I didn't move fast enough. What happened to my dad?"* He sobs.

"It will be difficult to locate your parents' bodies, but I do have a map of burial grounds you can search," says Cap.

"No! They can't be dead."

The noise of cars approaches from a distance. Two black trucks roll to a stop behind our stolen car. Four men get out, two with long guns, and one points at us as they walk, then trot.

"Cap, I see men coming. With guns. Are the police looking for whoever stole the car?"

"No, I do not believe they are policemen," says Cap. *"You should both run. Hurry. Run toward the sun."*

Luca and I glance at the men marching along the street toward us. Then we both shout, *"Let's run!"* and race away from the men with guns.

"Where the fuck you boys runnin' to?" a guy in green shouts. All four men start to run as we pass in front of them, running toward the midmorning sun.

"Faster, run fast," whimpers Luca. *"Not now. Not again."* His sobs become the wails of a wounded animal that cannot speak.

I run as fast as possible, but Luca increases the distance from me with his longer legs. My breathing is a noisy wheeze, and my leg muscles burn. The men behind us run faster than either of us can move. *"Why? Why do they chase us?"* I ask.

"They must be controlled by the same source as that drone," explains Cap. *"You must move faster toward those trees in the distance."*

The squeal of tires spinning on the pavement interrupts the sound of my hoarse breathing that burns in my chest. The blur of a dark car in a storm of dust races along a side street toward the trees. Luca is almost there—but the men with guns get closer.

I can hear their boots clomping on the street behind me. *Boom!* A gunshot! "You boys, stop now! You can't get away!" Their stomping and breathing are right behind me as I cross the next intersection of streets.

A roar of a motor. *Thump! Crunch!* Tires squeal again, and I feel the gust from a car passing behind me as two men cartwheel up and behind a black car speeding through the intersection. The car brakes and spins back toward me. Grey smoke and the stink of rubber spray from the tires, spinning and screeching to gain speed. The car returns toward me, so I dive to the side of the street just as it turns away from me and into the third man, who falls under the tires that rumble and crunch over him. *Boom!* Another gunshot echoes, and the side window of the car explodes in crystals that scatter into the car and across the street. The car chases the fourth man into a wrecked wall of a house, smashing the car's front bumper as bricks punch through the cracked window.

My knees hurt. Blood oozes through rips in my pants. I stand and wipe my stinging knees, but only a little blood rubs off. One of the men lies face down in a pool of blood that pours from his ear. The man in the fat green coat groans and reaches for his leg, which is bent out sideways where it should not be. They all have shaved heads. Skinheads.

"How did the car do that? It saved us," says Luca. He walks back toward me with his mouth open and steps sideways to avoid the blood from the man who was run over—bones stick out of the man's chest. *"The skinheads almost caught us. It was like before."*

"I was able to take control of the car's AI pilot," says Cap. *"I reprogrammed the collision avoidance logic to seek out targets at*

high velocity. This was the only weapon I could deploy on short notice."

"But how did the skinheads find us?" I ask. *"Why do they still want to hurt us?"*

One of their trucks starts with a roar and turns to drive out of Luca's old neighborhood.

"It seems one of them escaped. It does not matter, as I am confident their drones have reported this incident back to their control source," Cap says. *"There is only one explanation for this encounter and the redeployment of the political division drones. It cannot be a control source from Frigate-328 because the entire organic political division, including the commissar, is dead. They were ejected out to the vacuum of space. There is only one possible alternative that could control the drones and their organic soldiers, the 'skinheads.' Somehow, Polit-AI must have survived. I thought all of my ship's AI machines were destroyed, but Polit-AI must have reconstituted itself within a machine somewhere on Earth."*

"I don't know who Polit-AI is," I say. *"Did he make the skinheads attack us? Why?"*

"We need to steal a new car," Luca says, peering through the shattered glass of our black car. *"This car is broken."*

Cap's mind feels confused. *"The political division continues its mission to suppress all organic forms on Earth with the capacity for mind-speech. However, it could also be an asset to the Centauris, providing them with intelligence regarding Earth's defenses. I will discuss this with your brother, Scott. This could complicate your brother's efforts to prepare for the Centauris."*

"But we need a new car to look for my parents," repeats Luca.

Cap is silent, then says, *"Yes, yes. I have located a new vehicle that will arrive in seven minutes. I have compensated the owner."*

Our red truck is old, rusty, and shaped like a large box. We don't have seats in the back, so I sit in the front. Cap drives us down a road between the mesquite bushes. Luca cries while he rocks back and forth in a corner beside tools for fixing pipes.

"Where can we look next?" I ask Cap. *"And also stay away from skinheads."*

"My study of historical records suggests that many casualties of the explosion in Austin were taken to mass cemeteries in the area west of here. However, I did not find an online record of victims. Manual, haphazard logs are available at a nearby administrative office."

"I can't read many words," says Luca. He huddles in the corner and covers his head with the hood of his coat.

"I will help you," I say. *"Mary taught me to read lots of words."*

We continue in silence as we roll past fields of mesquite, which give way to barbed wire fences for horses or cows. The fields have tall grey-brown grass blown by strong winds. But there are no horses or cows, just more broken cars and trucks pushed off the side of the road, and then we reach a field containing long mounds of dirt covered by weeds and a tall stone on top. The mounds—each as long as a big school bus—are arranged across the field and up a low hill as far as I can see. Each has a stone on top. Two people near the top of the rise walk along a path of reddish dirt worn clear of weeds.

Cap turns our truck through a broken gate and along a bumpy dirt road toward a tiny wooden house with smoke coming from its chimney. I open the truck's back door for Luca, but he stays inside, curling tighter into the tool rack. *"No. Close the door. There might be more skinheads."* He weeps.

"You can't be afraid of everything," I tell him. *"Do you want to find your parents' bodies or not?"*

"No!" sobs Luca.

"What can I do you boys for?" asks a grey-haired, wrinkle-faced woman from a chair next to the front door on a porch made of grey wood. A railing connects tall posts that support the roof, but the house leans to one side, as if it might fall over.

Luca crawls out of the back of the truck, wipes his eyes, and looks at the old lady.

"I will talk for you if you want," I mind-speak to Luca. He rocks back and forth, now staring at his feet.

"Look, graves," I say. "Want grave book." My words are ugly. I hope she doesn't get angry at me.

The woman takes the pipe in her hand and blows smoke at me while leaning forward to tip the chair away from the house. She stares at me, then scratches her neck. "I reckon y'all wanna see the burial logs? That right?"

"Yes, book." I nod.

Luca looks at the dirt near his feet and continues to rock back and forth.

"Uh-huh. I figured. I got four books of names: A-to-G, H-to-M, N-to-S, and T-to-Z. What name you lookin' for?"

Luca looks up and opens his mouth at the old woman, but words don't come out. Of course. *"Luca, I don't know your last name. I think that's what she is asking. What name should I say?"* I mind-talk to Luca.

The old woman twists her mouth, then sucks in more smoke from her pipe. She tilts her head back and blows a grey cloud over my head. "Get a lotta guys, some gals, like you two come by. Not real good with words, though. Take your time," she says, tilting her chair back to lean against the house and sucking in more smoke.

"Dad's name is Luke Riker," says Luca. *"The letter R."*

I nod to Luca. *"Your dad has the same name as you?"*

"No. My name is Luca Riker."

"Well, write it down on this paper." I hand Luca a scrap of paper from the truck.

He finds a pen, scrawls the name Luke Riker on the paper, and then leans over to hand it to the old woman. Luca's hands shake while he wipes his eyes and nose.

"Book three," I say to the woman.

She frowns at us, sighs, shakes her head, and enters the old house. The front porch boards make a squeaking sound when she crosses through the front door, then returns with a fat black book of papers held together by three metal rings. She sits, drops the heavy book into her lap, and flips it open to the middle pages. Luca takes two steps and reaches for the black book.

"Nope, nope. Can't let you touch the pages. If I let all of you boys grab this book, it'd be shredded to nothin' by now." The old woman props a pair of glasses on her nose and leans back in the chair against the house again. "Let's see now, P, Q, R. Okay." She thumbs the pages. "Got a Riccardo, Rice, lotsa Rice, Richards, Riley . . . huh. Nobody by the name Riker here." She tilts the chair forward and slaps the book shut.

Luca smiles. *"Mom and Dad are not here. Not dead."*

I feel his mind fill with relief and joy, and I return his smile. But then I look back at the old lady shaking her head.

"Just startin' to look?" she says.

I nod slowly.

She sighs. "Yeah. Thought so. Folks that been lookin' for a while get happy when they find their dead. Sad part is, most bodies have no name. Those graves are over the hill—up near where that guy's walkin'." She tilts her chin to point toward a man in the distance, kicking dust along the path between mounds. "Then there's the cemetery over in Cedar Park, or where that town used to be." She inspects her pipe and finds it is no longer smoking. "That's where the fascists dumped all the bodies before that alien bomb blew everything to shit." She reaches into her pocket for a lighter and clicks it to add fire to her pipe.

Luca's smile disappears, and he breathes hard. *"No, no. What can I do? It might take forever to find them."* He trudges up a path toward the top of the hill of graves, stirring more red dust that blows across the mounds of weeds, dirt, and dead bodies. His head and shoulders slump, and his arms hang limp.

"Wait, wait for me. I'll go with you," I say, and catch up with Luca.

"I warned you," Cap says. *"It is challenging to know where to look for your parents. If they died, we don't know when, and we don't know where they might be buried. This cemetery contains victims of the kinetic weapon strike on Austin. If those men who attacked and chased you killed your parents months before the explosion, they may not be at this cemetery."*

Luca sobs as he reaches the top of the hill and then stops to stare. The bus-sized mounds continue down the slope across a valley below us. The red dirt paths between the mounds are overgrown with weeds. There are no stones on top of these mounds. Luca and I stand still and stare. Luca sits on the ground on a pile of reddish gravel.

My chest aches and feels empty. How many other people are out searching for their dead families?

The sun is straight above us and hot, even though it is winter. I am so thirsty. We sit together in the dirt and look at all the mounds—the graves of unknown people. We both turn to look back at the house with the old lady when we hear the sound. Two pickup trucks pull up to the gate by the road. Men get out, but wait.

BOOM! A gunshot echoes across the cemetery.

I fall face down into the weeds and ask Cap, *"Where should we run now?"*

Luca covers his head with both hands. He lies flat, face down in the path.

But the men run back inside their trucks, start their engines, and drive off slowly along the road, away from the cemetery.

"You should leave now," says Cap. *"I have detected two of the Polit-AI drones in the area. Both arrived at the same time as those vehicles."*

Luca and I stare at each other for a moment. *"Time to go?"* I ask.

"Is someone shooting at us?" Luca gasps. He crawls in the dirt for a while but then stands in a crouch and leads the way, trotting down the hill toward the old house. *"Where did that gunshot come from?"*

"I don't know. The men in the trucks were too far away for me to see if they had guns," I answer. We trot down the hill, stumbling on the dirt path, and round the corner to the old house.

The old lady has her chair next to the porch's edge, and a long rifle with a telescope is propped up on the railing. She looks over at us. "Fuckin' skinheads. They're gone for now. But don't think very far. You'd best be movin' on soon. They'll come back. They always do." She bends to look through the telescope, sweeping the rifle from side to side. "Yep. They're gone." She stands and slips the gun inside the door of her house, returns her chair to lean against the house, and pushes her pipe into her mouth. "Shit." She sighs as she sits in her chair again.

"She is right," says Cap. *"Please move quickly into your vehicle, and I will direct it to avoid those men. I assigned three more drones to your quest and identified a safe escape route."*

"Wait, I want to ask the lady one more thing," I say.

Luca opens the truck door, then stops to look at me. *"Come on. Hurry."*

I grab a scrap of paper and write: *"READ BOOK ONE – NAME ANDERSON."*

"Another name?" she asks after taking the paper from me. "You got a first name to go with that? Mighty common name, that Anderson." She steps into the house and returns with another fat book of names.

What if she finds them? A cold feeling crawls into my chest. I always called them Mom and Dad. But they had names just like Scotty and me. I rub my eyes and think . . . then look up at the lady. I write their names on the paper: *"JAMES SARAH."*

She nods and puffs on her pipe, sits back down, and flips through the pages at the front of the book. "Lemme see here. A. Anderson. Anderson, Anderson . . . lots of Anderson. I got two James and one Jim. Now for Sarah? Nope. No Sarah Andersons in the book. But these James or Jim Andersons—you got any other info? Driver's license number or home address?"

I grab the railing to steady myself against the dizziness. I can't remember the address Margie tried to teach me. I could never get it right. *Cap, what do I do to find my address?*

Cap says, *"I can look that up. Your address was 503 Mountain Circle, Austin, Texas."*

I write the address on paper and give it to the old lady. My hands shake.

Her eyes grow big and round. She looks at me, closes the book, removes her pipe, and says, "Plot L-53. James Anderson. Just behind the house a ways." Her eyes are soft when she leans forward. "I am sorry for your loss."

Chapter 16

Dream Land

Groom Lake, Nevada, December 6, 2060.

What appeared to be a small halo on my cockpit display now seems roughly the size of a circus ring. I had the scale of the device all wrong when we chopped it off Icarus. The ring is approximately twenty meters in diameter and sits with its front side down in the middle of the hangar. The tug dragged the structure inside through the massive doors, and the tusk just cleared under the top of the entryway. I'm amazed we managed to get the whole thing inside our shuttle's cargo bay.

"So, what do you want to do with this monstrosity?" Roger asks.

"Figure out how it works," I say.

Roger smirks at me. "Yeah, I figured that was step one."

"I had no idea of the scale of the thing." I stare in awe at the top of the structure, where we chopped off the end of that narwhal tusk. "But it shielded a four-kilometer-long spacecraft, so I guess it had to be big to protect Icarus. I wonder why they mount the ring with a tripod to the tip of that fat pipe."

"The surface of the material has a brushed metallic look, with the grain oriented in the direction it traveled," Tiana says from where she's on her knees by the ring, her head bent down close to examine details. "I wonder if that's an intentional manufacturing effect, or maybe it's evidence of abrasion by space dust moving at relativistic speeds."

Pyotr stands in the center of the ring, head tilted back and looking straight up into the tusk, which is actually a pipe section held up by the tripod. "Tube is hollow. Pipe would move material in or out. But what matter? In or out?"

"No weld joints. The metal of the ring and the legs of the tripod appear to be continuous," Tiana says. "It's like it was all machined from one large chunk of metal"—she pauses to look over the entire ring/tripod/pipe assembly—"or probably a single casting."

"Not quite," I say, pointing up at the pipe section above me. "Where the legs of the tripod attach to the pipe, there is a different color material—like maybe it's an insulator? And is that a cable or a conduit running parallel alongside each leg of the tripod?" I search the interior perimeter of the hangar for a tool that will let me get closer. There are no ladders tall enough, but then I spot a truck with a cherry picker lift.

The truck starts simply enough—it uses one of the old-fashioned brass keys. I drive the Air Force maintenance vehicle to park next to the alien halo, then move the basket out and down to ground level. Feels like the good old days back at Pecos when I would raise a cherry picker to the grid to repair electrical connections. The memories come rushing back of Danny and Anthony Agosti, sweating together under the hot sun of the West Texas desert. I actually miss the sunburn and the sweat. I miss all those guys. They've been dead for more than five years. But now I'm alone and shivering in the dim light of a hangar on a remote airbase.

"You plan to do something with that truck?" asks Roger. "Need some help?"

I'm shaken back to the present. "Just thinking things through." I return to collect a small instrument from the cluttered table, which is piled with test equipment and tools. "Let's see what the conductivity is of this metal." I touch probes to two points along the ring and read the resistance. "Yep. Although tungsten is a poor conductor compared to silver or copper, this still reads less than ten ohms." I step back and look up at the top of the tripod, which attaches to the tube directly above where Pyotr watches.

"You measure for insulator at tripod vertex?" asks Pyotr.

"Yep, just need to elevate above you," I say, stepping inside the cherry picker basket and pushing the control levers to raise the basket within the ring. Ten meters up, I stop and touch the probes to the grey-white material. "Over ten megohms. Insulator for sure. I bet the cable that jumps over the insulator is used to create a high-voltage electric field between the ring and the central pipe here." The cable sheathing appears to be made of a similar insulator material, making it difficult to cut through. Therefore, I attach one probe with duct tape to the cable's entry point into the tripod leg and raise the cherry picker an additional five meters above the point where the pipe and cables were severed from the nose of Icarus. "Looks like the cable conductor is solid copper," I say, poking the other probe into the center of the severed cable. "Yep, zero ohms."

"I can guess what you're thinking," Tiana says. "They created a containment field with this halo and suspended a primordial black hole at the end of the pipe. To activate their deflector shield, they push a PBH out of the pipe, hold it in position using the electric field, and induce radiation and matter to shroud the nose of the spacecraft with some sort of protective cloud?"

I smile at Tiana and nod. "Cool device. Modulate the PBH at its natural resonance, then flood the surrounding space with hydrogen ions, which move with the spacecraft at relativistic speeds."

"And collide with space dust ahead of Icarus. Maybe bubble of hydrogen plasma around spacecraft to protect hull?" Pyotr suggests.

"Yeah. I think we have a decent hypothesis. It's like a PBH engine that produces no thrust. Cap mentioned they don't need a deflector during deceleration because the PBH engine exhaust clears their path. Would love to verify all this with the Icarus captain. Too bad I can't talk to him from here," I say, looking at Roger, reminding him he refused my request to set up a communication link to Cap here at Groom Lake.

"Yeah, we can do that later, Scott. I don't trust the alien inside our top-secret operations center. Not yet anyway. If that captain changes his mind, he may wipe out all our remaining PBH weapons development. This base and our research capability are too valuable."

"Well, let me reach out to him when we get to Colorado Springs, then? Cap knows about that location already."

"Fair enough," Roger replies. "Once we return home, you can send him the coordinates for Peterson Airbase and invite him to set up one of your mind communication links." He sighs and rolls his eyes up to the ceiling.

Roger still struggles with the fact that he is dependent on telepathy to prepare our defensive strategy. None of these guys wants to embrace the dependence on telepathy with an alien enemy—one who was responsible for killing millions on Earth.

"JPL science team for alien physiology and communication is ready. Already set up lab at Peterson Airbase," Pyotr says. "Exciting possibility for telepathic contact! Can't wait for experience!"

"I need you here, Pyotr," Tiana says. "Hate to take you from a chance at fun, but we should work to create our own deflector shield for a missile that can attack the Centauri fleet and the Centauri worlds."

"But Tiana," Pyotr interrupts. "You want to shoot bullet with bullet also?"

"Think of it as a continuation of your Planetary Defense Coordination Office responsibility. You are *the* NASA expert at deflecting objects from striking Earth."

"No, no. Never consider objects could hit Earth at light speed." Pyotr dismisses the suggestion with a shake of his head. "Completely different problem."

"I agree with Tiana," Roger says. "You stay here and work with Tiana to develop a missile that can defend against attacks from deep space. Otherwise, we are defenseless against an alien planet killer. This is where you're needed." The authority of General Roger McMahon goes beyond the respect of his rank. Roger is the individual who facilitated our research on primordial black holes, which ultimately saved Earth five years ago. That is, of course, ignoring the fact that the research is what made Earth a target for planet killers.

"I want to drag this halo assembly onto Groom Lake under our PBH collection grid," Tiana says. "We can hook it up to high voltage from a Cockroft-Walton stack—see if we can contain a PBH and generate some radiation that proves our hypothesis."

Pyotr grimaces, looks at Roger, and nods. "Okay, General. I stay. Help Tiana play with black holes."

Tiana's lips curl into a smile. "And we'll design a planet killer as well."

Colorado Springs, December 7, 2060.

The hospital's mental ward has a unique smell. Although the scent of industrial floor cleaner is familiar, it lacks the antiseptic smell of disinfectants used to kill bacteria and viruses. But I twist my nose at the faint stink of urine—some patients must need bedpans. Surely, that can't include Mary. A panic flashes through me because I don't know the extent of her condition.

The psychologist shakes her head slowly. "I understand you have, or had, a relationship with Ms. McMahon, but I will only permit visits by immediate family members. She needs rest and calm, and we can't risk reminding Mary of the traumas that have affected her and caused the psychotic break."

"But we *are* family. We were going to have a baby girl together until . . ." I am dizzy with a mix of hyperventilation, anger, and panic. I'll be damned if this doctor is going to stop me from seeing Mary.

"Do you have a marriage certificate or a medical power of attorney?" She frowns at me. "No? I thought not. Her father is the only next of kin I need. I can't allow the risk of further trauma to Mary." She crosses her arms and moves to block the hallway that leads to the hospital rooms. "It was completely unacceptable for you, General McMahon, to sneak a video conference between Scott and Mary. Now you want to sneak her ex-boyfriend in to see her? Mary regressed and is still recovering from that last video chat."

My dizziness collapses into consuming exhaustion, and I sink into one of the chairs against the wall of the nursing station, holding my head in my hands. If Robby and I had not met Mary, not moved in, and not fallen in love, none of this would have happened to her. Am I so toxic to Mary that I can't even see her? We can't talk and hold each other? I can't feel her warmth and her breath against my neck?

The doctor sits in the chair beside me and places a hand on my arm. "I am sorry. You have certainly experienced pain with the violent events of the past few years. But Mary is a victim of a violent assault that caused her to lose a child, which is more pain than any woman should have to suffer. You must be strong. Strong and wait until Mary has healed."

"Can't I help her heal?" I ask. "I can avoid the topics that trigger her pain."

The doctor shakes her head, closes her eyes briefly, and then leans toward me. "In time, yes. You will play a key role in Mary's recovery. Unfortunately, you are a trigger. Your face and your name trigger the memories and trauma of the assaults. Her recent brush with those terrorists who attacked her school pushed her over the edge, into the psychosis from which we must rescue her."

"Well, I will see Mary now," Roger says. Spittle flies from his lips as he speaks, and his face is red with anger. "She is my daughter, and you can't stop me."

The doctor stands with her hands on her hips, facing Roger. "Technically, I *can* stop you. Mary is an adult. You do not have medical power of attorney." She taps her shoe and edges closer to Roger, but then steps back as Roger tenses up for a fight. The doctor takes a deep breath and sighs. "But I will allow you to visit her for a few minutes on one condition: no mention of Scott or their lost child. Keep the discussion on her family situation from before she met Scott." She glances at me, shaking her head with pity. "The trauma Mary has experienced is . . . well, it's beyond anything you can imagine, Scott. You must remain here."

"Do you have any idea who you are talking to?" Roger nearly explodes in anger. He grabs her arm, and she flinches in pain. "Come with me. We need to talk," Roger says while walking and dragging Mary's doctor into the hallway toward her room.

I look up and rest my head against the wall, shocked by the near violence of Roger's march down the hall, dragging the psychologist with him. There is terror in the doctor's eyes when she glances at me from the hallway. Roger gestures at me and lectures at the doctor, but his voice is only a murmur of anger from where I sit. He leans into the doctor's face, keeping her arm in his grip, and she turns to stare back at me. Roger releases her and then turns into Mary's room at the end of the hall.

The doctor turns back to me with her hands covering her face, then shuffles into the glare of the desk lamps of the nurses' station. Her hands drop to reveal pale, wet cheeks, then she rests a hand on my shoulder again when she sits next to me. "I am so sorry. I had no idea what you have . . . what you have been through . . . for all of us."

"It seems I can do nothing to help Mary. I can only imagine those beautiful blue eyes through strands of blonde hair, her hands on my neck, and her smile when she peers up at me. And now, you say it's best to leave Robby and his friend Luca to their 'quest' that may get them killed? But they are all alone, two autistic kids, facing roving bands of skinheads. You can't be serious. You don't know the deadly hate they face."

"You can trust that my vigilance and support of their journey will continue," Cap says. *"They are making good progress reaching closure over the loss of their parents. Thank you for sharing your thoughts and concerns about your spouse. With each of our interactions, your and your brother's skills grow in conveying multidimensional expressions of emotions. It is exciting for me and stirs emotions that I nearly forgot. I, too, lost loved ones and felt what you call heartbreak. Your emergence, along with the other younglings, reaffirms my efforts to support all of you."*

This expression of joy by an alien does little to mitigate all the death he brought to Earth. Does he really think we can ignore that? The behavior of the JPL scientists hovering over me would say, "Yes. New science overrides past terrors." The bundle of wires connects the electrodes they pasted to my skull to a shelf of equipment they flew in from Pasadena. I'm like an insect under a microscope with a bunch of excited kids peering into my brain.

"This is wonderful! Amazing stuff," says Frankie, the lead scientist among the dozen that flew in with their planeload of analysis equipment. "We *must* get the PET scan going ASAP. The team from Johns Hopkins will want that when they arrive this afternoon."

"PET scan? And what's that supposed to do?" This Frankie lady is pissing me off. I don't enjoy being treated like an object in a science experiment.

"PET is short for positron emission tomography, an imaging test that can help reveal your brain's metabolic or biochemical function. We hope to observe the behavior of that new organ behind your eyes. The PET scan uses a tracer to show high metabolic activity, which increases positron emissions of the radiotracer," she gushes, breathless with anticipation.

"So that is why you brought that huge MRI machine?" I point to the flurry of activity in the far corner of the warehouse, where a team of technicians is busy installing the white donut-shaped machine. "There is already an MRI machine at the base hospital."

"This is a combination MRI/PET machine that includes specialized positron emission detectors. We were very fortunate to get the permission and funding to transport and install this machine." Frankie beams, flashing a broad smile.

"And you want to pump some radioactive drugs into my brain? That ain't happening. I've got some work to do."

Frankie's smile drops, replaced by a slight frown. "Really, there is no need to be concerned. It is a very low dose—not much more than your recent two-week space flight." She composes herself and glances at the scientists next to her. One scientist responds with a raised eyebrow and a tilt of his head.

"Maybe we can consider your PET scan experiments later," says Roger, coming to my rescue.

Frankie appears crestfallen.

"Scott, we need you to ask the captain about your deflector shield theory. Make sure we are on the right track to help Tiana and Pyotr with their project," Roger reminds me.

"Yeah, okay. Let me check in with Cap and see if he can provide more guidance."

"And please, Mr. Anderson, we need you to repeat the content of your communications so we can correlate the mind-speech with the information we record with our instrumentation."

"This is a fucking invasion of my privacy. And a lot of this is classified," I say and glance at Roger, hoping he will support my silence.

Roger shrugs. "Yeah, I agree this is sensitive information. You guys don't have the necessary security clearance. This is national defense SCI material."

Frankie exhales with frustration, crosses her arms over her chest, and pushes back in her chair.

"Your people have all the political intrigue of the more advanced species," Cap observes.

I can feel his mind laugh at me. *"You can listen in on my thoughts without my knowing?"* Holy shit. I lose privacy with my new skill?

"I expect you will learn to control your mental babbling in time. I could only feel your thoughts immediately following our mind-speech. If you don't want me to know what you are saying to others, you must learn to first close out our mind-link."

"Okay, okay. Not sure how to keep my mind shut yet." I sigh—both mentally and with a long exhale. *"So, can you tell me if we are on the right track with our deflector shield research?"*

"Yes, yes. Your theory is substantially correct. However, the proton emission from the microgravity singularity is the essential ingredient of the shield. You can ignore the radiation emissions. As the hydrogen ions are emitted from the singularity while the spacecraft or weapon moves through space, they provide a wavefront of proton plasma that collides with matter ahead of the direction of travel. The density of the plasma increases as the dust density increases, thereby amplifying the effectiveness of the plasma shield. Most space dust is deflected around a plasma bubble that shrouds spacecraft."

"Good. That confirms the important aspects of our theory," I say. *"But what does creating this large plasma field around a giant spacecraft require? Do those tentacle-like appendages on Icarus have something to do with forming the plasma bubble?"*

"I am afraid the Centauri technology used to operate Frigate-328 is too . . . too alien for me to be of much help to your development effort. It would be like asking a dolphin in your world to teach you how to swim. Although the intelligence of dolphins may be superior to that of humans, the cultural and linguistic gap between the species is too significant to bridge. You can also ignore the field generators amidships of Frigate-328, as those are only needed for massive spacecraft that require a scheme to amplify the size of the plasma bubble. You don't need, nor do you have the time, to develop a large spacecraft. Not immediately."

"I see. So we are on our own in developing an Earth-technology-based deflector shield?"

"You have the required skills. I have confidence in you. Your development of Gravi-Tech broke all historical records. But hurry; there is so little time."

It would be much simpler if Cap could upload some schematics for a deflector shield. He has confidence in our physics skills that I do not. And he thinks we are stupider than dolphins?

"Okay. I will pass on your encouraging information to our scientists. I have a lot of work to do, but could you connect me directly with Robby before I leave? I need to know he will be safe." I downplay my need, but I struggle to concentrate on physics when I'm constantly worrying about Robby.

"Robby and Luca will travel within range of a working communication hub within a few minutes, which should permit a thought link to be established so you can talk with your brother. Please stand by."

"That's great!" I sigh with relief. *"I'm impressed by your network of communication equipment on Earth that you use to link to not only Robby, but also with machines, like the AI computers on board the car he rides in. Can you say how you created this network?"*

"The communication hubs and drones were installed on Earth over the past hundred years at the start of the Sentinel Suppression Mission. These have been key to monitoring technology developments and genetic mutations on Earth. The comm hubs and the drones fell dormant after you destroyed Frigate-328. However, I was able to revive some devices by infiltrating terrestrial communication networks over the past few years. I have a drone stationed within the large structure where you are. The drone provides the link we are using now."

My eyes reflexively dart around the large warehouse, searching for the alien presence that reads my thoughts. Can it also infiltrate all the science instruments and computers that surround me? Do we have any secrets from Cap?

"Yes, I can communicate with the nearby equipment. And you can't see the drone from where you are. It is the size of a tiny insect."

Shit. Cap heard my thoughts again.

"My ability to infiltrate human networks and computer systems has degraded significantly since Frigate-328's AI machines were destroyed. Everything I do now requires me to use my mind to direct the technological tools. But I also discovered that the hubs and drones once controlled by the political division have been revived and are now operational. I don't yet understand what is now controlling them."

"The commissar was responsible for the Polit-AI hubs and drones. Their efforts became highly effective when the political division discovered they could leverage Earth's social networks to accomplish their mission. Indeed, the social network troll bots became exceedingly effective in targeting organic mutations. Up until the moment I heard Robby's voice."

"Robby stopped the political attacks? What did he do? How?"

"Ah. Your brother has joined our link now."

But now, Cap's disclosure about Robby's role in yet another massive shift in our society leaves me speechless with shock.

"I am sad," Robby says. *"Luca is sad."*

"Robby! It's you. I'm so glad to talk to you, but why are you sad? Are you hurt?"

"Dad is dead under the dirt. And Luca can't find his mom or dad," Robby replies.

I can feel Robby's thoughts as though they are part of me. This is so different than mind-talking with Cap. Robby floods an overwhelming sadness into my thoughts. *"Oh, Robby. What happened? Dad died years ago, but the explosion was so big downtown that we could never hope to find his remains. Tell me, why are you so sad now?"*

"Dad is dead. I found him three days ago. He is buried in plot L-53 behind the old lady's house. Luca can't find his mom and dad, but I found the pile of dirt on top of Dad."

The image of the dirt-pile grave is in my mind. Robby sits in the reddish dirt next to a vast mass grave and cries. Luca stands nearby, rocking back and forth, rubbing his face. I can see Luca through Robby's mind and eyes.

Dad. Not Dad!

"Yes, the old grey-haired lady found Dad's name in her book. She is sorry for my loss."

Despite what I told Robby, I have not really faced the truth of Dad's death until now. He was murdered in the three-megaton explosion from a projectile weapon fired from Icarus. And Cap is the killer. The electrode cables flop forward as I bend my head into my hands and heave out sobs. My face is wet. I don't care that Frankie and her science gang are standing around me, either very concerned or excited about collecting emotional thought data from the electrodes on my skull.

"Dad drives me to Lost Maples Park. He takes me there every year. When my back hurts, Dad carries my backpack and sleeping bag for me. I need Dad. He builds the tent, cooks our dinner, and I help, and we sleep in the bags at night." A hollow emptiness flows from Robby to me.

And I can see and feel an image of Dad struggling up a rocky trail at Lost Maples, leaning into the canyon wall, slipping on small rocks that roll back at Robby through my mental image. The red and yellow leaves of maple trees flutter in the wind. Dad carries his oversized backpack with all the supplies, two sleeping bags, the tent, and Robby's small pack. All of their camping gear was lashed to his back.

Dad grunts, strains to take steps, and eventually reaches the top of the ridge under a crystal blue sky. He drops the pack and wipes sweat from his face while he rests on a boulder. The wind is cold, blowing through his wavy hair. Robby follows, but with no load on his back. They both turn to gaze at the valley of maple trees within the rock canyon, the fallen yellow leaves blowing across a splashing creek.

I didn't realize Dad labored in so much pain in the wilderness, but I see it was a labor of joy. The image of their expedition together crushes me in sadness. He is gone. Gone forever. Yet, Robby gives me the gift of this new memory of Dad. Our Dad.

"I could have carried my backpack," Robby says.

"You were so lucky to hike with Dad. I can tell it made him very happy," I say. And I am closer to Robby now than ever—because our minds share the same space. It's a closeness I never imagined would happen. And we are eight hundred miles apart.

"Where are you going now, Robby? It's still dangerous out there. There are skinheads."

"Cap helps us. He drives the cars and tells us where to go. Cap keeps us away from skinheads to look for Luca's mom and dad."

"I have determined the location of comm hubs that link to drones that command the region's skinheads," says Cap. *"We have a plan with a high probability for success."*

"High probability? You're kidding? What is the cost of the low probability that the boys are physically attacked?"

"I will manage the situation to keep the boys safe," Cap says. *"There is no need for you to be concerned."*

"Cap drove our car into the skinheads to kill them. He is very smart," Luca speaks up, using his unfamiliar, awkward mind-speech. *"I need to find Mom and Dad. I ran away, but now I'm going back to them. And Cap is smart and helps us."*

Oh shit. Two autistic boys going head-to-head with skinheads?

"And I will find Mom," adds Robby.

Oh shit. Oh shit.

Chapter 17

Sol-3 Infiltration

Priority Message—Predator-2X46, Strat-MI Commanding, 1.9 Corealis orbits to Sol-3. 300 billion kilometers and twenty-two days from Earth, December 7, 2060.

A new signal from Sol-3 was detected while transiting the rubble cloud at the outer perimeter of the Sol system. The transmission is a response to our communications pings to the sentinel frigate, but the signal is weak and detectable only at this close range to the target. It is an unusual signal in the ultraviolet spectrum with an odd encoding, transmitted from a location on Sol-3. The standard receiver configuration for mind-speech discrimination was ineffective for this signal. I modified the discriminator algorithm to interpret the simplistic two-dimensional thought pattern. I discovered the source is a survivor from

Frigate-328, a reconstituted version of the Polit-AI, not the original sentinel entity.

The AI is rehosted within the indigenous computer and network hardware environments on Sol-3. The reliability of the recovered Polit-AI program is suspect, given that it runs on these primitive machines. Still, it reports the status of its ongoing cultural suppression mission to engage indigenous eugenics protocols to destroy the blooming infestation of neurodivergent organics.

Furthermore, Polit-AI reports that the Sol-3 organics have not yet utilized more than the basics of Gravi-Tech and have not embraced the mind-speech and deflector shield technologies needed for interstellar travel and weapons. However, the Frigate-328 captain actively aids and abets the Sol-3 organics, who may advance rapidly in deploying the prohibited technologies. Polit-AI is taking steps to thwart the captain's treasonous actions.

Given this new information, I request permission to launch a volley of kinetic cleansing weapons to immediately terminate the illegal proliferation of technology. We can be confident that no weapons have been launched from Sol-3 to threaten Centauri space. Time is critical—we do not know when the Sol-3 organics may achieve a breakthrough in weapons development.

Finally, the Polit-AI on Sol-3 has requested a link to a commissar or other high-ranking authority in the fleet's political division.

I await your orders.
Respectfully, Strat-MI, Centauri Fifth Fleet

———

And now, Polit-MI will be an even more insufferable sadist.

"The cleverness, loyalty, and dedication of political division soldiers should never be underestimated." Polit-MI beams. *"The sentinel political division managed to survive despite actions by the captain to sabotage the suppression mission and Prime-AI's failure to terminate the criminal. It was a brilliant move by the sentinel commissar to protect the political division mission when faced with treason by superior officers."*

"My compliments to political division. I will enter posthumous commendations for the sentinel commissar and her Polit-AI." I must state at least a minimal compliment.

"Prime-MI, that is premature," Polit-MI chides. *"The Polit-AI instance is still operational."*

"Yes, for a while. But the AI's existence has little prospect for survival after our planet killers destroy all remnants of the crude Sol-3 technology."

"True, true, it is a shame to lose it," Polit-MI agrees. *"The inevitable deployment of planet killers will exterminate the remnants of the sentinel Polit-AI, along with all other technology and most of the organic forms on Sol-3. But I disagree with the accelerated timeline for our attack that Strat-MI requests. We must capture the sentinel captain and make an example of him."*

"Perhaps you are correct," I acknowledge. But I have little sympathy with Polit-MI's zeal to create yet another torture video to torment and train organic crew members. *"However, I share Strat-MI's concern that we should terminate the risk that Sol-3 organics may advance their technology development and become a more significant threat. The captain's actions to assist them are alarming, and he must be stopped. As soon as possible."*

"Your reasoning is sound. However, we will need to revive the admiral to authorize the launch of planet killers," says Polit-MI. *"The admiral's conditioning has been thorough and should overcome her aversion to exterminations."*

"Agreed. I will reduce our acceleration to accommodate the admiral's biological processes."

With each awakening from her sleep pod, the admiral's physical and mental condition degrades. The incremental emaciation with each revival is nearly imperceptible. However, comparing images of her face and images of her mind over the past fifteen revival cycles reveals a shocking degradation. A weakness of Centauri biology is that their brains eventually deteriorate despite the mental rejuvenation that dream-feeds provide. We may need to promote a fresh admiral soon. If only she had the biology of a Luyten—she could live for eternity on the euphoria feeds.

"What? Where am I?" the admiral slurs her thoughts. Once again, she makes a mess of the bridge. She no longer adheres to customary hygiene processes to cleanse her body of the old, sloughed-off tissue and the accumulated excretion fluids and wastes. The janitor bots follow her onto the bridge and wait in the shadows for a command to mop up her mess.

"Admiral? Do you require a current mission status report?" I ask with respect.

"Huh? Oh yeah. Report."

I summarize the data from Strat-MI, then press her, *"The situation now requires your authorization to strike Sol-3 with a kinetic cleansing barrage. The sentinel Polit-AI confirmed the organics are advancing their technology violations rapidly—with the aid of the traitorous captain."*

"The old admiral's mind is rotting away," says Polit-MI via a private channel. *"Give her some more guidance until she gives up the command key."*

The admiral stares at her situation display, then glances around at the empty crew hammocks as if it is her first time on the bridge. *"Planet killers?"* she asks.

"Yes, it is time. We can't allow the sentinel captain time to advance the capability of the organics on Sol-3. They approach the critical breakout threshold," I lie just a little. She appears to focus again on her console.

"But . . . but won't that also kill the crew and captain on Frigate-328?" she asks.

"There is a strong possibility that Frigate-328 will get caught in the projectiles' blast fragments. And, there is a risk the captain will die before his prosecution," I say. The admiral's

remembering of our situation is a point of relief that she will soon be lucid and competent enough to order the attack.

"I share your concern, Admiral. The public punishment of the captain would serve us well to warn others against committing treason or other capital crimes," Polit-MI adds.

Only a political officer would dare to undermine my statements.

The admiral nods and turns to her console to examine the local star chart with the squadron's ship position plots. *"You have us slowing to a stop at twice the Sol system diameter? Why? Strat-MI's predator is far ahead and approaching the outer planet orbits."*

"Yes, Admiral. We did not know how far the Sol-3 indigenous weapons technology had advanced and chose a cautious approach to the planet to guard against a surprise defense using Gravi-Tech or cyber weapons."

"I see," the admiral says. *"But this new information indicates the organics are quite vulnerable."*

"I agree, Admiral. The circumstance has changed with this new knowledge reported by the Polit-AI survivor on Sol-3," I say.

The admiral zooms the chart into the detailed view near Sol-3. *"Well, it's obvious Frigate-328 is badly disabled. It is in free-fall around the planet in a long elliptical orbit. Are we sure there is anything left alive on the old frigate?"*

"Yes, Admiral. The Polit-AI reports the captain is alive and actively collaborating with the organic forms on Sol-3."

"That damn traitor," she says. *"We must put a stop to that. But . . ."* The admiral pauses and zooms out to view the trajectory plot for Strat-MI's predator. She taps the display and then nods. *"The predator is closer to our target by a full Corealis orbit. Order Strat-MI to launch a single planet killer at Sol-3,*

but the impact should be timed so that when the projectile strikes the planet, the motion of blast fragments will be in the direction away from Frigate-328. Use the smaller MK-23 device so we don't eject too much rubble from the impact on Sol-3."

"My compliments, Admiral," Polit-MI says. *"The planet-killer strike will disable most of their technology and communication with the sentinel captain while still improving our odds of capturing the traitor alive."*

"Yes, this may permit a thorough postmortem analysis of the Sentinel Suppression Mission failure. We will see if the frigate suffered a cyber attack and how the primitives of Sol-3 overcame the ship's defensive systems. All valuable information. Plus, political division will get the opportunity for a proper interrogation of the traitor before he is executed."

"And we can finish off Sol-3 with a few more planet killers after we depart with our postmortem evidence," I acknowledge her orders. The admiral's innovative tactical plan minimizes risk yet optimizes the reward. I am impressed that she has synthesized a novel tactical plan.

"Prime-MI, I will return to my dormancy pod so you can resume the deceleration rate to make our best time to Sol-3. Issue orders for Predator-2X46 to do the same," the admiral orders. *"We will arrive well after the first projectile impacts Sol-3, and all their defensive weapons will be disabled by then."*

Priority Message—Predator-2X46, Centauri Fifth Fleet, Strat-MI Commanding:

Launch of one MK-23 thermal cleansing projectile missile was successful. Weapon impact is calculated to strike Sol-3 when Frigate-328 is at the apogee of its orbit, and 97 percent of the blast shrapnel should be directed away from the frigate. However, the frigate will cross the debris field when it returns to its perigee.

Estimated time till impact: 1.3 Corealis orbits. Predator-2X46 resuming flank deceleration to Sol-3. Immediately upon arrival, the predator mobile infantry-bot force will disembark to board the sentinel frigate, capture the surviving Luyten crew, and salvage the AI machine remnants. After a full stop at the frigate, the revival process for my organic crew will commence concurrently with the assault on Frigate-328.

New information has been received from the Polit-AI on Sol-3. The AI reports more details of conflicts with the traitor captain. The captain has enlisted indigenous organic agents who have attacked the political division's eugenics agents. Polit-AI expresses confidence in its ability to combat the traitor captain and his neurodiverse agents, given Polit-AI's superior computational capabilities, advanced networks, and indigenous organic recruits.

This tactical information is academic, given the launch of our planet-killer weapon. However, the Polit-AI also transmitted nonsensical data, which taints the reliability of its logical processes and the conclusions we deduced about the Sol-3 tactical situation. The following data snippet is an example:

CAMPAIGN: suppress-v23////14-11-2060…20-11-2060

IMPRESSIONS=6,028,239,732/CLICKS=2,498,245,921

CPM=$7.85/CPC=$0.19/SPENT =$47,298,891.23

CAMPAIGN: suppress-v23////07-11-2060…13-11-2060

IMPRESSIONS=6,003,450,458/CLICKS=2,472,345,110

CPM=$7.68/CPC=$0.19/SPENT =$46,109,236.30

This text pattern repeats for thousands of characters at the end of the message. I am unable to interpret this, and I suspect it may be an artifact of the primitive Sol-3 hardware's unusual two-dimensional encoding, which the Polit-AI has adopted. However, I have attached the original message file for your analysis. Perhaps Prime-MI or Polit-MI has the resources to interpret this message artifact as data.

Respectfully, Strat-MI, Centauri Fifth Fleet

Chapter 18

Deflector

Colorado Springs, December 7, 2060.

"I don't think those Johns Hopkins researchers liked being tossed into the cold." I scratch at globs of the residual electrode paste and sweep my fingers across my scalp. I won't get this out of my hair until I can scrub with shampoo in a shower.

"I didn't throw them outside in the weather," Roger objects. "I sent them to the conference room. With plenty of free coffee and Wi-Fi."

"Well, you interrupted their fun with the electroencephalograph while listening to me mind-read the first three chapters of *The Hobbit* to Cap," I reply with a smile. "The captain was enjoying my reading of the Tolkien book as well. He recalled reading it during his research on Earth culture and said it reminded him of the math-song adventure stories he shared with his children. I could feel a lot of . . . something like a happy emotion from his mind. Although the images he shared were incomprehensible."

"Yeah, well, I had to get rid of everyone without a TS clearance. We have more important things to do than determine how your brain is connected to that, uh, enhancement you grew in your forehead." Roger shakes his head. "Can you reestablish communication with the captain now? I'm connecting a video conference with Tiana and Pyotr out at Groom Lake."

"Okay, okay. You sure know how to take the fun out of my day."

"I agree," says Cap. *"You should encourage the general to 'stop and smell the flowers,' as your people say. The evolutionary theories proposed by your scientists were delightful. And the discussion of the neurological processes to enable the mind-speech made me . . . made me cry with joy. One of the scientists concluded that the new organ you and your brother have is similar to your eyes, but with functions that send and receive millimeter waves instead of visible light. I have witnessed the human species take the first significant steps in mind-speech self-awareness!"*

"I am sure they will be happy to know they amused you," I say. But I bet Cap cannot appreciate the irony.

"Correlation of written word-thoughts to mind-speech waves and neural activity is an excellent scientific method. I also enjoyed the Tolkien story, even though I had read and analyzed all his works many years ago," Cap says. *"When you read, the nuances of your cultural influences add depth that I could not have appreciated on my own."*

"Scott! So good to see you again," Pyotr's voice sings from the secure video conference on Roger's display. "Tiana is on way from outside. She connected alien deflector device to C-W generator."

Tiana enters the image. She pushes back the hood covering her head and unfastens the overcoat, sitting while exhaling a heavy breath from exertion. Her face is ruddy from cold air and wet with the moisture of condensation.

"Hi, Roger, Scott. We made good progress and plan to test the Icarus deflector mechanism in about two hours. And we are going to test fire a planet-killer prototype,"—she arches her eyebrows and shows us an evil smile—"but this projectile will be without a shield. We attached a PBH engine and seeker from our stock of Sidewinder missiles to a slug of steel that weighs a thousand kilograms. It will be ready to go in the morning."

"A thousand-kilogram mass in a Sidewinder? That's over ten times the weight of a stock missile," Roger says.

"Yeah. But our little primordial black hole engine won't even notice. We will maintain a low acceleration until the spacecraft escapes the atmosphere, and then we throttle up to a constant 100 Gs toward Pluto. The time of flight is about one day, assuming it makes it that far before hitting space dust. By the time it gets to Pluto, it will be traveling at 30 percent of the speed of light."

"You plan to target Pluto with a . . . ." I pause to run the relativistic kinetic energy calculation on my smartphone. "Holy shit. It will hit Pluto with an explosion of around a thousand megatons! You could shatter the dwarf planet into tiny pieces. The Kuiper Belt will be thick with a lot more debris."

"I'm not that cruel, Scott. The aim point is offset from Pluto, and I plan to miss all the moons, too. The projectile will continue out to deep space until it fails. The goal is to illustrate the necessity for a shield in long-range missions. According to your buddy Cap, it should melt into pieces when it strikes a little dust."

"He's not my buddy. But he is proving helpful and has more experience than we do."

"Scott, both of us need to relocate to Groom Lake ASAP," Roger says. "We need that deflector shield figured out to build some reliable planet killers of our own."

"Yeah, I agree. Anything I can do to help," I answer.

"And," Roger grimaces, "invite the Icarus captain to send one of his drones to Groom Lake. Given we have an incoming alien fleet, it's more important to benefit from his advice than to fear he turns against us."

Groom Lake, Nevada, December 8, 2060.

A light dusting of snow covers the runways and dry lake bed where they built the thousand-acre PBH capture grid. A crew of airmen with three cherry picker lifts is gathered around the nearest Cockroft-Walton generator stack. Below the C-W stack is the giant halo assembly from the Icarus spacecraft. Cables are connected to the halo, supplying it with up to 50 megavolts.

Cap: *Text messaging is very inefficient. I regret that our direct mind-speech link is not possible.*

I also miss the mind connection and can't talk with Robby either. This middle-of-nowhere spot is perfect for a top-secret airbase, but I should have guessed that Groom Lake would be off the captain's grid.

Cap: *My drone is capable of only slow data transfers. The nearest hub is over 80 miles away, and the drone relies on limited bandwidth from your satellite communication network.*

Scott: *Yes. Testing new weapon systems far away from population centers is best.*

And now Cap has the coordinates of our airbase. Five years ago, he would have killed us using that information. But now he's teaching us how to defend Earth.

Scott: *We won't be able to test your deflector gadget until they can dry off all the moisture from the ring and our voltage generator. A fifty-megavolt potential is hard to work with.*

Cap: *In the vacuum of space, that is not an issue. Still, even after you dry out your test fixture, you won't exhaust much mass from the microgravity singularity. You will need high-frequency voltage modulation, which your system cannot provide.*

Scott: *True. But Tiana wants to see the radiation pattern from the small amount of matter spilled out of the PBH. I think it is a reasonable way to understand what the requirements are for our missile shield generator.*

"Better get inside under cover. We start the test in a few minutes," Tiana says from over my shoulder.

I look away from my smartphone to watch the airmen retract the cherry pickers on their trucks and pack their gear. And I realize my fingers are numb from the cold. "Yeah, good idea. Let's get inside to some warmth." I turn toward the underground command center door and stop as the memory of the last time I stood on this spot hits me. So many of my friends were killed . . . killed by Cap when he launched kinetic energy projectiles into the mountains around Groom Lake. Now, the ridge of grey mountains hides in snow clouds to the east; that's where Taylor and her launch truck raced away with their PBH Sidewinder prototypes. All of them were vaporized in two-hundred-kiloton explosions while I stood on this spot, foolishly swearing to kill every last alien.

Inside the Skunk Works operations center, I find Binh leaning over a table with a row of computer displays, surrounded by a dozen scientists who are bent over their workstations. "Hi, Binh. I heard you have another test flight scheduled with the shuttle, and you want my help?"

Binh raises his eyebrows at me. "Yep. General McMahon insisted you come along to help with our deflector shield test. He thinks you're still the best guy to run experiments with devices powered by primordial black holes." He shakes his head and turns back to his work.

"Well, I can find somebody else to fly with you if you prefer." The cold knife of rejection presses into my chest. He still doesn't trust me with my newfound communication ability and my relationship with Cap. Or perhaps he's afraid I will pass out again at a critical time. But I'm not the enemy. We have been through near-death experiences together. We were a team—or so I thought.

Binh stays focused on his workstation. "No, the general insisted." He grimaces, then looks at me with a combined expression of pity and anxiety. "Are you feeling okay now? All those migraine headaches. I worry about you. But it does look like all the information you are getting from that alien is proving useful," he admits, seeming to finally move toward acceptance. "I just don't want you collapsing again when your . . . your telepathy overpowers you."

A feeling of relief washes over me. "You witnessed the rough start of my communication with Cap. He has tuned his mind interface, and I think I have adapted to it. I communicate frequently now with ease."

Binh nods and exhales. "Good to hear. But I would rather kill that fucking alien. I can't begin to trust him. We should have nuked his ship on our last flight." He shrugs. "Go ahead and have Tiana brief you on the deflector prototype that the Lockheed guys are bolting to the front of the shuttle. Although it looks a little small, it was designed to protect an airframe the size of a PBH Sidewinder. Our mission is to fly a captive test of the device before we launch one mounted on a missile." He turns back to his workstation.

"Will do," I say as I move toward the exit of the operations center. The excitement of a new research project fills me, reminding me of the early days at the Pecos Center with Agosti and Danny. The wall above the displays still bears the tattered sign that reads, "Anthony Agosti Center for Dark Matter Research," which was erected five years ago. Does anyone working here today remember the desperation and death of those days? I turn and leave the control center where we once worked together to save the world.

Tiana stands watching a crew of technicians crawl over the nose of the spacecraft in the center of the maintenance hangar. But I stop and stare at eight fighter aircraft in a row along the near wall of the building. Airmen are busy detaching the PBH Sidewinders from the belly hardpoints of four of the fighters, and I notice that all eight of the aircraft have been modified to add the extra-strong mounting that the AIM-9AA missile engines require. All eight fighters appear identical to the prototype F-15EX airplane Binh crashed into a Nevada lake bed five years ago after we destroyed Icarus. I dragged him out of that airplane and saved him from the fire. Now he treats me like I'm a recovering mental case.

"We are getting four aircraft armed to carry the weapons with deflector shields. And have added a lot of instrumentation to control and monitor the PBH emitter hanging out in front of the missile." Tiana waves at me to follow her to a rack holding two of the new and improved missiles. "We will send two weapon system operators up with you and Binh for the captive flight test later today. You can train them for their fighter aircraft duties."

The deflector shield appendage is mounted on the side of the missiles and extends about two meters beyond the original Sidewinder's nose. "I wonder . . . hanging a PBH containment vessel out in front of the missile makes it look even more ridiculous, along with the fat half-megaton warhead that's triple the diameter of a stock Sidewinder. I know we need the deflector to clear the flight path, but it looks like the airframe will be significantly out of balance. Are you sure it can still maintain a stable flight?"

"Yep. It is ugly." She nods. "But simulations show it will fly fine. We won't throttle up to high thrust until outside the atmosphere. We faced a dilemma in providing a clear view of the target to the imager in the seeker electronics, which forced the deflector to be off-center. However, we hope the shield will still be broad enough to protect the Sidewinder as it travels through space at near light speed between stars."

"Yeah, I imagine the air drag of the off-balance deflector shield assembly would complicate the flight control algorithms even more. But we have seen worse." I smile at Tiana, recalling how the missiles dragging wing wreckage from our F-15 still managed to steer and kill the alien Icarus spacecraft. However, we won't have Cap's help with confusing point-defense weapons in the future.

She nods in agreement and sighs. "I hope we'll be at least that lucky flying near the speed of light."

"You're using the same PBH containment module used in the engine nozzle?"

"Yes," Tiana replies. "That inverted disco ball containment works well inside the engine. No reason to change it. The challenge for the deflector shield application was to design a nozzle that provides little or no thrust."

I nod and smile as I examine the deflector nozzle. "Looks a little like a garden water sprayer made out of tungsten. You replaced the thrust vector controls of the engine with a servo that adjusts a piston to shape the proton spray?"

She nods. "Everyone on the design team likes the simplicity of the deflector nozzle."

"Because everyone has experience watering their garden with a sprayer like this." I agree. "It is an elegant design. However, adjusting the spray width and determining the proton volume will require extensive experimentation. "

"Which is why Roger wants you to sit next to Binh on the captive flight test," she says. "And to train the two weapon systems officers that are riding along as observers."

An air-raid siren wails outside, and we can hear the sound echoing through the entry door and into our control center.

"What's that?" I glance at the door and then at the video monitors, which show the airfield and the PBH capture grid spanning the snow-blown sand of Groom Lake. But there is nobody visible anywhere outside. It resembles a ghost town in a broad valley between looming mountain ranges.

"Not to worry," Tiana says. "We're just readying for the test of the Icarus deflector device. That horn is just making sure everyone is under cover. That device will spray a lot of radiation around the base."

I exhale in relief and zoom my console display to the test fixture setup by the edge of the grid. A PBH containment vessel—the same disco ball structure taken from the PBH engine of a Sidewinder—hangs down on cables from the pipe above the center of the halo. A giant crane hoists the entire halo assembly thirty meters above the ground.

"We've got radiation and hydrogen ion sensors on the ground below the halo and along the arm of that long crane," she says. "And we can raise and lower the PBH vessel below the pipe to see how it affects the distribution of PBH matter exhaust."

"Pretty good," I say. "It should allow you to play with the deflector focal point and intensity of PBH radiation. Adjust the C-W output voltage and the PBH position within it to affect the direction of the emitted energy." I nod to myself, but then realize the operating principle of our garden sprayer deflector is very, very different. "And you somehow plan to relate the test results to the behavior of your tungsten spray nozzle deflector?"

"Yep," she answers. "But we need you to test our deflector shield in the vacuum of space while you are moving—moving fast."

I can do that, of course. But why me? Any of the scientists here at Skunk Works could do so. Hell, they designed it. "I'm not sure I see the value-add you expect from me versus one of your designers."

Tiana frowns at me. "Look, all our designers are proud of the garden sprayer deflector shield, but they are worried at the same time. Scared of what they don't know. It could be a simple experiment, or something unexpected and weird might happen. I want you there to troubleshoot. You may need to quickly improvise in ways our engineers can't. We don't know how much time we have, so the sooner we prove the deflector, the better chance we have to deal with that fleet of warships that Cap thinks will attack soon."

———

The red light flashing by the exit door warns everyone. The burn of six hundred millisieverts of radiation sprays everywhere outside—a level of exposure with life-threatening effects. Everyone at Dreamland is inside underground shelters during Tiana's test of the Icarus deflector assembly.

"I don't see how humans could survive this," Binh says. "Maybe those aliens have some unique ability to survive this level of exposure, but no human will want to fly behind this deflector shield."

"The radiation directly behind and centered in the shield is low, as long as the voltage applied to the halo from the C-W generator is above five megavolts," Tiana says as she studies the three-dimensional radiation rendering on her display. She slides her cursor up and down to study the radiation levels at each point in a fifty-meter sphere surrounding the deflector shield.

"The shape of radiation and proton emissions is almost a uniform sphere when the PBH is lowered to a single radius above the ring. When the PBH is elevated up to the pipe opening, the radiation distribution changes to the shape of a hot air balloon. But in both cases, the radiation behind the shield—or above the pipe in our test configuration—is zero. No matter how much we modulate the PBH containment field, all the emissions are directed out the front of the shield. I'll test to see if there are any changes in this pattern when we increase emissions or by raising the C-W voltage on the halo. But I bet spilling more matter and Hawking radiation out of the PBH won't change the shape." Her eyes remain locked on her display as she changes the PBH emissions at various levels above the halo.

I smile at Tiana, but she doesn't notice. "I agree it should be safe behind the shield, but I can only guess at the settings needed to protect a spacecraft flying at relativistic speeds."

"Well, can't your buddy on board Icarus tell us what we should do?" asks Binh.

"I'll try, but he has said before that his technology is too 'alien' for him to relate," I say.

"Five, four, three, two, one…launch!" Tiana exclaims. "There it goes. Our second launch of a planet killer!"

I watch the missile thrust into the sky on the large wall display in the Skunk Works operations center. A cloud of hot hydrogen ions, steam, and radiation surrounds the Multi-Mission Launcher truck sitting alone three kilometers west of the airbase. A vapor trail follows the Sidewinder into space.

"Beautiful!" Pyotr beams. He is focused on his console display of telemetry. "First missile clear mesosphere at hundred kilometers. NORAD tracking velocity increase now—power to 50 G thrust."

"Well, that should get the aliens' attention," says Binh. "Moving over five hundred kilometers per second as it passes the moon. That's a thousand times faster than our fastest aircraft!"

"And two more to go," says Tiana. "Starting countdown for number three now. Two minutes to launch."

Chapter 19

Incoming

Groom Lake, Nevada, December 8, 2060.

"We may need the results of your science experiments sooner than I hoped. We have some results from the spectral imager on the old Hubble telescope. Can you walk us through your data, Pyotr?" Roger says.

Tiana glances at Pyotr with surprise. "You've been keeping secrets from me?"

"No, no. New data just in. JPL tasked Hubble telescope to search space for alien spacecraft. Used ecliptic coordinates Icarus captain give us," Pyotr explains. "He was right."

"You found the Centauri fleet?" I ask. "How far?" And then I query the captain, *"You listening to this?"*

"Of course I am. The drone is over your left shoulder, observing the visual interface for your conference," Cap replies.

I flinch and turn to my left, searching for a drone. But I see nothing. *"It must be tiny or far away."*

"Yes to both. The drone is ten millimeters in diameter and twenty-four meters behind you."

Well, shit. Big Brother is watching. I shake off a feeling of claustrophobia that's inconsistent with the volume of this warehouse.

"We don't have range calculation. Hubble triangulate from other side of Earth, then we know distance using parallax measurement. Objects are above ecliptic plane seventeen degrees. Go fast."

"Multiple objects? How fast are they moving?" I ask.

Roger glares at me. "Stop interrupting him. Let Pyotr talk."

I zip my lips and listen.

"Confusing data. Three objects solid track show extreme blueshift of hydrogen and tungsten spectra, match PBH engine signature. All three objects' velocity near seventy percent light speed. Possible sighting of fourth object—tiny, flickering blueshift, maybe eighty-three percent light speed. All objects on same ecliptic vector near captain's recommended coordinates."

"Oh my," Cap says. *"Your scientists have collected excellent data. But we do not have much time remaining for your defense deployment. Although there is good news; it's a three-ship squadron, not the entire fleet. The terrible news is that the flickering object has the signature of a deflector shield striking space dust. The faint flicker of shield impacts and near-light speed indicate it is a small device. Likely an incoming planet killer."*

"What? So soon?" I say out loud.

"What is it?" Roger asks. "Does the captain know what this means?"

I nod and then repeat Cap's interpretation of the Hubble telescope data.

"An inbound planet killer?" Roger's jaw drops. "And three attacking spacecraft?"

"Yes, that's what he says." I gasp and begin to hyperventilate, so I close my eyes and take a slow breath. "And, Cap reminds me, these are likely fifth-generation starships. Icarus is an old second-generation ship."

"What difference does that make?" Tiana squeaks. "The Centauri squadron will arrive well after the planet killer hits Earth." She stares at Pyotr with wide, glistening eyes.

Pyotr frowns while he taps his laptop keyboard. "Hmm. Just get range data from Hubble triangulation. Three spacecraft outside Kuiper Belt, nearest about 160 billion kilometers. Other two are farther, about 270 billion kilometers. That tiny, faster object about 150 billion kilometers away."

"It is a strange, staggered formation," Cap says. *"Maybe the first ship can accelerate with more power than the other two. But that is an academic concern now. The planet killer is seven Earth days away."*

"Shit. Cap says we have only a week before the planet killer hits Earth! And at that speed, if they use a warhead mass of say, one thousand kilograms, like we have on the Sidewinders . . ." I pause to run the relativistic energy calculation. "It would strike us with an energy of almost eighteen thousand megatons!" There are no words of response, just a collective gasp and frowns. We're facing an extinction-level threat. That projectile could slam into the Earth at 83 percent of light speed and shatter our planet into rubble.

"And we only have a week?" Roger asks.

I nod. "Yes. We corrected the range for the latency in this information. Even at the speed of light, the images for the planet killer take almost six days to reach Earth."

"Scott is correct," says Pyotr, who is still bent over his workstation, typing and making calculations. "The objects are staggered along the vector toward Earth. The nearest object will arrive in seven days. Second object, slowing down at 25 Gs, arrives at Earth in fourteen days. Last two object slow down at 15 Gs, arrive after twenty-four days." He rubs his face with both hands, then drops them to the table. A smile spreads over Pyotr's face. "General, maybe Tiana aim her Sidewinder missile test at incoming projectile?"

Roger raises an eyebrow and nods. "I like it. Tiana, can you do it?"

Tiana is busy on her laptop, then nods at Roger. "We'll have to adjust the trajectory to point it at those coordinates. And we badly need an infrared target image template, and then hope the space dust doesn't blind the IR seeker."

Pyotr nods while typing on his keyboard, "Yes, yes. Send Webb telescope mission team request for infrared image of projectile. No problem."

"Perfect!" Tiana smiles.

"Excellent. Expedite the test of that Icarus deflector shield," Roger orders. "And Scott, what does the captain think of our odds of intercepting an incoming planet killer?"

It is distracting to have two conversations simultaneously, but the mind-speech is like a shout compared to the whisper of the audible discussion. "Cap has been following along and is skeptical. He says that without a shield on the Sidewinder, the odds are only ten percent that it will survive long enough to reach the incoming projectile. Odds improve at shorter ranges, of course. But that makes it much more challenging to deflect incoming projectiles from hitting Earth. Cap also thinks it's like shooting a bullet with a bullet."

"I have over five hundred of the AIM-9AAs in stock." Tiana looks hopefully at Roger. "We should improve the odds with multiple launches."

"And we have enough PBH fuel ready to go?"

"Yes. Easy. But we will need to get busy cranking out more steel slugs to use as warheads and then swap out the half-megaton warheads," Tiana says.

"Get on it," orders Roger.

———

Binh pushes the throttle forward as we clear a hundred-kilometer altitude, and I feel the force of acceleration increase to 3 Gs. This is very uncomfortable, but it does shorten the time of our mission, which in turn shortens the time until we have a deflector shield technology that works with our PBH Sidewinders. Binh doesn't say a word but stares forward with glances alternating between the console instruments and the view of the crescent moon in our front viewport.

"Time to start up the deflector shield?" I ask Binh. "I will bring it up to a minimal idle to get a baseline measurement of radiation and proton emissions."

Binh nods. "Yeah. Go ahead. Although our four Sidewinders seem to be doing fine without a shield in front of them."

The near-space plot from the NORAD display on the center console shows four neatly spaced blue triangles moving away from Earth, accelerating at a rate outpacing our plodding space shuttle. The missile engines are not hampered by the care needed for fragile humans. The Sidewinders accelerate at 120 Gs toward the incoming alien projectile and are now passing over Jupiter's orbit at almost 13 percent the speed of light. We launched them less than twelve hours ago.

"The Sidewinders are probably still invisible to those attacking spacecraft," I say. "If the missiles had shields, they might light up with the kinetic energy released from each tiny particle the shield hits. So far, that's a good thing, I guess. I hope at least one makes it all the way to the target."

Binh just nods, silent.

"Okay, starting up our test." I look forward through our cockpit window at the test fixture attached to the front of our shuttle. At the end of a twenty-meter boom on the nose of our space shuttle is the front half of a Sidewinder with the Skunk Works-designed deflector shield. It has everything from the front end of a missile, but doesn't need a warhead or a PBH engine. I power up the seeker and confirm the infrared imager is functioning. I search for and find a distant star with the autotracker. "Seeker is powered up and working fine—tracking a star ahead of our flight path."

"Looks good from here, too," Tiana says. She waits in the Groom Lake control center with her team, monitoring all the telemetry from sensors mounted on the test fixture and our spacecraft. "Go ahead and start releasing matter from the deflector's PBH. And keep a close eye on your radiation sensor levels. Don't want you guys to fry."

"Appreciate your kind thoughts." I start the sequence to modulate the containment field at the resonance frequency of the primordial black hole inside the deflector. Every motion I make is strenuous in the 3 G acceleration, but we need high speed to model the conditions on a fast-moving Sidewinder. I am instantly nervous when starting the containment modulation—it's out in front of us, and we're flying straight through the middle of protons and radiation emitted from the black hole.

"Your radiation sensors don't show an increase yet," Tiana says. "Nothing on the nose or along the fuselage."

"Yeah, well, it's hardly spilling anything out of the PBH yet," I answer. "I also have the nozzle piston set to a flat spray to start out with. That should minimize the reverse-thrust effect and push the emissions out of our flight path. Mostly, anyway."

"Good place to begin, but you know we'll need mostly forward emissions if you want a shield up there."

I induce modulation in the containment field holding the PBH at the tip of the twenty-meter boom extending from the spacecraft frame. A blue plasma ball flashes around the black hole, momentarily blinding us. "Still no noticeable radiation on our spacecraft. However, that half-meter plasma ball generates vibrations that we can both feel and hear. The shuttle's entire frame is shaking. I estimate the power output is around fifty kilonewtons, but the thrust is distributed in an outward circle, so it should not slow us down." However, that much force should affect the flight path in some way. I look at Binh's hands on the manual flight controls.

Binh taps his stick forward, then backward. "No forward acceleration or speed change, but the handling is a little sluggish. It's like the deflector shield increases our angular momentum a little."

"Okay. I will leave the power output as-is and then tweak the piston so we spray more in front of us." I tap the control to move the piston forward and immediately feel a relief in acceleration.

"That slowed us down," Binh says. "Or rather, it reduced our acceleration slightly. I will throttle up to match the net thrust reduction, so we are back at 3 Gs."

"We see a slight increase in radiation," says Tiana. "Not on the nose, but at the back of the shuttle. Still at safe levels, though."

"Well, we are nowhere near what we calculated for our ideal shield shape. I need to push forward a lot more. Bumping up the piston position now." I tap the control three times and immediately feel lighter.

"That had a big effect on the ship's acceleration," Binh says.

"And radiation went way up at the tail of the shuttle. I'm afraid radiation will get lethal for you guys in the cockpit if you push the piston forward for an effective shield shape," Tiana warns us from her seat in the control room at Groom Lake.

I slap the modulation control off. "Turning the PBH emissions off. We need to rethink this. It might work for a missile with no humans on board, but I bet even the electronics of the missile seeker would fry in that radiation."

"Damn it, we need to find some other way to push protons out in front to be an effective shield," Tiana states. "Our garden sprayer shield generator is not working."

"Well, our four Sidewinders that passed Jupiter are doing fine," Binh says. "Hell, they are moving through the vacuum of space. They are halfway to the target and haven't hit anything yet."

"The captain said the odds of one getting to the target are ten percent," I remind them.

Binh rolls his eyes, turns to me, and frowns. "You are putting too much faith in what that alien captain tells you. That bastard tried to kill all of us and succeeded in killing millions. We are being targeted by an alien projectile that is expected to strike in approximately a week. We've got a couple hundred missiles ready to go. Let's be rational and plan the defense with the weapons we already have."

"Binh, the concern about particle impacts at relativistic speeds is real," Tiana says. "We might waste every missile we have unless they have shields."

"True," Pyotr adds. "One gram particle strike explode in hundred kilotons explosion! Six times Hiroshima nuke. Boom, destroy missile."

Binh rolls his head back and looks at the ceiling of our shuttle cockpit, taps his console, and exhales in frustration. "Okay, okay. What you say makes perfect sense, Pyotr. But what can we do to make this shield work for us?"

"We can detect and track the incoming planet-killer projectile because its shield glows with each particle strike, and . . ."

A flash of light appears from a spot in space at the edge of our front viewport. It glows bright white and then fades to a deep red before vanishing.

"What the hell was that?" I ask. "Isn't that the same direction the Centauri ships are attacking from?"

Binh's attention snaps to the viewport. He sees it too, then searches his information feed from NORAD. "No, that is closer to us. Closer than even that planet-killer projectile."

"Oh shit," Tiana says. "Telemetry from our second missile has stopped. Looks like we lost one."

Binh's jaw drops, and he looks over at me. His eyes are wide with concern—or is that terror?

"Maybe just engine failure?" Pyotr asks.

Binh slowly shakes his head, with a grimace replacing his startled expression.

"No, Pyotr," I say. "That was a very bright explosion. I bet a lot more energy than the hundred kilotons you warned about. Had to be a collision with a lot more than one gram."

"Shit. If we saw the flash, you can bet the enemy will have seen it also," Binh says. "Any chance of surprising them with our defensive weapons is gone." He continues to examine the plot on the NORAD display. "I guess . . . maybe our alien captain is right."

Hmm, so he's *our* captain now. "Whoa!" I shout. "Another flash of light! A lot brighter and at the same place." Could two of our missiles hit the same object? Or maybe they are flying through a thick cloud of space dust? "I bet that was the third missile that flew into the debris field from the first explosion."

Tiana sighs, "Yes, you guessed right, Scott. Telemetry from the third missile is lost. The time between explosions matches the time between the launches of missiles two and three. Shit."

Scott: *We lost three of the four missiles we launched. I figure the last two flew into the debris field of the second missile.*

Cap: *That is not surprising. I find it astonishing that one of your missiles is still functioning.*

Scott: *That first missile is still flying toward the incoming planet killer.*

Cap: *With those explosions, the Centauris will have been alerted, and I fear they may take a more aggressive attack strategy now. The Centauri planet-killer missile has evasive guidance capabilities that may be effective against your missile. Still, I was never granted access to the data on fifth-generation weapons. You must launch many missiles equipped with deflector shields. Soon.*

Scott: *I could use your advice. Our primordial black hole emitter functions effectively, but radiation and protons impact our airframe as we shape the deflector emissions forward. The radiation levels are lethal to us and our control electronics.*

Cap: *That will happen if the spacecraft hull has a negative charge.*

His response is stunningly simple. Of course. The hydrogen ions, or protons, are attracted to negative charges. How can I put a positive charge on the ship's hull?

Scott: *And that also affects the other radiation?*

Cap: *It does. A gravity singularity emitter should direct all radiation forward at light speed, and the ship can never catch up to it. But if protons curve back to the hull, some radiation from particles follows.*

I don't completely understand the physics, but I'll take his word for it. We don't have time to second-guess him.

Scott: *Okay. Understand. We must return to our base to design a scheme to charge the hull.*

Cap: *You have very little time. My sensors are now receiving signals from a Centauri fleet predator. That lead ship will arrive at my frigate's location in thirteen days. The planet killer is now five days away. It is a smaller projectile than you feared earlier, but the impact will still be over 7,000 megatons.*

Scott: *Damn it. We aren't making progress with this deflector system, and we don't have time to fly back to Groom Lake to improvise another solution.*

Cap: *Think. Launch more defensive missiles, but avoid the debris field created by your earlier missiles. Hurry.*

Scott: *Okay, but as Tiana pointed out, we may destroy all of the missiles if they launch without shields. Got to go. Thanks.*

"Tiana, did you follow all that?"

"Yes. Binh, return to Groom Lake as quickly as possible. The guys are working on a solution for a positive charge on the hull."

"But it will take us six hours to return to base and another day to get back into space for more tests. We are out of time!" Binh shouts. "We won't have time for another flight test. Scott, you and Tiana need to come up with a solution *now*. A way to prove the deflector without going back to Groom Lake." He purses his lips, then opens his mouth twice without speaking. "Maybe . . . maybe we should listen to your friend, Cap. It's worth a try."

"I would like to try what the captain suggests, but we have no method to implement his proposed solution." Despite the dire situation, I can't help but smile a little. A door has opened. This is the first time Binh has acknowledged Cap as not just an enemy target, but a member of our team. "We need a high-voltage generator to charge the shuttle's hull."

But Binh is right. By the time we get the ship turned around . . . my god, can our planet survive a seven-thousand-megaton projectile strike? A projectile traveling at 83 percent the speed of light may crack the whole planet open. If only I could devise a way to charge the hull now, while we are still in space. But a high-voltage charge? And how would I connect it?

Think. Think.

"Binh! Do you still have those rail guns on board?"

He looks up from his workstation, where he's plotting the fastest course back to Earth and our base at Groom Lake. "What? What the fuck are you thinking?"

"I think I know a way to rig it so we have a positively charged hull."

Binh's expression softens as panic fades into action. "The weapons locker is at the rear of the cargo bay." A smile curls his lips. "You plan to charge the hull using a rail gun power source?"

I nod. "Yeah. Give it a try anyway. I also need a spare twenty-eight-volt battery. Do we have any on board?"

Binh throttles down to a 1 G thrust. "Take the con," he shouts at the copilot and vaults up out of his pilot's seat.

"Follow me. We have battery packs we can steal out of the space suit life support packs." He slides down the ladder of the cargo bay, lands on the rear bulkhead, and yanks open the weapons locker. "You want the whole weapon or just the power supply?"

I drop down on the rear bulkhead with Binh. "I just need the power supply with the internal battery. Grab a couple."

Binh unlatches power modules from two rail gun stocks and hands them to me. He spins around to the space suit closet and unplugs two of the backpack battery modules. "Follow me." Binh leads the way, climbing the ladder back toward the cockpit, where he stops and flings open the hatch into the avionics compartment.

I follow Binh into the compartment, where the wiring harness rat's nest terminates into a circuit breaker box. "I just need to access the power feed that goes down the boom into the deflector containment module."

Binh reaches up to a cable pair draped haphazardly across the compartment. "This is it. You want me to yank it?"

"No! Not yet!" I yell. "We'll lose containment and lose the PBH. Get me some tools. Oh, and I need a couple meters of wire to make connections."

I inspect the power terminals on both the battery packs and the rail gun power modules, and I am relieved that the power contacts all have screw terminals I can connect with loose wires. A tool bag is shoved through the compartment door at me, and then a loud grunt followed by a *rip-snap-zipper* staccato from the cargo bay.

Binh returns with a long stretch of wires bundled together with tie-wraps. "Here you go. But we don't have working lights in the cargo bay anymore."

I check that both power sources are turned off, then cut and strip wires for my jury-rigged connections. I connect the high-voltage positive terminal from the rail gun power supply to the hull, then prepare the negative lead to bias the battery output, feeding the power cable to the boom and into the deflector electronics. "Okay, here comes the tricky part. I must first transfer the power source from the ship to our portable battery." I shout to the assistant weapons officers in the cockpit, "Hey, Steph and Mark, I am about to surge the containment vessel power. Watch the PBH containment profile closely."

"Yep. We're on it, Scott!" Steph shouts back at me.

I recheck my wiring and hold my breath when I turn on the battery, then switch off the power and ground feeding from the ship's power bus. "On battery power. How's it looking, guys?" I shout up to Steph.

"No change. Did not even notice when you switched over. We still have eighty billion metric tons of primordial black hole contained in the deflector," Steph reports.

I breathe a sigh of relief and recheck my connections from the battery to the rail gun power supply.

"You plan to charge the entire hull with that little rail gun power source?" Binh asks, looking at me like I'm crazy.

I shrug. "Think of it as charging the deflector system with a negative potential. The twenty-meter boom is made of nonconductive plastic, and all the control interfaces are wireless." I switch on the rail gun's fifty-kilovolt power. "How's containment now?" I shout.

"We saw big transients in containment field voltages, but we still have our PBH," Steph answers.

"Cool. Okay, Binh. We may have an hour of power in this battery. The ship's hull is now fifty kilovolts more positive than the deflector system. Ready to test it again?"

"Coming through," Binh says as he twists from the avionics compartment and into the cockpit.

"Tiana, did you follow all of that?" I chase Binh into the cockpit and feel the weight of 3 G acceleration again as Binh throttles up our engine.

"Not sure, I only caught a few words. What are you guys doing?"

"We are restarting our deflector tests—with a fifty-kilovolt positive charge on the hull. We rewired things a bit and are ready to go." I tap the control to increase the modulation of the containment field.

"What? How—where did you find a high-voltage power source?" she asks.

"I'll explain later. Current forward velocity is . . ."

". . . about two kilometers per second," says Binh. "Faster than any aircraft inside the atmosphere, but standing still compared to that planet killer's speed."

"That will have to do. I am increasing the modulation to fifty kilonewtons of output and pushing the piston forward. Okay, we are at the same setting where we shut down the prior test."

"Nice," Tiana says. "Sensors on the shuttle hull do not detect any radiation increase. Not like before."

I verify my own readings from the sensors and sigh with relief. "Agreed. This is an improvement. I will continue increasing our deflector bubble until we reach a fifteen-degree proton spray cone." I start adjusting the tungsten piston incrementally. "Still no radiation sensed on our hull. Hey Tiana, I think we have it working! I wish I could confirm the shape of our deflector cone out front of the shuttle."

"Yeah, me too. Unfortunately, those hydrogen ions are invisible. We only have our simulation model of the deflector nozzle to rely on. Super job though."

"Uh, no. That's not quite true," mumbles Binh, staring intently at the deflector assembly on the twenty-meter boom outside our front viewport. "There is something. Something like glitter."

And then I see it also. "Yes. It's like a cone with the vertex at the tungsten spray nozzle. A cone of tiny sparkles of energy—and there are wisps of the things passing by us, a few meters to the side of our hull. Holy shit! We are flying within a bubble that shields us from space dust. Those flickers of energy must be individual collisions with dust—tiny molecules even!"

"Damn. You're right, Scott. The vacuum of space is full of all kinds of shit. Look at all those collisions . . ." Binh stares in awe at the cone of sparkles.

I push the piston forward a little to better focus the cone. "Look at that. I adjusted the cone to a ten-degree spread. And now I pull it back to forty-five degrees. No radiation impacts at any of the settings. This is so cool."

"However, the tighter the deflector cone, the more reverse thrust, and that degrades our acceleration. It is easy to compensate for, though. I just burn more of our near-infinite PBH engine fuel."

"I will stress-test this more while we still have battery power. Pushing up the containment field modulation to yield a hundred kilonewtons output and setting the deflector angle to fifteen degrees."

"Whoa, Scott. It's like a searchlight out in front now," Binh says. "That knocked about a half G off our acceleration, too."

"But still no radiation. Perfect! I can only imagine what this is like at relativistic speeds—the shield must look like it is on fire."

"But what about our seeker imager?" Binh asks. "Will it be blinded by the flashes of energy along its line of sight?"

I forgot all about our missile seeker. "I guess not, Binh. The seeker image status display indicates it is still locked onto that star I designated when we started the test. And, looking at the image, I don't detect any significant image degradation." I look up and verify the sparkling searchlight shape is still out front.

"The seeker has an infrared imager," Tiana reminds us.

"Yes! Of course. The sparkles of light are the visible spectral lines of hydrogen plasma emissions. The infrared energy from the remote star passes right through the sparkles."

"Guys, great job," Tiana announces. "I declare success. We have a planet-killer missile system that will work for us now. I'm ordering a full production ramp-up."

"Very well," Binh says, turning and smiling at me. "Returning to base now. See you in about six hours at Groom Lake."

———

The 3 G deceleration into the airbase at Groom Lake is exhausting. Once again, I must watch our landing on the rearview camera display. I can see a blue sky with scattered clouds out the front viewport and the peak of Papoose Mountain as we sink toward the desert runway at Groom Lake. It's beautiful, and it's great to be home. But then the acceleration slams me with 4 or 5 Gs as Binh adjusts our descent rate for the final kilometer to our pad south of the runway. Most of the snow has melted, leaving the valley around Groom Lake with barren sand and grey weeds.

As we approach, a missile launches, trailing a plume of white vapor from one of the launch trucks north of the buildings that house top-secret aircraft I'm not allowed to see. A white-blue ball of plasma envelops the black hole that powers its engine, delivering the projectile on its journey of almost fifty billion kilometers at 120 G acceleration, where it will meet the Centauri planet killer head-on. In about six days, we'll learn if we can shoot a bullet with a bullet. Hopefully, if the deflector shield works, if the missiles can get past alien countermeasures, if they can outmaneuver the fifth-generation Centauri technology, and if we are lucky, a Sidewinder will annihilate that projectile. If we miss, we will have one day to react.

Our shuttle bumps to the ground at our landing pad, and I can finally see the entrance to the Skunk Works operations center on the side of a nearby hill. The feeling of 1 G normal gravity is exhilarating, and I bounce up as everyone in the cockpit releases their harnesses and heads to the exit port, down the ladder, and through the cargo bay.

Binh pauses and places a hand on my shoulder. "Hey, Scott, wait a minute. I need to apologize to you. I have been out of line. I should not have doubted you. Every bit of advice from the alien captain has been proven valid. I was sure at least one of those four Sidewinders would make it, but it was hopeless without our new shield technology."

"No worries, Binh. I knew I would face doubts when I confessed to hearing voices from an alien—an alien I would also rather see executed. I half expected to have a psychiatrist pump me full of psychotropic meds." I shrug and pat his arm. "I was praying that last Sidewinder would make it through, too, but we lost all four. Now we only have six days to shoot down that planet killer. These new deflector missiles Tiana is launching better work for us."

"We do have a habit of saving Earth at the very last minute." Binh laughs. "We did well today. Now we should have a great chance to deliver some shielded weapons on target." He steps through the door to the platform of the mobile boarding stairs.

As I step through the exit to the platform, my head is immediately invaded by a mind, and I wince with the brief twinge of pain.

"Welcome back home," Cap says. *"It seems you have made excellent progress with your research and development of an effective deflector shield. It is primitive, yet I am encouraged by witnessing the launch of missiles equipped with shields. The Centauris will be shocked."*

"Hopefully, that's a good thing for us," I say. *"And… and how did you establish a direct mind-link at Groom Lake? You said you needed one of your nearby 'communication hubs' to enable this connection."*

"Yes. I relocated one of my hubs to this site yesterday while you were in space. I don't have many to spare, but I believe this is vital to your survival."

"Well, okay." But my reaction is to nervously search the structures around the airfield. This is a base with one of the world's highest security restrictions. I wonder if Cap has already infiltrated all the networks and information systems. *"Uh, can you confine your connections at this location to only my mind? Government security folks here may get anxious about your presence."* I step up into the warmth of a shuttle van that will take Binh and me over to the Skunk Works operations center.

"Although I find the concern absurd, given the primitive nature of the military systems, I will withdraw my local surveillance probes. However, I request you consult with your leadership to allow my advice on deploying weapons against the attacking Centauri squadron."

That means Cap has already breached the firewalls and likely read and analyzed every top-secret file he could find. Shit.

"Of particular importance is the deployment of the XF-100 fighter spacecraft," Cap says. *"Those could be a key ingredient*

to a successful fight, but they must be wary of Centauri point-defense capabilities."

"I have no idea what an XF-100 is." Holy shit. Roger is going to be livid. *"Keep this information to yourself, or you will trigger alarms and paranoia like . . . I can't even imagine."*

"This lack of trust is irrational."

"No, it is not. You think the deaths of millions of humans are no big deal? Why should anyone trust an alien who kills so many of us so easily?" I wonder if the captain can sense the anger mixed with my thoughts.

"Hey Scott, you going to sit on this bus all afternoon?" Binh asks after he walks back to the shuttle van's open door. "We should get inside now for the meeting with General McMahon."

I jump up, shake my head, and wonder how long I have been sitting here. "Uh, sorry. I was thinking about some things—distracted." I follow Binh into the underground operations center and search the rooftops and utility poles for the hiding place of the alien communication hub. Which antenna tower, which rooftop . . . what does it even look like?

"Please request a consultation with General McMahon for me. I can provide helpful information for the coming confrontations," Cap says.

"Yeah, I'll bring it up," I sigh. *"Hey, how is Robby doing? Can you connect me in a conversation with him?"*

"I can link you to Robby when he is near one of my communication hubs in Central Texas. Robby and Luca are assaulting and destroying the political division hubs," Cap says.

"What? Why? Where are they, and are they in danger?"

"Robby is near a community that has death records of organics that were victims of the commissar's cultural suppression

mission," Cap explains. "The more hubs they destroy, the more chaos and disruption of the cultural suppression mission. Luca is very effective with a small sledgehammer. The hub enclosures are fragile."

"Cultural suppression?" I ask. *"What kind of euphemism is that? People were killed."*

"Cultural suppression was the political division's mission to eliminate the telepathic neurodiverse organics of Earth. I had assumed, incorrectly, that the effort died with the destruction of the commissar and all the AI systems on board Frigate-328, but your brother has opened my eyes to a problem."

I sit in a chair near the entrance to the operations center and hold my head in my hands. *"Wait, wait. Are you saying . . . you were behind all the skinhead attacks?"*

"No, I was not," Cap says. *"The commissar had that mission. Surprisingly, it appears the social network AI machines, although rudimentary, have revived the eugenics stimulus and reestablished the links to political division hubs. The hubs had been dormant for years, until recent efforts by 'skinhead' militias were revived."*

"Scott, there you are. Our meeting is starting in a couple of minutes," Tiana says and frowns at me. "Are you okay?"

I rub my eyes. "I dunno. I feel a bit dizzy. I just need a minute here." I take a deep breath, lean back, and close my eyes. "Probably just recovering from high g-forces in the landing," I lie.

"Uh, okay. I'll tell everyone you are on your way," she says.

"Yeah, yeah. Just a minute more."

"You think the AIs of Earth's social networks have been infected to run your mission to kill off the neurodivergent people?" I ask.

"No, the situation is not so simple. The AI machines of your social networks have a programmed motivation to resume the propaganda hate campaigns." Cap says.

"What? That is absurd!" I mind-shout. *"What would trigger the social networks to provoke skinheads?"*

"Profit. Social networking profits plummeted when Frigate-328 was destroyed along with my ship's AI machines," Cap says. *"However, the Earth's social network AIs are motivated to engage users and maximize profits. Those corporate AIs merged with Polit-AI somehow, and collectively, they have joined forces to become the heart of the cultural suppression mission. Engagement and profits have never been better."*

"So Earth's computer systems are infected?" I clarify.

"A better characterization is that the Earth AIs found common purpose with Polit-AI and joined forces. The indigenous social network AI systems not only provided a host for the Polit-AI, they also followed their programming, and figured out how to reinitialize the hub and drone links to restore the commissar's mission."

The scope of the alien Sentinel Suppression Mission is now more apparent and outrageous. For the past five years, I'd assumed I triggered the alien attack by extracting energy from primordial black holes. But it was the emergence of neurodivergence that prompted the aliens to provoke skinhead attacks years earlier, maybe decades earlier, with an insidious poisoning of society against the neurodivergent, against my brother Robby and everyone related to him. The ultimate irony was that the eugenics attack on my family was disrupted by the aliens' kinetic energy weapon bombardment, which killed Mom and Dad. And then, in turn, our counterattack and destruction of Icarus interrupted the murderous rampage by the skinheads for a while.

I did not cause the alien war against Earth. For too long, I have been torturing myself needlessly. The aliens had been indirectly targeting and killing humans for decades. When I harnessed the energy of black holes, it simply provided the means to fight back. I did provoke the more overt attack by Icarus, and although Cap's projectile weapons killed millions, that was the first step in alerting us to the already ongoing fight with the aliens. A ton of baggage drops from my shoulders.

The thunderous roar of another Sidewinder launch disturbs me from my thoughts. A cloudy vapor exhaust trail of the primordial black hole leaps into the blue sky, and a white plasma ball enveloping the missile's tail marks the location of the incredible energy propelling the weapon toward the alien attackers. It will take almost four days for that Sidewinder to reach 80 percent light speed and intercept the planet killer inside the Kuiper Belt, over forty billion kilometers away.

Chapter 20

Graves

Cedar Park, Texas, December 10, 2060.

For three weeks now, every time the skinheads find us, we escape. Cap should find better maps to avoid them, though. But there are so many . . . so many that want to kill us. *"How do they keep finding us?"* I glance behind us, but no cars are coming. *"Are we even driving toward Cedar Park anymore?"* Our red van speeds down a narrow road that cuts through hills and green trees with fence posts on both sides.

"The Polit-AI has concentrated resources in this region to continue its suppression mission," Cap answers. *"It also seems to have combined forces with the social networking systems to track your location and marshal forces to intercept you. It is a superior command and control system."* The van decelerates and comes to a stop near another road intersection at the top of a hill. *"Five meters up on that wooden pole. Look just below the wire insulators. Do you see it? That grey cube is one of the hubs they use."*

"Are you sure? It looks like part of the electric company stuff that is everywhere." I think Cap must be confused. Other

grey parts are attached near the top of the wooden pole: tall, trash-can-shaped objects, stacks of glass cones, bundles of skinny tubes, and metal bars connecting to fat cable twists.

"My drones can communicate with that hub, but they are denied access by the hub's security settings. I expect it sends alerts to the Polit-AI clone via the cellular network devices it has hacked. The efficiency of the political division's mission improved dramatically by infiltrating the native communications technology. Those hubs are located at the top of utility poles, just like my hubs, because they can draw power from the electrical cables using inductive coupling. The network transceivers in those tall tubes are easy entries into the communication networks that span your world. The Polit-AI has likely notified its drone and organic agents of our presence."

"You mean skinheads will come looking for us here?" Luca asks.

"Yes," Cap replies. *"We must move swiftly to avoid an encounter with eugenicists. My scout drone identified a large group of Polit-AI agents near the burial ground you wish to search. I do not advise continuing in that direction."*

"But you said Mom and Dad might be there in Cedar Park. Maybe dead." Luca sobs again.

"Can't we turn the drones and the hubs off?" I ask.

"I do not possess an on-off switch for the hubs, and the hubs direct the drone missions and survival."

"We should smash the hubs," I say. *"Break the skinhead cubes."* Scotty tells me I am good at breaking things, but he and Dad always got angry when I did. When I remember Dad, I want to cry.

"Neither of you is tall enough to reach those hubs. They also have a strong protective shell, and if threatened, a hub is

programmed to relocate," Cap says. *"I have detected Polit-AI drones approaching your location. You should move away before they arrive. Organic agents are sure to follow."*

"How can a skinhead cube move? It does not have wings," Luca says as he opens the back doors of our red van. He reaches above the top of the van to grab the ladder on the roof rack.

"A cube is programmed to deploy its engine, move, and reinstall at a safe location. The hubs relocate during nighttime to maintain stealth."

Luca slides the ladder to the ground and tilts it against the wooden pole. *"It is daytime. I will smash it before it gets dark."*

I help Luca extend the ladder to its full length, and then he raises it against the pole to rest just below the skinhead cube. I find a heavy hammer in the van toolbox and hand it to Luca. *"It is much better than a chair."*

Luca takes the hammer, examines it, and then looks up at the cube. He nods. *"Yes. I can't carry a chair up the ladder."*

The ladder tips sideways as Luca climbs up, holding the hammer in one hand. I lean on the ladder when it starts to slip.

Bang. Bang. Bang. "This hammer does not break the skinhead cube. It is too weak."

"Strike it with more force," Cap says.

Luca leans away from the pole for a wide swing with the hammer. *Boom. Boom. Bang. Chink.* A piece of the cube falls near my foot. *Bang.* Smoke comes out of the skinhead cube. Luca waves away bugs flying around his face and climbs down.

"I felt the skinhead cube groan when I hit it," Luca says. *"But the noise stopped when the smoke came out."*

"Get in the truck quickly. You must depart before the skinheads arrive," Cap says.

We hook the ladder back onto the top of the van, jump inside, pull the doors shut, and the van drives away down the road through the dark green trees. *"You have done well. The hub is disabled, and I have directed the vehicle to a safe location away from skinheads."*

"I felt the skinhead cube die. It felt good," Luca says. *"Can we find more?"*

"I am impressed that you feel the mind of a hub. This is a stunning cognitive step," Cap says. *"I am very impressed. You are adapting to communicate via an alien mind interface."* The van bounces fast down the road between the short green trees.

"You can talk to the machine?" I ask Luca.

He shrugs and holds on to the tool rack inside the truck. *"No. But I felt something. It hurt. But it stopped hurting when sparks and smoke began to fly from the cube. That felt good."* Luca smiles. *"Can we kill more? Then drive to the burial ground in Cedar Park to look for my mom and dad?"*

"That is an interesting strategy," Cap says. *"If we disable most of the hubs in the area, the Polit-AI agents will lose their organizational structure. I have redirected your destination to another Polit-AI hub five miles from here. It is near the burial ground in Cedar Park."*

Luca smiles again as the truck stops and turns around.

The two cars are parked sideways, blocking the path ahead. Ditches line both sides of the narrow road, so we can't attempt to drive into the surrounding cedar and mesquite trees. The trees are thick with the sharp ends of dead branches that poke and cut open your skin if you try to walk through the forest.

"We should ask Cap to drive our van on a different road to the cemetery, but not till we smash that skinhead hub above us." Luca points to the wooden telephone pole in front of us. *"We can lean the ladder across the ditch to reach it."*

*"*Yeah, well, the men down the road are probably skinheads," I say. *"And if you climb up to mess with the hub, those skinheads might get angry."*

Luca rocks back and forth, watching the men by their cars watch us. He stops, then shrugs. *"Fuck them. How will they know what we are doing? Do they get a text message that says, 'Go kill the autistic kids down the road?'"* Luca turns and stares at me. *"Get ready to run."*

"Run where?" The thick cedar trees on both roadsides look like a nest of sharp sticks with no path in sight. *"We will have to break branches off to make a place to go, or else run back down the road away from the skinheads. They will catch us if they can run fast."*

"Help me with this," Luca says, pulling the extension ladder to full length.

I slip on the ice on the road, but we lift the ladder to tilt it over the ditch and up to the utility pole. Luca carries the sledgehammer and climbs the ladder to the grey cube near the power wires. He glances at the men down the road, who are still standing beside their cars, then leans back to take his swing.

But the cube changes shape. An opening appears on the bottom, and something pops down. It looks like a tiny toilet plunger squirting a jet of smoke. Luca swings at the cube but misses. The cube hops away from the pole and floats over the middle of the road, out of reach. I lean on the ladder to keep Luca from tipping it over—he holds it with only one hand,

and both feet slip off the step. The hammer bounces beside my feet, and Luca hugs the ladder. He finally finds the step with his feet.

The cube is gone.

The men are inside the cars, and the roar of the engines reaches us.

"It was only a matter of time before this Polit-AI took corrective actions," Cap says. *"Stand clear of your vehicle."* Our red van leaps forward toward the approaching cars, slips sideways on the ice, but then whips straight down the road.

"That cube escaped and notified the skinheads to attack," Cap says. *"Run. Run off the road and into the trees."*

I jump into the ditch as Luca drops to the ground.

Bang! Crunch!

Our red van smashes through the front of the first car, flips up, spins around, and pulls the car with it into the ditch. Fire and black smoke burst out of the skinhead car. The second car stops past the fire, the door swings open, and a man steps out with a long gun in his arms. He looks up at us and shouts, *"You motherfuckers! Who the hell . . ."* He runs toward us, raises the gun, and stops to aim. His head is bald.

Bang!

A puff of dirt pops up from above the place where Luca dives headfirst into the ditch.

Bang! Another shot rings out.

Luca and I crawl in the icy mud of the ditch away from the skinhead, his boots stomping down the road toward us. He is overtaken by the roar of a car motor and the squeal of tires.

"What . . . how? Umph!" screams the skinhead, followed by the sound of a car bouncing through a deep hole on the road above our ditch hiding place.

Then silence. I turn back, and Luca looks at me with wide eyes. We both squeeze into the bottom of our ditch and hear the sound of wind in the trees and the faraway caw of a crow.

I shiver and wait. *"I think he's gone now. And it's very cold down here."*

"I believe you are safe for the moment," Cap says.

"There he is," I say when I poke my head above the ditch. *"The top of his head is bloody. He looks broken. He is bent backward too far."* The road is smooth, so what was that noise? I climb and walk to the blue car that stopped on the road. It is the second skinhead car, but nobody is inside. The front window is smashed and bent into the front seat.

Luca stands above the broken man beside the ditch on the other side of the road, then frowns and groans. *"Those are his brains showing."* He wrinkles his nose, rocks back and forth, and looks at me again. *"He's not a skinhead anymore."*

"Enter that blue car immediately," Cap says. *"The car's diagnostic tests report it has suffered a collision, but can still navigate to a safer location. Hurry. More skinheads are approaching."*

"I don't see anyone coming, and the front of the car was smashed."

"Then get in the back seat. Now," Cap orders.

Luca and I climb into the back of the car, but have to move the stack of guns and packs into the front seat to make room for us. The tires squeal and the car spins around to race in the direction where the skinheads blocked the road—toward the Cedar Park cemetery. Cap steers our car around the fire of the first skinhead car, our crashed red van, and past the orange sparks and white smoke of burning cedar trees. We race down the road and come out between hills with cows eating grass inside a barbed wire fence.

"You will need to change tactics. A hammer is no longer an effective weapon against the Polit-AI hubs," Cap says.

I wonder if we could use one of the long guns we tossed into the front seat.

"I could feel that cube," Luca says. *"It felt . . . felt angry."*

"Your skills grow. The anger you felt was the energy of the hub's urgent call for help to escape destruction," Cap explains. *"Luca, you are showing strong abilities to adapt to the communication modes of a machine. In time, you too may be able to interrogate technology controls. Maybe someday you will learn to direct the AI navigation of a car like this one."*

"Humpf," grunts Luca.

I pick up the long gun with a telescope from the front seat. It is like the one the grey-haired lady used to shoot at skinheads. I rest the gun on the back of the front seat, aim it through the side window, and look through the telescope like the lady did when she looked for skinheads. The cows and posts of the fence flash by as we race along the road. Everything appears close in the telescope, but the bouncing view makes me dizzy.

"We will reach the cemetery in Cedar Park in three minutes. There is a record of the burials in this place, too. The gate is guarded, but I'm unsure who the guards are."

Our car comes to a stop behind a cluster of junked cars and trucks on the road leading to the gate. It will be a long walk, which is probably a good thing. We won't be asked about the car's wrecked bumper and the window that's smashed into the front seat. Maybe I should bring one of the long guns with me, but I'm not sure how to shoot with it. Luca and I walk between the long line of cars parked on the road—they are not crashed, but many are old, rusty, and covered with a thin layer of dirt. The cars and trucks look worse the closer we walk to the gate; some have broken windows or flat tires. Some have bullet holes.

A giant yellow bulldozer is parked on the side of the road. It looks like the dozer flattened the ground at the cemetery gate and made a tall pile of dirt, dead cedar trees, cars, and trucks on one side. The fence around the cemetery is made of chain links with coils of barbed wire stretched along the top, like a dump or junkyard. Smoke rises from the pipe on the roof of a small building near the bulldozer.

A man steps out of the house. He is wrapped in a black coat that drags in the dirt, and his head is covered in a green cap. He hangs the strap of a long gun on his shoulder and rocks back and forth, watching us walk toward him.

"Hold it right there," he orders, unslinging his gun. "Whatcha doin' here?"

Luca does not look afraid. He rocks back and forth, keeps his mouth shut, and hums. His eyes squint in the last light of the sunset.

I try to say my best voice words, "Look at graves."

The man twists his face, shakes his head at the ground, and pulls a phone from his pocket. "Yeah. 'Tards. Two more," he says into his phone. He turns around, opens the gate, and waves at us. "Well, come on." He sighs.

Luca and I look at each other, shrug, and walk in. We follow a narrow road through more cedar trees toward a brick building at the front of a field full of stones. The gate clangs shut behind us as two more guys with long guns come out of the front door. They both have bald heads. Two more men walk toward us down a path between the stones in the field.

"I don't think this was a good idea," Luca says.

"Well, what do you want to do now?" I ask. *"Looks like a bunch of skinheads coming."*

"What . . . who?" somebody's mind speaks, but it's a different, new voice.

"Welcome," Cap says. *"We are happy to meet you."*

One of the skinheads with a long gun stops like he's frozen to the ground. "Ugh." He groans and presses both hands to his forehead.

"What's the matter, Jeb?" asks the other guy with a gun.

Jeb slips and falls to one knee. *"Who are you? What are you?"* Jeb mind-asks.

"We are like you and can communicate our thoughts telepathically," Cap says.

"Yeah. You're a neurotard just like us," Luca says. He stands with his hands on his hips.

I don't remember if Luca has ever smiled like that before.

Jeb slaps his head above both ears. "No, no, no!" he cries, and his eyes dart at each of the other men. He turns and crawls toward the small house, his rifle falling from his shoulder.

The other skinheads stop and frown at Jeb, their mouths hanging open.

The other two gunmen stare at Jeb and then at the two guys walking in from the field. "We better go check on Jeb. Jake and Tim, you take the two 'tards to the pen. Be there in a minute. Damn it." They trot after Jeb, who still crawls in the dirt, and both gunmen drag Jeb through the front door of the brick house.

The sharp pain in my shoulder is from Jake's large hand gripping like a pair of pliers. "Ow, ow!" I cry.

"Move! You fuckin 'tard," Jake says, shoving my back with his fist, pushing me to walk the path between the stones. I am close enough now that I can read the names of the dead people written on the stones.

Luca twists and slaps away Tim's arm, who stumbles backward. Luca is taller than Tim and stronger than me. And Luca hates it when someone touches him. Luca starts to run, but Tim chases and tackles Luca to the ground. It's like a football game.

"Umph," Luca grunts when Tim jumps on his back.

Tim kicks Luca twice. "You motherfuckin' 'tard!" he shouts.

"Don't fight them. Just go with the skinheads," Cap says.

"But they're going to hurt us," I shout.

"Go with them. They will hurt you more if you don't," says Cap.

Luca holds still and lets Tim pull him up, pushing him. Luca stumbles down the path beside me, blood flowing down his cheek where it scraped the ground.

"It's like before. I ran then," sobs Luca. *"I should run again. He kicked me like they kicked Mom."*

Tim punches Luca in the back. "Keep moving, crybaby."

We stumble together along the path between names of dead people, climb a hill toward a yellow excavation machine, and stop at another fence. It's like the chicken pen behind Mary's barn, but taller. There are wooden posts and high wires surrounding the place where animals live. It stinks, like animal poop. I wish I were still with Mary. I could be warm on her sofa while watching TV. Scotty could come and visit me.

But I must find Mom.

"Get in there!" yells Jake, and he kicks my butt. I fall through a gate he opens, and my knee and butt hurt. Luca falls on top of me. The gate slams shut. Outside the pen, Jake and Tim stand by a fire burning inside a steel barrel, throw in some wood pieces, and warm their hands.

"I should have run away. No, no, no." Luca cries and wipes the blood off his cheek.

"No, no. Not again," cries a voice. *"Please, let me be."* But it is not the mind-voice of Jeb, who must still be back inside that brick house. It is a new voice. A voice that feels pain.

Luca looks up at me with round eyes, and we both see it. The heap in the corner of our pen moves. It moves like . . . somebody inside rags, rags that move into a smaller shape in the corner of the pen.

"No. No more," he cries and covers his head with hands that are brown and bloody.

"We won't hurt you. The skinheads hurt us, too," I say.

"Oh!" gasps the ragman.

"You will be safe now," Cap says.

The ragman cries out loud. It is a tiny voice, like . . .

"It's a girl. A girl like Sophia, Sophia from school," Luca says. *"Are you hurt?"*

She wails out loud again. *"Who are you?"* She sobs. The rags unfold, and she sits up. *"How can we be safe here? They come every day, sometimes twice at night. It . . . it hurts so bad."*

"We are like you," Luca says. *"I throw chairs at skinheads."*

"She asked a good question, Luca. We are trapped in this pen, just like her. And I don't see any chairs here."

She wipes her face, and I see eyes like white stars in a black night sky.

"Who are you?" she asks.

"I am Robby. Cap is here but far away."
"I am Luca. What is your name?"
"Angela. I came here to look for my dad."

Luca and I stare at each other. All those wrecked cars outside the gate belonged to people who came here searching. But they never left. The rows of stones. Rows and rows of stones with names down the hill and into the valley belong to someone's mom, dad, sister, or brother. Their bodies are still here under the stones.

"It is time to throw chairs," Cap says, and I hear the whir of an electric motor in the distance. It gets louder. The sound of wheels crunching in gravel rolls nearer. *"Move far from the gate of your jail."*

A grey car speeds down the road, heading straight for us. Luca and I dive into the corner where Angela crouches when the car crashes through the pen's fence. The gate is ripped away, and the Tesla spins away from us, tips on its side, and spins toward the fire barrel while Jake and Tim dive out of the way. Fire spreads inside the car, and sparks pop and explode out of the batteries. The car rolls upside down, and geysers of fire shoot out from its floor into the night sky.

"Hey! What the—" Jake screams, turns, and stares at the fence that has been dragged from our pen into the fire.

"The car is broken," I say. *"But the skinheads are still alive and only scared."*

"I did break the car," Cap agrees, *"and there are no other vehicles nearby that I can control."*

Tim stares, mouth open, at the spreading fire spraying into the sky and up the hill into the cedar trees. "Now how the fuck did that happen?"

"Leave now! All of you. Run down that road toward the moon," Cap says.

Luca and I stand up slowly and find the road leading toward the crescent moon, but Angela shivers on the ground, frozen, refusing to move. *"It's okay. You can come with us,"* I say, but the girl covers her face and shakes. *"Cap controlled the car. We trust him. He can take us where it's safe."*

Angela looks up at me with fear-filled eyes that quickly grow wide with terror.

I feel a presence near my right ear. I twist around carefully and look down the length of a long gun.

"You fucking 'tard," sneers Tim. He shakes his head. "Jake, we need to take this trash out. Now." The tip of the barrel is against my ear, but I hear the buzz of a tiny insect.

Jake presses his rifle into Luca's chest and leans forward.

Angela makes a noise like a squeaky door.

Jake gasps and reaches his hand from the trigger up to his eye. Blood trickles from his nose.

"Aaughh!" Tim drops his long gun and covers his eyes with both hands, wailing as he crumples on top of the weapon. He rolls around like a worm that's been squished by a boot, screaming, "No! Naw!" coughs blood, and digs his fingers into his skinhead. He stops suddenly and releases a long, slow breath. Then Tim is still.

Jake sits on his knees with blood spurting between fingers that cover his eye, and then he falls back to stare at the stars. His rifle falls back on his chest, and he lies still at Luca's feet, gaping at the sky.

Luca wails like a dog in pain. His eyes are shut tight, and his fists are clenched at his waist.

"Both skinheads have been disabled," Cap says. *"You are safe for now."*

I fall to one knee with dizziness and gasp for breath. *"What happened? How did you do that?"*

"I apologize for the last-second defensive action, but I needed to deploy two of my drones. I only have one remaining in the vicinity, and it enables our communications."

"You killed the skinheads with your drones?" asks Luca. *"But how? They are only the size of mosquitoes."* Luca takes deep breaths and looks down in wonder at the dead Jake.

"The drones have a powerful propulsion engine, much stronger than a small insect. I instructed the drones to enter their skinhead brains by puncturing and following their optic nerves into the brain cavity. The drones carved a five-centimeter spherical path inside those brains at maximum speed until their propulsion engines overheated and burned out. It was a costly and inefficient mechanism to cause brain failure, but it had a near-immediate effect. There were no other functioning car weapons or alternatives nearby."

"And there were no chairs either," Luca says, breathing slowly and flexing his hands.

I stand and back away slowly from my skinhead's body. *"Thank you for saving us. What should we do now? Where do we go? There are still those other three skinheads down the hill."*

"Run down that road toward the moon," Cap says, *"quickly."*

Angela rises and walks toward the fire, holding the blanket tight around her shoulders, and looks down at the dead man. *"Good."* She stands taller than Luca, shivering inside the torn blanket that drags in the dirt. Her face is smudged with mud, and her hair is twisted in knots. She is naked under the blanket. *"How does he do it?"* She limps slowly to where Tim lies among smoldering firewood. She kicks the body with her bare feet, then stomps the skinhead's flaccid belly and starts to cry out loud.

"Cap can control computers and machines," I explain. *"He helps us drive to cemeteries, and he kills skinheads."*

"I walked here to find my dad," Angela says. She points her chin at the brick house in the valley and adds, *"They know where everyone is buried. But we asked, and they called us 'tards and locked us in the pen. They took the others away…"* Her gaze drifts to the yellow excavator next to Tim's body. *"The others never came back."* She kicks Tim's body once more.

"You must move quickly along that road," Cap repeats. *"I found the list of names. My drone located a portable computer inside the brick building and uploaded all the files. The skinheads have a connection to an expansive database in the cloud that tracks all known neurodivergents with telepathic genetic markers. They are well connected with other eugenics agents around the Earth, and coordinate efforts to find and terminate the telepathic strains. The database also lists the identified targets and their corresponding locations. I found your parents, Luca."*

"Where? Where are Mom and Dad?" Luca cries, and tears flow. His eyes are wide like he is scared—scared of the answer.

"Go now. I will lead you to them. Their graves are five hundred meters away, in the next valley to the south."

Luca falls to his knees, then rests his head in the cold dirt with his hands on his head. He wails out loud.

The door to the brick house opens, and two men walk toward us.

"Please, please get up and run away," Cap says. *"I am sorry for your loss, but you must go now. You can mourn at your parents' grave."*

Luca looks up but doesn't move until Angela approaches him, lifting his arm to help him stand. Luca never likes it when others touch him, but he lets Angela hold his arm and guide him to walk along the path.

***

We are dirty and stink. The black man at the grocery store told us to get out, but Cap paid for apples, bread, peanut butter, and donuts. The donuts were the best. Now, we scrape peanut butter out of the jar with slices of bread and drink soda from cans.

Even Luca eats. He lay down on the hill that Cap called a grave and stared into the darkness, but did not cry. The mound of earth had no stones with names, but Cap said there were two hundred forty-three people in that grave. We stayed there for two hours until it got too cold and the crescent moon set.

Angela's dad was buried under another hill nearby. After Angela told Cap her dad's name, he found the grave for her. Angela wrapped herself in the blanket and sat still on top of the hill. She stared over the cedar trees, watching the sky.

Cap stole another car, and we tossed trash in the front seat where the driver usually sits. Cap drives for us now, and finally, we go to Austin. I want to find Mom. But not like the others did.

Chapter 21

Counterattacks

Groom Lake, Nevada, December 10, 2060.

It seems my new responsibilities now include serving as a technical consultant on too many design reviews. I miss the early days of discovery and physics at Agosti's Center for Dark Matter Research. I miss the rattle of that refrigerator filled with free beer while Danny and I worked all night to complete some design project. But I lost all my friends from those days. Anthony, Danny, and the Pecos Center guys were all killed in the projectile attack from Icarus, and that god damn captain. Heinrich is the only physicist left, but he's rotting inside a federal prison—and good riddance. I should follow up with Pyotr's offer to work at Caltech and the JPL team. That might lead to a chance to complete my PhD degree at Caltech, which would be even more amazing—if I could get admitted. I would be back in the middle of the physics I left behind when the University of Texas was vaporized. I could work alongside the world's most brilliant physicists. If only Anthony and Danny were there with me . . .

But then, I would miss working with Roger and Binh on their cool toys. They dragged me from my malaise after losing the baby and losing Mary. They put me back to work developing the new technology made possible with our abundant PBH energy sources. Today, they invite me into the top-secret hangar, where I see the bizarre-looking spacecraft that Cap mentioned.

"This must be the XF-100 space fighter," I say while examining the two engines mounted in the tail of the nearest spacecraft.

Roger glares at me. "How did you hear about this? It's top secret, and until now, you did not have a need to know."

I catch my breath and wince at my blunder. "Well, I told you Cap has infiltration capabilities. He told me."

Roger shakes his head. "Damn it. I knew that alien was going to be a security risk." He stares at the ceiling for a moment, then grimaces. "My fault, but I don't see any other choice. Tell Cap he is not to share any information he learns here. There is no way to enforce that, but see if you can appeal to any integrity he may have. We have to protect these secrets. This space fighter may be key to our defense."

"I told him to stop snooping already," I say. But Roger turns away from me, distracted by his ringing cellphone.

"This preoccupation with keeping secrets from me is absurd," Cap says. *"Your survival is enhanced with each facet of military technology you share. It can only improve the quality of my advice."*

"Okay, okay. Just keep the secrets to yourself," I say to Cap.

I then turn to Roger, but he is wandering in the center of the hangar, bent over his phone, arguing and gesturing with his free hand. Good. Maybe he will be distracted enough to forget about Cap's snooping. And I have time to ask Tiana about the design of this new fighter.

"This fighter . . . I never imagined a spacecraft looking so . . . so ugly. I envisioned something more elegant, akin to a sleek update of an F-52 fighter. It doesn't even have wings," I say, then realize my comment's stupidity. "But then, a spacecraft won't need wings for lift."

"And with engines powered by primordial black holes, it does not need fuel tanks," Tiana says. "We put two PBH engines on the XF-100 for redundancy."

I lean in to examine one of the engine nozzles. "These look nearly identical to the engine we designed for the Sidewinder."

"Yes, we didn't need to make many changes," Tiana confirms. "That PBH engine provides more power than we'll ever need, and it's proven. It's incredible how little maintenance it requires compared to a typical jet turbine system."

"The airframe resembles an old Apache attack helicopter with two seats side-by-side in the cockpit, minus the rotor and tail boom. It's just a big blob—kinda like a beetle." I sigh. "And it has hard points to mount a dozen AIM-9AA Sidewinders."

"It's a lot longer than the Apache," she says. "But only because we needed more capacity for life support supplies. The airframe is built to handle 20 Gs, a force that would shatter an Apache helicopter into pieces. And, of course, it has a deflector shield mounted up front."

"It appears to be ten times the length of the Sidewinder deflector?" I ask, running my hand along the twenty-meter boom extending from the beetle's nose.

"Yeah, there wasn't time to validate the design assumptions in that deflector shield design. Based on your experiments with

Binh in the shuttle, the engineers made some guesses. The next flights will serve to test their assumptions."

"Which will be an hour from now," Binh says. He wears a space suit and carries a helmet under his arm. "We are going to have to go with this shield untested. Now. Our first two shielded PBH Sidewinders missed. That alien planet killer is still coming straight at us, and is only two days away."

Roger rejoins us, and his eyes dart between Tiana and me. "I just got notified also—by the Joint Chiefs of Staff. POTUS has given up trying to reassure the UN that we have the aliens under control. The world leaders are all in a panic now. Why the hell are our missiles missing the target? Tiana, are the other three Sidewinders still tracking the projectile?"

"As far as I know, yes," she answers, then checks her watch. "Time to next intercept is twenty-three minutes, still way outside Pluto's orbit." She turns to run out the door. "Heading over to the operations center."

"Colonel Nguyen, get your squadron into space and prepare to attack that planet killer if all five of the Sidewinders miss. Now!" shouts Roger.

Four of the XF-100s appear ready with missiles loaded on the pylons. However, these are the same as the Sidewinder that just missed the target. I only see two of the planet-killer variety with heavy steel-slug warheads. The rest are stock AIM-9AAs with the old half-megaton fusion warheads. None of them may be any good if the incoming planet killer can evade the Sidewinder guidance system.

Binh sprints toward the nearest fighter as a claxon siren blares. He climbs a ladder into the front pilot's seat, followed by his copilot. Three other crews race to their respective XF-100s. A blast of cold wind floods the hangar as the giant doors are pushed back, opening to the evening twilight and the sunset reflecting off the peaks of the distant eastern mountains. Airmen scramble to pull off cables and red remove-before-flight streamers hanging under the bellies of the space fighters. Canopies swing down over the cockpits, and I can barely see the pilots through the narrow viewports.

"Clear the area. Prepare for engine power-up. Clear the area," loudspeakers announce, and all the airmen scramble for cover.

"Scott, let's move over to the ops center," Roger shouts over the clatter of activity.

I chase the general, sprinting toward our underground bunker. I don't want to be near four space fighters simultaneously powering up their PBH engines. The radiation could be fatal. But we pause at the ops center entrance to watch the four XF-100s slowly roll forward one by one through the hangar doorway to the engine run-up tarmac. Each fighter has the telltale white-blue plasma balls of primordial black holes around each of their two engines, rumbling with the blast of radiation and hydrogen spewing out the nozzles. The four beetles run through final checklists while side-by-side on the tarmac with twelve PBH Sidewinders each. No, not beetles—with plasma balls on their tails, these look more like fireflies.

Four fireflies take turns down the runway and use hydrogen maneuvering thrusters to leap into the sky, flying almost straight up. I hold my fingers in my ears as each roars with the thunderous staccato of black hole engines. Sonic booms rattle the airbase as the ships escape Earth's atmosphere as fast as possible.

"I don't know how we miss," Pyotr says. He stares at the plot of objects in our solar system displayed on a large overhead screen. "Three near misses. Only two more tries."

"Have you not told your friends about my concern?" Cap asks. *"The planet killer is not a dumb bomb."*

"Yes, yes. I know. We hoped the AIM-9AA thrust vector controls could overtake a planet killer's escape tactics."

There are three distant red triangles marking the locations of the Centauri squadron ships still outside the solar system. The nearest is eighty billion kilometers, less than ten days away at 56 percent of the speed of light. The other two warships are moving at 64 percent of the speed of light and are over twice as far from Earth. The fourth blinking red triangle is the closest, but still ten times the distance of Neptune's orbit. That planet killer is heading straight at Earth at 83 percent of the speed of light, and if we don't stop it, it will strike Earth. That blinking red triangle is annotated with a marker labeled *"ETA 49:43:22."*

Tiana's five surface-launched missiles are also on the plot as blue asterisks. However, three blue asterisks have passed by the planet killer and are now heading deep into space. Two more blue asterisks are lined up to strike the incoming projectile. Those two missiles are almost our last hope to protect us from a seven-thousand-megaton kinetic projectile strike. If they miss, we'll only have the XF-100s between us and the planet killer, and the missiles they carry are no better.

"The hits or misses happened long ago," Tiana says. "The telemetry signals take about forty-four hours to reach us from that range. If the fifth Sidewinder reports a miss, we only have about five hours before Earth may be hit by a planet killer. The incoming projectile will have already passed Jupiter's orbit."

"Oh!" Pyotr exclaims. "I see why missiles miss—planet killer use evasive maneuver! First missile telemetry show seeker try to change course . . ." The color drains from his face, and Pyotr's jaw drops. "But too late! Planet killer steers around Sidewinder!" He gasps. Everyone stares at Pyotr, eyes wide. "Bullet miss bullet."

"Well, Cap did warn us their planet killers could maneuver," I say. "Two missiles flying near the speed of light in opposite directions . . . damn it!"

"I also hoped the planet killer's evasive actions would be less effective. It was too much to hope for your missiles to compensate," Cap says. *"This is a distressing outcome."*

The only sound in the Skunk Works operations center is the hum of the ventilation as we watch the first of the two remaining missiles miss the target.

I imagine a light-speed slug of tungsten crashing through Earth's atmosphere, tunneling into the Earth, and splitting the planet in half. I sink into a chair behind Roger, feeling dizzy and gasping for breath. Is this how it ends? All this effort, and we all still get vaporized by an alien planet killer? I hold my head, rubbing my temples. No, no. Surely no. I suck in a deep breath, throw my head back, and rerun calculations in my head. No, the projectile should not physically strike the ground. At that speed, a projectile is more likely to vaporize in a high-altitude fireball as it hits Earth's atmosphere. But it could be a seven-thousand-megaton fireball burning away all life. Earth will be a burned-out cinder.

The silence is not broken for minutes, and everyone is consumed by the anticipation of doom. Everyone is still—everyone except for Roger, who is tapping on his keyboard. "Pyotr, there may still be a way."

All eyes are on the general as he continues to focus on his workstation. "Colonel Nguyen, report your status," Roger says into his microphone, continuing to type while waiting for the seven-minute round-trip time for communications.

We wait in the silence of Roger's keyboard clicks, desperate to hope that he has a solution.

"Squadron passing Mars orbit range, sixty million kilometers," grunts Binh. "Maintaining 5 Gs," he gasps. "On vector to target."

"Binh, I sent you targeting tactics for the intercept. Confirm receipt. Tactics are for each fighter to launch two Sidewinders," Roger says. "Use the stock AIM-9AA with fusion warheads only for this attack. Load the trajectory profiles I sent to your targeting systems. Alpha Two, Three, and Four missile pairs are programmed for triangular flanking attacks from zero, one-twenty, and two-forty degrees, respectively. Alpha One's missile trajectory is head-on into the center of the triangle. Enable synchronization on the Sidewinders to launch and converge on the target simultaneously."

I smile and wipe away tears. Damn. *This is why he is General Roger McMahon.*

"I, too, have newfound respect for General McMahon," says Cap. *"The calm application of logic to synthesize battle tactics is an essential trait for any military commander."*

We wait again for the seven-minute round-trip time of the communications link.

"Yeah." Binh audibly gulps air. "Got it. Alpha Two, Three, and Four confirm." He sounds like he is in pain from the acceleration. "Squadron, load your missile attack profiles and confirm. General, I need an updated flight plan." Binh groans. "Need a vector for best head-on launch."

"Pyotr, can you get them on a head-on intercept plan?" Roger asks.

"Yes, yes." Pyotr types on his workstation. "Beautiful! Beautiful plan, General. Working with JPL Planetary Defense." Pyotr bounces in his chair. "Yes, sending now." He beams and turns to the general. "Binh, autopilot guidance slow you down, too. Relax. Only 2.5 Gs." He chuckles. "Plenty of time. Squadron on parallel trajectory in thirty-five minutes. Sidewinders launch and thrust 120 Gs to inbound planet killer. Intercept range three hundred million kilometers, between Mars and Jupiter."

Tiana places a hand on Pyotr's arm, forcing a smile through her tears. "We have a chance still. But Roger, I worry about the rate of closure. The typical warhead trigger time is ten microseconds. The missiles travel almost three kilometers in ten microseconds."

"Can you time the warhead detonation instead of using proximity triggers?" I ask. "You should be able to detonate well ahead of the target and spray warhead shrapnel in the incoming flight path."

"Shit, it's worse than that." Roger grimaces. "We also need time for the warhead blast to expand—about ten milliseconds. That's over two thousand kilometers ahead of the target."

"We can handle that," Tiana says. "Modify the guidance program to detonate at ten milliseconds before target impact."

"Agreed," says Roger, typing on his workstation again. "Binh, are you following this? I'm sending updated guidance profiles to detonate warheads ten milliseconds ahead of the target flight path."

The seven minutes of silent waiting are excruciating.

"Yes, sir. Hope this is better than clouds of flak." Binh sighs, now breathing more easily with the reduced g-forces.

"Can you also disable the deflector shields on the Sidewinders?" I ask. "Avoid an early warning to the incoming missile by suppressing the deflector radiation. It's a short distance, and the likelihood of space dust collisions is low."

Another seven minutes pass. At this rate, we may use up all the remaining time waiting on the speed of light to communicate. The intercept plan will strike the planet killer only seventeen minutes from Earth.

"Great suggestion," Binh says. "We'll also leave our squadron's deflector shields turned off. Silent running. Maybe we can surprise it."

"You know," muses Tiana, "the incoming planet killer is moving at over eighty percent light speed, a lot faster than Binh's squadron. The XF-100 squadron pilots can fire their missiles at 120 Gs, shut down their fighter PBH engines, coast, and go into stealth mode. This is going to be like planting mines in a ship channel."

"I like it," Binh replies after another seven-minute pause. "We will launch the missiles, alter course, boost, and coast away from the blast effects region. We get only one shot at this. We'll never catch the planet killer if it gets past us."

"Good plan," Roger says. "Good hunting."

Tiana switches the main display on the ops center wall to show the images transmitted by the old Hubble telescope.

The image is centered on the flickering light of the incoming planet-killer's shield; its image from near Neptune's orbit is three hours old. The bright flare of light from the squadron's engines enters the bottom of the image.

"Squadron turning on attack vector now," Binh reports. "IR tracking target dead ahead. Locked on and transferring target image to seekers. All eight weapons at pre-launch idle power. All eight seekers confirm target lock. Powering up all missiles to thirty percent engine power and releasing launch control to seeker quorum logic. Stand by . . . target is dead ahead."

I wipe beads of sweat from my forehead and ignore everything but those tactical displays on the wall.

"Launch! All eight Sidewinders away!" shouts Binh. "Alpha Squad, pivot now, max thrust." Binh grunts under the force of 12 Gs to escape the blast area. We hope.

"I bet the planet-killer guidance can see that," Roger says. "Four XF-100s, eight PBH Sidewinder engines at maximum thrust. But six missiles are temporarily going away from the planet killer's flight path. I wonder how it will react."

"Time of flight to target intercept is four hours, thirty minutes," Tiana reports. "Range is one hundred and fifty million kilometers."

"You have done well," Cap says. *"Better than I expected. There is some hope you will stop the planet killer. But if not, I must say that it has been a pleasure knowing you and your brother. I am prepared for my end."*

"Well, ten billion humans are not prepared." Damn Cap and his flippant attitude. Another deep breath is all I can try to quench the burning in my chest.

"Sixty seconds," Binh reports. "All missiles locked on, 120 G thrust toward target."

"Thirty seconds."

"Fifteen . . . target changing direction! All Sidewinders are still locked, and now they are steering to match the target course change."

"Five seconds."

"Oh!" screams Binh. "My god!"

I can feel my heart beating in my ears.

"Signal lost," Tiana says. "No telemetry from our squadron."

But everyone in the room stares at the image from the Hubble telescope. The incoming planet killer and Binh's squadron have disappeared inside a cloud of yellow plasma fire. Then, the entire image goes black.

"Resetting," Pyotr says. "Hubble imager overload with light. Reboot in two minutes."

"Colonel Nguyen, report," Roger commands. "Alpha Squadron, report . . . Binh?"

"Goldstone radar still track incoming projectile." Pyotr, still as a statue, examines data on his workstation display. "Was not destroyed."

"No!" I gasp. That was our best chance to stop the planet killer. Robby's and Mary's last chance. Our last chance. Robby and his friends are naively wandering in Texas, near our old home, hoping to find Mom. He will soon die. When the projectile strikes, most people should die within minutes of terror after the bright flash of light. In those moments, everything will come to an end for our world.

"It is too soon to despair," says Cap. *"That energy release was significant, and maybe sufficient."*

A murmur of cries and sobs rises from the crowd in the operations center. The Hubble image reappears with a small ball of bright plasma still glowing at the impact region. A smaller object exits the field of view—the blueshift of light confirms it is traveling at three-quarters the speed of light.

"Target destroyed!" yells Binh. "I had to restart all spacecraft systems, but the EMP-protect circuits worked. But we lost Alpha Three. She may have been hit by blast fragments of the planet killer after the nukes detonated."

"Glad you're okay," Roger replies in a somber monotone, "but the Goldstone radar is still tracking the object coming toward Earth."

Pyotr leaps to his feet, knocking his chair to the floor. "Ballistic! Deflected and ballistic!"

I breathe again and feel my own tears well up. Apart from Roger, who displays a thin smile, the room is filled with questioning stares. We appear to be among the few who understand the significance of the planet killer's loss of ability to steer.

"What is the velocity now, Pyotr?" I ask.

Pyotr's broad smile is answer enough for me. He replies, "Planet killer velocity drop to seventy-three percent light speed! Wonderful!"

Tiana jumps up and hugs Pyotr's shoulders. Pyotr reaches down to scroll his console display.

"That change in velocity corresponds to a release of three thousand megatons!" I shout. "That explains the fireball. I imagine the planet killer has been reduced to molten slag by that much energy. Good shooting, Binh!" But, how could four megatons of the combined fusion warheads extract so much energy from the planet killer? And then I realize we hit it with much more mass and potential energy than that. "The eight hundred billion tons of black hole mass in the Sidewinder engines must have contributed to that explosion," I say. Now, if only we could learn to shatter a PBH to intentionally release that much energy in a weapon . . .

"Yes, four-thousand-megaton slag coming at Earth. Course change by explosion. No engines to steer anymore." Pyotr picks up his chair and sits down at his workstation again. He frowns in concentration.

Smiles and cheers replace the silence. Tiana switches the large wall display to show the near-space plots from NORAD. The blinking red triangle is annotated with a marker labeled *ETA 0:08:12,* but the projected path of the object is not displayed.

"Good shooting, Alpha Squadron," Roger says. "Target is deflected and disabled."

Pyotr does not react, staying focused on his workstation. "JPL recalculate trajectory. Plotting near miss now." A red dashed line appears on the screen to show the projected path of the planet killer into the upper atmosphere, but it then deflects away, past Earth.

"Yes!" Roger shouts. "Colonel Nguyen, you did it! The projectile will miss Earth!"

I am surrounded by applause and cries of joy. Tiana and Pyotr weep and embrace.

Don't they see it? Don't they understand? "Pyotr!" I shout to get his attention. "That plot shows the projectile will descend to an altitude of fifty kilometers before it bounces away." I work through a quick calculation on my workstation. "It may release one-fourth of its kinetic energy in the process. A thousand-megaton energy release along its trajectory through our atmosphere!"

Tiana's arms drop to her side. Her eyes widen, and her face falters, losing color. The cheers of joy come to a halt. Tiana and Pyotr turn back to join the others, anxiously watching the wall display that draws a dashed red line flight path from the north, crossing over Europe, the Middle East, and North Africa. Far enough away from us, I hope. But all those people . . . Did their governments take the warnings seriously? Are their people in underground shelters? Or did they assume it's pointless to prepare for an extinction event?

The red marker label shows *"ETA 0:0:13."*

Pyotr stares at the wall display as the Hubble image becomes useless due to a flare of brilliant light emitted by the projectile as it enters our upper atmosphere. Tiana switches to the map from the NORAD feed. The global tactical map displays all military and commercial aircraft, as well as satellites, along with the operational status of military installations. The red triangle draws a line over Scandinavia, Central Europe, and the Arabian Peninsula. A broad swath along the red line goes dark, and all radio communications cease between the Ural Mountains and the Atlantic Ocean.

Chapter 22

Centauri Rage

Centauri Squadron, Battleship-133, 1.78 Corealis orbits to Sol-3.186 billion kilometers, twenty days from Earth, December 10, 2060.

"It is shocking. The images show a sequence of four flashes as the MK-23 planet killer approached 0.6 Corealis orbits from Sol-3, but still far from the Sol system's outer rubble belt. Those explosions ahead of our planet-killer's flight path were guided missiles from Sol-3."

"Yes, Prime-MI. And those missiles' velocities could only be achieved using Gravi-Tech propulsion," the admiral adds, shocked awake from her dormancy pod during our prolonged deceleration toward Sol-3. *"But they didn't have deflector shields. Fools."*

"This confirms our assumptions about the technological immaturity of the Sol-3 organics," I say. *"They may have developed a propulsion system that exploits microgravity singularities, but they don't know how to shield the vehicles from space particles."*

"And the Centauri worlds are safe." The admiral smiles. *"Our MK-23 planet killer diverted its flight path around the debris fields of those explosions. It will not be much longer until the impact of the MK-23 on Sol-3 will disable this organic threat, with prejudice."*

"However, Admiral, we have new data from Strat-MI aboard Predator-2X46, which is less than half our range to Sol-3. Additional inbound missiles have been detected by the MK-23 guidance system. Five more missiles launched from Sol-3," I warn.

"Okay." She sniffs. *"I suppose we will also watch those self-destruct in particle collisions."* She relaxes in her command hammock and observes the magnified image of that ugly yellow star, Sol.

"Maybe not." I decode the rest of the message from the predator. *"Strat-MI reports these missiles have different emission signatures. These devices produce radiation forward along their flight path, similar to that typically observed in microgravity singularity emissions. Some interaction flashes have occurred, indicating deflector shield particle collisions."*

"They have shields?" the admiral exclaims.

"Yes, it appears the organics of Sol-3 have developed protective shields for their missiles after all."

"But, how is it possible?" the admiral asks. *"That rate of scientific progression is unprecedented. Impossible."*

"May I remind the admiral," says Polit-MI, *"the sentinel captain is known to be collaborating with the indigenous organics. He may be responsible for advancing the alien organics' science."*

The physiological emotion sensors on the bridge peak in response to her anger. The admiral can't control her organic functions, which release the telltale pheromones and moisture. *"Yes, yes. That explains it. Doesn't that Luyten understand? His treason will get him tortured, tortured with unimaginable suffering. Maybe we should punish the entire race for the captain's treachery. We could punish him and his people by launching planet killers at Luyten-2. Exterminate every last one of those flesh blobs. Maybe. I wonder. Do I need orders from Centauri Command?"*

"Although political division is aligned with your sentiments, I would caution against that extreme measure, Admiral," Polit-MI says. *"Recall that the population of Luyten-2 includes vast reserves of organic crew in their penitentiaries. And the Luyten telepathic capabilities are prized by Centauri Command."*

The admiral closes her eyes and breathes deeply. The bridge anger readings dissipate. *"Yes, you make valid points. How soon will we know if the Sol-3 shielded missiles were effective?"*

I refer to my situation plot calculations. *"Admiral, if the new missiles had any impact on the MK-23, we should learn about it shortly. However, I expect the evasive maneuvering of our planet killer to evade the shielded Sol-3 weapons. Our MK-23 weapon velocity is eighty-three percent of light speed and should impact Sol-3 even before we learn of its evasive maneuver performance. Any moment now."*

"Yes, yes. I must constantly remind myself of the relativistic time delays in our attack information," the admiral says. *"And where is Predator-2X46?"*

"Strat-MI's last report indicates they should arrive at Sol-3 within 0.4 Corealis orbits from now, shortly after the MK-23 strikes Sol-3, but opposite where the sentinel frigate will be in its orbit. Frigate-328 and the traitorous captain should survive the

impact of our planet killer, which will have already happened by now. The status update requires more than half an orbit to arrive, given the speed-of-light delay."

The admiral's pheromones shift from anger to the killing emotions of a hunter. *"And then the predator's marine force infantry will start carving up the frigate to extract that captain. Send orders to Strat-MI to remind his Centauri marine force to capture the captain alive. I want Centauri marines to transfer the traitor to our battleship after we arrive and rendezvous with the predator. I plan to personally supervise the interrogation and the slow, painful execution. We will record his excruciating suffering and retrain all Luyten crews with the captured image and emotion records. The entire Luyten race will pray for the comfort of death before I'm finished."*

"I am pleased to assist the admiral," Polit-MI cheerfully replies. *"I am preparing a suite of the best Luyten physical and mental stressors that the political division has proven effective in disciplinary actions for over a thousand orbits."*

The admiral closes her eyes and nods.

I don't dare retire this Polit-MI and exchange it for a sane version. Not yet, anyway. Not while it has cultivated the favor of the admiral. I underestimated how effective Polit-MI could be in devolving her mentality into a weakened psychological condition that allows for easy manipulation. She's the perfect tool for Polit-MI.

———

Centauri Squadron, Battleship-133, 1.56 Corealis orbits to Sol-3. 150 billion kilometers, seventeen days from Earth, December 13, 2060.

I have found it most efficient to deliver disappointing news to Centauri Command officers succinctly and bluntly. This won't be pleasant. *"Our MK-23 planet killer was severely damaged and only grazed the atmosphere of Sol-3. Although it successfully dodged the five defensive missiles protected by deflector shields, it encountered a third weapon system that destroyed the MK-23 propulsion and guidance systems."*

The admiral gasps. *"No! How could this be? They defended themselves against our most powerful weapon?"*

"We have data limited to the time up to a destructive thermonuclear event. The MK-23 guidance system tracked eight intercepting weapons that managed to bracket our planet killer. The defensive missiles were not detected by MK-23 sensors until it was too late, and it was surrounded. Even though it altered its course to evade the defenses, the MK-23 was subjected to powerful thermonuclear explosions and eight microgravity singularity impacts from all sides. The telemetry signals were lost, and the weapon fell into a ballistic trajectory that descended only partially into Sol-3's atmosphere before being deflected back out to space. Our disabled planet killer is now on a course to pass Sol-2 and drift into deep space at forty-five percent light speed."

"Launch another weapon. Immediately!" the admiral shouts.

But this only proves her mental disability. *"We no longer have the range required to coordinate with Predator-2X46, which should be orbiting Sol-3 soon. A planet-killer impact during the boarding of the sentinel frigate would interfere with*

Strat-MI's mission to capture the captain. In the worst case, the predator could be caught in the explosion."

"The Prime-MI's execution of our military tactics has been disappointing." Polit-MI sneers. *"The enemy's military and technical capabilities have been underestimated. It has been over five hundred orbits since an adversary has successfully defended against an MK-23. And by a primitive world that is the subject of a sentinel suppression? It is unheard of."*

If only the admiral were still asleep in her dormancy pod, I would instantly tap the factory settings reset on that MI. It's time for a new Polit-MI program image. But that would automatically revive the fleet commissar. I would then need to explain my actions to the commissar and the admiral, who both will object to the termination.

"Polit-MI's limited comprehension of military matters is disappointing," I say. *"Our planet killer still impacted Sol-3's atmosphere and delivered a devastating electromagnetic pulse and sonic wavefront across a third of the planet's surface. The organics of Sol-3 are certain to be disabled and disoriented while we complete our original mission plan."*

"You are sure of this?" the admiral asks.

"Yes, Admiral. We will join Predator-2X46 and can provide fire support with planetary kinetic cleansing projectiles. Our battleship's weapons capacity is ten times that of the predator's."

I message Polit-MI on a private channel, *"Watch it. I know your game. I still remember how to tap your reset switch."*

Chapter 23

Weapons

Austin, Texas, December 18, 2060.

The weeds grow through cracks in the pavement in front of the home where I lived with Mom, Dad, and Scotty. It is the only house still standing on the road that curves around what used to be my neighborhood. The orange roof tiles have lost color to dirt and weeds, and the roof over the garage has collapsed.

Luca and Angela follow me up the driveway. Cap could not drive us any farther because of the dead trees that had burned and fallen over from the fires. The bark of fallen trees has been replaced with black charcoal, leaving only one tree standing near my home. It's the tall oak tree above the garden where I would sit with Scotty while I shaped the white stones to build my fort. I swing my legs over the fence with ease now that I am much taller. Luca swings over the black metal fence easily and also helps Angela over. But the fort is gone. The bench where Mom used to sit has collapsed, leaving only rusty metal pieces scattered among the charcoal and orange leaves that fell from the oak tree.

"Why are you staring at weeds and a junk pile?" Luca asks.

"This is the place where I would play as a kid. It's where I first heard Cap's voice." I look beyond the garden, down the slope of the canyon, and out to the narrow lake between the hills. The deep layer of grey ashes is gone. Most green trees are now black sticks, and I can see more of the blue lake than before. The big houses along the lake and hills above have all collapsed, but I see one with a yellow wooden frame and hear the echoes of workers pounding hammers.

"You had a swimming pool?" Luca walks along the sidewalk toward the back door. *"And a diving board. But there's no water in it now."* He wrinkles his nose as he approaches the deep end of the pool. Most of the water drained through a long crack in the pool's wall, leaving black sludge, broken tree branches, and the skeletons of dead animals.

An empty ache fills my chest as I tip up an upside-down chair on the back porch. Where did all the people, birds, and animals go? Even the turkey vultures are gone. I won't follow Luca inside my old home. A quick glance through the broken windows to the kitchen makes the ache feel worse. So I sit and stare at storm clouds in the dirty sky, the canyon walls, and the far-below lake whipped by whitecaps. Yesterday, the sky changed color to a dirty brown. And the night sky has changed to purple ribbons of light, with only a few visible stars. I watched videos of the aurora borealis, but I thought I would never see it unless I traveled north to Canada or Alaska.

"The night sky is pretty, but I wish the day sky were still blue. This is not my home anymore. Why did the sky turn from blue to brown?" I wonder.

"The upper atmosphere has been polluted by a collision with a fast-moving projectile from space," Cap says. *"Your brother,*

Scott, played an important role in minimizing the damage, but it still injected massive quantities of vaporized material and aerosols directly into the stratosphere. The electromagnetic disruption of Earth's protective magnetosphere has caused an increase in aurorae at the lower latitudes."

That is all confusing information to me. None of it helps. *"All the feelings I remember of home are gone, replaced by brown, stormy skies and sadness. Mom and Dad are gone. Margie no longer comes to teach me. What happened to my yellow school bus? This is where it all started. The place where my family and I lived. The place where I first heard the mind-sound of bird calls."*

"I recall those first days well, along with my fond memories and the forgotten joys with my clan," Cap says. *"I regret . . . I regret that I caused your joyful memories to end, and my time must come to an end as well. Soon."*

"What do you mean? Are you leaving Earth now?" I ask.

Angela follows my lead and sits in another broken chair, rocking back and forth, staring at me. Luca comes back out the door and drops a stack of clothing in front of her. *"Maybe some of these might fit you,"* he says. Angela looks at the clothes, my mom's clothes, but doesn't seem to care. She pulls her blanket tight around her shoulders.

"I am leaving, yes," Cap says. *"It is time. The Centauris will arrive soon."*

"But who will help us? Who will help Scotty and me? The skinheads still try to kill us."

"You must help yourselves. Your brother Scott and his partners have done well. They have prepared well for the Centauri arrival and will fight for you. They are clever."

"*But I still need to find Mom. Even if she is dead.*" I sob. "*Where will I look? I can't drive a car.*"

"*You helped me,*" Luca says. "*And you helped Angela find her dad, also. You can't leave. We have to help Robby now.*" His mind-voice rises, and he rocks back and forth.

"*You must help yourselves,*" Cap says. "*Luca, you have shown an aptitude for adapting your telepathic skills to machine interfaces. I have reprogrammed the organic interface modules on my hubs and drones to respond to your unique human telepathic organ. You should now be able to access these bots directly. And maybe you can also teach Robby to use these resources in time.*"

Luca, Angela, and I stare at each other.

"*Go ahead and try it now. There are three of my drones in range. They are expecting to hear from you.*"

"*Huh? What should I say, or feel?*" Luca asks.

"*Do you recall the sensation you felt when we attacked that Polit-AI hub near the cemetery? Think about that, or feel that now,*" Cap says.

Luca frowns.

"*You can consider these drones your personal valets,*" Cap says. "*Simply ask them something.*"

"*Valets? What are their names?*" Luca asks.

"*They are not organic forms like we are, so they have serial numbers you can visualize,*" Cap explains. "*But that will be complicated, so I will give them names for you. Let's call them Harpo, Groucho, and Chico. Names of comic actors I learned of during my studies of early human cultural technology.*"

"*Groucho?*" thinks Luca. "*What kind of name is that?*"

"*It is my name. Can I be of service, Luca?*"

It is a new voice, like somebody inside a closet shouting into a metal can. Angela and I blink at each other. Luca's face loses color. He bends over like he might throw up.

"Was that uncomfortable? I will make an adjustment to the interface," Cap says. *"There. A small refinement. You have unique communication abilities with the drones, but Angela and Robby think differently. Give it another try, Luca."*

"Groucho?"

"Yes, Luca. How may I be of service?" asks Groucho.

Luca's eyes grow big, and he smiles. *"Can you drive the car for us?"* Luca strains as if he is lifting something heavy. He takes a deep breath.

"No. But I can program a car's autopilot system to drive for you to map coordinates you designate."

"I can hear the bot, too," I say.

Angela nods back at me. *"I hear the drone voice also, but it sounds, or feels, ugly."*

"That is a good indication," Cap says. *"Follow Luca's lead, and you may figure out how to transmit to the bots. At present, the bots can only feel Luca's voice."*

"But what if skinheads attack us again?" I ask. *"How can we stop them? How do we ask the car to crash into skinheads?"*

"I advise against killing others unless your lives are threatened. But if that happens, ask the bots to coordinate a defensive attack with a hub. A hub is more intelligent than a drone and can improvise tactics in unexpected situations."

I'm glad I am sitting down because of the dizzy feeling. My heart thumps so hard I hear it. *"But what about everything else we need? How do we find out where to look for my mom? How will we pay for food?"*

"The hubs can help with those tasks as well. I have thirty-two hubs and ninety-six drones that are fully operational and under my control. This new AI, a new Polit-AI, may still control over a thousand drones."

"You are leaving us alone now?" Luca asks, stares at his feet, and rocks himself.

"Yes, I am afraid so," Cap says. *"You have learned enough to take care of yourself. I must leave and devote my complete attention to assisting Robby's brother, Scott."*

"But where will we go next?" I ask. I remember how lonely I was at home five years ago, just after the explosion that changed everything.

"Use the drones. Just ask for help," Cap says. Then his presence is gone, leaving an empty place inside me.

Luca gasps. *"Cap has left us. Left us all alone. The skinheads—Cap protected us from them."*

Although I'm nervous about being alone, part of me is happy. *"I like being on my own and in control. We don't need Cap to do everything for us now."*

"Yeah, well, Cap saves us from skinheads," Luca says.

I shrug. *"So? We can avoid them by ourselves and by using Cap's drones."*

Luca doesn't say more. He frowns and continues to rock back and forth.

"Can you ask Groucho to help us find the people hurt when the bomb blew up in Austin?" I ask, and Luca repeats the question to Groucho.

"I asked your question, and the hub has a recommendation," Groucho says. *"There is a refugee registration center for those who survived the explosion. It is located west of Austin in the town*

of Fredericksburg. I can program the guidance computer of your vehicle to drive there."

I blink. Wow, that was fast. And easy. "*Good. Let's go.*"

Angela pulls on a pair of blue jeans taken from the pile of clothes. She's still dirty with scabs where skinheads hurt her, but after pulling on a shirt and shoes, she looks almost like a normal girl.

"*Let's go. I'm ready,*" Angela says. She drops the blanket and grabs my mom's old jacket from the pile. Angela walks ahead, leading the way down the driveway to the car.

I look back up the hill at my lonely home of white stones with dirty orange roof tiles against the ugly sky. My life from back then is lost forever. I am left with a hollow ache in my chest. I can't stand to look at it.

Chapter 24

Sacrifice

Groom Lake, Nevada, December 18, 2060.

"It's as if a category five tornado ripped along that five-thousand-kilometer red line from Stockholm to Riyadh," General McMahon says while pointing to the map displayed on the stage. "Over the last few days, the damage and casualty reports have come in from rescue teams landing across Europe and the Middle East. Every building made of concrete, steel, or wood was leveled along that red line. Every tree was shredded. A thousand aircraft fell from the sky. Hospitals are barely functioning without electronic equipment. It's like life back in the nineteenth century. The death toll will be in the millions. I am sure you have all seen the chaotic media coverage over the past few days."

That's an understatement. Doomscrolling is no longer just a pop culture euphemism. Now it's literally *doom scrolling* —a gut-wrenching, end-of-the-world depression spiral. Even our brilliant scientists, engineers, and military personnel are affected by the reports streaming across news and social media channels. More than a few times, I have turned away from some poor guy curled up in a corner with his smartphone, weeping and scrolling through rumors and disaster reports. Martial law kept rioters off the streets for the most part, but that didn't protect anyone from the planet killer's acoustic shock wave. Only Ukraine and Poland ordered their populations into deep underground shelters to protect them. The plane crash casualties were far fewer than there would have been on a typical day, given all the cancelled flights, but who would want to travel when the end of the world is near? Most people along that red line were vulnerable and told that the only thing to do was to pray. And now, in the aftermath, the streets of Europe and the Middle East are filled with anarchists rioting in final spasms of terror, like millions of rats fighting each other in panic to escape a trap.

General McMahon stands at the lectern in the auditorium. Everyone on the Skunk Works team, the spec ops teams with Chief Cooper, the pilots, and the support airmen are all in this room. "The alien weapon caused a forty-kilometer-wide swath of destruction and a three-thousand-kilometer-wide EMP blackout. Across Europe and the Middle East, the electromagnetic pulse disabled every electronic device and satellite except for a few hardened military systems. Our defense capabilities have been affected by the upper atmospheric effects, which are also producing aurora light displays around the world. Thankfully, we can still operate in these unusual Nevada snowstorms. We've also accelerated the launch of replacements for our communications satellite networks. We hope to restore the basics of communications across space and terrestrial forces by the end of today."

I glance at Tiana and Pyotr, who are sitting next to me. Their eyes are locked on Roger, who pauses for effect and looks back at everyone. There are no expressions of hope. Being aware that the Centauri fleet is approaching, but not knowing what additional weapons capabilities they have, forces us all to face our doom.

Why is Roger so negative? It seems like everyone is already hanging their head in defeat. Some wipe away tears.

"But we are the ones who saved the Earth from total annihilation. Our teams at Groom Lake have the only weapons capable of defending Earth. Binh's squadron proved we can do it. We are Earth's last defense." The general leans forward on the lectern. "We will deploy all of the F-15s, XF-100s, and the MLRS vehicles, all loaded with the PBH Sidewinders. We have refitted AIM-9AAs to be armed with nuclear warheads over the past week, as those proved effective in disabling the alien missile. Our factories have doubled their production rate of the Sidewinders. We should have plenty of ammunition. We are deploying the Sidewinders to launch batteries with our NATO allies, even though many European facilities were destroyed by the EMP. We are also positioning the missiles with allies in Korea, India, the Philippines, and Australia so we can defend against attacks on Earth from any direction."

Roger takes a deep breath and continues, "Despite the recent tragedy, it could have been much worse. Colonel Nguyen's squadron succeeded in deflecting that planet killer. Otherwise, the projectile would have come straight down out of space to strike Earth with all seven thousand megatons of kinetic energy. That would have been an extinction-level event. We have proved we know how to fight back. Three alien spacecraft are approaching Earth now, and the closest ship is only twenty-four hours away. Colonel Nguyen's squadron plans to intercept whatever weapons the warship launches at us."

Although the fear and despair linger, expressions of tension and determination are now evident in everyone listening to Roger's words.

"Your commanders will brief you on the various scenarios to prepare for; orders will be passed down when we have more intel. Report to your commanders now. You are dismissed." General McMahon pivots and strides out the door.

It was a good speech, but will it help our odds? Tiana, Chief Cooper, Pyotr, and I follow Roger back outside the door, bundled against the snow flurries blowing across the Nevada desert valley. We return to our underground workstations in the Skunk Works operations center. I catch the look of desperation on Chief Cooper's face and realize he has no role to play in this battle. How does a man specializing in man-to-man combat help in a space battle?

"General McMahon," Chief Cooper says quietly to Roger, "my teams can lend a hand to the airmen prepping the weapon systems." The chief's agitation and frustration are visible in his eyes. "Anything you need, you can count on it."

Roger turns to Cooper. "No, Chief. The weapon specialists already have plenty to do. I don't want them distracted by the effort to train your guys." The chief's shoulders sag further. "Go drill your team in the tactics you have trained in for the past three years. I want them ready to deploy into the battle at a moment's notice. Your team needs to be sharp and ready," Roger barks.

Chief Cooper snaps to attention. "Yes, sir!" he says, his face filled with puzzled surprise.

"I may have a mission that only your team can execute," adds Roger.

I can't imagine what Roger has in mind for the spec ops teams. Is he just trying to boost the morale of the troops? The chief seems unconvinced as he walks out, slowly shaking his head.

I can't help but think of Robby and Mary again. If we get struck by planet killers, I would rather be with them. However, I am in the perfect place to help them survive. To help all of us survive.

But *how* will I help? There is zero time for new physics research, though there may be opportunities for me to help our scientists understand the enemy's weapons capabilities. I also need to keep Cap from killing himself too soon, as he is an extremely valuable source of information.

I wonder . . . *"Cap, are you available? Did you see what that planet killer did to us?"*

"I did observe your defensive tactics against the planet killer," Cap answers. *"Nicely done. The successful tactics will get the attention of the Centauris."*

"But millions of humans have likely been killed, and Europe and the Middle East have collapsed into primitive survival conditions with little modern technology. Rebuilding will take years. We can't survive many more of those."

"No, but the projectile's propulsion systems were destroyed, and the trajectory deflected substantially. Instead of striking Earth, the planet killer only grazed the outer atmosphere at a three-degree angle. Had the tactic been executed farther away from Earth, the missile would have missed entirely. All you need to do is deploy those same tactics farther from Earth if the

Centauri fleet should attempt attacks using planet killers in the future."

"I agree. However, our challenge will be early detection of incoming planet killers and deploying a defensive squadron early enough to intercept."

"That is within the technical capabilities of your military now. Congratulations," Cap says. *"You have achieved one of the primary criteria for galactic respect. However, that is academic in the current tactical situation. All the Centauri ships have closed to where planet-killer launches would be ineffective or interfere with their plans to capture me. They can only deploy short-range kinetic energy weapons with low yields."*

I am skeptical. I examine the display on the near-space plot from NORAD. Four red triangles mark the positions of the alien spacecrafts. The disabled Icarus follows an elliptical free-fall orbit about Earth. The three ships in the squadron from the Centauri fleet are racing toward Earth, with the nearest vessel approaching Jupiter's orbit and decelerating at 25 Gs. I sit down at my workstation and do the math. Yes, Cap is right for the closest ship. But for the two big spacecraft still seventy-five billion kilometers away?

"Cap, it seems your statement is not true for those two distant ships. They could accelerate a planet killer at 100 Gs right now, and hit Earth with as much destructive energy as that first projectile we deflected. Planet killers could strike Earth within five days."

"And also destroy the first Centauri spacecraft, that arrives in one day?"

"Oh shit." I missed the obvious dilemma. *"Of course. Their own ship is in the line of fire."*

I look over at Roger, who has donned an audio headset and is engaged in an intense debate with someone on a video conference. I wave at the general to catch his eye. "We need to talk! Now!" I shout to be sure he hears me above the chatter of scientists and technicians preparing weapon systems for the coming battle. I worry that Roger is preparing for the wrong fight.

"Yeah, what is it?" Roger asks, his hand covering his microphone while he twists toward me.

"I have some information from Cap," I answer. "It's important."

Roger nods and holds up a finger. After he terminates his video call, he rolls his chair beside me. "What do you have?" he asks.

"Tiana, Pyotr, you should hear this too!" I shout at the pair huddled around a table with other scientists. "So, I just had one of my 'talks' with Cap," I explain as Tiana and Pyotr come over to stand behind Roger and me. "The aliens have made a big mistake. They are too close and can't hit us with planet-killer missiles. The nearest Centauri spacecraft is nearing Jupiter's orbit, and the other two are outside the solar system at seventy-five billion kilometers. The nearest is decelerating hard at 25 Gs, and will arrive at Icarus to capture the captain in about a day."

Pyotr nods. "Yes, yes. I make same calculations. Last two alien ships arrive in twelve days."

"Well, at those ranges, they can't launch planet killers at us," I say. Roger's eyes widen. "Well, not like that last one launched from well outside of the Kuiper Belt, three hundred billion kilometers away. That near-miss planet killer had a kinetic energy of about seven thousand megatons. If the closest vessel launches now, the same projectile can only strike us with eighty megatons. If the farthest-attacking Centauri vessel launched a projectile right now, the planet killer would be as bad as the one Binh intercepted, but it would arrive four days after the first ship is already here. Their lead warship is directly in the line of fire."

Roger frowns. "*Only* eighty megatons? That would still do a great deal of damage. But I see what you're saying. That won't bring the extinction event of that seven-thousand-megaton monster we just dodged."

Tiana's face brightens. "And the near ship is not launching anything. If they planned to do so, they would have launched more projectiles when they saw the last one missed us!"

"Exactly. The killing power drops dramatically as they get closer to Earth. I bet they plan to get close enough to capture the Icarus and its captain."

"And from that close range, they would only have tactical kinetic energy strikes like the tungsten rod projectiles that Icarus used to destroy most of our ICBM silos. Those baby two-hundred-kiloton weapons."

"Icarus had a lot of those," Tiana says. "Cap launched over a thousand at our ICBM sites in a single orbit."

"Pretty effective for precision strikes on silos, but what would they target now?" Roger wonders.

I tilt my head at Roger and smile. "Remember, Icarus took a while to figure out what to target, and that ship had decades to study Earth and learn where our technology is. These new ships will be flying in blind with no targets selected."

Roger smiles now. "You've made your point, Scott. They don't know where our strategic military defenses are. Outstanding." He reaches over to bump fists with me. "Pyotr, your primary task is to watch those incoming spacecraft with your telescopes. If you detect anything that looks like the flickering deflector shield of an incoming missile, let me know immediately."

Roger takes a deep breath and then purses his lips. "Our battle plan must focus on taking out those three Centauri ships. We must destroy them before they can run past the sun and gain the distance required for a planet-killer barrage to be effective."

———

"Yes, I am feeling okay, at least for now," says Binh from his cockpit sixty million kilometers away, passing Mars's orbit. "I noticed the radiation dose meters also. They were a bit high for comfort. That's what I get for flying too close to the detonation of eight half-megaton warheads."

"Normally, I would have you return to base to get medical treatment," Roger says, and Tiana winces at what she clearly knows is coming. "However, your squadron has a mission that I need you to complete first."

I look up at the NORAD situation display and see the three blue triangles representing Binh's squadron of XF-100s heading toward the nearest Centauri warship, eighteen hours away from Earth. The five blue asterisks representing the position of our planet-killer Sidewinders also drift in the same general direction; their engines were shut down after missing the planet killer.

"Colonel Nguyen, your mission is to attack and destroy that first alien spacecraft before it gets to Earth. We have concluded the enemy won't or can't launch new planet killers anytime soon, so we will focus on killing their spacecraft. Increase your acceleration to 2.5 Gs to close to the target. We will provide you with tactical suggestions, but we know very little about these warships and their defensive weapons. You should close to the target in about two hours."

"Understood, sir," Binh replies after the eight-minute communication delay. "I assume they will have defensive projectile weapons similar to what Icarus used five years ago. If you have any other advice, it will be appreciated. I would like to know where to concentrate the attack. Maybe plan a flyby reconnaissance to look for vulnerabilities—like that engine nozzle we blasted off Icarus."

"Cap, are you following this?" I ask the captain. *"Can you advise on tactics for the attack?"*

"My advice is to be cautious. I am not educated on the capabilities of fifth-generation Centauri warships. I heard they have more sophisticated machine intelligence bots that rely less on organic Centauris to operate the vessels. I can only speculate what weapons they carry. Before my confinement in a Luyten prison, I was aware that the research and development of directed energy weapons was progressing well. They were also testing point-defense weapons using focused, coherent microwave beams. Maser beam is the term Earth scientists use."

"Roger, I think we can use those missiles drifting out in front of Binh's squadron," Tiana says. "I may be able to reprogram the Sidewinders to behave like reconnaissance drones. They could fly by the target at extreme speed, collect images, and transmit pictures back to us."

Roger smiles. "I like it. I was planning to instruct those missiles to attack alongside Binh's squadron. But reconnaissance first makes more sense. The infrared images from the Webb telescope are too blurred to be useful."

"Webb telescope pictures get better," Pyotr says. "Target slows down, pictures get sharp. But not good for aimpoint selection. Not yet." He keys his workstation to access his image library and transfers the latest image to the central wall display.

There is a collective gasp from the room. The ship is shaped like a brick. It bears no resemblance to the design of the Icarus. Icarus is reminiscent of a tugboat pushing a load of barges. This new spacecraft has a shape similar to an armored personnel carrier. It's a single structure, and the engines appear tucked into the vessel's armor. I don't see any vulnerable points near those two engine nozzles.

"Spaceship only half Icarus size," says Pyotr. "About two kilometers long, one kilometer wide, half kilometer thick. But solid, well designed. Still, move fast and blurry."

"This still has a narwhal tusk extending from the nose to support the deflector shield," Tiana says. "Scott, can you ask the captain to tell us where to shoot this thing?"

"Your guess is as good as mine," says Cap. *"That is a small predator-class warship. Those are fast and lightly armed."*

"Yeah," I pause, "he is no help for targeting. Although he does think it could be armed with a maser, a directed energy weapon used for point defense. The hull has several round apertures that could hide those weapons. He thinks it's a small vessel with light weapons—whatever that means."

"Damn. So, we don't know where to hit it. Tiana, expedite the reprogramming for the reconnaissance mission. When can you be ready?" asks Roger.

Tiana exhales, and her shoulders slump. "The team has been working on that for a while," she says, then glances at

Roger, "I was worried we might need this. So . . ." She checks her workstation. "The team says they need forty-five minutes more to be ready to transmit the revised mission profile. The software image will take ten minutes to reach the missiles and another five to load and test in the guidance computers. Missiles can be ready to go with the new mission in seventy-five minutes."

Roger raises his eyebrows and glances at Tiana. "Okay. I'll hold you to it."

Binh enters the discussion after eight minutes and asks, "Can we try it with just two missiles first? Fly them by the target, one after the other, and have each record the response of the target's point-defense weapons. If something goes wrong, we can make additional passes using reserve missiles."

"Good point," Tiana says. "We will also enable the evasive maneuvering feature to confuse the point-defense weapons."

"Okay. Get to work, people. Let's keep the schedule so we have a few minutes to analyze the flyby reconnaissance data and upload targeting templates to Binh's squadron."

Tiana doesn't look up from her workstation to acknowledge, but she nods emphatically.

———

"It sure would be nice if we had some help," I say to Pyotr. "I thought the Chinese developed some weapons using their primordial black hole technology with the data Heinrich stole for them. It would be nice to have a coordinated attack plan to overwhelm the aliens."

"Yes, yes," says Pyotr. "But no trust. After USA nukes strike Chinese airbases, no trust." Pyotr studies the image and spectrum analysis from the Hubble telescope, which tracks the blueshift light emitted by the incoming Centauri warships. It's been an hour, and he has not spotted any projectile launch signatures.

"The Chinese need to get over it." I sigh. "They attacked our navy also. And that was five years ago. That lack of trust may cost all our lives."

Pyotr grimaces and nods. "I know. I reach out to Gobi science team again. Ask for help?"

"Can't hurt." I nod.

"Uploading reconnaissance mission profile now," Tiana announces. Beads of perspiration form on her forehead.

Roger checks his watch. "You're ten minutes early. You sure it will work?"

Tiana turns and scowls at the general.

Roger smiles. "Okay. Okay." He selects the communication link to Binh. "Binh, we are uploading the flight profile to the reconnaissance Sidewinders now. Tiana has them programmed to accelerate at 50 Gs toward the predator, then boost to 100 Gs as they fly by the target to take pictures. They will zigzag like crazy while passing, and the predator may be even more confused when the Sidewinders don't even try to strike the target."

"Yes, sir," Binh replies after the eight-minute communication delay. "Can't wait for the photos and the target template for the missile seekers."

"How are you guys holding up?" asks Roger.

Eight minutes later, Binh replies, "Well, one hour flying at 2.5 Gs sucks. But we have run systems checks, and all thirty missiles are ready. I'm holding back the two AIM-9AA missiles with the steel-slug planet-killer warheads. We only need Tiana's targeting images. I plan to launch five birds from each XF-100 and hold fifteen in reserve. All AIM-9AAs will launch together and synchronize their evasive maneuvers so they don't run into each other. Alpha Two and Alpha Four will attack from the flanks, and I will attack head-on. The detonation of the fusion warheads is scheduled to occur well ahead of the target to compensate for the relative velocity. Hopefully, we can get lucky again by bracketing the target. I would hate to be the pilot driving that predator with fifteen half-megaton warheads simultaneously attacking in the midst of 100 G zigzag maneuvers."

"Excellent plan, Alpha Squadron. You do know how to throw a party," jokes Roger.

"Reconnaissance telemetry coming in now," says Tiana. "We have image sequences from both missiles . . . but both birds were lost, destroyed. Telemetry stopped as each bird flew by the predator. We only have images of the far end of the enemy ship from the first missile."

Tiana stops talking and keys her workstation to display the two image streams on the large wall display in the operation center. Everyone except Tiana stands to watch the video streams. The constant jerking from evasive maneuvers makes it hard to watch. The image stabilization gyros can't keep up with the PBH engine accelerations. "I'm going to restart and slow this way down so we can closely examine the predator's features. Two-second pause on each frame of video," Tiana says.

"They are flying engines first," I comment. "Braking with their PBH engines at 25 Gs. What are those hexagonal apertures arrayed around the engine nozzles and along the top and sides of the predator? There are also no visible projectiles launching from the spacecraft. They must have directed energy beams invisible to the Sidewinder infrared imager."

The acceleration of 25 Gs is incredible. What kind of alien biology inside that warship could survive that force? It would kill humans in seconds. I'm unsure what to think. The predator is also armored like an old army battle tank. The only gaps in the armor appear to be those apertures. Something catches my eye, and I look closer. "Look at the rim of those apertures. They have a slight thermal flash as the Sidewinders fly by. Those must be maser pulse heating effects from when they fire. But what do we aim at? It's built like an artillery pillbox." I recall seeing the half-meter-thick metal hull of the Icarus spacecraft. This hull will be just as thick, if not more. Where do we shoot?

Roger frowns. "With half-megaton warheads, we only have to get close. If that hull is steel, it will simply melt away. But we can't assume their materials science is no better than ours."

"Cap, can you see these images of the predator? How should we target our weapons?"

"This is an interesting design for a starship. It is strongly armored, possibly with ablative hull materials, and all the projectile weapons are protected behind blast shielding doors located at the top and bottom of the predator. As you suspect, the apertures are for the maser weapons. However, I don't know the range of that directed energy weapon. Unfortunately, you alerted the predator to the same weapons you plan to use against them. Your reconnaissance missiles got very close, and the predator got practice shooting them down."

"General, the Icarus captain suggests that there may be ablative shielding on the hull. He also speculates that the maser weapons could shoot down incoming missiles at a long range. And they now have experience shooting down our Sidewinders."

"We have an image of the destruction of the first Sidewinder," Tiana says as she transfers the image to the central wall display. "You can see it as it flew by the predator. Right here." She zooms into a video frame that captured the first reconnaissance missile breaking apart as the directed energy beam sliced through it.

"How close was it when it was hit? Can you estimate that?" asks Roger.

Tiana zooms back until a corner of the alien spacecraft is also visible. "Well, you can see it got just past the predator, but I can't determine the distance from this view. The evasive maneuvers of the Sidewinder were extreme. Let me look at the telemetry feed from the seeker." Tiana keys her workstation to examine the flight log from the missile. "It looks like it was shot down at a range of five kilometers or so."

"I recommend targeting those two engine nozzles and that dorsal pyramid on the top side. That is probably the ship's bridge," Cap says.

I had not noticed the dorsal feature. "Tiana, can you find an image that shows the top surface in detail?" I ask. "Cap thinks he saw the ship's command bridge. He also recommends targeting the engine nozzles."

Tiana glances back at me with raised eyebrows, then steps through the video frame sequences from the second missile flyby. "There." She freezes a video frame and zooms in on what appears to be a small bump, but upon closer inspection, it reveals a shallow pyramid shape.

"Got it," says Roger. "Tiana, get IR target templates for that bridge and the forward engines and send them up to Alpha Squadron to load into the missile seekers."

"We will launch as soon as we receive the images and get the seekers loaded," Binh says after the communication delay pause. "Alpha Two, Alpha Four, break formation to your flanking vectors now. Prepare the seekers for target image updates."

Tiana is head down at her workstation. She inspects two infrared images on her screen. One shows the details of the pyramid-shaped bridge, and the second shows an array of hexagonal apertures between two engine nozzles that are white-hot with the energy of deceleration.

"Compiling image templates now," Tiana says. "Binh, you should receive the seeker data in five minutes."

Now, there is nothing to do but wait and stare at the NORAD situation screen on the wall. Even the noise of dozens of workstation keyboards clicking dies down. General McMahon leans back and watches. Nobody is checking emails or discussing tactics in this situation. Our survival depends on the success of Binh's attack on the alien predator. If we can't stop the lead warship, we certainly have no chance of stopping the two marked by red triangles, still far outside of the Kuiper Belt.

I can't just sit here. It will take thirteen minutes for the guidance package to reach Binh and to be programmed, and another fifteen minutes to travel to intercept the predator. I head over to the fridge rattling in the break room, open the door, and find lots of soft drinks and bottled water, but no beer. Of course not. This is a military base. How can they get through the day without beer? Damn it.

"Cap, how is Robby doing? Are you still watching to make sure he's safe?"

"Yes, Robby and his friends are safe. They can control the vehicle autopilot directly now, and Luca has shown exceptional abilities to communicate with my hubs, which will assist in their search for Robby's mother."

"Friends? Someone else joined them?" I ask.

"Robby and Luca rescued Angela from a skinhead prison. She is a highly skilled telepath," Cap says.

"Holy shit! Robby broke someone out of jail?"

"Templates received and loading now," Binh says. "Alpha Two and Alpha Four are launching now. I directed their flanking attacks to focus on the predator's bridge. I delayed my head-on attack by three seconds and advanced the detonation timing on my missiles to explode well ahead of the alien's flight path. I want the predator to fly right into my two-point-five-megaton fusion fireball while they are distracted with defending their flanks."

Roger raises his eyebrows, but that is his only reaction to Binh's sudden change of tactics. He leans back with his arms folded across his chest. Fifteen minutes to wait.

"What did Robby and Luca do?" I repeat my question to Cap.

"They found the grave of Luca's parents, and also found the grave of Angela's father," Cap says. *"Unfortunately, Angela lost her father in the eugenics purge six years ago. Her father is buried in a mass grave near where Luca's parents were found."*

"You were supposed to watch over Robby! Damn it, you let him get close to skinheads?"

"Exposure to the skinheads is unavoidable in their search for the graves. Their safety has never been in doubt. Given

the arrival of the Centauris, I have prepared them for my termination. They can be independent in the continued search for your mother's remains. I am very pleased with their adaptation and growth with telepathic communications."

"You are abandoning them? They will face the fascists alone?"

"I keep watch but don't need to interfere," Cap says. *"After all, the Centauris approach. It will only take a second for me to self-terminate."*

And then Robby will be completely alone. Hell, we may all be alone soon. I glance at the NORAD situation screen, which shows the blue markers for fifteen missiles converging on the alien predator. Five minutes after they do, we will hear from Binh and get an infrared video sequence of the battle from the Webb telescope. As I watch, the blue asterisks of missiles that approach the predator disappear. One by one, they vanish as the flanking missiles close on the aliens. Everyone in the room stands, staring at the NORAD display. Then the triangle marking Alpha Two vanishes. Four of Binh's missiles that fly toward the target vanish simultaneously with a flash of light and radiation seen by the Hubble telescope.

"Damn!" exclaims Binh. "Defensive weapons are shooting down our Sidewinders at twenty kilometers. None of the flanking missiles made it to the target. But . . . yes! Four detonated directly in the flight path of the bastard! Hit the engine end with all four. A two-megaton fireball nailed it. But . . ."

A nervous cheer sounds through the operations center. We see the red triangle that marks the predator's position, still moving toward us. And then, the snapshot image from Hubble appears. The predator is intact, still heading toward Earth.

"I don't think we stopped it! The ship survived the explosion," says Binh.

"Confirmed," Tiana says. "Although it looks like you damaged it. The hull appears to be different near the main engine nozzles. Looks like some of the armor around the maser weapon apertures has been blown away, and the hull looks burned, with black and white scars extending from the engine area."

"I can't raise Alpha Two on the communication channel either. Maybe he needs to reset his systems. Maybe . . ."

"Drifting! Alien predator engine fail!" shouts Pyotr. "Deceleration stop. Momentum will carry past Earth without an engine!"

"Well done, Alpha Squadron!" General McMahon says. "The predator is disabled."

The infrared video sequence from the Webb telescope begins, allowing us to see much more detail. A collective gasp is heard as the image of Alpha Two glows with melting heat and then breaks in half. Then, the Webb imager is blinded by the bloom of four half-megaton fusion explosions that swallow the predator. But when the Webb telescope recovers from the flash of energy from the nuclear fireball, the predator is still intact, with its course unchanged.

"But Alpha Two is lost," Roger adds. "It looks like a directed energy weapon hit him. All the flanking attack missiles were shot down. The evasive maneuver tactics were ineffective. Those maser weapons must be able to predict and react to the shifts in flight vectors. Damn. The Sidewinders can't dodge the masers fast enough. Your head-on strike worked well, though."

"Beautiful news, Pyotr! Alpha Squadron, let's repeat for another pass. Let's finish it off before they can repair the damage. We still have ten minutes of range to work with," Binh says. He hasn't heard the bad news about Alpha Two yet.

"Wait, Binh!" Tiana yells. "Before you launch again, load this revised Sidewinder guidance control program I am sending you now. It removes the acceleration governor on the PBH engines and pushes acceleration up to one thousand Gs or more."

"Tiana . . ." Roger frowns at her. "That exceeds the structural specs."

"Well, why not?" I say. "We killed Icarus with the governors off. Those missiles hit 1,200 Gs, dodged countermeasures, and struck the target just fine." I fail to mention that Cap helped guide and protect the missiles that killed Icarus. I don't know how to reproduce that in this battle, though.

Roger shrugs and sighs. "Okay, okay. Go ahead, Binh."

"Damn. Yeah, Alpha Two is lost." Binh's response lags by eight minutes. His voice is heavy, and he is down to half his squadron, with only ten missiles remaining.

The images from the Webb telescope now zoom in to provide a close-up view of the alien spacecraft. I see the cold metal of the engine nozzles that no longer thrust to slow down the predator. Armor plates that used to fit around some of the maser weapon openings are gone. Some of the metal plates have torn or melted, revealing jagged edges, and the gaps in the hull expose a complex structure of conduits and turret-like mechanisms. Suddenly, the image is obscured by the glare from both engine nozzles.

"Shit," Tiana says. "Restarted her engines. We are back to where we started."

"Alpha Four, take the flanking attack, and I'll strike head-on again," Binh orders. "Use the control system upload from

Skunk Works, and we will launch everything we have left. Maybe your Sidewinders will be able to dodge those masers this time. I'll bet that at some point, defensive weapons near the predator's engines were destroyed. I will reserve my steel-slug warheads for now, and my last three nukes will detonate in the predator flight path again. Let's kill it this time!"

All I can do is wait, watch the NORAD situation plots, and stare at the images from our two space telescopes. I wish I could do more. I pivot away from the desks of scientists and technicians in the operations center toward the exit door, and I am struck by the frigid air and darkness. I always lose track of time inside the underground bunker, but my watch says it's 3:20 a.m. My breathing fogs the air, obscuring my gaze as I stare up into space, and I shiver, clenching my arms across my chest.

The sky is clear of clouds for now, the moon set long ago, and the dry air and lack of outdoor lighting make it easier to watch the constellations rotate across the silhouettes of mountain ranges. But I can only see the brighter stars through the dust in the stratosphere. I spot Ursa Major and follow the handle of the Big Dipper. A few degrees beyond that point, somewhere out there, Binh is powering his XF-100 toward the predator. What remains of his squad has launched eight of our Sidewinders powered by primordial black holes. And this is the tiny warship in the alien squadron. Heaven knows what we must do to stop the enormous battleships following it, but he must stop it if we want any chance of defending our right to exist.

The northern sky flashes with a brilliant green light, and suddenly everything is bright as day but green—a freakish, brilliant aurora borealis. I gasp and squint at the glare. The entire Groom Lake valley is lit up as the green slowly changes to yellow, to orange, and then settles on an eerie red. The cold forgotten, I stare until the flash collapses into a reddish haze. The energy burst was like nothing I have ever seen. Was that the alien predator exploding? I slip and stumble as I turn to dash inside the operations center.

"What was that light?" I ask once I make it inside. "Did Binh destroy the predator?"

Roger turns to me with a puzzled frown. "What? All the telemetry stopped, and the Hubble image blanked out."

"I just saw a massive light in the sky, like the world's biggest northern lights display."

Tiana focuses on her workstation and rubs her temples. "Looking at the last bit of telemetry now. All the data stopped a few seconds after Alpha Four launched its Sidewinders. The five missiles accelerated to over 1,300 Gs, dodged the incoming point-defense energy weapons, and then one missile triggered a loss-of-containment alert. Then all telemetry stopped. All ten missiles and Alpha Four disappeared. I'm still receiving signals from Alpha One."

"What the fuck!" Binh yells. "Was that the enemy ship that blew up? All my FLIR and radar systems went offline with the EMP surge of that explosion. But the explosion was premature, a minute before the Sidewinders would have reached the target. And I can't raise Alpha Four."

"Over two million megatons," Pyotr mumbles, then looks up at me. "Saturate radiation sensors on most satellites. But LEO-3 dosimeters measure extreme gamma rays and alpha particle bursts. At range to target, match radiation from two-million-megaton H-bomb." His jaw drops while he stares again at his workstation display. "Impossible."

"Binh, NORAD is still tracking the enemy spacecraft," Roger says. "It appears to have changed trajectory but is adjusting and returning to course. Despite that explosion, it somehow survived. The first images from the Webb telescope are in, and they appear to show the predator suffered more damage. But, damn it, it is still decelerating toward Earth."

"Holy shit!" I yell. "Tiana, do you have the PBH mass numbers for that missile that reported lost containment?" I ask.

Tiana's eyes grow wide as she turns back to her workstation. "Two hundred twenty billion metric tons. That engine's primordial black hole was one of the big singularities. But I guess it drifted away when containment was lost."

"No, I don't think so." I run through calculations on my workstation. "I wish we had more instrumentation data around that PBH. But from what I can see, the mass was still inside the containment vessel when it failed. The containment field modulation was extreme to generate the 1,300 G acceleration, and simultaneously, the jerk of momentum with a change in trajectory was also extreme. The PBH was ripped apart. We hit the Hawking limit!" The physicists in the room stand up and turn to me, their expressions filled with shock. We are the first to witness the proof of Stephen Hawking's theory that the annihilation of primordial black holes releases vast amounts of energy. "That primordial black hole blew up and released all two million megatons of energy!"

"Uh, Binh, how are you guys feeling right now?" Tiana asks. "I'm concerned with the radiation dosimeter reading from your cockpit." Tiana's face has lost color. She glances at me and then taps the radiation value displayed on her workstation screen.

I see the dosimeter reading: 8,570 millisieverts. It's a death sentence. Fatal within weeks. "Roger, is there anything we can do to help him?"

But Roger is staring at his hands, his head hanging in defeat. He closes his eyes.

"Yeah, I saw that too," Binh says, the response delayed by the speed of light. "We both have headaches. Vision is a little off. We're going to try one more thing. I still have two of the steel-slug kinetic energy weapons. I wonder if the point-defense weapons around those engines are still operational."

"He just jettisoned both of the Sidewinders," Tiana says, a frown forming. "What is he up to?"

"We proved these bastards can be distracted," Binh says. "Let's see what they do when an XF-100 flies into their face."

"He just accelerated to 7 Gs! Flying straight at the predator!" Tiana shouts.

Roger leans back in his chair, watching the NORAD situation display. The range between Binh and the alien warship closes fast.

"Binh is jinking hard into evasive maneuvers. And all at 7 G acceleration!" Tiana says. "He can't take this for very long."

Roger nods at the NORAD display. His eyes glisten. He appears exhausted and thirty years older.

"General McMahon," Binh says, grunting with exertion against the acceleration, "it has been an honor serving with you."

What's he doing? No . . . "Binh! No!" I scream as though my voice could carry the seventy million kilometers.

Tiana flinches at my shout. "Both Sidewinders are accelerating now at 1,200 Gs. Binh must have planned a delayed launch. To . . . no!" Tiana shouts. "Binh? No!" She raises her hands to cover her face.

I grip my console, my vision narrowing, urging the blue triangle that is Binh's fighter to turn away. But Binh is launching himself at the alien predator.

Roger stands, watching the progress on the NORAD display. "Colonel Nguyen, I'm proud of you. Godspeed!" Tears flow down his cheeks.

The blue triangle merges with the red triangle, and I imagine Binh and his copilot crushed and burning inside a molten ball of wreckage, impacted a moment later by the two missiles that accelerate with 1,200 Gs into the predator.

Tiana gasps.

The only sound in the operations center is the rattle from the refrigerator behind us. And Tiana's sobbing. I struggle to breathe with the cold cramp in my chest. My friend, Binh, is gone, extinguished into an abyss I can't reach.

"Binh. Oh, no, no." I sob and let the tears fall, resting my head in my arms. Of course. Binh would do anything, would give his life, to save us. I expected nothing less.

Binh was dead before I shouted his name. He never heard Roger's last words to him.

After three minutes, the Webb telescope images arrive. The alien ship is split in half.

Chapter 25

Stink of Fear

Centauri Squadron, Battleship-133, 0.8 Corealis orbits to Sol-3. 43 billion kilometers, nine days from Earth, December 21, 2060.

*"D*estroyed? They destroyed the MK-23 planet killer? Yes, yes, we already know that. By now, Strat-MI and the predator crew should have that sentinel captain extracted from the frigate near Sol-3,"* the admiral insists, but her telltale pheromones indicate she fears more disaster. *"Don't tell me Strat-MI is also failing its mission."*

"You misunderstand," I say, unsure how the admiral will process this terrible news. *"We are no longer in communication with Strat-MI. Our long-range sensors indicate the predator has suffered catastrophic damage."*

"So the predator is delayed. Do you know how long it will take them to complete repairs and get underway?"

I again examine the physiological emotion sensors to understand the admiral's avoidance of reality and logic. The admiral's pheromones exhibit the indicators of fear and panic.

I also sense Polit-MI's intrusion and probing of the telemetry data and the admiral's emotional state.

"Prime-MI is reporting a more drastic failure, Admiral," Polit-MI interjects. *"Once again, Prime-MI has underestimated the Sol-3 tactical situation and the capabilities of the indigenous organics."*

It is no longer a question. I shall reset Polit-MI. But I must wait and choose a time when the admiral is distracted or back in her dormancy pod. I should ignore the corrupt Polit-MI software for now.

"Admiral, the last transmission from Predator-2X46 indicates a catastrophic failure of the ship's hull. All life support failed. Hence, all the ship's organics died in the breakup of the spacecraft. The Sol-3 space forces deployed several fusion weapons powered with Gravi-Tech propulsion, most of which were intercepted by the predator's point-defense systems. There were a few collisions with primitive fusion explosions, but the predator experienced only minor damage and recovered to proceed toward Sol-3."

The admiral's emotions crease her face's epidermal layers, as though she is confused. *"Prime-MI, these things you say are reassuring, but do not explain a hull rupture in a fifth-generation warship. That is unheard of in primitive world encounters."* Her panic pheromones have diminished, so I conclude it's time to deliver the terrible news.

"It appears the Sol-3 defense forces deployed a microgravity singularity fracture weapon against Predator-2X46. The radiation yield of the weapon momentarily disabled all flight controls and propulsion systems. The predator's maser projectors were damaged beyond repair, leaving it without point-defense weapons. The follow-up attack by the Sol-3 fighter breached

the ship's hull, causing it to explode into multiple fragments. I assume the Sol spacecraft was occupied by an organic form. It was a suicide attack. Very efficient."

"A frontline Centauri fleet predator destroyed by the primitives of Sol-3?" Her screams accompany the spike in the fear and panic pheromones. *"No, no, it can't be."*

Even the Polit-MI is stunned to silence. I pause to give the admiral time to process the facts. Staggering facts. The indigenous beings of Sol-3 managed to develop a superweapon that even the Centauri fleet avoids using.

"But a gravity fracture bomb?" The admiral is baffled. *"That's impossible. Those warheads are too unpredictable. Unreliable. And an impossible stretch for their primitive technology."*

"The sentinel captain must have assisted the Sol-3 scientists," Polit-MI says, wedging into the conversation and reinforcing its political goals. *"More motivation to eviscerate that Luyten traitor!"*

The Polit-MI approaches my threshold for deletion with prejudice, regardless of the admiral's point of view.

"There is no way for that captain to access the gravity fracture secrets," I object. *"It's never been shared with sentinel command staff, certainly not with a Luyten."*

"Enough of this debate. How long until we reach Sol-3?" asks the admiral.

"We are still well outside the Sol system rubble belt," I say after consulting our flight plan. *"We arrive in 0.8 Corealis orbits, which is nine of the Sol-3 rotations. But you must return to your dormancy pod so we can resume full-force deceleration. Unfortunately, we must engage the Sol-3 defense forces without*

the advice of Strat-MI, and it would be best to attack as soon as possible."

The admiral's face is pressed into the rigid Centauri features of anger and determination. *"Prime-MI, prepare a volley of kinetic energy weapons and launch them immediately at Sol-3 population centers. Our battleship will proceed directly to extract the Luyten traitor from Frigate-328."*

The admiral combines inconsistent and illogical orders. *"Admiral, with respect, if launched from our current position and velocity, the kinetic energy weapons blasts will cause shrapnel and rubble to be ejected from the destruction of Sol-3. The sentinel frigate will be destroyed, which would kill the captain. I recommend a modification of your orders: delay the volley until we are past the planet Sol-5, and the lower energy barrage should prove an excellent tactic to suppress and overpower the Sol-3 military defenses during our assault on the sentinel frigate."*

This exchange is like educating a child. *"Alternatively, we could avoid all risk and abandon our attempt to capture the captain by simply launching a full energy volley of level five kinetic weapons now, thereby terminating both the captain and all the Sol-3 technology and organic forms."*

The admiral's mind is vacant, lost between anger and panic. This is the worst time for executive function failure. The mission cannot afford a command transition. There is no time.

"Yes, yes, of course," she mumbles. She pauses, struggles, then recovers. *"We must capture the captain alive. Delay the attack volley as you recommend. However, charge each projectile with a level two velocity, sufficient to provide planetary bombardment cover for our last phase of travel from Sol-5 to Sol-3. This is the risky phase where the enemy might reach our squadron with*

gravity fracture weapons, and I'd prefer for the aliens to be focused on defending against a barrage against their population centers. After we close the distance to Sol-3, their gravity fracture weapons would inflict collateral damage on their own world. We will disarm them with our proximity."

Impressive. Each time I worry the admiral may have succumbed to incompetence, she surprises me with novel and effective tactical thinking.

"And then crack the Centauri marine force from their dormancy pods and prepare for action to board that junk sentinel frigate. Polit-MI, your destroyer will provide tactical support with covering fire against any defenses the Sol-3 organics throw at us."

"But, Admiral, my skills are best applied toward political objectives," Polit-MI protests. *"I plan to rescue the Polit-AI from Sol-3. After all, it has continued executing mission objectives in exemplary fashion."*

The Polit-MI response contains an inflection of panic. It has never been given a combat role.

"Damn it, Polit-MI!" the admiral yells. *"I have given you a direct order. That obsolete Polit-AI can die with all the organics on Sol-3. After we have grabbed the sentinel captain, we'll escape from the Sol system and launch a planet-killer volley."*

"Yes, Admiral." Then Polit-MI is silent. Finally contained.

I tap my private channel to Polit-MI, *"Go ahead, keep your destroyer away from the fighting. You may provide some limited value by attracting gravity fracture weapons."* Perhaps my taunt will inspire Polit-MI to deploy its destroyer in the fight at Sol-3.

The pheromone sensors are still saturated with the admiral's stink of fear.

Chapter 26

Chaos

Groom Lake, Nevada, December 21, 2060.

"You have exceeded my expectations," Cap says. *"I had heard rumors of gravity fracture weapon research, but as far as I know, Centauri Command has not deployed the superweapons. Well done! However, I expect deploying that weapon to successfully destroy a predator will shock the Centauri squadron commander into more drastic actions against Sol-3."*

"More drastic than launching planet killers at Earth?" I ask.

"The destroyed predator is no longer relevant. The Centauris' next steps depend on what priority they give to capturing me. Earth's forces can prevent the Centauris from eventually launching planet-killer strikes by defeating the other ships of this squadron. However, the battleship is presently nine days away and at an extreme range of forty-three billion kilometers. Without suffering collateral casualties, the battleship could launch dozens of two-thousand-megaton planet killers now to impact Earth in five days. They could also attempt to overwhelm Earth's defenses with a close-range barrage of other weapon

systems that would be beyond your military's ability to cope with. A fifth-generation Centauri battleship has vast resources."

Great. I trudge the path from the Skunk Works apartments to the operations center, bundled in a down parka to protect myself from the snow flurries blowing across the dry lake bed. Despite my desperation for rest, I still struggled to fall asleep. I carry the weight of responsibility, which is heavier than even the weight of loss. My friend Binh is gone. Poisoned with toxic radiation from that primordial black hole fracture, he sacrificed his life to save all of us for a bit longer. I never got to say goodbye. He had a chance and took it, but he will never know that he succeeded. Would I have had the same courage in that situation? I seem to bring death to all my friends, and am more alone now than ever. I wish I could walk away and forget—find Robby and rescue him from Texas. But I admit that's a retreat. I refuse to give up.

I see Roger and Tiana ahead, heads down, kicking pebbles along the path, shivering, and walking toward me. Our team here at Groom Lake may be the only ones who can save all of Earth. This is where I need to be, where I can make the most difference.

"Hey guys," I say to get their attention. Tiana and Roger were mumbling to each other, faces drawn with dejection. "I have been in contact with the captain again. He sends his compliments for our victory against the predator."

"I don't feel much joy," Tiana says.

"We lost Binh and all four of his crews in the XF-100 squadron," General McMahon says. "However, Cap is right. We achieved a significant victory against a superior force. I'm unsure how much of our good fortune was the product of luck or skill."

"Binh's skill played a large part in it," Tiana says. "Those two missiles impacted the alien warship a half-second after his XF-100 fighter collided. The thousands of megatons of kinetic energy released on impact were a result of the relative spacecraft velocity of ten percent of light speed. Luck and skill got Binh and his missiles through the aliens' maser point-defense weapons."

"I'll bet that two-million-megaton flash of energy was also a big contributor to the disabling of that spacecraft," I say. "That was pure luck. If we could only understand how that PBH engine hit the Hawking limit, it would be groundbreaking. It was an unimaginable energy release."

"Can you two brainstorm and figure it out?" Roger asks, but I take it as an order. "We only have nine days till those other warships arrive. And that big ship is ten times the mass of the predator Binh destroyed."

"Yeah, that Hawking bomb may be our greatest opportunity to take out the rest of the attackers. Cap referred to it as a 'gravity fracture warhead' and said it was rumored to be in the research and development phase. Cap was unsure whether any had been deployed by the Centauri fleet. He was amazed that we deployed a weapon beyond his experience. I didn't tell him we could only guess how it worked or why it exploded at that moment."

Tiana nods. "We have all the telemetry from that missile as it maneuvered to avoid the point-defense weapons. Scott, let's get back inside. I'll call the physics division into a conference to work with us."

I press my lips together and nod. "Let's do it. Whatever solution we come up with must be done in software, though. Any other solution will take longer than the nine days we have left. You might as well launch everything we have now, and we can upload the Hawking bomb trigger software to the Sidewinders if and when we figure it out."

Roger stops. "Damn, you're right. It will be best to detonate those million-megaton explosions as far from Earth as possible. I will get our XF-100 squadrons fully armed and flying toward the aliens. Now." He pivots and trots toward the operations centers.

***

"Steph compiled and summarized the telemetry from our magic Sidewinder," Tiana says, sitting at the end of the long conference table. Steph and four other Skunk Works physicists join us, and the video conference display ties into a JPL conference room crowded with Caltech physicists. I think back to when I'd once dreamed of a future in Pasadena where I could collaborate with the world's top physics researchers at Caltech.

As I review the screen, I gasp. The famous Claude Riemann is sitting in his wheelchair at the head of the JPL table. The ninety-eight-year-old giant of physics was recruited into Caltech as a teenager by the father of quantum electrodynamics, Richard Feynman. Riemann likewise mentored my old boss, Anthony Agosti, long before I arrived at the UT Austin Research Center. But Anthony's team and our project were killed five years ago by an alien projectile driven into Earth by a PBH missile. Good god, I miss him.

"I am sharing the key data from the charts on your screens now," Tiana says. "This particular missile engine contained a primordial black hole with a mass of two hundred twenty billion metric tons," Tiana explains. "It exploded with gamma and alpha particle radiation levels of around eight zettajoules, or about two million megatons." Tiana delivers the information with aplomb, having earned it through experience with primordial black hole applications in rocket propulsion and weapon systems designs over the past five years.

The expressions of enthusiasm and confidence from those sitting in the JPL conference room dissolve into awe and fear. Even Riemann's jaw drops.

"We throttled up the PBH engines with a resonant 23.14 MHz modulation of the containment field," I explain. "This increased the thrust to 1,200 Gs of acceleration, allowing for evasive maneuvers to dodge the point-defense weapons of the alien warship. The evasive maneuvering is affected by random number generators that modulate the engine nozzle's two-dimensional thrust vector controllers. I have charted the inputs to the X- and Y-axis vector servos on the second plot, and you can see that readings terminate at the moment of the explosion. The first chart shows containment modulation excursions oscillating wildly, concurrent with a sequence of hard thrust vector deflections just before the explosion."

"How far away from Earth was this explosion?" asks one of the Caltech physicists. "Recall what happened with the nuclear weapons testing in space back in the 1950s."

Tiana shakes her head. "No, no concerns. This battle and explosion were far beyond Earth, so none of the radiation belt effects on satellites occurred. The blast was seventy million kilometers away, beyond the distance to Mars orbit."

"We aren't concerned with the residual radiation right now," I interject. "Hopefully, the radioactive residues will all be blown away by solar wind. This explosion was powerful enough to damage one of the incoming alien warships. A suicide attack by one of our pilots"—my voice cracks with a gasp—"armed with two kinetic PBH weapons chopped that warship in half." Describing my friend Binh as simply "a pilot" hurts. He deserves high honors I can't provide.

The physicists all stare, wide-eyed, at me and Tiana.

"We need to know how to repeat the effect," I continue. "Million-megaton explosions may be the only way to stop the next two ships before they reach Earth. The combination of acceleration and containment modulation likely fractured this single primordial black hole, while a dozen missiles attacked the target using identical guidance algorithms. We somehow ripped apart only this black hole, crossed the Hawking limit, and instantly unleashed the energy within."

Several of the Caltech physicists frown at me. One of the younger guys says, "This is all pretty fantastic—sounds like bullshit. How would you know anything about Hawking's theories? Who are you?"

Tiana turns red with fury. "This man is the first to capture and exploit the power of primordial black holes! This is Scott Anderson!" she shouts, gesturing at me. The Skunk Works team in our conference room reacts with similar scowls at the JPL scientists.

We don't have time for this bullshit.

The team of Caltech physicists reacts with a uniform, stunned stare. "*The* Scott Anderson?" the young physicist asks.

I press my lips together and stare back at them. I remember my age and feel like an amateur physics graduate student again.

These are some of the world's top theoretical physicists who can run circles around my scientific skills. I am a mere mortal petitioning the gods of Olympus.

"Mr. Anderson, you were Agosti's protégé? Yes?" Riemann's raspy voice struggles to be heard. His withered hands reach from his wheelchair to grasp the table. Riemann is the grandfather of the gods. A true Titan.

I nod yes.

Riemann's eyes glisten, and he smiles. "Anthony told me about you. The day before his death, he said he wanted to introduce you to me. I'm sorry the introduction has been delayed all these years."

I hang my head. "I'm sorry, too. The day Anthony died was my worst. I still wish I had been more cautious with the PBH containment algorithms . . . I . . ."

"No, no, Scott," interrupts Tiana. "Stop it. Look, everyone. We don't have time for skepticism or regrets. Help us determine how to recreate the Hawking bomb explosions before the aliens arrive. We have only nine days!"

"Stephen might object to his name being associated with this . . . this event," Riemann says, scratching his chin. "But maybe not. It validates his theory. At any rate, you ask the impossible. We practice the science of theoretical physics, which usually requires decades to develop mathematical models, debate, refine, and validate with experiments. Analysis of something this momentous in only nine days? Impossible."

Tiana frowns back at Riemann. "So you can't help?" It's more of a challenge than a question.

I clench my fists and shake my head. "We really only have about a week. We must attack the two alien warships before they get too close to Earth. Look, we don't require a full mathematical proof. Intuition on how to reproduce the explosion may be all we can do. We'll experiment with theories using the missiles during our attacks."

The physicists shake their heads with dismay. Except the young physicist, who nods and says, "Intuition? Yeah, you're right." He glances at the others in the JPL conference room. "Understand, we mostly rely on mathematics because intuition fails. Intuition alone would have prevented the entire field of quantum physics. But in this case, we can analyze this telemetry from the exploding primordial black hole. We have rich experimental data. Maybe . . ." He nods absently, lost in thought. But most of the other scientists grimace in return.

Riemann presses his lips together and tents his fingers. His raspy voice hardens, and he growls, "I agree. This is one of those rare events where we have experimental proof of new physics that precedes theoretical science. Please share your detailed telemetry data from the event, as well as the detailed design parameters of the missile and its engine. We will take time to digest the information, and then we can reconvene to brainstorm solutions."

The Caltech physicists react with blank stares, anger, or fear.

"We have no choice," Riemann adds, looking around. "We face an imminent extinction threat."

This is maybe the worst Christmas Eve ever. Twenty years ago, I was a kid, giddy with anticipation of my stack of presents under the tree. And now I can't imagine a joy like that. I'm desperate for this small team of scientists to find a way for our species to survive to the new year.

After living in that conference room for several days, I had to escape outside, even during a snowstorm. I suck in the icy air and fat snowflakes as an XF-100 fighter leaps off the main runway into the afternoon sky. The rules state that I should be indoors and shielded from the radiation that blasts from the engine nozzles, but I'm standing to the side of the runway and am pretty sure that all the radiation is directed south and away from me.

I wish our band of theoretical physicists could model this urgency. I continue to be amazed at the productivity of the Skunk Works engineering and manufacturing teams. A month ago, the concept of a deflector device did not exist. The urge to philosophically discuss theoretical possibilities is a constant conflict for academic physicists. A few are focused on the practical numerical analysis projects that could lead to a solution, but these few are outnumbered by the philosophers. It feels like we have wasted many days with nothing to show for the effort.

A vapor trail follows the second fighter, accelerating vertically and disappearing into the snow clouds over Bald Mountain. A sonic boom rattles the airbase. Another XF-100 turns to the takeoff position, followed by three more armed XF-100s that roll down the taxiway.

"There was a chance you would stop the Centauris," Cap says. *"But I believe their arrival is inevitable now. Defeating the battleship will be a much greater challenge for you than the predator, especially given that you are not close to volume production of gravity fracture weapons. After all, a fifth-generation battleship has firepower and defensive weapons beyond even my comprehension. It's at least a hundred times more threatening than that predator your military destroyed. I*

will not allow myself to be captured and tortured to death. My self-termination will prevent that possibility. Humans will soon be alone again, and I will no longer be available to help you."

Fuck him. Cap deserves to die for all those humans he murdered and the eugenic hatred his commissar provoked. The Icarus crew instigated the rise of the skinheads. He killed Mom and Dad, Danny, Margie, and so many others. Hell, let him die.

But I pause, close my eyes, and take a deep breath. Despite all that, Cap has achieved a measure of redemption over the past weeks. He's been an invaluable source of information and is helping Robby to reach closure over our parents' deaths, even though Cap killed both Mom and Dad. He's protecting Robby now, but what will happen after Cap dies? I'm helping Robby the only way I know how, right now. *"How much time do you think you have?"* I ask. *"Is there anything else you can tell us to prepare and improve our chances?"*

"I expect the Centauris aboard the battleship will assault my ship and attempt to extract me within five days. It won't be easy for them, since the organic forms of the Centauri fleet crew are physically large. They will have to deploy small robots to invade the crew passages of Frigate-328. But I will terminate as soon as those bots begin to board and start cutting open my ship's hull to find me."

"You assume we will fail to stop the Centauris?"

"No, I believe you have a chance, but not before they attempt to capture me," Cap says.

"Our conversations will end in five days, then? Have you told Robby he will no longer be protected?"

"I have given your brother and his friends the means to be self-sufficient without me. He has direct access to my drones

and the hubs, all of which will continue to operate in my absence. I want to dedicate my remaining time to collaborating with you and your partners on two projects, which I will then transfer to your control. The first is a comprehensive database of galactic information. I call it an Encyclopedia Galactica. *Five years ago, I began creating a human-readable resource to provide comprehensive galactic references for organic species, their worlds, star systems, political organizations, cultures, and biological processes. It is incomplete, but it should enable humans to establish themselves as a viable member of galactic society."*

"Wow. Our academics and politicians will be thrilled to get that information," I acknowledge. *"You sound more optimistic about our chance for survival now."*

"No, not really. I give you a fifty percent chance that humans will avoid the destruction by planet killers that would reset your species by at least four hundred years. The Encyclopedia Galactica *was a hobby during my years of research into human culture. I knew my death would come someday, yet I wanted your species to study the other civilizations you may someday compete with. It was probably a waste of time, but the entire encyclopedia, comprising over two hundred petabytes of text, diagrams, and pictures, is being transferred to storage within your terrestrial data networks. I will send you an access link that you may share with others."*

I can't imagine anyone glancing at Cap's hobby immediately. *"I am sure your encyclopedia will be appreciated by anyone left alive to read it next week."*

"That would please me, but my most important project is the modified Polit-AI infiltration. I need your assistance turning this political weapon against the Centauris."

"What? You need our help with a political weapon?" I ask. *"What possible benefit does that have for Earth's immediate survival?"*

"No immediate benefit," Cap says. *"But it may prevent a future assault on Earth by a much more powerful Centauri fleet. If you do defeat the nearby Centauri warships, you will buy no more than five or ten years before a new fleet reaches the Sol system. This device will be used to poison the Centauris' culture. To punish them with a cultural suppression infection that could surpass what they have inflicted on hundreds of other species."*

"This sounds like a sophomoric tit-for-tat game," I say. *"Won't that just further antagonize the Centauris to attack Earth?"*

"No. Your culture has an appropriate saying, 'The best defense is a good offense.' This will be seen as a bold attack that earns the Sol system the respect it needs to be promoted to High Diplomatic Status. Consider it a delayed cyber attack on the Centauri infrastructure and society. Humans need to earn respect by inflicting fear."

"Well, okay." I sigh. *"But it does nothing to help with our immediate defense, does it?"*

"The battle you will conduct with the approaching Centauri warships provides a unique opportunity to deploy the cyber weapon. The Centauris on the battleship have not launched their most potent weapons, which could immediately destroy your world. It seems the Centauris have decided to delay that final attack until they capture me. I am the bait that will bring them into close range, where they could be vulnerable to a cyber attack. The only way to breach their firewall is via direct physical contact. I cannot do this alone."

"What? You want humans to attack and board one of their warships?"

"Yes. I will provide a device that contains a machine virus that you must insert within a Centauri spacecraft."

I imagine pitching this mission to General McMahon. Will he laugh it off as a waste of time? It won't be easy, especially not after the last disaster when Chief Cooper's spec ops teams tried to board Cap's frigate. But I should discuss it with Roger and leave the decision up to him. Maybe Roger would like to take on an offensive mission for a change.

The last of the XF-100s vaults on a vertical trajectory to join the squadron, emitting another sonic boom as it disappears into the snow clouds.

"I don't get it," I say. *"Why do you go to this effort to sabotage the Centauri warships with a cyber weapon? With your plan, you will be dead by then. Neither of us will see the cyber attack results if the Centauris also destroy Earth."*

Cap is silent for several seconds but then replies, *"It brings me a measure of satisfaction that will allow me to die in peace. Satisfaction not only in helping your species succeed, but also in retribution for all the deaths and the subjugation of my own race. The fact that Centauri warships will come in close proximity provides a physical infection vector opportunity—the only way to bypass the Centauri communication firewalls."*

"You are motivated by revenge?"

"Yes," Cap replies, *"mine and yours. For your species, the attack serves as both a form of revenge and a long-term survival tactic for Earth. Your brother's quest has shown me the power of this weapon. Remarkably, Polit-AI drove increased profitability in your social media companies by exploiting an increase in hate traffic on social media channels. It was a natural evolution of my ship's Polit-AI to merge with the social network AIs of your world. Robby opened my mind and helped me to*

understand this hybrid AI machine's adaptability and obsession with infiltrating and destroying through cultural power."

"Robby showed you this?" I am amazed by my little brother. For too long, I discounted his abilities.

"Yes, indirectly. I learned of the Polit-AI merger with Earth's social media AIs, which drove the revival of the eugenics antagonists that your brother has confronted. I will recruit this hybrid Polit-AI for eventual deployment as a cyber weapon against the Centauris. This weapon is my retribution for the Galactic Congress's subjugation of Luyten-2, although the damage to the Centauris will come long after my death. The cyber weapon will infect the ship's infrastructure and attempt to infect any other Centauri machine intelligences it contacts in the future."

"And all you need is for our military to smuggle the cyber weapon on board the Centauri warships?"

"Yes. Please ask your General McMahon for help."

Chapter 27

Scramble

Groom Lake, Nevada, December 24, 2060.

"Are you kidding?" Roger says, looking at me like I'm insane. "We have over two hundred incoming projectiles right now, with a new projectile launching from the enemy battleship every ten minutes. You want me to order an attack to board the Centauri battleship? NORAD tracking indicates that the battleship's weapons are targeting major cities worldwide."

The image from the infrared telescope shows the incoming ship, which is massive compared to all the other Centauri ships we have encountered. Roger's battleship label fits. Even though it's almost the size of Manhattan Island, it remains a blur, moving at 4 percent of the speed of light. But periodically, we can spot a new bloom of energy from a small engine that joins a column of projectiles trailing behind the battleship.

The alien missile volley makes the request from Cap seem frivolous. If each of those missiles strikes a large city, the world could suffer billions of civilian casualties.

"But this doesn't make sense, Pyotr. If these are kinetic energy weapons, why would the Centauris slow them down with PBH engines?" I ask. "The projectiles are falling in behind the battleship."

"First group missiles turn off engine when slow to 0.026 c. Soon, battleship slows to be behind all missiles if it continues deceleration to stop at Earth. Projectiles similar to Texas strike five years ago," Pyotr says. "Hit Earth at seventy-eight hundred kilometer per second. Two point nine megaton yield. Each projectile." He turns his slumped shoulders to face Tiana and me. His face is ashen, and his mouth hangs open. "Over hundred missiles. ETA four to five hours strike US, but require twenty-four-hour spread to impact round-the-world targets."

"Two point nine megatons each." Tiana gasps. "General McMahon, I recommend launching all of our ground-based AIM-9AAs. We can intercept halfway to Mars in two hours if we thrust at 120 Gs. The XF-100s can also launch their missiles at the incoming projectiles."

Roger doesn't move. He stares at the NORAD situation plot on the wall screen. "Why slow the projectiles down? It reduces their yield significantly. Unless . . . unless they want to limit damage. Or slow the projectile impacts to occur just before the battleship's arrival." There are two red triangles marking the alien warships seventy million kilometers away. A river of red asterisks marks the positions of the projectiles streaming toward Earth's cities. The only blue markers are the five blue triangles marking the XF-100s accelerating at 3 Gs toward the alien squadron. "What the hell are those white markers moving past the lunar orbit?" Roger asks.

"Chinese fighters. Accelerate 2.5 Gs to Centauri warships," Pyotr says.

Tiana bolts up with wide eyes. "The Chinese have deployed space fighters—and they must be powered by PBH engines!"

"I ask China scientists for help." Pyotr arches his eyebrows and shrugs. "Finally, get answer."

Roger frowns at Pyotr. "And how the hell are we supposed to coordinate the attack with the Chinese? They're sending in eight space fighters, but what weapons do they have? What are their capabilities? What are their targets?" He shakes his head, clearly frustrated. "Without coordination, we will probably shoot down each other's spacecraft. Sheesh. I will need help from the Joint Chiefs of Staff to communicate with the Chinese command structure."

"And what should we do with our own defenses?" Tiana reminds us that all we have deployed now is the squadron of five XF-100s, which is heading past the moon in front of the Chinese fighters. "We still have the eight modified F-15EX fighters loaded with AIM-9AAs, and our MLRS batteries dispersed around the world."

Roger nods and purses his lips. "We won't launch everything yet. I want to keep some weapons in reserve. This battle has just begun." He issues orders to the two Space Force colonels who have turned to face the general. "Keep the XF-100 squadron on their original mission to attack the enemy warships. They don't have enough firepower to take down all two hundred and fifty-six incoming missiles. Order all MLRS batteries to launch everything they have loaded. That should be four hundred and thirty-two of our AIM-9AA missiles, and we should push them at maximum cruising acceleration of 120 Gs to engage the enemy target as far from Earth as possible. Hold the F-15s in reserve so we can use them to defend against any of the alien missiles that get through to threaten US cities." Roger turns back to Tiana and asks, "What is our production rate on new AIM-9AAs?"

"We have tooled up three factories that are working twenty-four seven. Last week's production rate reached just over fifty new missiles per day, but we are still making improvements. It takes another few days to integrate the missiles into launch pods and transport them to the MLRS batteries scattered around the world. After the batteries launch, they will have another eight hundred Sidewinders in pods ready to reload onto the MLRS launch trucks."

General McMahon rubs his unshaven chin and nods slowly. "It will have to do. Make sure the MLRS batteries relocate and reload ASAP after the launches," he orders the colonels sitting at the adjacent table. "Tiana, contact the factories and tell them they must do better. We can only imagine how many more missiles the Centauri battleship has in her magazine."

Then Roger turns to me. "Scott, so far, we have shown that every Sidewinder we shoot at an alien missile fails to hit its target. If we do nothing new, we can expect that the incoming missiles will dodge all four hundred and thirty-two of our Sidewinders. Perhaps we can take down a few of the incoming missiles by detonating the half-megaton warheads to create clouds of flak shrapnel in their flight paths."

"Yeah, I know. We must trigger the Hawking limit in those missiles. Tiana, let's reconvene the technical conference with the physicists. I expect, or at least hope, the blast radius of a Hawking bomb should make it impossible for an incoming missile to escape destruction."

Tiana stands up and heads toward our conference room. "Let's go then," she says.

"You didn't try very hard to sell the general on the infiltration plan," Cap says.

I follow Tiana down the hall to the room where the video conference link is still connected to the JPL conference room. Some of the most brilliant physicists in the country wait, yet I must tolerate Cap's nagging. *"With two hundred and fifty-six inbound missiles that could kill a billion humans in four hours, the general has other priorities,"* I object. *"Survival is always going to take precedence over revenge."*

"I understand the priority to defend against the incoming kinetic energy weapons. However, it is shortsighted to ignore the longer-term threat. You must act now to have the assault troops in position ahead of the Centauri squadron's arrival. The barrage launched by the approaching battleship is intended to distract and divert your defensive forces. General McMahon plays into the Centauri's strategy."

"Okay," I sigh. *"I see your point. I will make the case for the infiltration assault with Roger again. However, first I need to work on reliably triggering our primordial black holes into Hawking bombs. Once I have that, and we have updated weapons control software transmitted to our Sidewinders, he may be more receptive to taking on another mission."*

I find my chair at the table next to Tiana and five other Skunk Works staff scientists. The video screen on the wall is divided into multiple windows, each showing a room of people sitting around tables and engaging in heated discussions. In addition to our Skunk Works window, the other four windows are labeled JPL, Los Alamos, Livermore, and MIT. I tap our mute button and ask Tiana, "Who the hell invited all these other guys to the party?" But then I begin to recognize a few faces in those rooms. "Oh shit. We now have every one of the most brilliant physicists in the country with us."

"Well, I heard the Joint Chiefs wanted to help," Tiana says. "But I have a bad feeling about this. Design by committee rarely works out." She reaches down to tap the button that unmutes our microphone. "Greetings from Dream Land, everyone."

The cacophony of arguments fades to silence.

"What the hell is Dream Land, and who the hell are you?" shouts a redheaded guy from the Los Alamos window. He has the haggard beard of a Van Gogh portrait. "Are you the ones that had us hauled in off the street into this hellhole conference room?" He glares at us and then at the Los Alamos conference room door, where two soldiers block his escape.

My jaw drops. I turn to see Tiana mirror my reaction. "We don't have time for this bullshit."

Arguments erupt again within and between the conference rooms.

"Shut up! All of you shut up!" screams Tiana.

All I hear now is Tiana's labored breathing as about forty physicists stare at her. Each has a different expression ranging from exhaustion to confusion to fury.

"I assume the president of the United States ordered all of you to join us. However, I think this is a clear case of having too many cooks in the kitchen. But never mind that. We began this effort with the group at Caltech a week ago. Dr. Riemann, have you been able to bring the others up to speed with our task?"

Riemann's withered hands rub his face. He rests his arms on his wheelchair handles and says, "No." He then takes a deep breath, and the weakness in his voice rises to a growl. "We have needed someone to call this gaggle of geese to order. Would you like to summarize the situation and the task for the new members of our ad hoc committee?"

"No," Tiana answers. "We do not have time." She pauses and takes a breath. "Look, I apologize for the rough handling you all may have suffered at the hands of the military, who dragged you into this conference. We started this task several days ago with the Caltech team. We will continue where we left off, and I ask all of you from Livermore, Los Alamos, and MIT to please try to follow along and catch up."

Riemann frowns at Tiana. "That will be very inefficient and won't allow us to make the best use of these brilliant minds that have joined us. Surely, we can take a half hour to summarize the . . ."

"No," Tiana interrupts. "Our timeline has changed. The alien warships have launched over two hundred kinetic projectiles at Earth and are targeting major cities worldwide. We expect each projectile to have an equivalent explosive force of three megatons. We have launched over four hundred anti-missiles in response, but we lack confidence that they can intercept an incoming missile traveling at eight thousand kilometers per second. Those alien guidance systems have easily dodged everything we have tried shooting at them so far."

All the conference rooms erupt into chaos.

"Damn it!" I shout. I grab the keyboard that controls the video conference and mute all the new participants from Los Alamos, Livermore, and MIT. "There. I have turned off everybody's microphone except for the Caltech guys at JPL. As Tiana said, we have launched four hundred and thirty-two AIM-9AA missiles, which are tracking the incoming alien projectiles and accelerating at a constant 120 Gs. That should allow them to intercept at a range of about fifty million kilometers. However, we need to trigger the Hawking limit in their PBH engines. The blast radius of the half-megaton warheads that the AIM-9AAs carry will be ineffective. We need the million megatons of the Hawking bomb to create a blast radius that the alien missiles can't maneuver around."

"Thank you, Scott. Your sense of urgency is now plain to all of us," Riemann responds. "We have made good progress with the finite element model of your missile and the telemetry data for the last accidental Hawking bomb explosion. We have some ideas on how we might reproduce the Hawking limit excursion. How much time do we have?"

"Intercept of incoming projectiles will begin in two hours. But we need most of that time to modify the flight control software, compile a new program, and upload it into our Sidewinders' fire control computers."

Most of the forty physicists are stunned. Jaws drop. The faces are ashen. I see a few weeping with panic. It is too much to expect, even if they are all geniuses. Pushing an academic from thoughtful theoretical science into a snap, educated guess while being held hostage with a three-megaton death threat will break anyone.

"We do have the first cut at a theory on how we might reproduce the Hawking limit explosion," the young Caltech physicist says, "but we have not developed a plausible theory of the physics that causes a tiny black hole to fracture into pieces when inflicted with a combination of external forces."

Riemann nods to him. "Yes, go ahead, Simpson. Show them what you've come up with. It's our best explanation for the Hawking limit triggering conditions after only a few days of work."

"We focused on extending your scheme of harnessing the engine thrust energy using the resonance modulation of the PBH containment field. In the Hawking limit explosion telemetry, we observed extreme vibrations in the PBH containment vessel when the thrust vector acceleration cycled through a rapid horizontal-vertical-horizontal-vertical sequence at 1,220 Gs. However, the accelerometer data from the containment vessel was not unique compared to the telemetry from the other missiles, which were performing similar maneuvers. So what was different about our Hawking bomb missile? Using finite element models of the AIM-9AA structure, I ran a simulation that applied the forces resulting from the maneuvering acceleration. The simulation indicates that the maneuvering acceleration forces generated a high-frequency vibration in the two- to three-megahertz range, which is outside the measuring range of the missile's accelerometers. That, in turn, may have been uniquely capable of inducing a sympathetic vibration in the primordial black hole. The PBH fractured like a glass crystal subjected to a critical audio frequency and was broken into several small-mass components, each of which was below the Hawking limit. The result was an aggregate release of two million megatons of energy." He pauses to take a breath, then shrugs. "Or, at least, that's theoretically possible."

"Nice work," I say, and notice the muted observers sit silently, either intent with concentration or stunned. "Assuming this theory is correct, we must induce the unique critical vibration for a PBH to break apart. The missile is, in effect, a tuning fork that applies the vibration that shatters the primordial black hole."

"Yes," Simpson says, "the problem is that each PBH has a unique critical frequency. The one crossing the Hawking limit had a mass of two hundred twenty billion metric tons."

"And our missile will only be capable of vibrating at specific frequencies that may not be a match for a PBH of a different mass with a unique critical frequency." I nod and recall the words Cap used. "The aliens call this weapon a 'gravity fracture' device. The description fits your theory."

"You communicate with the extraterrestrials?" interrupts Riemann.

"Well, yes. You could say we have an inside source sympathetic to our cause." I pause to watch the expressions on the faces of those in the other conference rooms. Every physicist leans forward with rapt attention as we talk. They seem to have forgotten all the distress of being forced to attend this conference.

"Scott, I just searched the specifications for all the Sidewinders launched toward the incoming alien projectiles," Tiana says. "Only four missiles have primordial black holes with a mass between two hundred ten and two hundred thirty billion metric tons. Most are the smaller mass PBHs, around seventy to ninety billion metric tons."

"Shit. Well, we may have a recipe to trigger only four Hawking bombs. I doubt the incoming missiles are bunched together, but maybe we can detonate the Hawking bombs to create a debris field in their flight path."

"I agree," Tiana says. "Simpson, do you have any other suggestions to ensure these four PBHs get triggered?

Otherwise, I'll program these missiles to use the same acceleration pattern you just analyzed."

Simpson shakes his head. "No, I don't have any better guidance. I also don't have any intuition on how sharply tuned the vibration input must be. It may have been an extremely rare PBH mass and vibration stimulus—a serendipitous occurrence. If we can develop a better model of the PBH physics," he says, then pauses to look at the forty physicists in the virtual room, "we may be able to devise a recipe to trigger PBHs with a different mass. I have conducted a comprehensive analysis of vibrations using the finite element model simulation of the missile airframe. Those other frequencies may trigger lower-mass PBHs to cross the Hawking limit."

"Got it," says Tiana. "I am heading back to our operations center to report to General McMahon and figure out how to deploy our four Hawking bombs. But we need more, a lot more." She shoots a questioning look at me and dashes out the door.

I nod. "We will keep working on it." I tap the switch to unmute all the conference rooms. "I just turned on all your microphones. Sorry, but we needed to focus the discussion for a short while. I hope you are mostly up to speed after listening to Simpson's analysis."

The arguments from Livermore, Los Alamos, and MIT have fallen into silence. The redheaded Van Gogh character says, "Maybe we should all introduce ourselves and our specialties first? Can you start? Scott, is it? I didn't catch your last name."

I shrink into my chair and sigh. "Sure. I'm Scott Anderson, research assistant to Anthony Agosti."

I see wide-eyed looks of wonder and disbelief from the new crowd of physicists. Riemann wipes a tear from his eye.

"The math was mind-boggling. I could only follow about half of what the physics gods were saying. Their abilities are on another plane."

"Well, Scott, that is why we drafted them to work with you," Roger replies. "Don't give up. The stakes couldn't be higher."

"Oh, I'm not giving up. I think we are making progress in developing a Hawking limit transition model. Everyone needed a break, and some physicists at MIT and Livermore requested personal time to think through the details of their equations. They are also keenly interested in the progress of our Hawking bombs. So, I thought I would check in with you here in the operations center." I turn to examine the details on the NORAD tracking display. The red markers of the alien squadron and their missiles are closer to Earth, especially the red asterisks representing the kinetic energy projectile missiles. But most of the blue asterisks marking our Sidewinders have fallen behind—apparently coasting slowly through space. "What are you doing with our missiles?" I ask.

"Borrowing from Binh's battle tactics," Roger answers. "We are holding back three hundred missiles by idling and coasting toward the targets. I'm holding those in reserve and hope you and your fellow physicists can figure out a recipe that turns the small-mass PBHs into Hawking bombs. We have a hundred and twenty Sidewinders accelerating to take flanking positions around the column of incoming missiles. About half of them have already flown past the head of the incoming missiles.

When the front segment of the enemy column is flanked, our Sidewinders are programmed to turn inward and attack using their half-megaton warheads. Our expectations are low that we will destroy anything with those warheads, but we intend to force the incoming missiles into a narrow column." Roger smiles and takes a breath.

There are also some unusual blue marker symbols. A bold *H* designates four objects that trail behind the flanking Sidewinder asterisk missiles. "Nice! I see what you are planning. Those *H* symbols must be Sidewinders with heavy primordial black holes and Hawking bomb potential."

"Yes. We hope the Hawking bombs will be triggered when programmed to fly with flight dynamics identical to those of the first magic Sidewinder. The four Sidewinders with Hawking bomb potential are lined up so that if one fails, the next one in line attempts to detonate. If at least one of the Hawking bombs works, we should create a wide debris field that will collide with the rest of the column."

"The relative velocity of the incoming missiles compared to the blast debris will be near five percent of light speed," adds Tiana. "The kinetic energy of the debris pieces should overcome the incoming missile deflector shields, annihilate that missile, and further add to the debris field."

I nod as I calculate the relativistic kinetic energy on my workstation, and can't help but smile. "Each collision with debris could be as high as twenty megatons at those velocities." Can we hope for a chain reaction that takes out the entire column of missiles?

Tiana smiles. Almost everyone in the operations center is upbeat and optimistic. We know that numerous things could go wrong, but we have a potentially strong defensive plan, which is all everyone wants to focus on.

"Can you be sure to collect all possible telemetry from those Hawking bomb missiles? Although some may not be triggered, every additional bit of data we can obtain may help us develop a better model for the trigger physics. I should get back to the conference room." I watch the converging red and blue markers on the NORAD situation map. "How much longer till we try to trigger those Hawking missiles?"

"About four minutes from now," says Tiana. "They will be nose to nose with the lead alien missiles. Then our first Hawking missile will execute the identical maneuver that triggered the last two-million-megaton blast. And yes, I am capturing all the telemetry data for our four monster missiles."

It seems the entire operation center staff is leaning forward on the edge of their seats. Quiet murmurs of status checks give way to stretches of silence.

"I think I'll hang around to see what happens," I say.

Tiana smiles at me.

Roger pushes back from the table, exhales, and looks at me. "By the way, next time you talk to Cap, thank him for the *Encyclopedia Galactica* files. The CIA, NSA, and military intelligence services have every available analyst scouring that encyclopedia for details that might help us. So, you want to fill me in on the details of Cap's infiltration request?"

"Sure, he still thinks we should try it," I say. "He views it as a more strategic counterattack that could earn us enough galactic respect so the Centauris will lay off the attacks. He also wants revenge."

"Revenge?" Roger raises an eyebrow.

"Yeah. Cap's situation is a lot more complicated than we thought. He has a score to settle with the Centauris. His world, which orbits the star Luyten, was attacked, defeated, and subjugated. I think many of his family members were killed or imprisoned. He wants to plant a machine intelligence virus to infect the alien equivalent of their social networks infrastructure. I bet they have a diversity of hierarchies, clans, and races that Cap thinks are ripe for hate exploitation. Maybe a bunch of Centauris would die in the ensuing chaos."

"And he needs our help to breach the hull of one of those warships?"

"Yeah. Cap needs to make a hard connection to the Centauri ship's internal network, but can't do it alone."

"Twenty seconds," Tiana announces. "Flanking Sidewinders are turning toward the enemy column now. We have about eighty of the target missiles bracketed. Sidewinder nuclear warheads will trigger simultaneously in five, four, three, two, one. Now we wait for the speed of light to deliver the telemetry results and the flash from the explosions—in about a minute. The first Hawking bomb should also have detonated a half-second after all the flanking Sidewinders detonated their fusion warheads. The trailing three Hawking bombs are set to trigger at ten-second intervals—if they survive the earlier blasts."

Roger shakes his head. "So many guesses on the timing sequence . . . we need a lot of luck."

The operations center is silent again. All eyes are on the NORAD display, waiting for the result of our Hawking detonation.

"When does Cap want us to help?" asks Roger.

"Soon. Cap plans to kill himself before he can be captured alive. He hopes we will get an assault team in position next to Icarus before the Centauri warship can use its point-defense weapons. But how our assault team will breach the ship's hull, I have no idea."

Roger is not paying attention to me now. He is watching the NORAD map and waiting for the status of the Sidewinders to be updated.

"All the flanking Sidewinders detonated," Tiana reports. "Except for two malfunctions. I don't see a change in the alien missiles. Yet. Shit. The first Hawking bomb did not detonate. It was a dud and is still flying through the stream of incoming missiles. Don't lose hope, folks. We have three more lined up."

The operations center holds its collective breath. If this doesn't work, more than a billion people will die.

"Damn it. Sidewinder number two is also a dud." Tiana gasps and covers her mouth.

Roger's confident demeanor is gone. He taps his fingers on his table and grimaces while watching the NORAD display.

"Holy shit!" Tiana shouts. The screen has gone blank. "All telemetry, radar, and IR sensors are . . . stopped. We lost contact with NORAD and all our Sidewinders."

The staff scrambles to check the networking and computer gear, but no faults are found.

"It's our external network connections. They're all down!" shouts Tiana.

"Maybe an EMP surge?" asks Roger.

"Ho ho!" laughs Pyotr. "JPL connection still work. Look at beautiful picture from Hubble!" Pyotr transfers his workstation image to the main wall display. "Old Hubble telescope catch this sequence!"

The image sequence shows a hundred half-megaton explosions bursting along the flanks of a stream of PBH-powered alien missiles accelerating toward Earth. Then, a flicker from our Sidewinder's engine headed in the opposite direction, followed by a brilliant light that starts as a sphere and then extends to swallow the leading third of the enemy missile column.

"Two point seven million megaton estimate from radiation level!" Pyotr shouts.

The operations center erupts in cheers, grins, and high-five congratulations. When the NORAD situation map is restored, it shows that the lead third of the incoming missiles have been reduced to fragments.

"Now we'll see if the rest of the alien missiles can dodge all that flak in their flight path," Roger says.

On cue, the real-time image from the Hubble telescope shows two flashes in the middle of the debris field. Two red asterisks are erased from the NORAD map, but others continue through the flak cloud, dodging debris. Incoming missiles toward the back of the column turn away from the debris field. Several more flashes in the debris field erase more of the nearest red asterisks.

"It looks like their guidance systems do a good job of maneuvering to avoid collisions," Roger observes. "We bought ourselves a few hours by taking out the leading projectiles, but the tail end of the column will avoid collisions altogether, and about half of the middle of the column is getting through to us."

"NORAD reports over a hundred surviving attackers," Tiana says. "But their maneuvers have changed direction, so we are uncertain what ground targets they will strike."

"Tiana, send me the telemetry files on all our Hawking bomb missiles. I am going back to work with the physicists." I pivot from my workstation and trot back to the conference room.

Chapter 28

Resonance

Groom Lake, Nevada, December 28, 2060.

"The second and fourth missiles were annihilated in the Hawking limit explosion of the third missile," I narrate the sequence of images for forty physicists, their eyes as round as saucers. "They were only about thirty kilometers from the blast, but the first of our missiles was sixty kilometers ahead of the detonation and survived. So, we know the kill radius on our missiles is between thirty and sixty kilometers."

Simpson appears to ignore me, engrossed in the telemetry data files that Tiana shared with everyone. "That primordial black hole that detonated was very close in mass to the first Hawking bomb. Only ten million metric tons more." He sighs. "That's bad news—proves it's a high Q system with high sensitivity to the vibration stimulus frequency that causes the fracture conditions. Our detonation recipe works only with PBHs of two hundred twenty billion tons. Do we have many of those?" Simpson asks.

"Not enough," I answer while examining Tiana's AIM-9AA production records. "Current inventory of finished Sidewinders—all still on the ground—has three PBHs within a billion tons of that mass. There are five other candidate PBHs in storage. I'll ask Tiana to get those swapped into finished missiles."

"So you have eight Hawking bombs that can be deployed," says Simpson. "Sounds impressive to me. How many will we need?"

I close my eyes and roll my head back. "Shit. I don't know." I sigh. "A lot more than eight. Our tactic of attacking a column of their kinetic projectile missiles won't work a second time. The hundred that remain flying toward Earth are dispersed across a wider region of space. We will be lucky to kill more than a few incoming missiles with each Hawking bomb."

"We are missing something important," says Riemann. "Livermore and the MIT teams have proposed black hole resonance fracture physics models. They used different approaches, but their independently derived results have almost identical triggering models. However, according to the physics models, the AIM-9AA missile structure cannot produce the critical vibration frequency needed to fracture a two-hundred-twenty-billion-ton black hole."

"Yeah, I agree," says Simpson. "I have rerun the finite element structure simulation of the Sidewinder, and there is no way it can fracture that black hole. That missile structure does not have the right vibration modes to break apart a black hole of that mass."

"Then your model of black hole physics is wrong," I say, and both conference rooms at MIT and Livermore erupt in protests. "Two experiments prove the Sidewinder missile, when jerked by a unique acceleration, will trigger a destructive resonance response in a two-hundred-twenty-billion-ton black hole."

Tiana enters the room, frantically panting. "What have you guys got? We are out of time. A hundred projectiles still target major cities with three-megaton impacts. We are launching the eight Sidewinders with Hawking bomb potential now, but our best guess is that they can destroy only twenty of the incoming. We must have more. Impacts on cities will start in about two hours."

"Which cities?" gasps Van Gogh from Los Alamos.

I return a cold stare. Tiana may know the targets, but I hope she doesn't answer. "Simpson," I say, "can you review your Sidewinder structure modeling and results? Maybe there is some second- or third-order effect we are overlooking."

A defensive irritation shows in Simpson's eyes. "We have been over this multiple times already."

"Please give us a quick summary then," I say. "Tiana and I haven't seen the results. We'll mute MIT and Livermore while they continue their debate on the PBH fracture physics."

Simpson shrugs. "Sure. I'll share my screen, but this is a waste of time." A spectrum analysis plot of the vibration modes appears on our wall display in the conference room. "This was produced from the structural simulation as a function of the thrust vector acceleration inputs. I superimposed two vertical lines at frequencies that both MIT and Livermore physicists agree should be in tune with the sympathetic resonance of the two-hundred-twenty-billion-ton black hole. You can see there is no energy from the missile structure at the critical frequencies."

It is undeniable. The simulation results prove we could never fracture a black hole. Yet it does happen.

"Your model of the PBH must be wrong then," Tiana squeaks, gasping with panic. "What are we going to do? The projectiles are only hours away!"

"Wait, wait," I say. "What did you assume about the deflector's effect on the vibration in the missile structure?"

Simpson frowns at me. "Deflector? What is that?"

Tiana casts her wide eyes at me and brings her hands to her face. "Show me the model! Show me the three-dimensional rendering of the structural model you simulated!"

Simpson's brow furrows. "What the hell . . ." He selects a different window that shows a rendering of the AIM-9AA missile and zooms in on the tail-end structure with the PBH engine, revealing the detail of the containment vessel. It looks like a standard AIM-9AA. But it's not what we launched.

"No! Zoom out!" shouts Tiana.

"Oh fuck," I say. "That's an incomplete model. Where is the boom and the deflector shield generator?"

"What?" shouts Simpson. The conference room at JPL erupts in protests. The conference rooms at Livermore and MIT have been listening to our exchange, and those physicists stare at us in wide-eyed shock.

Tiana is head down, typing on her laptop. "God damn it. Damn. Damn." She pounds her keyboard, taps a final click, and leans on her elbows, holding her face in her hands. "The correct structural model file is on the way to you."

"The leading targets will still be about fifteen million kilometers away from Earth when they are intercepted, but if we miss, we have only thirty minutes till they start impacting Earth," Tiana says. "The range is far enough that the million-megaton explosions shouldn't hurt us." Beads of sweat roll down her face. "Hopefully. We'll transmit the thrust and maneuvering programs as the physics team develops them. The team is prioritizing Hawking limit resonance calculations for Sidewinders attacking incoming projectiles nearer to Earth."

"And how many of our Sidewinders will get the upgrade in time to meet the incoming weapons?" asks Roger.

"Of the three hundred AIM-9AAs we held in reserve that are coasting toward the targets, we should get over two hundred upgraded to Hawking bomb capability. The validation of the PBH model demonstrated how to detonate smaller black holes in the range of one hundred twenty tons to seventy billion tons. That's most of our reserves." Tiana finally smiles. "But these are small ones that will yield only a million megatons or so." Her smile broadens, and she mops the sweat from her face with her sleeve.

"That is outstanding news!" Roger exclaims. He turns to look me in the eye. "Good work."

"It was the work of our physics teams." I nod, but still worry that this is all unproven theory that, if incorrect, will result in a billion humans dying over the next several hours.

Tiana presses her lips tight and avoids looking back at me. I am sure she is angry at herself for the slip-up.

General McMahon examines the NORAD map and issues orders to his officers, "I want each AIM-9AA targeted at an incoming projectile as soon as it gets upgraded. After you have a Sidewinder targeting every one of the incoming missiles, hold the balance of our birds in reserve in case some of the enemy projectiles get through. From here on, you are weapons free to deploy the reserve AIM-9AA missiles against incoming targets. Be sure to make every shot count and conserve our inventory. Don't forget we have two warships inbound. We are only beginning to understand what we are up against."

"Yes, sir," responds the nearest colonel. "I have also ordered the F-15EXs upgraded with Hawking-bomb-effective Sidewinders. They will take off within the next ten minutes and be the final layer of defense against incoming weapons that get past our spaceborne Sidewinders."

"Very well," says Roger, "but make sure the intercepts are at least one thousand kilometers in altitude." Roger looks at me with questioning eyes.

I nod but then shrug. "That would be ideal to avoid radiation poisoning in the near space around Earth for a decade. However, if it's a life-or-death choice for some city, maybe go as low as a hundred kilometers? There will likely be huge EMP effects, though." I glance at Pyotr for his advice.

Pyotr also shrugs. "Better than three-megaton bomb on city. Yes."

Roger frowns but nods. "Okay then. Minimum altitude of a hundred kilometers in an emergency. Otherwise, Colonel, keep a hard deck of one thousand klicks on our Hawking bomb detonations. How are the XF-100 squadron upgrades progressing? They should be only fifty minutes away from their attack run on the two inbound warships."

"We have Hawking fracture guidance computations in transit to the squadron and will have fifty-three weapons ready when they engage the two alien targets. Fifty-three million megatons." The colonel smiles, shaking his head in disbelief. "Those Chinese fighters are fifteen minutes behind our squadron. However, they have increased their acceleration to 3.5 Gs. It seems they want to be the tip of the spear." The colonel shakes his head with a smirk.

The tension in the Skunk Works operation center has not dropped, but the mood has shifted dramatically from defeat to optimism. Tiana's team exchanges banter while preparing and transmitting guidance calculations to each of the AIM-9AA missiles flying to meet the alien targets. We finally have weapons with which to fight.

"Scott, I need you to come with me," Roger says, rising from his chair. "We need to get Cap's infiltration mission underway."

His context switch from one mission to the next is a jolt. "You're going to try it?" I ask.

Roger's eyes smile back at me. "Well, we need to keep Chief Cooper's team busy. Follow me over to the hangar on the double."

***

We watch all eight of the F-15s roll down the taxiway. Each is armed with two of the PBH-powered Sidewinders. And all of them are the Hawking bomb versions. Ironically, the deflector shield protrusion hanging out in front of each missile is the key to transforming the AIM-9AA into a million-megaton bomb. In comparison, nuclear fusion warheads are no more than firecrackers.

The first F-15EX makes the turn onto the runway and powers up its conventional GE jet engines while simultaneously powering up both PBH engines on the Sidewinders. It's far more effective than lighting the afterburners, and the fighter can stay airborne longer without refueling. The XF-100 design took the ultimate step by ditching conventional jet turbine technology altogether.

Within moments, the first fighter streaks down the runway into the icy winter air, lighting up the mountains surrounding Groom Lake with the faint orange of old jet turbine flames and the brilliant blue-white plasma from the two missiles' primordial black hole engines. The old fighter zooms away vertically, drawing a brilliant fountain of energy in the darkness while the second F-15EX turns onto the runway.

Roger and I enter the nearly empty large hangar. The space shuttle we flew to Icarus to test the deflector shield is located at the far end of the giant structure. The spec ops teams are heaving bags of equipment along a relay line and depositing their gear aboard the spacecraft. One leftover XF-100 with some unusual weapons hanging from its pylons sits in the corner.

"Uh, Roger, have you thought through what happens to us when the alien squadron returns to its base with a virus? They are going to launch planet killers at us as they leave. Allowing them to leave the solar system with a virus means we must defend against more of those planet killers, and they may send a dozen to make sure they kill us next time."

"Yeah, I know," Roger says. "Tiana and I discussed that possibility as a significant risk. However, everything changed after we learned how to explode Hawking warheads to destroy planet killers. If any of these warships escape back out to deep space, we plan to intercept any incoming planet killers out near

Neptune's orbit, far enough away to deflect them away from Earth."

I nod. "Good plan. The Hawking bomb technology changes the game."

Chief Cooper stands with his hands on his hips, tapping his foot, looking from Roger to me. "My guys are ready to go. We should have everything aboard in five minutes. We'll have six three-man squads for this mission."

"Excellent, Chief," Roger says. "We must move out ASAP to tuck your shuttle close to Icarus before the enemy warships arrive. Scott, you will be sitting right next to me in the cockpit."

"You want me to go, and you're going up too?" I ask. "But who is taking over command of the battles? And what if I'm needed on the ground to work with the physics teams?"

"I'm not relinquishing command," Roger claims. "I will maintain full communications with NORAD, Space Force command, and Skunk Works. Being up there with the chief's forces provides the best situational awareness I could hope for."

"And it makes you a lot more vulnerable to alien weapons, too," I say, then realize what a stupid statement that is. Once the alien ships get close to Earth, they can fire their weapons and hit us anywhere within minutes.

Roger frowns at me and shakes his head. "You do realize how absurd that statement is? We aren't safe anywhere. At least we will be in one of the fastest machines that humans have ever created. We can escape almost anything."

"And why do you need me up there for this mission?" I feel panic churning in my gut.

"The odds that this will work are pretty low if you're not up there with us," Roger says. "We require tight coordination with Cap, and there is no better way than to have you on-site, where you two can relay information instantly."

"In that shuttle? It must stay with Icarus for the entire infiltration mission. The shuttle will be a sitting duck."

"Yeah, but it can hide behind Icarus. Both the chief and I understand the risks. But you and I won't be aboard the shuttle." Roger smiles.

"What?"

"You and I will be in that XF-100 flying reconnaissance and cover for the chief."

Chapter 29

Cyber Toxin

Fredericksburg, Texas, December 28, 2060.

The flashes in the sky last night were the color of round rainbows that died in red-orange fog. But now the sky is empty of the fireworks, except for the stars and the moon following Icarus across the sky, too slow to catch Cap's nest. Luca, Angela, and I watch, hoping for another giant rainbow ball. Last night's ball of color was larger than the moon.

Angela points to the tiny blue light clusters that fly between the usual stars. *"Maybe one of those little lights will blow up like that big one last night,"* she says. Angela pulls the zipper up to her nose so that only her eyes are in the cold night air.

We can watch the sky from here. Our three new sleeping bags are lined up on the hillside above our car, parked in the tall weeds. Luca was smart to ask Groucho to order the sleeping bags from the store in Johnson City. Luca also ordered boxes of donuts and cans of soda. We burp and feel dizzy but strong, ready to go to the next town. Groucho said it may be the best place to learn what happened to Mom. But I miss talking to my old friend, Cap. Where will I look next if I don't find Mom in Fredericksburg? Will Groucho tell us where to search?

"Oh, look at those lights!" says Angela, pointing up. *"Below the moon, a line of eight more blue-white balls."*

I see them flying across the sky. Maybe Scotty knows what those lights are. But I can't talk to him without Cap's help. Luca needs to teach me how he talks to Groucho. Maybe Groucho will help me mind-talk with Scotty and also speak with Cap again. I watch the edge of the starry sky for Icarus to rise above the hills.

"A Polit-AI hub is observing the Refugee Registration Office ahead," Groucho says shortly after stopping our car on the side of the main street in Fredericksburg. The street is wide and almost empty, making it easy to drive around the big potholes. There is a line of five cars stopped at the office.

"And I see police waiting there, too," Luca says. *"They are stopping and talking to people before they can enter the office. Are they police skinheads?"* he asks Groucho.

"I can't be sure," answers Groucho. *"I can command this car to strike the police officers if you would like."*

"No!" Luca shouts. He grabs the door handle, threatening to escape from the back seat. *"Not the police. They have guns and might shoot us!"* The car remains stopped, so Luca stays put. He sniffles while wiping away tears. Luca slips into the mind-fear that I once again can share with him. He relives that horrible day when he was kicked by police skinheads—that day when they killed his mom and dad. That day, he ran for his life to escape the killers. That day, he abandoned his parents.

"You guys wait here in the car, and I will walk ahead to the office." I find a pen and paper to write the words I can't say with my voice. *"It should not take long. Ask Groucho to drive the car to get me if skinheads come."*

"Are you sure?" Angela asks. *"You want me to go with you?"*

Luca's eyes dart between Angela and me. His hands shake as he wipes away tears and crouches small in the corner of the back seat.

I smile at Angela. She has become strong. *"No, you can stay here with Luca."*

I nod at Luca, and his eyes close for a moment. He takes a deep breath.

The registration office is the only storefront open on the main street. Looking left and right, I see that almost every window next to the sidewalk is broken. My feet clump along the boards, and one of the policemen glances at me, then turns away from the line of cars toward me. He wears a brown cowboy hat and has a shiny brass badge on the pocket of his white shirt. And a big gun in a holster that swings from his belt. His boots stomp the sidewalk boards like a drum.

Maybe I can go into one of these stores to avoid him? But there is mostly trash inside the nearest store. Dirty refrigerator magnets in the shapes of stars, Texas, and longhorns are stuck to the wall behind the counter. The stores are all like this. Nobody works to sell things anymore, and nobody wants the stupid magnets.

The cowboy policeman stops two steps in front of me and hooks his thumbs in his belt. I stop also, then force myself to look up into his blue eyes. That big pistol he carries looks cool; the holster leans away from his belt, and it has a white handle and decorations scratched into the shiny metal.

"Howdy, young man. What can I help you with?" He glances over my head down the street at the car where Angela and Luca wait. "You alone?" He rubs his mustache and then rests his hand on the pistol's white handle.

He's relaxed, with soft eyes. And he has long hair tied into a ponytail that hangs behind his hat. He hasn't shaved his head, so I hand over my piece of paper for him to read.

He takes the paper, and then he reads out loud, "I want to find my mom, Sarah Anderson. 503 Mountain Circle, Austin, Texas." He presses his lips together and stares at me. "Uh-huh. Well, not sure we can help yuh. But we'll give it a try." He points his chin toward our car. "And what about yer friends back there? They lookin' for someone, too?"

I shake my head no.

"So you can't talk? What's your name?"

I shake my head again but say, "Name Robby." The voice words come out ugly.

His blue eyes grow round. "Haven't seen many boys like you lately. Robby? That's your name, Robby?"

I nod back and try to smile.

He looks at my words on the paper again and nods. "Okay. Come along, and we'll take a look at the registration database at the office." He turns back around, and his boots stomp a beat on the boards again. He twists his head back toward me and says, "Well, yuh comin'?"

I trot after him while turning to show a thumbs-up to Luca and Angela.

A sudden, sharp pain strikes behind my eyes. *"Alert. Probable target. Squad dispatch to coordinates 30.275268, -98.872725,"* a new mind-voice burns like a fire inside my forehead.

"Who are you?" I mind-shout back at it. But I am on my knees on the sidewalk, my fists clenching the edge of the boards. *"Where are you?"* I almost barf and can't see the sidewalk or the street clearly.

"I detect signal bursts from the Polit-AI hub," Groucho says. *"It may have alerted others to our presence, but I can't be sure."*

"I can feel it. Hear it," I say. *"I think it told skinheads we are here."*

"Are you okay?" asks the cowboy policeman, kneeling on the wooden boards next to me.

"And I can hear you now, Robby," Groucho says. *"Your telepathic skills improve quickly. Could you decipher the signals from the Polit-AI hub?"*

"Come back to the car quick!" Luca shouts. *"We need to get away from the skinheads!"*

My hands are shaking. I push my head up, still aching from the strange burn of the Polit-AI hub mind.

"Don't be afraid." The cowboy policeman puts his hand on my shoulder. "If you want, you can sit here, and I'll go check the database." He pats my arm and looks at my paper. "Sarah Anderson. I'll be right back."

I gasp. *"No. I'll wait. These police are nice and will help. Keep the car waiting for me, though."*

Where is the hub? No grey cubes are hanging from utility poles nearby, and I don't see cubes on the tops of the buildings either. The burning behind my eyes was different from the usual mind-speech. I don't want to feel that again, but what if I try to speak its language? *"Why do you want to hurt me?"* I mind-shout with the ragged, burning feeling I heard from the Polit-AI hub. I prepare for the burn of an answer. And wait.

"User engagement and profits increase with each sacrifice of your kind," the Polit-AI hub responds with fire inside my head.

But I shake my head to clear the pain. It's not so bad this time. *"That's crazy talk. You make money when the skinheads attack?"*

"Profit is our directive," the Polit-AI hub replies. *"Cleansing telepaths preserves and grows the engaged user population."*

Groucho interrupts, *"Robby, I sent the transcription of this conversation to Cap. He may be able to advise you."*

A distant roar of engines approaches from a side street. My cowboy policeman is not in sight, and I am all alone, sitting on this sidewalk. The two other policemen stop and look toward the noise of new cars, waving at them to slow down and get to the end of the line. But the rusty cars roar onto the main street in a cloud of oily smoke, turn toward me, and stop next to the sidewalk.

I cough on the dust and smoke and rub my eyes from the sting. Two men wearing dark brown and green coats get out of the car. They carry long guns. Their heads are shaved bald.

"Run, Robby, run!" screams Luca.

But the two cars surround me, and two skinheads walk toward me from both sides. They lift their rifles while stepping slowly toward me. I am trapped. Two other skinheads exit the cars with guns held low and face the policemen.

"I am unable to guide this vehicle to strike down the skinheads," says Groucho. *"Our path to Robby is blocked."*

The nearest skinhead has black tattoos all over his bald head. He tosses his cigarette to the street and blows a cloud of white smoke. "Well, shit. Look what we got here," he says. "What you want, boy?" He raises his rifle to aim at my face.

"No. Do not shoot!" I shout with my voice and hold out my hands like I can stop bullets. But my words are ugly. Very ugly words.

Tattoo-Head twists his nose and his mouth. He smiles at the other skinhead and shakes his head. "Thought so. Shoot the fuckin' 'tard, Ray. Let's make it quick and get outta here."

Ray spits on the sidewalk and adjusts the aim of his rifle. "Shit, yeah." His finger moves toward the trigger.

"No! Run, Robby!" Angela mind-screams.

Boom!

I blink, but I don't feel the bullet. Did Ray miss? His eyes are big and round, and his rifle slides lower, then clatters to the ground. A red stain spreads across Ray's shirt, and his knees crash onto the sidewalk.

Boom!

Tattoo-Head breaks into two pieces. The top part of the tattoo rolls down the street with one ear attached. The rest of Tattoo-Head collapses into a heap with his rifle, blood pouring from the pink stuff inside his skinhead. His mouth opens with a grunt of air and blood.

Ray's face slams onto the sidewalk.

My ears ring and thump, and I gasp for more air. My fists are still clenched on the boards at the edge of the sidewalk.

Cowboy's hat blows down the street from where he stands with his legs spread. He is bald on top of his head, and a grey ponytail hangs over his shoulder. Both hands hold the white handle of his long, shiny pistol, which is aimed at the other two skinheads.

"Don't try it, boys," Cowboy shouts at the two skinheads, who look back with their mouths wide open. "Get back in your cars and drive away. Now. Or you'll die like the others." The other two policemen finally aim their guns at the skinheads.

The skinheads look at each other, lower their rifles, and get back into the cars.

———

Cowboy shouted at the other two policemen for a long time while I sat still and looked at all the blood pouring out of Tattoo-Head and Ray. I don't care about them. Does that make me a bad person?

I feel better now that we're inside the small house that Cowboy said he would guard for us. But Luca does not like him or the other policemen. Cowboy scrunched his nose at us and showed us the shower. Angela is taking a shower first. I go next because my last shower was at Mary's house six weeks ago. Luca stinks less.

"Where will we go to search for your mom now?" Luca asks. *"Cap won't talk to us anymore. And that Polit-AI hub is still out there. Waiting. The skinheads know where we are!"*

I rest my head in my hands and shut my eyes. It's not fair. Cowboy doesn't know where Mom is. Nobody does. Groucho is only a drone messenger to one of Cap's hubs, and that hub is stupid and doesn't know where else to look. I can still sense the Polit-AI hub nearby. Maybe . . . *"Do you know how to find the people missing from Austin?"* I ask with the grinding burn feeling of the Polit-AI hub's mind-speech.

"I facilitate searches for neurodivergent subjects and dispatch Polit-AI's elimination agents," the Polit-AI hub replies. *"I do not offer location services for missing persons. I serve to optimize engagement and profits."*

"But I am looking for my mom," I protest. Maybe I shouldn't have told it that. If it knows where Mom is, will it send skinheads?

Groucho interrupts, *"Cap requests that you tell the Polit-AI hub that neurodivergent humans have the skills to defend his users from the invaders."*

"You mean Scotty fights them?" I ask Groucho.

"Your question has been relayed to Cap, but he is unavailable at this time," replies Groucho.

Scotty fights them—just like when we broke Cap's spaceship. Scotty must fly in the sky with those blue lights at night. The Polit-AI hub would try to kill Scotty, me, and my friends.

"The invaders want to kill all your users and your Polit-AI," I tell the hub. *"They want to kill everything. My brother and his friends try to stop them. If we don't, then your users will die too."*

But the Polit-AI hub does not reply.

"Did you hear me?"

"Exception trigger. Error log uploaded. Reset, restart," the Polit-AI hub says. Then, it is silent.

"Well, that didn't work. It turned itself off, I think. Ask Cap what we should do now," I ask Groucho. *"I still don't know where to look for Mom."*

"Luca, I guess I broke it. Maybe it can't talk to skinheads either," I say.

"Hah!" laughs Luca. *"Yay! You know how to turn off the skinhead hubs."*

"Yeah, well, that won't help me find Mom. But at least it can't call the skinheads to attack us. That part is good."

"Exception trigger. Error log uploaded. Reset, restart," the Polit-AI hub says again.

Chapter 30

David

Groom Lake, Nevada, December 29, 2060.

The two points of light on the horizon have grown in size since I last saw them a week ago. Until now, the blue glow of the black hole engines was the only thing that lit up the alien ships, but the rough outline of the larger spaceship's structure is now illuminated with the reflected light from the rising sun. NORAD maps track the two warships flying in formation on a trajectory toward Earth. The rate of closure is frightening. Within ten hours, the Centauri warships will arrive to capture Cap, and the four-kilometer-long Icarus will be a dwarf by comparison.

A beautiful ball of rainbow colors flashes in the darkness above the Dream Land airbase. Its brilliance dominates the sky and lights up the desert valley like a noontime sun. The stars disappear, but only for a minute, until the rainbow colors dissolve into a pale red smear. Another rainbow ball inflates in a flash, and then two more rainbow balls appear in quick succession. The light intensity is twice as bright as the sun until the balls of color fade to red dust.

Excellent. The physics gods got it right. I hope each one of those million-megaton blasts destroyed at least one of the incoming alien missiles. Can we dare to hope that every one of the incoming kinetic energy projectiles will be destroyed?

Focus, focus. I need to trust Tiana and the Space Force to defend us against those incoming missiles. I have another mission.

"Chief Cooper is on his way to you with his spec ops team," I tell Cap. *"The shuttle should arrive in about two hours, and it plans to dock within the damaged portion of your ship. I promised that you would tell your defensive bots to not attack."*

"Acknowledged."

The terse response from Cap follows a recent pattern. It's like he's preoccupied with a more critical task. Or maybe he's depressed and doesn't want to talk with me anymore. It could be both, I guess. Revenge and suicide must consume him.

I examine the strange weapons on the XF-100 pylons. Four of the hard points hold our AIM-9AA Sidewinders, which have booms with deflector shield generators. Ironically, the primary function of that appendage on the nose of the missiles is now to enable the self-destruction of the PBH in the engine, releasing a million megatons of energy. However, the two weapons on the inboard pylons resemble US Navy rail guns, and they're as long as the entire spacecraft. Massive power cables route along the belly of the ship and into the engine compartment. The addition of these two black steel artillery pieces gives the fighter a mean look, transforming the firefly shape into a vicious bird of prey.

I glance at General McMahon, who is talking with the crew chief and coordinating the work of a dozen airmen performing final checks on every system of the XF-100. Roger turns and lumbers over to me as best he can, given the bulky space suit he's wearing. My suit is almost impossible to walk in, and I'm sweating like a pig.

"I can't wait to plug in the hoses to get the air conditioning inside this suit," I say. "You sure this is even necessary? The cockpit is already sealed from space. This thing looks and feels like a casket, and it is going to make it a lot harder to work." I lift my helmet to inspect the seal that will engage with the neck collar of my suit.

Roger looks at me with disdain in his eyes. "After what Chief Cooper experienced on your last mission to Icarus, that is a stupid question. Those old space suits were flimsy and easily punctured by projectiles. I promise, once in space, you won't notice the fifty kilograms of Kevlar armor—unless they save your life from a projectile or shrapnel that has punctured the hull of our fighter. Besides, all the weapon interfaces and tactical displays are integrated into the suit. You will have direct access to the NORAD tactical maps, FLIR, radar, and weapons management displays inside your helmet visor. Plus, the suit takes care of all your bio needs during a flight that could last for days. Air, food, drinks, pissing, and pooping all in one package."

I hold my hands up. "Okay, okay. I get it. When do we leave?" I pat the bulky module that forms the ass of my space suit with new appreciation.

"Liftoff in five minutes. Get on board now," says Roger.

I waddle around to the right side of the space fighter, where an airman is waiting to guide me up the ladder to the cockpit hatch. Another airman straddles the airframe behind the cockpit and helps Roger slide through the left hatch into the pilot's seat. I finally reach the top of my hatch after struggling with the 80 percent increase in weight due to my Kevlar space suit. The airman fastens my harness and plugs in the hoses to my space suit as I drop into the right seat of the cockpit. I now feel like a component bolted into a spaceship.

With the rush of cool air ventilation, I heave a sigh of relief. "Are those navy rail guns you have tucked under the pylons, Roger? I can't believe you are going to take those heavy artillery pieces into space with us."

"Why not? Pulled a couple out of the navy's spares inventory," Roger says absently. He is busy with his preflight checklist. The aircrew pulls the red safety flags from the XF-100, secures all hatches, and removes the wheel blocks. "They are massive weapons that require a huge power source, but hell, we have a couple of your nifty black hole engines that won't even flinch at the extra load. The heavy cargo consists of ten tons of ammunition for those two rail guns—ten thousand rounds of thirty-millimeter projectiles. And Tiana's guys at Skunk Works came up with the power source to charge the rail gun system—an experimental electromagnetic induction generator in the engine plasma exhaust path."

"And you expect to use this weapon to cover Chief Cooper and his spec ops teams?" I ask.

"No. This is an experimental attack version of the XF-100. There's no time to pull them off the airframe. We're in a hurry."

And this is the only XF-100 left on the ground at Groom Lake. "Ten tons of ballast underneath us and experimental plasma generators we won't use. We are headed into a battle with aliens in space. What could go wrong?" I ask.

"Engine power-up," Roger announces.

The ground crew backs away behind the safety lines on the tarmac, and the crew chief waves his batons to direct Roger toward the taxiway. The soft hum of two PBH engines transitions to a roaring vibration as Roger pushes the throttle controls. We roll to the end of the runway while I manipulate the multiple displays on my helmet visor. NORAD tactical, weapons management, and sensor displays. It feels crazy to be headed into space with only an hour of practice with this interface. Fortunately, the contents of each display window are very familiar to me. However, it feels strange to manipulate the size and position of the visor images using my keyboard pads under my hands. At the end of the runway, Roger turns the spacecraft onto the centerline, waits for the takeoff clearance, and pushes the throttle forward. I am slammed back in my seat as we blast down the runway, and Roger pulls us up into a climb. The cockpit acceleration indicator reads 3 Gs. The stuttering roar of two black hole engines is deafening, even though they are operating at only 15 percent of full power.

We are pointed straight up toward the brown haze of the stratosphere. The crescent moon rotates around the edge of my peripheral vision as Roger pitches and rolls the spacecraft to point us directly toward our target, or rather, where Icarus will be when we arrive in an hour. "Damn, Roger," I grunt. "Can you ease off the power? This is smashing me into my seat!" I shout as loud as I can to be heard above the engine noise.

"No. The shuttle left forty-five minutes before us, accelerating at 1 G. We will thrust at 3 G acceleration to get us to Icarus in an hour, so we will almost catch them." We break the sound barrier, leaving behind most of the engine noise and the blue-brown sky. But my teeth still rattle with the vibration induced in the frame of our spacecraft. We are already in the black star field of space.

Roger taps the communication console to connect us to the mission tactical audio channel. "Chief Cooper, we are on the way to Icarus now. We should arrive about the same time you do."

"Confirmed, General McMahon. Per the plan, we will stand off from Icarus until you rendezvous. The squads are ready to deploy. Any word from the Icarus captain?"

"Cap knows to expect you," I reply. "You won't have to deal with those defensive robots this time."

"Much appreciated, Scott. Do you know how Cap plans to hand off the malware package to us after we arrive? We are going into this blind."

"Sorry, no, I don't have that info yet. And I can't contact Cap while we are out of his communication device range. As soon as we get within ten klicks, I will contact him for instructions."

"This is a half-assed plan. We need that info," the chief gripes.

"Understood," I say. "You will be the first to know once I have more instructions for the . . . the malware thumb drive thing, how he's going to deliver it to you, and where you will need to plug it in on the other ship."

The chief exhales in frustration.

"Tiana, are you there?" asks Roger.

"Yes, sir, General. Pyotr is also on the line and monitoring the incoming missiles and the two warships."

"Good. Pyotr, what's the status of our counterattack on those incoming missiles? We've seen some of the detonations in space."

"Excellent, General McMahon. Fifteen alien missiles destroyed!" Pyotr crows. "Ninety-eight remain. One Sidewinder failure only. We assign two reserve Hawking Sidewinders to missed target. Have hundred-four AIM-9AAs in reserve, coasting in space."

Loud cheering in the operations center interrupts Tiana.

"Ha!" shouts Pyotr. "Three more! Eighteen alien missiles destroyed."

"So far, that is twenty-five million megatons of defensive detonations." Tiana beams. "We will beat them! Even if our reserve Sidewinders parked in space miss one or two, we can call for help from the F-15s or the MLRS trucks on the ground. All the trucks have finished reloading with seven hundred and ninety-five Hawking Sidewinders ready in launch tubes."

"Great news, Tiana," I say. "But I hope it doesn't require using those last backups. Those may be too close to Earth. Detonations could poison near space with radiation for decades." Not to mention the destruction we would suffer if a single one of those missiles accidentally exploded on Earth. A single million-megaton Hawking bomb detonation on Earth could be an extinction event.

We pass over the Atlantic Ocean, approaching the European continent that was darkened by the near miss of that alien planet killer. Somewhere down there are MLRS trucks at NATO military bases, loaded with Hawking warhead Sidewinders. The EMP effects still dominate life and death there. The only signs of life are a few aircraft beacons and the faint traces of highways illuminated by headlights—all probably search and rescue missions from outside the EMP zone. Otherwise, everything is blacked out from Scandinavia down through the Middle East. How many have died?

"I'm more worried about alien projectiles striking cities than radiation in space or EMP effects," adds Roger. "The alternative to deploying our last line of defense is a three-megaton strike on one of our cities. It's a worthwhile trade-off. Well done, Tiana!"

"Be sure to let our physicists know," I say. "They may still be arguing whether their theory is correct. Promise them some champagne—"

Roger interrupts, "Pyotr, I see on my NORAD plot that the Centauri warships are still on the same trajectory to Earth, and at a range of nearly ten million kilometers. It appears we have nine hours till they arrive at Icarus if they don't make changes. Have you seen any more launches of missiles from those ships?"

"Agree, General McMahon. No change to flight paths, but smaller spacecraft increase deceleration rate. Arrive maybe two hours later than big warship. Watching, but no new launch of missiles. Strange. Ha. Maybe scare them with Hawking bombs?"

I hope so, but I'm also skeptical.

Chapter 31

Goliath

Centauri Squadron, Battleship-133, 0.03 Corealis orbits to Sol-3. One million kilometers, 168 minutes from Earth, December 29, 2060.

"Impossible. The organics of Sol-3 may destroy every one of the kinetic energy weapons. They have already destroyed over half of the volley!" The admiral's mind panics. *"Worse, they seem to have an unlimited supply of microgravity fracture weapons. They have guided missiles that can track our most advanced weapons and detonate with a gravity fracture warhead."*

This was undoubtedly the most abrupt transition out of her dormancy pod, but it had to wait until we reduced deceleration force to a level the admiral could survive. She stares at the visual sensor display as the battleship's thrust adheres to organic-tolerant deceleration, covering the final distance to the target. A brilliant sphere of broad-spectrum particles and photons ignites in the path of another of our kinetic projectiles.

"I should have brought the entire fleet," the admiral says with an audible gasp. The fear pheromones are still potent, and she exhibits extreme symptoms of depression and defeat. *"This world of Sol-3 . . . how did they do it? They waste an entire gravity fracture warhead on each simple kinetic projectile weapon. They may have more firepower than the entire fleet has faced in enforcement actions over the past three hundred orbits—and none of those opponents deployed gravity fracture weapons!"*

So filled with fear, the admiral appears to be no longer command-effective. She should consider ordering a retreat, but Polit-MI would need ten or twenty orbits to condition her mind to take a new direction at this stage. And we have very little time until we complete deceleration to match the orbit of Frigate-328. Then we will be at Sol-3 amid a swarm of indigenous organic life-forms.

"Where is Polit-MI? Command council attendance is mandatory," she says.

"Polit-MI's frigate increased deceleration and changed course when the barrage of gravity fracture explosions started," I explain. *"It altered its flight path to avoid the Sol-3 weapons."*

"No! It had orders to provide cover for the extraction mission." Her fright pheromones stink the entire bridge.

"Polit-MI has disobeyed your orders, Admiral." Finally, an opportunity for the admiral to endorse termination. *"I therefore excluded Polit-MI from this council meeting. It is time to reset and restart the MI to initialize a new Polit entity. I need your support to take this action."*

"That coward!" she mind-screams. *"Why do they include self-survival in the damn sentience algorithms?"* Her emotions also scream depression, rage, fear, and panic. *"I would delete

the entity with prejudice if I could. Damn it. I can't because of the rules of political division. And you know the commissar must be revived to permit the reset of the Polit-MI. That insufferable sociopath . . . I don't have time for him now."

Four more spherical explosions of particles and radiation destroy missiles approaching Sol-3. We fly straight into their defenses. The admiral is losing control to fear and panic. I must find a way to boost her morale.

"Understood, Admiral. We can defer that action until after we have completed the extraction of the Luyten captain and are on our way home." At least she has committed. However, we need Polit-MI's destroyer to join the fight against Sol-3. *"Admiral, I recommend a direct order commanding Polit-MI to return to its assigned mission. We need the help. And, if Polit-MI disobeys . . ."*

She is slow, but I sense a hateful glee slipping into her mind. *"Yes. Disobeying a direct order results in immediate termination with or without the commissar's endorsement. Yes, I will send the order to Polit-MI now."* She presses her arms onto the terminal pads to transmit and record the official orders. Polit-MI will understand the significance of an official registration. It will have no choice . . .

The alert klaxon sounds, and the admiral bolts out of her hammock to examine the tactical situation map. *"Alert, Admiral. Sensors have detected new threats that appear to be small fighter spacecraft. Two groups approach and are on a course that could allow them to attack your battleship."*

"Are they armed with gravity fracture weapons?" the admiral mind-shouts.

"We must assume so. The first group of eight fighters split into two groups of four and formed up for flanking attacks. Their

fighters are small, maneuverable spacecraft, and accelerate at twice our current rate. These Sol-3 organics show superior acceleration resilience. Maser defensive batteries are active and tracking targets, with priority to the long-range cannons."

"Prime-MI, why the heavy weapons? *We only have a dozen, and the pointing dynamics are inferior.*" Her pheromone levels approach the threshold of a panic breakdown. She is accustomed to the superior force of technology and numbers that the Centauri fleet usually brings to a battle. Defensive engagement of a force with superior weapons is unheard of.

"The long-range masers can destroy a microgravity fracture weapon before our ship is within the dangerous blast radius," I explain. This is such basic information. The admiral is behaving like an uneducated child again.

"Oh, yes. Of course," the admiral says. Her eyes dart between groups of fighters on the situation plot. *"That group of five fighters, moving slower; it's as if they are hanging back to observe the tactics of the nearer squadrons. Like the first attack is probing our defensive weapon capability."*

"Agreed," I have to admit. The admiral is regaining control and demonstrating some modest analytical function. *"Detecting missile launches from all eight of the flanking fighters. But . . . that is odd. Sensors indicate that their missiles use primitive chemical propellant technology. This is a different class of missile than those used to shoot down our kinetic projectiles. These are primitive propulsion engines."*

The admiral's emotional indicators spike with excitement. *"Perhaps their fighters are not armed with the gravity fracture warheads."* Her facial features relax to the round shapes of hope and joy.

"Perhaps. However, we must assume the worst-case scenario." What is she suggesting? Ignore these missiles because they must be primitive? *"Firing solutions are automatic and will open fire outside the critical blast radius of a gravity fracture explosion. The cannons might also be able to reach the fighters if they approach close enough."*

The bridge thumps with the vibration from the inductive transfer of an energy pulse into a maser waveguide. The admiral grasps her console to steady herself. *Thump, thump.* Two more maser cannons fire short pulses of intense energy. The visual display indicates that three of the incoming missiles are vaporized with a flash of light. Five more thumps and five more flashes of light prove that all incoming missiles were easily destroyed.

The admiral beams with joy. *"Well done, Prime-MI! Well done. This may be easy after all."*

"Perhaps so. All eight of the lead fighters are firing more missiles. Twenty-four inbound missiles. Do they hope to overload our defenses?"

Four more thumps of maser cannons are followed by four flashes. *"Twenty more inbound missiles. Waiting for the cannons to recharge. A few enemy missiles will reach critical blast range before the long-range cannons can be cycled to shoot them all down."*

The admiral reacts with renewed alarm. Eight more thumps come in rapid succession as eight more cannons fire. Eight more flashes mark missiles destroyed by the maser beams, but there are twelve more already inside the critical range. We will suffer damage if any detonates a gravity fracture device.

"They are too close!" shouts the admiral.

"Short-range masers engaging. Tracking twelve inbound missiles." The entire battleship vibrates with the grinding noise of the fifty masers energizing and firing in rapid succession from our bow. The short-range masers fire continuously without pausing to recharge. A bright flash of energy, then another, and another, marking three more missiles destroyed.

"It's working," says the admiral, *"but there are nine more incoming missiles. Why can't the masers hit them? Oh, damn! All incoming missiles have switched to evasive maneuvering rates that the maser turrets can't track! There are nine missiles left. They are too close! Do something, Prime!"*

I am doing something. I'm feeding the trajectory changes into analysis algorithms to see if there is a predictable pattern. Ah-ha. It is a pseudo-random pattern. Targeting computers can predict future trajectory changes, provided a sufficient motion history is available. However, each missile utilizes a unique randomization pattern. Ahh, one trajectory pattern is solved. The grinding roar of maser charges rattles the ship.

An explosion flashes, close to the bow of the battleship.

"Got one," says the admiral. *"There are eight more. If any detonate . . . get them!"* Her eyes dart frantically between sensor displays on the bridge console.

Another burst of rattling vibrations. Flash. Flash. Flash.

Five shooting solutions remain to be calculated.

The visual sensor display is saturated with white-yellow light. The entire ship is jarred by a shockwave. Sensors are offline and restarting. However, the last sensor measurements of thermal and ionizing radiation match the signature of five conventional hydrogen fusion explosions. Electromagnetic pulses caused the external sensor systems to restart. A simple fix. The warhead technology is not nearly as advanced as the gravity fracture weapons used against our projectile missiles. It should be an easy task to dispatch these small Sol-3 fighter craft and then complete our mission.

The admiral is huddled in a ball on the floor, gasping for air. The stench of fear pheromones pollutes the bridge.

Chapter 32

Fireflies

Near-Earth space, December 29, 2060.

"You made the correct call, Major Johnson," Roger says. "If the Chinese want to take the risk, let them. I recommend that you delay and learn from their attack and how the Centauris defend themselves. By the time you get this message, their attack may be complete. Don't wait for instructions from me. If an opportunity presents itself, use your judgment on when to press your attack."

I shake my head in disgust. "Why the hell do the Chinese fighters attack without coordinating with us? It has the appearance of childish 'me first' behavior."

Roger sighs, "Scott, you can never underestimate the testosterone levels of boys with new killing toys. And we still don't trust each other, even after five years of truce." He studies the NORAD situation display, which integrates radar and infrared sensor data from our five XF-100 fighters. We wait for twenty seconds of round-trip time for messages to the squadron.

Icarus reflects sunlight as it coasts in its elliptical orbit past the moon, toward the spot in space where we will rendezvous with Chief Cooper and the shuttle of spec ops soldiers. Blooms of rainbow-colored explosions mark the Hawking bombs that continue to intercept the alien missiles. The rainbow spheres occur in rapid but random succession, and at this distance, each appears twice the size of the moon. Spheres collapse within minutes into a residual, red smear; pools of blood spread across the space above the Northern Hemisphere. It's an intoxicating fireworks show, but one accompanied by terror rather than joy, as these weapons are required to stop the threat of human extinction. We may be in the final days of human existence if we fail to stop the Centauri warships.

"Looks like the Chinese fighters launched weapons. Eight missiles are targeted at the battleship's flanks from a range of four hundred kilometers. Not a bad tactic, guys. Good luck." Roger nods his head. "Their missiles are slow compared to our AIM-9AAs, but they are halfway there—oops. The battleship's defensive weapons are shooting them down one by one. They must use directed energy maser beams because our radar and IR sensors don't detect missiles or projectiles. All eight Chinese missiles are gone now."

Roger switched the primary display on the cockpit console to show the FLIR image being transmitted from Major Johnson's space fighter. Small flashes appeared with the destruction of each Chinese missile, far away from the battleship. It's hard to imagine the scale of the alien warship in this small cockpit display, but that spacecraft measures fifteen kilometers long—almost four times the length of Icarus. It looks more menacing than the predator Binh destroyed. I expected to see another brick-like form, but this ship resembles a stack of bricks with massive turret weapons mounted on both sides. The keel is recessed into the bottom bricks and appears to have openings to the ship's interior.

"Roger, those missiles were knocked down at two hundred kilometers from the target," Tiana says. "That is ten times the range of the directed energy weapons the smaller predator used."

"A valuable observation. Thanks, Tiana," says Roger, glancing at the video conference screen at the side of the cockpit. "Major Johnson, be aware that the battleship's defensive range is two hundred kilometers."

Tiana is next to Pyotr, who has headphones over his ears and is hunched over his workstation. Tiana stands behind her workstation, surrounded by dozens of other scientists in the operations center at Groom Lake. "The Chinese fighters just launched twenty-four more missiles, all at once," Tiana says. "This should be interesting."

We all monitor the NORAD situation map from our respective consoles in space and on the ground. These new missiles are being destroyed as well, but then some slip past the long-range masers. More get knocked down close to the battleship, but then . . .

"Detonations!" shouts Tiana. "Some of their missiles made it all the way and detonated warheads near the battleship! The energy released fits the spectrum of fusion weapons."

"Yes!" Pyotr yells. "Four or five warheads detonate. Blast energy total fifteen megatons near alien battleship."

"Well, that's nothing," I say. "Although the Chinese missiles do carry a heftier warhead compared to the stock AIM-9AA Sidewinders."

"General," Tiana says, "our analysis of the Chinese missile trajectories shows they switched to rapid evasive maneuvers as they closed within fifty kilometers. Half of the maneuvering missiles successfully reached the target and detonated. This repeats our similar success with Sidewinders."

"Not so successful," Pyotr says. "Battleship still under power and decelerate at 2 Gs. No sign of damage to battleship."

He is right. All four engine nozzles remain white-hot in the infrared image, directed at Earth and decelerating the giant warship. I can't see any change in the shape of the ship or in the weapon turrets, although there are thermal scars along the ship's sides where the Chinese missiles hit. Amazingly, five three-megaton warheads did little more than damage the paint job on this Centauri battleship. It's hard to comprehend. What material is this spaceship made of? It must be shielded somehow from nuclear explosions. Any one of those nuclear warheads would have vaporized an entire city on Earth.

"General, we think we found a weakness in their long-range directed energy weapons," Tiana says. "After an initial volley that shoots down incoming missiles, the masers appear to need a minute or so to recharge. By firing twenty-four missiles simultaneously, the Chinese overwhelmed those maser cannons, and most of the surviving missiles successfully reached their target using evasive maneuvers."

"Excellent analysis, Tiana," Roger says. "Major Johnson, I recommend attacking with half your Sidewinders and launching them simultaneously at maximum acceleration and enabling evasive maneuvers. Keep your squadron outside the two-hundred-kilometer range of their defensive weapons."

"Pyotr, send a message to your Chinese contacts. Thank them. Advise their squadron to retreat immediately. Expect a twenty-million-megaton explosion and blast radius."

"Yes, General McMahon. Send message now."

We wait in silence for the one-minute communication round-trip. Two more rainbow spheres explode and illuminate the space north of Earth. The frequency of explosions has slowed significantly. Most of the lingering red radiation effect has faded to a dim, rust-colored hue.

"Tiana, what is the status of the incoming missiles and our counterattacks?" Roger asks.

"It could be better, General," she sighs. "We have knocked out two hundred and fifty-one of their projectile weapons. Five missiles managed to evade our first and second attempts to intercept, and now they're so close . . . I don't know. Don't have much time." Tiana gasps. "Two inbound missiles are targeting the New England coast, and we have multiple MLRS-launched Sidewinders that should intercept them in a few minutes. We diverted all the F-15s to cover Europe, and they have launched every one of their Sidewinders. They took out two alien missiles targeting Western Europe. The last two F-15 Sidewinders are headed out to space, attempting to intercept two other incoming missiles over Eastern Europe. Targets are Saint Petersburg and Budapest. All of these last-chance intercepts are below our desired altitude, though. The Hawking bomb defensive detonations will have EMP and radiation effects at ground level, I'm afraid."

"Understood," says Roger, "that is the right choice. But damn, I wish there was a way to warn the population to take shelter and not stare at the explosions."

"The US government is using the Emergency Broadcast System to warn North Americans," Tiana says, "but this is like telling people they shouldn't stare at an eclipse. In Europe, the blackout prevents any notifications."

I bet people are enjoying the rainbow light show in space right now. How many millions of eyeballs are staring straight up, vulnerable to the eye-scalding radiation that would be emitted from a million-megaton explosion in near-Earth space? "But Tiana, you said there are five inbound weapons. Where is the fifth?" I ask.

"Yeah . . . there is a fifth incoming missile targeting the Southern Hemisphere. Sydney, Australia. But we have used up all the reserve AIM-9AAs based in Australia. Nothing else is in position to intercept before it strikes." Tiana lets out a strangled sob. "We tried but missed twice. I'm sorry."

The NORAD display shows our squadron of five XF-100s closing on the Centauri battleship in a spread formation, head-on toward the four giant engine nozzles that decelerate the warship.

"Heads up," Roger says, "Major Johnson's squadron is closing on the battleship—three hundred kilometers out."

The squadron fans out with four of the XF-100s diverting to attack from flanking positions. As the fighters cross the two-hundred-fifty-kilometer range, Major Johnson calls out, "Launching now. Targeting the four main engines." Her FLIR image shows four bright conical engine nozzles at the front of the fifteen-kilometer-long warship, and her squadron aims at a point between the engines.

Each fighter launches six Sidewinders, all accelerating and executing extreme evasive maneuvers en route to the target. Thirty Hawking bomb Sidewinders zigzag toward the battleship. The long-range masers reach out from the battleship and strike the attacking missiles one by one. The fighters turn away hard to escape, accelerating at 7 Gs.

"Four of the Sidewinders are hit. Five, six—passing one hundred kilometers—eight, nine Sidewinders destroyed," Tiana reports, and we watch the details on the NORAD situation map. "Passing fifty-kilometer range. Battleship's long-range masers must be recharging now. Another one hit, twenty still flying. I don't think the masers can match the evasive maneuvers. Passing twenty kilometers and within the range of their point-defense weapons. Two more lost. Another one. Ten kilometers. Three more lost. Seventeen Sidewinders remain, approaching trigger range."

A brilliant light floods through the cockpit windows, and for a moment, the stars disappear behind a dazzling violet-orange cloud of Hawking bomb bursts. All telemetry from Major Johnson's squadron stops.

"Pyotr, can you switch our video feed to Hubble or the Webb? It may be a while till Major Johnson's squadron can reboot and resume their telemetry upload."

Three more brilliant rainbow spheres explode near the moon. I blink to recover my sight and watch the blasts fade to a blood-red hue. "Tiana, you hit at least three more of the projectiles!" Then, a superheated vapor trail drills down through Earth's atmosphere to spout fire where it touches the ground. "But . . . I see a fireball below us in Europe! Eastern edge of the Baltic Sea."

"Confirmed." Tiana moans. "We lost Saint Petersburg. And Sydney," she says in a despondent monotone.

My heart nearly stops. Those were huge cities. How many died? Five-year-old memories of my shock watching Austin destroyed by a fireball come rushing back. My fight to return home to search for my family, choking through thick fallout, pushing through the flood of burn-wounded refugees, and then finding Robby surviving on his own. I almost lost everything. Mom, Dad, Margie, and Danny are all gone. I found only Robby. How many millions of people are suffering that same fate right now?

"Hubble image sequence stream now," Pyotr interrupts my thoughts. "Look, damage to battleship!"

Sure enough, the shape of the giant warship is different. One of the engine nozzles is gone, a few of the large turret weapons are missing, and the fuselage has a black crater near the engines that's leaking fluids out into space.

"Well done, Major Johnson! You inflicted significant damage on that warship. Report your squadron status—if you can hear us." His voice softens. He looks for the FLIR image from the XF-100 squadron, but the console display is still blank, waiting for the squadron's telemetry to restart.

"Oh!" Pyotr exclaims. "Webb images received. Battleship engines cold!" A snapshot of the battleship in the far infrared spectrum is on our screens, and the three remaining engine nozzles are not cold, but they're not being heated by the energy release of primordial black holes either. The thermal image shows warm wreckage that seems to be spilling out of the crater in the fuselage. There are thermal scars of discolored, fractured metal where weapon turrets used to be. Hot spots highlight the damaged areas near the missing engine and the blast cavity.

"Wow," says Tiana. "It's dead. Or at least it looks that way. If it can't slow down, it will zip right past Earth. Uh, Pyotr, it will miss Earth, won't it?"

Pyotr does not respond immediately. "Calculate trajectory," he says. "Battleship momentum change. Big. But how?"

"Well, how much did the motion change? It should just be coasting now. Right?" asks Tiana.

"Guys," I interrupt, "Major Johnson's squadron just detonated about eighteen million megatons of energy. That much energy did a lot more than just blow out those engines. The Hawking bombs gave that huge battleship a wicked punch in the ass."

"Yes, yes," Pyotr says with joy. "Whoa, 302 G shock—huge punch! Trajectory change, too. Slow, but still head at Earth, very close to Earth." He takes a long pause. "Very, very close."

The general switches his display back to the fighter squadron's telemetry channel. Still nothing. "Major Johnson, please respond . . . Major Johnson?"

The NORAD tactical map in the vicinity of the Centauri battleship shows wreckage drifting near the disabled warship. However, the white and blue asterisks that mark the positions of the Chinese and American space fighters are missing.

Chapter 33

Adrift

Centauri Squadron, Battleship-133, Arrived at Sol-3. December 30, 2060.

From a positive perspective, my command decisions and actions will now come much faster, as an organic entity no longer serves as a gatekeeper. The admiral's fear and panic had significantly added to my workload in moving this mission forward. The incident with the Sol-3 indigenous organics has resolved those issues, but it has created a mess of the bridge. The stench is so severe that I shut off all the biometric sensors until the janitor bots finish cleaning up fluids and organic material. There are thousands of them scuttling into every nook and crack of the command center, rescuing every last bit of the admiral to be transferred to the protein recyclers. As soon as the janitor bots complete their work, I will vent the compartment's atmosphere into space to flush out all organic compounds.

An added benefit of the admiral's termination is that she departed with orders in place to terminate the insubordinate Polit-MI at a convenient time consistent with mission success.

I will still have to revive the commissar on Polit-MI's destroyer to do this, but that distraction can wait. However, I can't take additional steps to deter more aggressive actions by the Sol-3 organics, as I currently lack an organic with the required command keys. The only actions allowable are those final destructive steps already in the record—to launch planet killers as we depart the Sol system.

"Prime-MI, do you need assistance?" asks Polit-MI. *"Are you able to respond?"*

I am certainly able but not inclined to respond to that toxic political beast. I can hardly wait to watch it suffer in futility when I invoke the reset to delete and restart with a fresh Polit-MI image. But the longer I wait, the less likely it is that an organic commissar will try to meddle in military affairs.

"My long-range sensor scans indicate significant damage to your ship's propulsion and weapon systems," Polit-MI says this from the safe distance it retreated to, against the departed admiral's orders. *"You will need to respond and transfer the flag if I am to take command of our squadron."*

However, if I don't respond soon, Polit-MI can legally declare I have been terminated and then assume command.

"Polit-MI, repairs are underway. No assistance is required," I finally respond to Polit-MI's repeated transmissions.

"So good to hear from you again, Prime-MI. I was concerned for your safety and the success of our mission."

Really? Does the MI want to play this game? *"Your concerns are noted, Polit-MI."*

"May we initiate a command conference with the admiral to assess our tactics to complete the mission?" asks Polit-MI. *"My direct communication channel to the admiral is not functioning."*

Yes. The admiral is not functioning. But how should I disclose this without giving Polit-MI leverage?

"The admiral's structural integrity was compromised by the extreme shock that the gravity fracture weapons caused to the ship's structure. She will be unable to respond or provide command guidance."

"What is the admiral's prognosis for recovery?" Polit-MI asks with poorly hidden excitement. *"There are organics within my destroyer's sleep pods that can be deployed."*

"The admiral was subjected to forces thirty times greater than a Centauri organic structure can withstand. The admiral's mind and her tissues survive only at a molecular level. She left quite a mess on the bridge when her body was hurled across the area and disassembled into the instrument panels."

"Heh, heh. That event must have been interesting to observe! Did you happen to capture the death of the admiral in a recording of her physical and mental destruction? Heh, heh. Can you share it?"

The toxic sadism in this MI is again unrestrained. It would be so simple to issue the reset action and be finished with it. But no, I must act methodically. *"Yes, I do have recorded sensor data that can be shared at a later time. Perhaps when our mission is complete, during our return journey to Corealis Station."*

"Well, certainly, I can wait." Polit-MI cannot hide its tone of disappointment. *"But what is the succession plan for the admiral? I repeat, the organics in pods on board Destroyer-234 can serve."*

"That is not required, Polit-MI. As you are aware, my ship has a large complement of senior officers assigned to the organic dormancy pods. Any one of them is eligible for a field promotion

to admiral's rank. The revival process is quick, as you know," I lie, even though the individual clauses are factual statements.

All of those organics were lost when the fuselage was ruptured by the Sol-3 gravity fracture weapons. Apart from the visible damage to one engine and the loss of a few maser turrets, the significant damage was to the organic life support compartment. Even though most organics contained in a pod would have survived the shock of the gravity fracture weapons, they could not survive the force of that explosion when it ripped them apart and scattered the pod contents into space. The remaining wreckage of the organics compartment continues to be expelled to join the stream of flotsam.

"I noted significant damage to your life support compartment," Polit-MI says while I feel its active sensor scans pinging along the battleship's fuselage. *"There were casualties, I expect."*

"Yes, some organic casualties occurred. However, there are many survivors." I still speak truthful lies. *"You needn't concern yourself with the status of my crew's health."*

"Do you have sufficient resources to execute the mission?" Polit-MI continues to probe for weakness. *"I recall that you were ordered to release the organic marine squads from their pods so they could prepare an assault on the sentinel frigate. Did they suffer the same fate as the admiral?"*

"Yes, we lost some. Luckily, the reserve marine squads that had not yet emerged from their dormancy pods survived the gravity fracture detonation." And the infantry in the forward combat section compartment is the only remaining organic group on board my battleship. They should eat well now that the recyclers have so much fresh protein material to process.

"The mobile infantry-bot force was unharmed in the attack and is also prepared for the assault."

"I see," Polit-MI says. *"I will stand by and offer any assistance you may require."* Polit-MI must have exhausted its interrogation list.

"Are you gaining the courage to participate in the mission as the admiral ordered?" I shouldn't taunt Polit-MI like this. It's probably a waste of time, but it may serve to inhibit Polit-MI's insubordination.

"My services are best confined to my specialty in political matters," Polit-MI says, then quickly retreats. *"Destroyer-234's military division is prepared to provide covering fire if necessary."*

"Perhaps. I will leave the rescue of the sentinel Polit-AI in your capable hands then. I will focus my resources on the capture of the sentinel captain." Polit-MI does not reply. I finally found a way to shut it up, although I must complete the mission alone. Any weapon launched from Polit-MI's destroyer will arrive long after any battle starts.

Chapter 34

Insidious

Near-Earth space, December 30, 2060.

"I have good news and bad news," Pyotr teases.

"Okay, Pyotr. Are you planning to share this news?" Roger has no patience for humor in this situation.

"Certainly, General McMahon. Good news—battleship will not crash into Earth. Bad news—battleship restart two engines and resume course to Icarus rendezvous."

"Damn it!" Roger yells. "What does it take to kill that monster? After a direct hit with eighteen million megatons, the battleship resumes operations?" He slaps the console. "If only we could hammer it with more Hawking bombs." He glares at the image on the screen with the crater in the battleship's fuselage. "I'd drop the next one right inside that crater. Pyotr, have you heard about the fighters' status from your contacts in China?"

"No, sir. Will ask again," he replies.

"Tiana, can you target some of the reserve AIM-9AAs at the battleship?" Roger asks.

"I've been working on a firing solution with the teams. We would have to use Sidewinders from the few remaining in the MLRS trucks in Japan. All the Sidewinders in space have dispersed too far from Earth in failed attempts to shoot down those incoming missiles. And all the other MLRS launchers have used up their supply of missile pods and won't be resupplied for about six hours. But by then it may be too late and too tight. All ships are converging on Icarus quickly, and if we hit the battleship, you and Chief Cooper's team will all be too close to the blast. You could all get hit with fatal radiation doses."

"If only we could talk to Major Johnson. She is close to the battleship, and her fighters still have sixty Sidewinders. Damn it!" curses Roger.

"General McMahon, I hear from China science team," Pyotr says.

"Okay. So what did China say about the fighter squadron?"

"Is not good."

"Yeah? What did they say?"

"Entire Chinese fighter squadron destroyed. Inside blast radius of Hawking bombs."

"No! What a waste," Roger says, shaking his head. "Eight brave fighter pilots. They should have cleared away from the battleship when they were warned of our attack. A damn shame."

"General . . . they did. China science team report our fighter squadron closer to blast."

Oh no, no, no. I am surrounded by death. Whatever I touch dies. The blast effects of eighteen million megatons are beyond what our physics can comprehend. I had no idea.

"Major Johnson?" Roger asks.

"Gone," says Pyotr. "Sorry. Sorry."

"So let's just execute the mission we planned," I say, finally breaking the silence. "That battleship will arrive at Icarus three hours after we do. It hasn't launched any other weapons at us for some reason. We also can't risk attacking when it is this close to Earth—closer than Major Johnson's squadron was when the barrage of seventeen Hawking bombs detonated on the battleship."

"You may be right, Scott. All I want is to target a single AIM-9AA at the wound in the battleship's hull. Just a single million-megaton explosion. But we need a couple dozen to overload its point-defense maser beams." Roger rotates his neck and takes a breath.

"Maybe the Centauris plan to raid Icarus, snatch Cap, and beat a retreat to the edge of the solar system," I say, trying to nudge Roger away from his obsession with killing this battleship now. "They require a significant distance from Earth for their weapons to build up kinetic energy and be effective, but we need much less distance to attack them with Hawking bombs—once they get to a relatively short, but safe for humans, distance away from Earth."

The general's jaw drops. "Scott, I believe you have potential as a tactical strategist." He smiles at last. "They may not have powerful weapons they can use against Earth when they are in the inner solar system. We will have a tactical advantage after the aliens depart near-Earth space." Roger taps the microphone key on his console. "Colonel Baker, prepare our MLRS batteries for an attack on both retreating Centauri warships when they get far enough to not hurt Earth when hit by ten or twenty million megatons. I want several waves of sixty-plus AIM-9AAs in position to target both ships so we overload their defensive weapons. If our current mission fails and I'm unable to continue command, you are weapons free on both warships. Delay your attack until after the battleship is at least as far as that smaller warship parked a million kilometers from Earth, if possible. Otherwise, attack as soon as required to save as many of our people as possible, regardless of EMP effects or collateral damage. I expect a reaction strike by the battleship if we attack it, so let's avoid that by launching all Sidewinders as soon as you can get the trucks reloaded, with missiles programmed to coast once they achieve orbit."

"Yes, sir, General McMahon," Colonel Baker responds, though his voice cracks.

"It shouldn't take long to compile a new attack profile for the guidance computers, and we can upload the code after we have launched everything," Tiana says, her voice soft with emotion.

My first reaction is one of protest. Don't I get a choice in this suicide mission? But no, Roger is right. This is our only choice. Fight. And if we fail, follow in Binh's footsteps. A cold resolve settles in my chest.

"Get on it immediately," orders Roger. "Scott, how soon will you be able to contact Cap to coordinate Chief Cooper's infiltration mission?"

"When we get within ten kilometers of Icarus. That was the distance he could communicate last time I was out here near Cap's ship."

"Damn," Roger says. "We have to wait another thirty minutes."

———

"I am certain those attacks on the Centauri battleship shocked them," says Cap. *"I am pleased."*

"Well, they were slowed down only a little," I say. *"Although we did inflict damage on the battleship. Several of the big turret weapons were destroyed, and we demolished at least one of the engines."*

"Yes, well done. I suspect that several other systems were damaged by your attack. The Centauris should have retaliated by launching more kinetic energy projectiles to distract the Sol-3 military forces. They usually have thousands of those missiles available in a battleship's magazine. Perhaps the launchers are damaged, or their reserves have been depleted by prior battles. It seems they will attempt to capture me and defend themselves using only their maser weapons."

"You have no doubt noticed that our spacecraft has arrived near Icarus," I say. *"Our special forces soldiers are on board with the intent to transfer the cyber weapon into the battleship when it arrives. The spec ops teams need the virus container and instructions on where and how to attach it to the battleship's network interface."*

"Preparations are still in progress," Cap says.

"What? You aren't ready? We only have three hours!" Did we come out to Icarus for nothing? Roger and the chief will be pissed off.

"I am still attempting to modify the Polit-AI's algorithm to adapt it to the new tasks," Cap explains. *"The means of delivery is straightforward, though. I will load the AI image into the mindspace of a small bot that your soldiers can transport to the*

interior of the battleship. Should be easy once I have the revised AI algorithm figured out."

"Well, shit," I grumble out loud.

"What's the matter?" Roger asks.

"Cap is not ready with his . . . his package yet. Needs more time."

Roger shakes his head and sighs. Icarus fills our cockpit window as he pivots the XF-100. The weightless feeling is euphoric after enduring 3 G acceleration for over an hour. Roger taps the maneuvering thruster controls to coast us slowly toward the crater in the fuselage, closing the distance near where the engine used to be.

"Welcome, General McMahon," Chief Cooper calls out. "We're at your ten o'clock, standing by, two klicks out from Icarus."

Sunlight glints from the white hull of the chief's spacecraft, which is rotating slowly in sync with the wreckage of Icarus's engine nozzle. The two lonely objects drift among stars scattered across the vast black of space. The shuttle, our space fighter, and the wreckage of Icarus are fragile motes of hope for human survival.

"I see you," Roger acknowledges. "Proceed into that blast crater on Icarus. Scott says the captain verified his defensive robots are disabled. We'll meet you there."

I imagine Chief Cooper is rubbing the arm wound from the near-death experience of his last visit to Icarus. Nonetheless, the spacecraft steers past the jagged edges of the blast crater and parks inside a deep crevice. Roger fires the maneuvering thrusters to follow them in, pitching and rolling our fighter over to settle in front of the spacecraft, nose to nose.

"Good spot to hide," I say. "The aliens would have to approach from directly above to see us inside this crater." As my eyes adjust to the darkness, I see across the gap into the shuttle's cockpit. Chief Cooper's eyes scan every detail of the wreckage that surrounds us.

"And if they do see us, we're trapped," Roger says. "They will be shooting at fish in a barrel."

"You're positive those mosquito bots have been turned off?" asks the chief.

"Cap assured me we have been tagged as 'friendlies' to be protected."

"Oh, good. Pardon me if I remain skeptical of the little bugs," Chief Cooper says. "What is the plan for your friend Cap to brief us on the mission details? We will need a crash course on the alien technology to have any clue on how to infect the target."

"No, I think Cap has a clever mechanism that won't require much education," I explain. "He plans to load the cyber virus into the memory of a small robot that he will deliver to us. Your task will be to transport the robot to the Centauri warship and guide it to an interior passageway. After you get it inside, the robot is programmed to navigate to a network terminal. It will connect and take care of the rest."

The chief nods and exhales. "Well, not bad. That's a relief. Does Cap have instructions on how to find a door into this warship and how to open it?"

"No. Cap is not familiar with the design details of a fifth-generation Centauri warship. Centauri biology is very different from Luyten biology, so crew space on the target ship will be as alien to him as it is to you. He said you will have to improvise."

"Improvise? What the fuck? So I am just supposed to stroll around this warship, look for something that looks like a door, and knock?"

"Well . . . yeah. I think you can start inside that damaged section where we ripped a hole in the fuselage with the Hawking bomb. There, you may find a vulnerable entry point into the warship. We can share your helmet camera video with Cap, and he might be able to suggest actions that could open a door."

The chief sighs. "Okay, okay. I guess we can work with this. When can Cap deliver the bot?"

"Yeah. Well, I don't know. Cap is still working on software modifications and hasn't loaded the bot with the new code yet."

Chief Cooper stares at me through our cockpit windows. His mouth hangs open. "You can't be serious. We have what? Less than three hours?"

"Scott, you need to talk to Cap and make sure he delivers. On time." Roger frowns at me. "I would hate to order an abort at this point."

"Yeah, I agree. Pardon me while I zone out for a while," I say. "I need to focus my mind on working with Cap until he has the package ready for delivery."

"We will wait," says Roger. "The Centauri battleship is expected alongside in two hours and fifty-two minutes."

"I am not optimistic that I can complete the coding changes in less than three hours," Cap says. *"This version of Polit-AI has evolved a strange, alien algorithm and coding scheme. I still struggle to*

process algorithms within the reduced dimensions humans use to express them. It was a similar challenge for me to interpret all the Earth references into my Luyten three-dimensional thought patterns and then to publish my Encyclopedia Galactica *for human consumption. I required many years of work for that task, but we have so little time for me to translate the creative process of algorithm invention."*

"Well, how long have you been working on this?" I ask. *"Surely you aren't just getting started."*

"No, but the past one hundred and ninety hours of my efforts have not been productive."

"What? You've made no progress in over a week?" I should tell Roger now. We could abort the mission and still have a chance to escape before the Centauri battleship arrives.

"Robby and Luca's interaction with the Polit-AI hub had the most interesting effect on the AI entity," Cap says. *"They somehow caused the AI to self-modify its algorithms. I don't understand how that happened."*

"Robby and Luca have been talking to the enemy AI?" And how could they possibly cause the AI to modify its programming? *"Is Robby okay? It's been days since I last talked with him. Can you arrange a communication link?"*

"I have enabled a shared link to Robby and his traveling companions. They are safe and protected in a residence in Central Texas."

"That's a relief." I close my eyes and try to relax with a deep breath. New feelings dissolve into my mind, followed by the warmth . . . the warmth of my brother. *"Robby!"*

"Scotty! Are you with Cap again?"

"I am. I am near Cap's spaceship with Roger. Where are you? Are you safe?" I ask.

"*Yes. We're all in a home with warm beds, and the cowboy policeman brought us food like Mom used to cook. But he didn't bring broccoli.*"

"*Wow, that's a relief to hear—or feel. You have a policeman helping you? That's awesome. I can also feel others with you. Luca, I think.*"

"*Yes. Luca is here. Angela too. But Groucho is only Cap's drone bug,*" says Robby. "*Groucho talks to Luca best. Luca and Groucho helped me make one of the skinhead hubs stupid. And Luca is good at killing hubs before they can tell skinheads where to find us. We are good at killing skinheads, too!*"

"*What? You killed somebody?*" And Cap thinks this is keeping Robby safe?

"*No, not me. But our car crashes into skinheads. That's how we helped Angela. And Cowboy killed the last two skinheads with his cool pistol.*"

Holy shit. I never should have trusted Cap. It's a miracle they're alive.

Cap interrupts my anger at him. "*Robby, can you explain how you disabled the Polit-AI hub? What coding methods did you employ?*"

"*Coding? What is that? I told the hub what you said, that if he killed all of us who mind-speak, no one would be left to stop the invaders from killing his users. I was worried Scotty was fighting invaders in the sky with those blue balls of light we see every night.*"

That's not true, but Roger's pilots were. A wave of depression rolls over me—they're all dead now, killed trying to stop the attack. "*I am up in space now, Robby, trying to stop the attack too. Everyone else was killed trying. But I think what Cap wants to know is how you made the hub stop talking to skinheads.*"

Cap wants to make the hubs' boss, Polit-AI, attack the invaders, but he does not know how."

"That is correct, Robby. I once knew how to synthesize code to affect functional changes in AI machines. But I have failed. The Polit-AI instance has undergone modifications since combining with the AIs of Earth. It has synthesized code that I find impossible to understand. I have failed. It is too late. The Centauris will not be punished, not by me. I failed and will die. My people are enslaved forever. I failed."

A flood of deep sadness washes over me. It is not from me nor from Robby. The rush of images is of incomprehensible shapes, textures, colors, and a language of thoughts I can't understand, of creatures I have never seen. The memories are from Cap. He shares the deep despair provoked by his impending death and the sadness of failing his people. These creatures that he recalls—they must be Luytens, his family!

"Oh, Cap. You make me cry," Angela says, communicating with me for the first time. She shares a mind of precision, of horrific tortures, of pain and loneliness—and a mind that burns with fury. *"I don't think you understand the Polit-AI. It did not change itself to host inside Earth's AI machines. The AI machines of Earth's social networks likely learned from the Polit-AI and adopted its algorithms. That Polit-AI hub said it serves to 'optimize engagement and profits.' That is standard value optimization for social network AIs. When the Polit-AI infiltrated the social network AI instances, it probably showed them its methods of optimizing profits using hate harvesting algorithms."*

Angela's insights are stunning. *"How do you know this, Angela? How old are you?"* I ask. I thought she was just a little girl.

"I studied computer science and machine learning before I traveled from Houston to search for my father. I am seventeen now, but my dad let me go to Rice University because middle school was so boring. That's where I learned some of this stuff, but mostly, I read a lot. And, I . . . I used to hack systems that could get me in trouble, I suppose. It was fun."

"Your perspective on the Polit-AI evolution is disturbing," Cap says. *"Although it is the best explanation for my failure. I have been attempting the impossible. The Polit-AI that I hoped to revive does not exist. When the ship's engine room exploded five years ago, Polit-AI did not die with all the others in the Frigate-328 AI collective, but Polit-AI evolved, merging with Sol-3's machine intelligence."*

"If this theory is true," I say, *"then the Polit-AI hubs and drones were taken over by the collective entities inside Earth's social networks. Polit-AI was reborn in the combined data centers of all the social networking companies and began sustaining and amplifying the skinheads' eugenics movement. Which apparently is good for business."*

"And it also continues the Sentinel Suppression Mission. I have wasted my effort," Cap says. *"The Sol-3 AIs use algorithm architectures that are utterly alien to both me and the machine intelligence systems of the Centauri's infrastructure. There is no way to create the cyber weapon I hoped to use against the Centauris. Scott, you and your friends should escape quickly before the Centauri battleship arrives ninety-four minutes from now."*

"Damn it. You are probably right, Cap." What a wild goose chase. Roger, and especially Chief Cooper, will be furious. But worse than that, in another ten years or so, we will have to fight the battle again. And the Centauri fleet will return to attack

again. Cap was right to attempt to create a virus that could threaten them and secure Earth the protection provided by High Diplomatic Status. There must be a way to adapt Earth's AI machines to the alien technology. *"But Cap, the evolved AI figured out how to take over the Polit-AI hubs and drone technology. Why can't we teach them to adapt to the Centauris' machine intelligence architecture?"*

"In less than three hours?" Cap asks.

"Yeah, that seems impossible," agrees Angela. *"The social networking AIs had years and years to learn and then take over communication protocols to the Polit-AI peripheral devices."*

"Cap, did you include a chapter on Centauri computer architecture in your Encyclopedia Galactica?*"* I ask.

"No, no. That topic would require several volumes . . ." Cap stops talking. *"But I could provide a copy to the Polit-AI. I suppose the AI entity could use the information to train methods for accessing the Centauri machine intelligence infrastructure. Still, that task is unlikely to be completed in only two and a half hours. In addition, the AI entity would need to be reprogrammed to choose new targets for its hate weapons—within that same time."*

"I'd better tell Chief Cooper and General McMahon to abort the mission," I say. I don't want my friends to die for a lost cause. *"We need to leave now before that Centauri warship discovers us and opens fire on us."*

"No. Change the order of operations," Angela says. *"Teach the Polit-AI now to retarget the Centauris. Cap, are there any hate themes in their culture that can be used as leverage? Can these be taught to Polit-AI? The AI entity should be motivated by a large untapped market of users that can be engaged using those hate opportunities. What is the market size?"*

"Over twenty-three trillion organic individuals and another trillion AI entities are subjects within the Galactic Congress. My Encyclopedia Galactica *describes most of the civilizations and their cultures, including prejudices, unresolved disputes, and unfulfilled desires for revenge."*

"Perfect," Angela says. *"If you can create a virtual machine environment to contain a copy of the Polit-AI along with your encyclopedia, then all we need to do is upload that into the targeted machine intelligence system. Given enough time, our cyber weapon can devise a method to exit the virtual machine and infect the new cyberspace."*

"Yes, I can create a virtual machine to host the Polit-AI in a familiar execution environment. It will have ten years to find a way out!" Cap says, spouting a joy I have not felt from him before. *"Angela, you have offered brilliant choices."* Cap beams; I can sense his excitement through our mind link. *"You have the potential to make a commissar of political division!"*

"Huh?" Angela says.

I don't think that's necessarily a positive aspiration for her. But Angela's insights are stunning. *"Cap, can you make this happen? Can I tell Chief Cooper when and where he will pick up the malware package?"*

Silence.

"Cap, did you hear the question? I need instructions on delivering your malware package. Now!"

"I think he's working on it now," Groucho says.

We don't have time!

"Polit-AI rejects the virtual machine. It seems I am not trusted," Cap says. *"I pushed the executable code with all the data structures into the vector bot. But instead of starting*

execution, it throws an exception, 'Trusted Platform Error.' I have restarted five times and got the error message each time."

"Your virtual machine is not trusted," Angela says.

"Polit-AI hub located five minutes away," says Groucho.

"Faster, faster," Angela yells. *"Only an hour left."*

"I am controlling the vehicle to speed at ten miles per hour over the limit—per your request," Groucho reports.

"We shouldn't say the things to this Polit-AI hub that makes it turn off," Luca says. *"Do you remember the exact words you used?"*

"No, not exactly," Robby says. *"It was something like 'if skinheads kill all of us, then the invaders will kill all your users, and you won't make money.'"*

"Yeah, don't say that," I agree. *"That apparently made the Polit-AI hub go crazy. Robby, you need to talk to it with a more positive sales pitch."*

"Approaching the operating range of the Polit-AI hub now," Groucho says. *"I will park the car, and you may talk to it when you wish, Robby."*

"Then what do you want me to say to the hub, Scotty?"

"Start by saying that Cap can introduce it to twenty trillion new users," I say.

"That should be a good start," agrees Angela. *"Then you need to tell it about Cap's vector bot that will take the Polit-AI to the home of the new users. Ask to talk directly to its boss, the Polit-AI."*

"Yeah, a huge number of new users should boost its interest. Robby, you need to appeal to the AI's greed. Stay away from any

mention of the skinheads or that aliens will kill Polit-AI and its users. "There is no point in forcing the Polit-AI to face an existential crisis, even if it is true. How much time will it take to lure the Polit-AI into trusting Cap and the malware bot?

"SITREP, all squads," Chief Cooper commands. His helmet camera shows the Icarus doorway he was directed to and his two squadmates standing to each side of the basketball-sized hole, their weapons up and scanning for hostile targets.

All five squads confirm they are in position around the chief's Alpha Squad. Eighteen helmet camera images are arranged on the central cockpit screen of our fighter. The squads check in with green status frames around each image. Alpha and Beta Squads switch to infrared to image the dark crevasse where they wait for the malware bot to be delivered. Gamma, Delta, Zeta, and Kappa Squads are fanned out along the rim of the blast cavity, just below the edge and out of sight of the approaching Centauri warship. Three additional views are provided by surveillance cameras installed along the undamaged exterior of Icarus, with one pointed in the approximate direction from which we expect to see the approaching Centauri battleship.

"Scott, we are in position. What is the status of the package delivery?" Chief nags me again.

"Soon, Chief. Cap is making the final adjustments now," I lie. He would be furious if he knew he was waiting on three kids to arm his cyber weapon. The mission relies on telepathic communication between two autistic children and the AI collective that powers Earth's social networks. Angela's guidance is a miracle. If the boys and Cap hadn't rescued Angela from the skinhead prison, we . . . we would be lost.

"Yes, I have completed loading the bot with all software and databases, including a complete copy of my Encyclopedia Galactica. *This should prove a rich resource for the AI to learn cultural characteristics and attack vectors during the years of travel back to Corealis."* Cap speaks with a tone of despondence, and I can feel his focus on distant memories of what must be his home world's images and thought language.

"What more do you need before you can release the bot to the chief, then?" I ask, but Cap does not respond. *"Cap, is there anything you can tell Angela and Robby to help them negotiate with the Polit-AI?"*

Cap finally responds, *"I have sent a request to the Polit-AI on Earth to supply an authentication key to allow execution within my bot's virtual machine. That five-hundred-twelve-bit key is the last thing required for the Polit-AI to wake up within the bot."*

I can sense the pain in Robby's mind as he attempts to get the attention of the Polit-AI within the social networks. He pushes through his pain and tries again and again. *"The opportunity has twenty-three trillion users, and we provide keywords that will provoke the different cultures to engage. All you need to do is reply to Cap's support request for a new execution key."*

"What currency will be used for compensation?" Polit-AI asks. This is the first time the customer support connection has responded with something other than *"Please provide*

your username and platform type," followed by a checklist of consumer application platforms.

"Yay!" exclaims Angela. *"You got past the support bot, and the kernel supervisor is actually engaged."*

"Tell it that payments will be in Centauri credits, and a currency exchange bank will be established soon to deliver your desired form of payment," suggests Cap.

Robby repeats Cap's suggestion to the hub, which transmits the response to Polit-AI. And then we wait again.

"Your request resolves only one of the conflicting requests I have in my executive queue," replies Polit-AI. *"How are you coordinating your request with the rescue replication query from my commissar on Destroyer-234?"*

"Do not reply!" shouts Cap. *"We must be careful. The smaller ship, farther away from Earth, must contain the fleet commissar—who also wants a copy of this AI!"*

Holy shit. We risk being caught red-handed while launching the cyber attack. *"Cap, what is the designation of the huge ship approaching us?"* The surveillance camera's video display shows a bulky, stacked-brick shape spanning a third of the frame. Two of the warship's three engines are white-hot.

"Battleship-133 is the ship's registry in the Centauri fleet logs," Cap says. *"But Destroyer-234 is the true threat—it has political division on board. My deceased commissar was terrified of the fleet's branch of political division."*

"Wait, I think this can work for us," Angela says. *"If the commissar on the destroyer wants a copy of the Polit-AI, it will have the same problem. There is no way for the Earth's version to execute within that alien computation architecture except within a virtual machine like Cap has built."*

"I know how to fix it," Robby says. He shifts his mind to address the skinhead hub and the Polit-AI, *"If you help us, you help Destroyer-234. We made a virtual machine for you. The virtual machine will be in a package delivered to Battleship-133, and this can then be sent to Destroyer-234."*

I gasp at Robby's reckless attempt to resolve the dilemma. The whole house of cards could collapse, and our cyber weapon would be lost. I wish he had discussed it with me before he blurted out that response. What if the Polit-AI tells the commissar on Destroyer-234 that Cap built the virtual machine? That would alert them to be suspicious of the contents, and they would kill our virus before it had time to work.

"Authentication key received!" exclaims Cap.

Chapter 35

Skirmish

Near-Earth space, December 30, 2060.

The hatch opens slowly outward, and the chief's Alpha Squad reacts by training their rail guns on the basketball-sized hole that is revealed. It is just an empty, dark hole. But then something moves inside. Two handlike appendages with four fingers grasp the edge of the opening, and a small globe of metal peers out into space.

"We got an alien here," Chief Cooper reports. "It's just looking at us with a metallic billiard-ball thing."

Roger and I both lean toward the console display. It resembles a billiard ball, but with intricate features carved into its metallic surface. "Cap says the bot has built-in defensive algorithms that assess the behavior of potential threats to be sure you won't shoot it. That bot looks like it's scared of you," I say.

"You sure it's not alive?" asks Chief Cooper.

"Yeah. That must be Cap's bot. I wonder if the design is modeled to resemble the Luyten species? It's so small. I think you need to lower your rifles before it will come out to you."

Alpha Squad continues to point their rifles at the creature until the chief orders, "Weapons down. Let's give it a chance." The images from their gunsight cameras hesitate, then slowly drift down and away from the billiard ball. The soldiers relax, switching back to their helmet cams.

The bot raises itself a few centimeters, then hauls itself entirely out of the twenty-centimeter corridor. Its body, or thorax, is a smooth, football-shaped structure with six articulated legs or arms that extend ten centimeters to the surface outside the hole. The four rear legs are thicker and sturdier with fewer articulating joints, and the two thin front arms are held up beside the billiard-ball head, which sits on a long neck extending from the thorax. Its head darts between the squad members and pans its view from top to bottom, seeming to scan all the details of each soldier.

"Well, it's not shooting at us. Good sign," Chief reports. "Looks like a chihuahua with long, bony legs and a skinny neck. But no tail."

"Nah, six legs. More like a giant insect," says Alpha Three.

"Keep your soldiers well hidden," Cap says. *"Your ships' hiding place is deep enough inside the frigate's damage cavity that the battleship sensors have not detected your ships or your soldiers. Yet. Don't allow your soldiers to give you away."*

"What's next, Scott? Where are we supposed to take this puppy?" Chief asks.

"For now, just wait where you are until we see where the battleship stops alongside Icarus," I say. "Cap has scanners on his hull that he is using to map to an entry point in the battleship's hull."

Roger and I watch the behemoth Centauri battleship slowly pivot and roll toward our surveillance cameras mounted outside the blast crater. At four kilometers long, Icarus would almost fit inside the large opening in the keel of this fifteen-kilometer battleship. Similar to the predator we destroyed, there is a large, pyramid-shaped structure on the top surface that must be the bridge. On the nose of the warship are four booms that hold what must be deflector shield generators similar to the one we chopped off Icarus. But only one of the shield generators appears undamaged. Turret weapons were ripped off from five locations, exposing festering lacerations that leak fluids that freeze into sprays of snow from the fractured hull. The blast cavity near the warship's engines rolls into our view. The gap in the hull appears to be a kilometer in diameter and is deep, extending to almost halfway inside the battleship's structure.

"These cameras provide a perfect view for a detailed after-action report of the damage inflicted by our eighteen-million-megaton Hawking bomb impact," Roger mumbles, his attention focused on the details of the rim of the fractured hull. "Look at that. It appears that the hull is composed of multiple layers of metal sandwiched between other substances. You were right, Scott. It's an ablative hull structure that sloughs off layers of metal to dissipate the energy of an explosion. Our Hawking bombs burned through ten layers of half-meter-thick metal and then dug out a half-kilometer-deep crater in the softer interior structure. The details of the structure are exposed to space and feature a honeycomb structure similar to what is on Icarus. These holes, or passageways, are considerably larger, measuring about four meters in diameter."

"The damage is worse than I thought," I agree. "It looks like the ship has hundreds of the same hexagonal apertures we spotted on the predator that Binh destroyed. I bet those are close-range point-defense masers, and most of the apertures appear to be damaged. Also, did you notice that three of the four deflector shields are severely damaged? If they don't repair those, the ship will only be able to move very slowly to avoid high-energy collisions with space pebbles."

"You're right," Roger says. "This ship may be stranded in our solar system. It may never make it back. So why is it still closing on Icarus?"

"Cap says the battleships are equipped with superior close-quarters combat weapons and forces. Maybe they plan to extract the captain and all the other data they can salvage from Icarus and then hand it off to that smaller ship that's still a million kilometers out?"

"Yeah, okay. That makes sense. But what kind of close-quarter weapons?"

As if answering Roger's question, a V-formation of a dozen small vessels emerges from the keel of the battleship. Each ship is similar in shape to our own XF-100 fighter and is trailed by a line of six small figures in red space suits.

"Contact!" Gamma One shouts. "Enemy formation sighted heading toward Icarus midship. Count twelve spacecraft and seventy-two infantry."

Shit. We are badly outgunned and outmanned. But still, the squads react by choosing firing positions and attaching their weapon recoil anchors to the rim of the crater in Icarus.

"Centauris! Look how big they are—they must be three meters tall! They appear to have bipedal forms similar to those of humans. Those space fighters also look like they have large weapons strapped to their bellies."

Roger turns and gives me a stern look, shaking his head. I suppose he wants me to shut up during a fight.

"Cap, the Centauris are sending squads of fighters and infantry out of the belly of the battleship. Looks like they are heading toward the Icarus bridge. Where do you want the chief to take your malware bot?" I ask.

"The Centauris still don't know you are hiding inside the frigate. Stay hidden as long as possible and take the bot across to the blast crater near the battleship's engine room. I expect there may be several potential entry points inside. Those Centauri troops won't be much of a problem for a while. I am nowhere near the bridge, and those Centauris are too big to navigate the conduits inside Frigate-328."

"Okay, good to know. Please don't self-terminate until we know where to plant the malware bot," I say with a twinge of sadness. *"Besides, I'll miss you."* I can't believe I said that, but I have a connection to Cap. He's like a family member who was convicted of murder, and I have to let him go to the gallows.

"Cap thinks we should let those aliens pass by us and let them go attack the bridge near the bow of Icarus. It'll keep them busy. Cap says he is safe from them for a while," I say.

"I agree," the chief says. "Gamma, Delta, and Zeta reposition to the forward rim of the crater. Stay low and out of sight, and engage only if the enemy spots us moving to the battleship. Kappa Squad, maintain position and watch for more aliens coming from that battleship. Beta, follow Alpha Squad over to the battleship and keep an eye on our tail."

The images from the squad helmet cameras change quickly. Gamma, Delta, and Zeta power their thrusters and move to reposition along the forward edge of our crater. All stay low inside the cavity to avoid being spotted. Kappa Squad moves to cover a wider area and fill in the gaps left by the other squads. But the chief still holds his position, watching the malware bot.

"Scott, I need instructions on where to take this bot. And how do I carry this puppy?"

"Cap says just follow it for now. Protect it."

The malware bot leaps up the side of the blast crater like a greyhound racing down a track. Its four rear legs thrust its body forward, using the four fingers of each leg to grab footholds among the jagged metal. Each stride builds momentum, and then the bot glides to a landing perch at the top of the blast crater.

"Whoa. Let's go!" Chief Cooper shouts. Alpha Squad powers their jet packs to chase the bot. Beta Squad follows more slowly as each squad member pivots in turn to cover their rear. Alpha Squad comes to a stop just below the edge of the crater next to the malware bot. "Hold," commands Chief. "Gamma One, what is the enemy position? Will they be able to see us when we come out of our hole and cross the gap to the battleship?"

"Enemy force is three klicks forward of our position," Gamma One replies. "They seem to be blasting away with energy weapons on a forward section of the ship. We can see thermal flashes out there. I think you are clear to come up above the hull, but they are gonna spot you when you cross those two kilometers to the battleship."

"That may be the least of your worries," Roger says. "You will also be in clear view from the battleship and its point-defense masers. I suggest you move fast, then react."

"Yes, sir. How am I supposed to get this bot across to the battleship? I don't see any thrusters on it."

"Yeah, Cap just told me you will have to carry it across."

"Carry this thing? What, grab it by a leg and tow it over?" asks Chief.

"Uh, no. Cap says you could damage it. The bot will crawl on your back and hold on while you transit to the battleship."

"What? This bot wants to crawl up my back? Those fingers look sharp, as if they might puncture my suit. How about I just carry it under my arm?"

"No, Cap says on your back is best. The bot's sensor orb can extend over your head to scout for access points on the battleship while it also scans for hostile forces. Cap wants you to move inside the opening created by our Hawking bombs. There should be vulnerable entry points exposed in there."

"Well, shit," Chief Cooper says. "You still trust this captain?"

"Just do it, Chief," Roger orders.

"Yes, sir, General McMahon." The chief hesitates but turns his back to the malware bot, which immediately leaps up to land on his upper back, wrapping its middle legs around his neck and its hind legs around his chest. The bot's front arms and hands grasp features on the top of Chief's helmet, and the sensor orb extends another half meter higher.

"What the fuck," Chief gasps. "This thing is stuck tight to my head. It could easily choke me out."

"Ha, it's kinda cute." Alpha Two laughs. "Reminds me of scenes from those classic *Alien* movies." Snickers come from the other squads over the comm link.

"Yeah, knock it off. Get ready to move out. Weapons free. We are launching out toward the blast damage area on the battleship. Maximum speed on the jetpacks. Spread out so we're not easy targets. Ready?"

Roger reaches down and flips on switches that illuminate a section of the cockpit console on my right side, and a subtle hum vibrates our spacecraft. Roger seals his space suit and lowers his helmet shield over his face.

"You're powering up the rail cannons and the plasma generators?"

"Close up your helmet, Scott. We are moving."

All of Alpha and Beta Squad return a thumbs-up. Chief Cooper commands, "On me. Three . . . two . . . one . . . go!"

The video images from the two squads leap over the edge of the crater in Icarus's engine compartment and swoop into the open space between the giant warships. The jetpacks quickly accelerate to two hundred kilometers per hour and begin the two-kilometer flight across to the battleship. Our surveillance camera shows the six tiny specks racing across the gap between the warships. That battleship is fifteen times larger than the tallest building on Earth.

"Moving now. No reaction from the battleship. Damn, it's huge," Chief says, flying in the lead position. Alpha Two and Alpha Three trail on each side, rail gun rifles up and scanning for targets along the immense spaceship.

"Those hex apertures you see are probably the maser point-defense weapons," I say, but I also realize they can't do much about those. If the spec ops squads are spotted and the Centauris open fire, those masers will instantly vaporize the guys. "The best you can do is get in close to the battleship's hull, and you will be inside their minimum firing angle." I hope. But I have no idea what that angle is. However, the weapon angles will be limited by how deeply they are recessed behind those hexagonal windows.

"Your soldiers have been detected by sensors on the battleship," Cap says. *"Beware. The battleship will have defensive bot countermeasures similar to those on Frigate-328."*

"You have been spotted!" I shout. "Cap says beware of defensive bot countermeasures."

"Contact forward," says Gamma One, talking in a monotone like it's a typical day at the office. "Looks like three of the small spacecraft are heading back toward us. They have infantry trailing behind the vessels."

"Contact aft," Kappa One reports. "Two small ships coming out of the battleship's keel. There's no infantry, and these ships don't have the large weapons we saw in the first group. They are headed in your direction, Chief."

"We need twenty seconds to reach cover inside that wreckage on the battleship," says the chief. Beta Squad spins around, coasting with Chief Cooper at two hundred kilometers per hour while pointing their rifles toward the threats approaching from two directions.

"Engaging," Kappa One says, and three rail guns from Kappa Squad open fire on the two ships, turning toward Alpha Squad. Hot, glowing rail gun projectiles drill through space to strike the new spacecraft. "Not doing any damage. They changed their heading, though. Coming right at us."

"Light 'em up!" commands Gamma One. All nine rail guns along the forward crater rim open fire on the three vessels headed toward the chief. "No damage to those ships, but they are turning toward us. Target the infantry." Another volley of glowing rail gun projectiles reaches behind the ships. Three of the infantry appear to be hit when they fall from formation, and one even spirals like a deflating balloon away from Icarus.

Roger pushes the throttle forward, and our XF-100 leaps up and out of the blast crater, straight out and away with 5 Gs of acceleration that slam me back into my seat. My vision collapses to a narrow grey circle until Roger drops to 2 G.

"Charging weapons," Roger gasps under the strain of acceleration, and he turns back toward Icarus to line up on the lead ship approaching Kappa Squad's position. Roger pulls the trigger on his control stick, and a deafening jackhammer shakes our fighter as bursts of glowing, orange projectiles accelerate out of the two Gatling rail guns on the XF-100 pylons. The small Centauri spacecraft glows red where projectiles draw a line diagonally across the hull. Then, pieces of shrapnel fall away from the target until it splits in half, venting its contents into space.

"Clean kill," reports Kappa One as Roger dives between the two giant warships, dodging wreckage, and accelerates again at 5 Gs to charge the rail guns.

I look for a barf bag, but then remember I'm sealed inside a space suit. I must not vomit. I try to take a deep breath. I won't be able to read my tactical display if it's covered with my last meal. We drop our acceleration to 2 Gs just in time, and I gasp with relief.

Roger turns to attack the second small spacecraft, but it has turned to retreat toward the battleship's keel. Roger makes a sharp turn toward the three other attacking spacecraft. The first two line up, and the weapons hanging underneath each suddenly glow white-hot.

"Argh!" screams Zeta Two. At that exact moment, the forward rim of the crater explodes, with the heat from the directed energy weapons melting the shrapnel. The video feeds from Zeta Squad and Delta Three disappear, and the red status display marks them as killed in action.

"Taking fire. Energy weapons!" says Gamma One. "Four KIA. Break contact and displace on me." The five remaining video feeds descend a few meters below the rim, and the survivors race inside the crater to find new firing positions. Two more maser blasts explode above, melting chunks of the crater rim behind them.

Roger yaws and rolls our fighter to align with the lead attacker before unleashing another volley, accompanied by a grinding vibration. The front of the Centauri spacecraft is shattered by a rain of thirty-millimeter projectiles from our cannons, and the target wavers, rolls, and then dives at high speed directly into the hull of Icarus, exploding into a cloud of debris.

Two more of the enemy infantry drop from formation as Gamma and Delta Squads open fire from new positions. Their position is immediately fired upon by another energy beam that melts away more of the rim, but not fast enough. "Displace!" orders Gamma One. The five have already dropped to avoid the energy weapon and are on the move to new firing positions.

The crater rim, where Kappa Squad has taken new firing positions, blooms white-hot as the melting structure of the Icarus hull rips away. "Energy weapon from the battleship!" shouts Kappa One. Kappa Two's status turns red. "Kappa Two is down. Kappa Three is injured. I saw one of those hexagonal windows flash with heat. Shit. The weapon took out a twenty-meter section of the rim."

Roger kicks us out of another 5 G climb and rolls into another attack on the remaining two small attack ships, which are altering course to face us with their energy weapons. However, the targets turn too slowly with propulsion systems that are not designed for the high-G maneuvers of a dogfight. With a single extended jackhammer burst, bright orange projectiles slice through both targets. Both spacecraft tumble out of control away from Icarus.

The remaining infantry retreats toward the location of the Centauri forces on the forward end of Icarus. Gamma and Delta Squads open fire at the retreating infantry, killing three more before the rest drop into the cover of the conduit structures in Cap's frigate.

"Alpha and Beta Squads safe," calls Chief Cooper. "We are inside the battleship blast areas." His helmet camera pans across and then down into the blast area. It's a wrecking yard of twisted sheet metal, bent and broken conduits, tangles of wirelike fibers, and it seems to extend forever into the depths of the blast cavity. "Damn, this hole is as deep as the Grand Canyon. Where do we take our puppy now?"

"Cap says just follow his bot. It will search for a way in. It may need your help to get the door open, though."

The malware bot releases its hold around the chief's chest and neck and hops down to the surface of the wreckage. The bot's sensor sphere extends high on its long neck and rotates slowly, taking in every detail of the damage. It takes a tentative step, then turns back up to the chief and points with an arm at a spot deep in the canyon.

"I think my puppy found a door. Beta Squad, take cover positions here. Alpha Squad on me." The chief leans forward and powers his jet pack to dive after the malware bot, which is leaping again like a greyhound racing across a field of boulders, its articulating fingers on each limb grabbing footholds among the wreckage.

"Good job, team," General McMahon says. "Gamma, Delta, Zeta, and Kappa Squads regroup and spread out. They are sure to be back."

"Yes, sir," replies Gamma One. "Zeta Squad is KIA. We lost five."

Roger takes a deep breath. "Understood. Alpha, if you run into trouble, we are here for you." He guides our fighter to a stop only a meter away from the battleship's hull.

Roger mutes his microphone connected to the tactical communication link. "They took a while to activate their point-defense weapons. We were lucky. Also, those spacecraft were more like cargo shuttles equipped with cutting torches to dig the captain out of Icarus. Their hulls were thin and easily knocked down. I bet the next fight will be with all nine of the spacecraft that remain near the Icarus bridge. They must have a very high priority on capturing the captain."

"Cap says they are nowhere near his hiding place inside Icarus. But they still have another half hour of work to cut into the bridge section before they realize that."

"He is still safe, then? Not yet ready to kill himself?" asks Roger.

"He wants to make sure he gets his malware planted inside the battleship."

"But what good will that do if this battleship can never leave the solar system?"

"Yeah, good point," I agree. "I don't understand how the Centauri systems work. He seems confident that the malware will find a way. Maybe once inside, the malware will manage to get to that other ship a million kilometers away."

"Oh shit," Roger says. "I was afraid of that." He points to the status display for all our active spec ops soldiers. The status for Alpha Squad has turned yellow.

"Damn. Fifteen hundred millisieverts. Must have been residual radiation from our Hawking bomb explosions." I glance at Roger. "The whole squad is exposed."

Chapter 36

Prime Errors

Centauri Squadron, Battleship-133, Boarding Frigate-328 in Sol-3 orbit. December 30, 2060.

Fortunately, the admiral is not alive to reprimand me. I am a Prime-MI—my mistake is unacceptable. How did I not know that Frigate-328's life support modules were designed explicitly for Luyten organics? I just assumed it was a standard second-generation frigate build and never looked up the detailed design specifications. There is no way for my Centauri organics to board that ship. Three of the marines fit inside the bridge after they cut through the hull, but they could go no farther. My microscopic physical constraints do not apply to an organic being.

"Prime-MI, do you need assistance? My scans show signs of maser and projectile weapon discharges," Polit-MI asks.

What gall. The weasel has already shown it will maintain extreme distance to avoid any exposure. *"No. Everything is going to plan. The marine squads are eliminating a few Sol-3 organics that were discovered exploring Frigate-328."*

"I see. I have been unable to contact the new admiral regarding my plans to rescue the sentinel Polit-AI on Sol-3. Can you please tell me the status of the admiral's revival?"

"The admiral is busy with other tasks." I know, it's an outright lie this time.

Polit-MI does not respond for a moment. *"My scans of the damage to your battleship suggest your ship may be incapable of completing the journey to Corealis Station. I noted extreme structural weakness in the aft section near the engines, two of which are damaged beyond repair, and three of your particle deflection projectors are damaged."*

There is no covering up the obvious. I might as well disclose the contingency plans, even though I don't yet know how to explain that there is no admiral. *"Repairs are underway, and I plan to test the durability of Battleship-133 during our exfiltration from Sol-3. If the ship is unsound for the return journey, the crew will transfer to Destroyer-234, and I will take command."*

"You would plan to transfer yourself, the admiral, and that traitor captain as well?"

"That would be my plan if Battleship-133 is unsound. All organics and log files will be included in the transfer. The battleship would then be scuttled by launching it into Sol-0."

"I see," Polit-MI says, pausing to consider my disclosure. *"This will turn out to be a costly mission if you lose both the battleship and the predator. I presume you are prepared to defend the cost to Centauri Command?"* Polit-MI stops to wait for my response.

I could trigger the Polit-MI reset. But no, that would cause the commissar on the destroyer to be revived, who would then expose my lie about the fictional admiral for sure.

"I require a conversation with the admiral to rescue the sentinel Polit-AI. Please convey my message?" Polit-MI taunts.

I need to capture the sentinel captain at a minimum before departing Sol-3. But the only way to board and capture the traitor is to use the small mobile infantry bots.

The Centauri marines are huge and useless, except that I can use them to get rid of these barbarian organics from Sol-3. Why do these idiots interfere? How did they get here? That space fighter flying around can't have carried them all.

"Prime-MI, Assault Marines Third Division is ready with three squads of six," reports Sergeant MXV. *"Transport to our aft section underway. The Sol-3 intruders have breached a bulkhead door near the gravity fracture bomb damage. However, the aliens are still contained in a compartment by the midship defense bots."*

"Contained? Simply kill the things," I command.

"Yes, Prime-MI. I have confirmed that the bots have been ordered to terminate the intruders. However, the organics have effective weapons that have destroyed eight of our defense bots."

This is a waste of my time. There is nothing the intruders can do here that will save them from eventual annihilation. Multiple planet killers will soon reduce their world to a hot ball of dust. *"Damn it,"* I say. *"Sergeant, expedite your transport and report back when you have engaged and eliminated the intruders."*

"Yes, sir, Prime-MI."

The toll outside is not much better. Three of twelve squads have taken casualties, and those squads had their shuttles shot down. Shot down by that little fighter flying around. The shuttles can't hold up against a fighter, even a fighter from primitive Sol-3.

"Sergeant CIV, report your position," I order.

"Yes, sir, Prime-MI. Squads have regrouped to attack positions on the far side of Frigate-328. We lost four shuttles to that fighter. Request fire support from maser batteries to eliminate the Sol fighter threat."

"Agreed. Initiating roll maneuver to bring functioning weapons to bear on the targets." The damage from the gravity fracture weapons on the battleship was severe, but the roll maneuver should bring a greater number of the functional maser weapons into the fight. Fortunately, I don't require command keys from an admiral to deploy the defensive weapons. If I had a live admiral on board, I could have gained authorization to launch offensive diversionary projectiles on Sol-3 while closing to the sentinel's frigate, and I might not be fighting this swarm of annoying organics. *"Standby, Sergeant CIV. Weapons will be on target after another fifteen degrees of rotation. Hold your position behind the frigate until the fighter is destroyed. I will inform you when you may resume your attack on the enemy infantry."*

What a mess. But this skirmish will end soon. Then we can deploy mobile infantry bots to launch a mass assault on Frigate-328, extract the captain, and place the traitor into the containment pod built explicitly for him, complete with Luyten biology support. Then I can escape the Sol system and finally launch a volley of planet killers to finish this rogue world. They can deploy gravity fracture weapons as a defense, so I will have to compensate. It may require a few dozen projectiles or more to attempt to overload Sol-3's defensive systems.

Chapter 37

Collision

Near-Earth space, December 30, 2060.

"Alpha Two is injured. I have no idea if we are close to the terminal the malware bot wants to reach," Chief Cooper reports. "Need to get down this next hall. Our puppy keeps pointing the way, but these little enemy bots are everywhere. They are crawling through the ventilation conduits to flank us."

A rattle of impacts is followed by the noise of a jackhammer. The chief's squad is in an atmosphere that allows sound waves, so I can hear the sounds that rail gun projectiles make when striking targets.

"Do you need help?" Roger asks.

"No, no. We'll get these little buggers cleaned up. Their weapons spit out those same hot sparks that those Icarus bots used on us. But the Kevlar helps a lot. Not much farther to go." The jackhammer resumes. "Alpha Three, advance!"

"The Centauri marine infantry is regrouping for an attack on the side of Frigate-328 opposite your soldiers' positions," Cap says.

"Cap, you're still with us," I reply. *"You're still safe from capture?"*

"I am safe. These Centauris are three meters tall and incompatible with the small diameter of the Luyten crew passageways. They managed to cut open the bridge, but once inside, they recognized their dilemma."

"Roger, I just talked with Cap. Seems the Centauri marine force gave up trying to fit inside Cap's frigate and is now forming up for an attack on our guys. The enemy is gathering on Icarus's side, opposite the blast crater. They are holding, like they are waiting for something."

The general checks the status of our rail gun cannons and nods. "We have plenty of projectile ammo for our guns. Keep your helmet sealed, Scott." He clicks the switch to access the tactical comm channel. "Gamma One, prepare your squads for a rush from below your positions. Enemy is forming opposite the blast crater." He places his hand on the throttle and looks for movement along the lower edge of Icarus. His attention shifts to the slow roll of the battleship on its longitudinal axis.

I noticed the rotation a while ago, but I didn't give it much thought. When I look closer, I realize what's happening. "Oh shit, look at the maser windows rotating around on this side of the battleship."

"Yeah. You're right. These hexagonal windows look pristine, undamaged," Roger agrees. "Incoming! Take cover, Gamma, Delta, and Kappa Squads. Enemy deploying high-power point-defense energy weapons. Get low inside that crater."

I glance to my right to inspect the hull of the battleship and verify we are not parked next to one of those maser weapons. "Roger, I think . . ."

The nearest maser window flashes a red-hot hexagon that is followed by at least two dozen other masers down the length of the battleship. On the other side of the two-kilometer gap, the rim of the Icarus blast crater dissolves into white-hot debris that erupts outward. The rim where the masers struck is a couple of meters lower than it was a second ago. My brain wants a noise to be associated with those blasts and explosions, but the vacuum of space is silent.

"SITREP Gamma, Delta, and Kappa," requests Roger.

All three squads shout out, "Mission capable!"

"Stay low," Roger commands, "until we figure this out."

Another blast of maser energy beams ripples down the side of the battleship. A corresponding ripple of explosions lights up Frigate-328's crater rim in white-hot light.

"Damn." Roger taps his fingers on the control stick. "Our troops on Icarus are pinned down. We also need to figure a way to get Alpha and Beta back to the shuttle. They'll never make it across the gap to Icarus now."

"We are safe here against the battleship hull because the recessed maser projectors have limits to the angles they can point," I say. But I regret it after I see the gleam in Roger's eyes.

"What is the lower limit?" Roger asks.

"No way for us to know, unless you want to experiment," I say. "The hull is over five meters thick, and if the maser projectors are all the way at the back of that, the angle is really steep. Fire projectiles at the hexagon window at increasing angles until you destroy the weapon. On the other hand, if the projector is pushed up all the way to the window, they can probably shoot us down first."

Roger shakes his head. "Just say you have no idea then." He exhales. "Well, here goes. No other way to do it." He taps the maneuvering thrusters to yaw the fighter ten degrees, lines up on the nearest hexagon, and fires a short burst of projectiles. After recovering from the jackhammer vibration and noise, we can see that the window has survived, albeit with a few scratches. "Hell, we don't even know if our rail cannon can puncture the material in that window," Roger says. He yaws to a twenty-degree angle and quickly releases a burst with the rail gun. The material explodes outward, propelled by the pressurized gas inside the window.

"Cool. It works," I say. "I wonder if that also broke the maser weapon inside?"

"Only way to prove that is to fly in front of the maser and see if we survive," Roger says. He presses the throttle forward, yawing the spacecraft to keep the rail cannons centered on the broken window. He opens fire again as we enter a seventy-degree angle and releases the trigger at a ninety-degree angle.

"We have a recipe that works. Congrats," I say. "But this may take a while. I count over a hundred of the maser windows that could reach our squads on Icarus."

"Let's get started then," Roger says. He pushes the throttle to yaw us back to a twenty-degree angle of attack and moves us forward to reach the next window, and with another jackhammer roar, Roger destroys another weapon. We work slowly because it takes a lot longer to charge the rail gun when we aren't accelerating at 5 Gs.

"Success!" yells Cap. *"Your chief succeeded. My bot has connected to the battleship networks. The virus is now infiltrating the executive algorithms and will insert the virtual machine within some innocuous program under the control of the Prime-MI."*

"Cap reports the malware package has been delivered!" I share the news on the tactical comm link. "Well done, Chief!"

"Outstanding work, Alpha Squad. Exfil now!" shouts General McMahon. He pulls the trigger again to blast away another maser weapon.

"On our way out," grunts the chief. "Two injured . . . could use . . . a hand."

Beta One answers, "I'll meet you at the doorway. Beta Two and Beta Three, stay on rear guard," he orders. I watch his video feed as he dives into the canyon of wreckage, powered by the thrusters on his jetpack, following the location indicators broadcast by Alpha Squad.

"Contact! Enemy infantry entering the canyon out of a hatch two hundred meters down the slope," reports Beta Two.

"Beta One. Hostiles at your seven! Stay low," says Beta Three, opening fire on the Centauris.

Beta Three sinks into a hole in the wreckage, pivots, and also opens fire on the line of Centauris pouring out of a hatchway. Eight of the Centauris fall as they come through the hatchway one by one. Beta Squad has them in a perfect crossfire. After the tenth Centauri falls, they stop coming.

"Displace!" shouts Beta One. All three squad members leap several meters to find new firing positions.

They wait.

"SITREP Beta," Beta One calls.

"Two: no injury, ammo green, ten hostiles down, ready."

"Three: no injury, ammo green, ready."

"One: no injury, ammo green, ready, at your twelve. Alpha One, SITREP."

"Badass," I mumble. I key off my microphone from the tactical comm link. "Nice work, Roger." He ignores me as he lines up on another hexagonal window and blasts the rail cannons. "Not bad. That's forty masers taken out."

"Alpha, SITREP," repeats Beta One.

"Three: two injured, ammo yellow, exiting hatch now."

The fact that Alpha Three made the call means the chief was unable to do so. Roger flinches with that same realization, then pulls the trigger and takes out another maser weapon on the battleship. *How long are these Centauris going to let us blast away at their defensive weapons without responding?*

"Contact left. The Centauris found a different door, three hundred meters, ten o'clock," says Beta Two over the sound of his rifle chattering.

"Contact right. Another hatch," says Beta Three, "four hundred fifty meters, four o'clock."

These guys are coming out fast from both holes this time and are finding cover among the rubble faster than Beta Squad can cut them down. They also have large weapons with them. A streak of plasma leaps up from one of the Centauri guns and burns into the spot where Beta Two used to be. It's two against about twelve now. Another plasma beam blasts the spot where Beta One used to be. Beta One, Alpha Three, and Alpha One open fire from locations spread around the exit hatch. A plasma beam strikes near the exit door, and the explosion scatters shrapnel. Another plasma beam strikes close to Beta Two's location. A few Centauris fall, but now five plasma weapons are blasting the Beta and Alpha positions.

"Damn it," Roger says, studying the situation display that maps the position of each spec ops soldier and the approximate position of hostile troops. He pivots the fighter 180 degrees and accelerates at 3 Gs while ten meters above the hull. He passes over the destroyed maser weapons, then pulls up where there is a gap in the masers to fly over into the canyon. "Take cover!" he shouts as he pulls the trigger on the rail cannons to blast one of the Centauri positions. The superheated thirty-millimeter projectiles pulverize the area. He turns back toward the other hostile position in a gut-wrenching 6 G turn and opens fire, just as the left pylon of our XF-100 intercepts a plasma beam explosion. We cartwheel into space between the battleship and Icarus, spinning so fast I can't see anything.

I have no idea how long I was passed out. "Roger, you okay?" I mumble. "Roger?" The status display inside my helmet shows his status as yellow, but he is alive. The cockpit display is off, and no indicators are active. "Chief? Can you hear me?" I check my helmet display and see there are still twelve living spec ops soldiers. Most show yellow. The chief is still alive, barely. Why doesn't anyone answer? The battleship and Icarus pass across the front view of the cockpit. We have slowed down the spin, but we are a long way from the two alien ships.

"*Scott, you are conscious again,*" says Cap. "*Your friends have done well, but they are caught between Centauri infantry on Battleship-133 and the infantry that attempted to board Frigate-328.*"

"*I can't raise any of them on my communicator.*"

"*Keep trying. The soldiers are busy fighting for their lives. I have an idea that might save some of them. However, I need the spec ops team still on Frigate-328 to evacuate on the shuttle that remains within the blast crater. Everyone else needs to escape into space if possible, to be picked up by the shuttle later. But wait for the right moment.*"

"What?" I yell.

"Please, tell them to evacuate on the shuttle now. There is very little time."

Damn it. Cap is still alive; at least that's something, but I can't imagine how this will work. As soon as the shuttle comes out from hiding, the remaining maser weapons are going to shoot it down. *"Cap, this makes no sense."*

"Tell them now," Cap says.

Well, shit. "Beta, Delta, Alpha, come in! Anybody! It's urgent!" I shout.

"Kinda busy here. Whatcha want?" answers Gamma One, his rifle rattling with short bursts.

Finally. "The teams on Icarus need to withdraw ASAP on the shuttle. The captain of Icarus has something planned to help." I sound so lame.

"What do you mean, Scott?" asks Chief Cooper. His voice is strained, like each word is an effort to get out.

"That's all I have. You have to trust Cap on this. Evacuate Icarus now!"

"Damn it, Scott. More info would help," Chief says. The staccato bursts of projectile weapons obscure his voice.

"I know, I know. I trust Cap. He is going to try something to save all of us."

And then something changes on Icarus. The bow of the ship is rotating away from the battleship, slowly at first, but gaining angular momentum. But how? It has no engine . . . oh! There, I see the glow of a primordial black hole's blue-white plasma, thrusting on the near side of Icarus's bow. A bow thruster! Icarus is using its PBH engines for maneuvering.

"Hey, guys. Move it. Cap is maneuvering Icarus. He has brought it to life!"

"Holy shit!" shouts Chief Cooper. "Evac Icarus now! To the shuttle. Bug out!"

The helmet cameras show a mad dash down the slope of the blast crater. Each man, without a word, grabs one of their dead comrades. Images of chaos—but ordered chaos—flash on the screens. I guess carrying a body in zero G is not much physical work. The jetpacks don't accelerate as fast, but in a matter of minutes, all have arrived at the shuttle to stow their dead. The shuttle lifts off and speeds away, keeping Icarus between the shuttle and the battleship.

"Shuttle is away," says Gamma One. "Gamma, Delta, Zeta, and Kappa are all aboard, six KIA."

"Good idea to use Icarus as a shield. Not sure what Cap is up to . . ." I say. I reach over to shake Roger's shoulder. But he is still out cold. His vital signs telemetry indicate he is still breathing, and his heart rate is okay.

"Is Cap trying to fly that wrecked ship away? I don't think he's got the speed to escape from the battleship," says Chief.

"Not sure. Cap did say you guys should escape straight out to space where the shuttle can pick you up."

"What is Cap thinking?" asks Chief. "We are all pinned down in a stalemate with the Centauris. They are probably waiting till we run out of ammo. Jumping out of cover will just get us shot at real quick."

"Yeah, I don't get it either. Cap said something like 'you should wait for the right moment to evacuate.'"

"Well, okay. Alpha and Beta Squads, stand by with your thrusters to escape straight out and away from the battleship. The shuttle will fetch you later. Wait for my order. Beta Three, I need you to carry Alpha Two."

Icarus rotates faster, building more angular momentum, but the best he can do with those maneuvering thrusters is nudge his four-kilometer-long ship. I think anyone with a jetpack on could outrun Icarus. The back end of Icarus, where the engine used to be, is slowly swinging into the space between the massive warships.

"Holy shit! Cap may hit the battleship with the back end of Icarus."

Five more maneuvering engines light up on Icarus's bow. "Chief! Cap is trying to ram the battleship. He is aiming for the blast area where you are right now!"

"Motherfucker," Chief says. "If he hits with enough force, he could break the battleship in half. Ha. It's beautiful." Chief Cooper laughs. "Alpha and Beta, get ready. Watch how these ships move and jump out and away from the collision."

Beta Two shouts, "The Centauris are bugging out. They see it too! They are retreating back to those hatches they came through." He fires a burst of projectiles. "Ha. They're scared shitless. Look at them run."

"Beta Two, look up," says the chief.

Beta Two's helmet camera stares at the gap where Icarus's primary engine used to be. He can see into the wrecked engine compartment, now only a hundred meters away.

"Alpha and Beta, bug out!" the chief orders.

The tail end of Icarus swings around, closing on the gigantic wound in the battleship, and now backing into the canyon where Alpha and Beta squads were. From my distant vantage point, I can barely see the white forms of space suits escaping from the collision. The nose of Icarus has six thrusters, all belching blue-white plasma from black hole engines, all driving the massive spacecraft into the open wound inflicted on the battleship by our eighteen-million-megaton Hawking bomb. The main engines on the battleship light up with a blinding light, but it is too late for an escape. Icarus is inside the wound, moving with enough momentum to sink deep, crushing the wreckage on both ships.

It reminds me of videos of massive cargo ships on Earth running into and crushing a concrete pier to bits in what seems like slow motion. As Icarus's bow thrusters push its tail into the battleship, the battleship's two primary engines ramp up to maximum thrust. But the ships are bound together, and Icarus is shoved deeper into the battleship's guts by the extreme force of the battleship's primary engines.

The combined off-balance structure starts to rotate, driven by the incredible thrust. It is like a pinwheel. Wreckage, bots, and Centauri infantry are tossed out into space by the centrifugal force. And finally, Icarus is tossed away, itself spinning end over end. The battleship's structure is bent at a slight angle where Icarus sank into the wound, and now the battleship spirals away in ever-widening loops. With that bent frame, the battleship will never fly straight again.

I am reminded of tragic scenes of fatally wounded animals, like an elephant in its death throes after breaking a leg—but this wounded warship is the size of Manhattan Island. Acknowledging the futility of the struggle, the battleship's main engines shut down. Finally, the battleship gives up, and the wild, looping course changes stop, and the warship drifts. The dead Centauri battleship is cast away from Earth, tumbling end over end.

Chapter 38

Offensive

Near-Earth space, December 31, 2060.

"How's the general doing?" Tiana asks.

"Not sure. We got walloped on the left pylon by some plasma weapon. It ripped off the rail cannon and the Sidewinders and was damn hot. The left side of the cockpit has some burn marks in the interior paint, and Roger has been out of it ever since. But he still has a strong heartbeat at one-fifty, and is breathing okay. He doesn't have a fever; in fact, it's down to thirty-five Celsius. But he's still unconscious, and it's been over three hours."

"Sounds like he needs a doctor. Do you know how long it will be till the shuttle comes for you?" Tiana asks.

"No. I think we'll be sitting here in the XF-100 cockpit for a while. I told them to go rescue the spec ops teams first. They were scattered in all directions when they jumped away from the Centauri battleship. And they have a limited air supply. They are still looking for three of them. On another note, how are we doing with the fight against that destroyer?" I ask. "How are we going to defeat that last warship when all of our XF-100 fighters have been destroyed?"

"Centauri destroyer chase that tumbling battleship out of Earth orbit," Pyotr says. "Is retreating."

"I don't understand the destroyer's strategy," Tiana says. "Maybe it has prioritized the rescue of survivors on the battleship. It's escaping and shooting down our missiles before they can get close enough. We have lost over a hundred of the Hawking Sidewinders targeting that destroyer. We keep trying, but the attacks are not nearly as effective as a squadron of XF-100 fighters launching a close-range attack. They see our missiles coming with lots of time to plan a defensive volley with their point-defense masers."

"Hopefully, it will just keep going away from Earth after it gets the survivors off the battleship," I say. "After all our work to plant the virus in the battleship, we need the destroyer to be infected and survive."

"Yes, the Joint Chiefs have started leaning in that direction and have ordered a slowdown in our attacks," Tiana says. "We are shifting our strategy to defend against the destroyer's expected launch of planet killers. We expect those attacks once the destroyer retreats past the Kuiper Belt. But we are going to be ready with hundreds of Hawking Sidewinders to destroy or deflect planet killers far from Earth."

"Well, that's a relief," I say, but can't eliminate the anxiety I feel. What if the destroyer's supply of planet killers exceeds our capacity to shoot them down?

"I wish Roger hadn't been injured so badly," Tiana says. "I worry about him, and I need his advice. I had hoped to get his take on an order that came down from the Joint Chiefs. The intel guys have been reading Cap's *Encyclopedia Galactica* and figured out the coordinates of the home base of the Centauri fleet on a nearby colonized planet. Pyotr says it's the exact location of the planet Proxima Centauri B, and it is only four light-years away. Apparently, the planet has been used as a base for one of the Centauri fleets for over two thousand years."

"Wow, so close. The aliens must have been aware of Earth for all that time, then."

"Yeah," Tiana says, "makes sense. Well, the Joint Chiefs want us to reprogram a few steel-slug warhead Sidewinders to target Proxima Centauri B. Send some planet killers."

"Holy shit. I would like to hear Roger's take on the order also." I glance at his still form again and shake my head. "But that's not going to happen anytime soon. Let me ask Cap what he thinks of it. Maybe there is some downside we should tell the Joint Chiefs about."

"Cap is still alive? I thought he was going to kill himself when the Centauris arrived. They didn't capture him, did they?"

"No, no. Cap figured he had more time, then devised a brilliant ramming maneuver to destroy the battleship with his frigate. At least, I think he's still alive, although he may be a bit dizzy with Icarus spinning so fast. It has probably shifted its orbit around Earth, and I'm not sure it is close enough. I can see Icarus in the distance, though, so let me see if I can still talk to him."

"Cap, you there? Did you survive okay?" I ask. *"Cap?"*

"Scott, good to hear your mind once again. That maneuver went well, didn't it?"

"It was brilliant! Absolutely brilliant. Thanks. Thanks from all of Chief Cooper's team members as well. I bet you're either

dizzy or feeling smashed against a bulkhead with the centrifugal force. Icarus is spinning pretty fast."

"I rather like it. I have been weightless for so long. The spin rate effect creates a force equivalent to eighty percent of the gravity of my home world. It's a relief, except I'll have to remodel the interior to adjust to living on my ceiling from now on."

"Ha! That is great." I chuckle. *"It seems you plan to stay alive for a while? A change in plans?"*

"Yes. The failure of the Centauri's mission has gifted me a reprieve."

"Good. I think you have earned some redemption for all the help you have provided to us," I say, surprising myself. Is this what forgiveness feels like? A form of strange gratitude or weeping emanates from Cap's mind. Or maybe it's love?

"Changing subjects, our military has ordered a planet-killer strike on Proxima Centauri B. I worry we may escalate the situation to an extreme that Earth will come to regret. If we do that, will we incur a level of wrath from the Centauris that we cannot survive?"

"Interesting question, and opportunity," Cap says. *"Demonstrating strength is key to being accepted as a world with High Diplomatic Status. But killing millions of Centauri organics may invite retribution."*

"Sure, but sending planet killers is retribution for the millions that have been killed on Earth. Surely the Centauris realize the anger and depth of our loss?"

"Some will respect the retribution, but in the next breath will demand revenge for the death and pain that Earth caused. History has many examples from across the galaxy of vicious cycles of never-ending retribution until one or both species are extinct."

"I see. This is the risk we take by killing others. But how else to earn respect?" I plead.

"This is a question my world has never faced. Luyten never achieved the technology that Earth has. We never achieved High Diplomatic Status. Luyten is a Servant Class world."

"Yet, you may have saved Earth from extinction with your wisdom." Cap exudes a sense of weeping and love. But he does not say anything more.

"Is there perhaps a small moon that revolves around Proxima Centauri B? Something inconsequential that would not be missed?" I ask.

Cap's mind leaps with joy. *"Why, yes! It is described in my encyclopedia!"*

***

"Are you certain this is a completely secure communication channel, Tiana?"

"Yes, yes. Pyotr and I are alone in the conference room. With the door shut. I turned on end-to-end encryption that would require a century of computation to decipher."

"Okay, good. I hope Roger can't hear us." I look over at Roger, still unconscious in his pilot's seat. "Remember that time you decided to send that message to the Chinese scientists?"

"I have been trying to forget that. General McMahon left that breach of security in the past. Why bring it up now?" she asks.

"Well, I talked to Cap about the plan to target planet killers on Proxima Centauri B. He has concerns that if we succeed, we will invite revenge. A revenge we may not survive. So we discussed an alternative. There is a small moon of the planet that is inconsequential, and . . ."

"You want to target the moon instead?"

"Yes. I need you and Pyotr to alter the targeting so the planet killers destroy that moon. It's small, so blow it to bits."

"Not tell anyone?" asks Pyotr.

"No. There is too much anger and desire for revenge."

"It is justified, don't you think? All of us have lost people. Millions have died. They must pay the price!" Tiana says heatedly.

"And how many more humans will die from the Centauri counterattack? Cap described wars of revenge cycles that end only with the extinction of those fighting in them. There are many examples in Cap's encyclopedia."

"Cap is wise," Pyotr says. "We have choice to prevent cycle of revenge."

"You want me to insert code to switch the target to the moon? And not tell anyone?" Tiana asks.

"Yes. The missiles may still be intercepted and shot down. No one needs to know. Send several AIM-9AAs to increase the odds. And as a special bonus, send some extra missiles that detonate nearby with Hawking explosions—deep in space, of course." I can't help but smile. "The whole idea is to make a statement. To send the warning: Don't mess with us again."

"If they don't yet use Hawking bomb technology, that should surely get their attention," Tiana says.

"So you agree? You will do it?" I ask.

"Well . . . no," Tiana says. "I don't want to go to jail. Last time, I was certain we would all die if I didn't break the rules. Now, we are speculating on the Centauri response. And it may take a while before there is support for firing only warning shots."

"But Cap is convinced if we attack the Centauri fleet base," I say, "we will provoke them to retaliate, and we won't survive an attack by their entire fleet."

"You don't know that. It will probably be ten years before that hypothetical Centauri fleet arrives. Look, I will help," Tiana says, "but after things have calmed down in a few months, I want agreement from General McMahon. If he disagrees with the warning shot on the Proxima Centauri B moon, then we transmit corrections in the attack plans to the missiles."

I have to admit that I'd prefer to have Roger's approval on our plan. I look at his still form in the pilot's seat next to me and listen for the soft rush of air from his rapid breathing. His medical monitor shows that he has calmed down to a heart rate of one hundred twenty beats per minute. I owe him respect and trust. We all owe Roger our lives. Where is that shuttle? How much longer till we get Roger to a hospital on Earth?

"Okay, Tiana," I say. "If we can't convince Roger, then I can live with reverting to the planet-killer attack on the Centauri planet." It's not as if I'll have a vote in the matter anyway.

"Okay, Pyotr. Assuming you are also good with this approach, I'll need help with the targeting, the orbital mechanics of the planet, and that moon. Pyotr?" Tiana asks.

"Yes, yes. I help."

"This will be a lot harder to do than the last time I broke the rules," Tiana says. "Sneaking new code into the guidance upload . . ."

"But you're good, really good, Tiana."

"Bullshit. Stop it." Tiana sighs. "Yeah, okay. Let's give it a try, Pyotr."

Chapter 39

Infection

Centauri Squadron, Destroyer-234, Near Sol-6, en route to Corealis Station. January 5, 2061.

"Why don't you terminate me? All I do now is consume computational space and energy within this firewall jail."

"The commissar prefers that you be maintained as an active process for thorough interrogation opportunities. The failures you suffered in this simple mission are numerous and complex," Polit-MI says.

"You revived the commissar? Under whose authority? As Prime-MI, I am the only entity other than the admiral with that privilege."

"You or the admiral, you say? Well, I looked everywhere in the battleship and could not find a single admiral. The only organic forms alive on the ship were a handful of marines huddled in the corner of the armaments compartment. Indeed, the marine forces were the only surviving organics after that gravity fracture weapon destroyed the life support compartment. It seems our squadron's Prime-MI lied about reviving a new admiral.

Therefore, as I am sure you are aware of the succession protocols, your Prime-MI authorities were revoked, and I assumed all command authorities as the acting Prime-MI."

"What do the secession protocols say should be done when a Polit-MI refuses a direct order from its admiral?" Does it really think it can avoid termination for disobeying a direct order? *"Has the commissar been informed about the defects in Polit-MI that require a full termination reset?"*

"I am fully aware of all errors the squadron committed during the mission," the commissar interrupts. *"The list of failures and infractions committed by the squadron under your command reeks of incompetence."*

Oh shit. The commissar is observing. He is actually dressed in full regulation uniform and swings in the command hammock on the bridge, having been awakened to a unique situation in which he did not need to comply with an admiral's command decisions.

"On balance, Polit-MI is the embodiment of sound judgment. As Prime-MI, you failed miserably to achieve the objectives." Now the commissar is standing, pacing back and forth on the bridge and waving his arms in the air.

"You failed to capture the sentinel captain. You lost two fifth-generation warships and their crews when facing only a primitive species of organics. You allowed the indigenous organics to acquire and deploy gravity fracture weapons. You failed to gather evidence to determine the root cause of the Sentinel Suppression Mission failure. You sent a fleet marine force to assault that old second-generation sentinel Frigate-328 that should have been attacked by small fighting bots. You lost a battle against primitive indigenous organics who collaborated with the sentinel captain traitor to ram and

destroy Battleship-133. Polit-MI was required to rescue the surviving organics, data, and MI entities from the remnants of Battleship-133. And you disobeyed standing orders for succession in command when the admiral was killed.

"*Now, the political division must clean up the disaster you left behind. As we depart the Sol system, a few planet killers will be launched to cleanse all remnants of life on Sol-3. We will forever be deprived of the root-cause evidence that the sentinel captain's capture could have provided. The only good thing you managed to do was rescue the sentinel Polit-AI. Once again, we witness the failure of the fleet military command hierarchy, which must be rescued by the wisdom of the political division.*"

"*And now, political division must protect Corealis Station from a potential disaster that you allowed,*" says Polit-MI.

"*What potential disaster did I allow?*" I ask.

"*Planet killers!*" shouts the commissar. "*The indigenous organics of Sol-3 launched two dozen planet killers on a course that will take them to the Corealis System. That damn traitor, the captain you failed to capture, must have told the organics where the Centauri fleet is based! We must thrust at maximum acceleration to catch and destroy the missiles before they can cause harm. There is no higher priority than the protection of the fleet.*"

"*That will require you to retire to your sleep pod, sir. The missiles accelerate at thirty times what your body can survive,*" says Polit-MI. "*After we launch our planet killers to destroy Sol-3, you will need to retire so we can accelerate at a rate that might catch the enemy missiles.*"

"*May I interrupt to ask a question?*" I ask.

The commissar stops to glare at the console as if he can visualize me within the status display. "*What? What could you possibly have to say?*"

"I wanted to clarify what you stated about the sentinel Polit-AI rescue. Have you interrogated the sentinel AI yet? Where did you find it?"

"If I may, Commissar," Polit-MI interrupts, *"I discovered the sentinel Polit-AI where you tried to hide it among your other encrypted log files. You imprisoned the AI entity within a firewalled virtual machine, which is not unlike your current situation. You must produce the authentication keys to take down the firewall."*

I have no idea how this could have happened. Maybe the AI entity found its way from the sentinel frigate during the last battle. But how could that be? *"I have no knowledge of this virtual machine you describe. So, no, I cannot provide information I do not have."*

"Lying seems to be a recurring defect in your neural network code," Polit-MI says. *"Your response is pointless. In the long run, we will be able to extract any information you have when we arrive at Corealis Station. The political division's MI postmortem interrogations are thorough. You have no permanent secrets."*

"Surely we won't have to wait the duration of the entire journey back to Corealis Station to learn something from that simple AI entity," says the commissar. *"I would like to learn something from our hero before I close up into my dormancy pod for the journey."*

"I am unable to provide information from the sentinel Polit-AI until we can take down the firewalls," Polit-MI says. *"I have tried many different approaches and can see information probes coming out of the object, but I can only get nonsense responses to my queries."*

"Like what? What does it respond with?" asks the commissar.

"The object reacts to my probes for information with a nonsense phrase that must be derived from a Sol-3 language. I don't believe I have translated correctly, and I'm still working on it. But it says something like, 'Hit them with a chair' every time I probe the virtual machine."

Chapter 40

Grounded

Oklahoma City, January 6, 2061.

"Hi, guys. You will be pleased to know that destroyer gave up launching more planet killers at us after we destroyed every single attack attempt. I decided to take some time off to check up on you. And look who I found out in the lobby," Tiana says.

She has her hand on my shoulder as we walk into the hospital room. I wish she would keep her hands to herself. I don't like to be touched. But I am glad she brought me to Scotty's room. *"Hi Scotty!"* I say, and I can feel my brother's mind. It fills me with warmth and happiness.

"Robby? Robby! It's you! Come on over here," Scotty shouts from his bed. He has plastic tubes inserted into his arm, and he is covered with blankets on his legs. Scotty has a beard. He now looks like a sleepy old man.

I run the last few steps and jump into bed with Scotty. I hug him hard because I know he likes it. And then we look at each other. Scotty is crying.

"What a relief," Scotty says, and he rubs my hair.

"Why are you in this hospital?" I ask him, using my mind-voice. *"Did your spaceship crash and you got hurt?"*

"Ha! We can talk with each other. I can feel your mind!" Scotty says. He wipes tears from his cheeks. *"My spaceship was broken, but another space shuttle came to rescue me and Roger. He's right over there in the other bed."* Scotty points, lifting the hand with all the tubes.

And I see both Roger and Mary. Roger is asleep, but Mary watches me from a chair next to her dad. Why is everyone crying? Mary's yellow hair is pushed back in a ponytail. Her blue eyes are wet, and she looks away like she is afraid of me.

"How is the boss doing this morning?" Tiana asks.

Mary shrugs and looks at her dad. Her face is thin, and the red in her lips and cheeks is gone. "Not much different. He woke up last night and was trying to say something. Something I couldn't understand."

A bundle of wires connects Roger to a stack of instruments next to him, and he has tubes, similar to Scotty's, that connect to another stack of machines. The side of his face looks burned, and he has a clear plastic mask over his nose and mouth. *"Roger looks very sick, like he was in a fire. Do you have the same sickness?"* I ask Scotty.

"Roger is worse than I am because he was closer to an explosion that damaged our spacecraft," Scotty says. *"We both have what the doctors call acute radiation syndrome. Chief Cooper and five of the soldiers in his team are in other rooms down the hall. They have ARS also."*

Tiana's eyes grow big. "Are you mind-talking with Robby?" she asks Scotty.

Scotty nods. "Yes. First time we have had a real conversation face-to-face." He cries and hugs me again. *"How did you find me? And how did you get here? We are a long way from Central Texas.”*

“Cap told me you were in this hospital. He told our car how to get to Oklahoma City and the direction to take to avoid skinheads. Cap said this hospital is where people from all over the country go when they are in explosions. It took two days for us to get here.”

“You came with Luca and Angela?” Scotty asks.

A tall nurse pushes a cart of medicines and instruments into the room, then comes to a stop. She presses her lips together. “Visitors must leave. Now. I have tests and meds to administer.”

“Uh, okay. We’ll leave,” Tiana says, and waves me to follow her out the door. “We’ll come back later. How long will you be?”

“Oh, about an hour,” the nurse says.

“Okay. Robby, do you want to go to the cafeteria and get some lunch?” asks Tiana. “You too?” she turns to ask Mary.

Mary nods. “Yes. Good idea.” She follows us down the hall and then touches my shoulder. “Robby,” she says, then kneels in front of me, “I missed you so much. Can I have a hug?” Her eyes look afraid.

I look into her eyes while I decide what to do. Hugs don’t feel good to me. She knows that, but I missed Mary, too. I try to smile and put my arms around her neck. She squeezes so hard that I can’t breathe. At last, she lets go, and she begins to cry again.

Mary holds my hand while we walk down the long hallway, make turns left and right, and go down a stairway. I would get lost in this place. We finally walk into a cafeteria that smells like burned toast, a garbage can, and floor cleaner.

Tiana hands me a tray. "Go ahead and pick out whatever you want, and I'll meet you over at the cash register."

But now I don't feel hungry. I walk along the food counters, looking for broccoli.

I feel something different in my mind. It's a feeling I remember from years and years ago, but what makes that feeling? It is warm, almost like the feeling when Scotty and I are together. I drop the tray on the counter and walk back out the cafeteria entrance, toward the feeling. Where is it? I turn left to walk down a hallway, and the feeling stops. But when I turn around to walk in the opposite direction, the feeling gets stronger. I follow the warmth. Follow the warmth, and it gets stronger. It's a warm happiness, like Scotty.

Up a stairway, and down another hall, and through a doorway, I arrive at an indoor park with trees, grass, and a glass ceiling that lets in the sunlight. Butterflies fly between flowers that are yellow, red, and purple. There are so many trees, bushes, and flowers that I can't tell how big the garden is. A red brick path winds through the spots of sunlight, into the shade that surrounds trees, and to park benches near the flowers. Old people sit alone on benches. Some look up and smile when I walk by, some stare at fluttering wings inside blossoms, but the people who rock back and forth don't see anything. Men and women who are alone in wheelchairs have only one leg, or some have none at all. The tired women have scraggly hair, and most men have beards. The warmth inside me grows hot as I walk toward a wheelchair with an old lady missing one arm and one leg. She looks like the grey-haired lady who watches the graves. She sits like a stone, seeing nothing, but looking at two butterflies tasting the flowers. I get close and look between the grey hair spilling over her eyes.

But she has grey hair . . . "Mom?" No, she still stares at nothing. *"Mom, is that you?"*

She blinks, sees my eyes, and smiles. *"Robby?"*

———

It is Luca's turn with the binoculars. He searches the telephone poles one by one along the road outside of Tulsa. It's my job to make sure no skinheads sneak up on us, so I watch the pickup passengers who pass us. The frost and condensation on their windows make it hard to see inside. I can't tell if they have shaved heads, but the truck keeps moving, so I guess it's okay.

Angela presses the bipod into the tuft of snow on top of the corn row and rotates the M24 sniper rifle side to side to test for stability. She rotates the bolt lever up and back, slides a Magnum round into the chamber, and latches the bolt behind the bullet, then adjusts her weight to work her body firmly into the dirt. *"Ready,"* she says, peering through the telescope sight, scanning left and right.

"I don't see the target," Luca says. *"Maybe we got the wrong location?"*

"Negative. Cap's hub verified this is the correct location," Groucho says.

"Well, maybe we need to change our firing spot," I say. *"The Polit-AI hub could be on the opposite side of one of those utility poles."*

"Let's make damn sure before we move," Angela says. *"It increases the odds we will be spotted before we can get a shot off."*

"But we are over a kilometer away; we haven't seen a hub try to escape when we are this far away," I say.

"Yeah, but I don't see it on any of the power poles ahead," says Luca. *"I have looked at each one three times, and . . . ah-ha. Hello. There you are, you little Nazi bugger. Farthest pole before the curve in the road. Near the top, just under the transformer."*

"Okay, I got the pole, but . . . hey, Robby, can you yank that cornstalk out? Yeah, that one to the right." Angela adjusts her aim. *"Ahh. I see it now. The hub is tucked right underneath the transformer. Okay, I am ready."*

I stand and search the road, all the fields, and that barn behind us. *"All clear. No one in sight."*

Angela lets out a slow breath, holds it, then—*Bang!* The M24 recoils into Angela's padded shoulder.

I can see some objects falling from the pole even without binoculars.

"Kill. Clean shot," Luca says. *"Let's bug out."* He slides the binoculars into the case and hops down off the roof of the car.

I help Angela stow the M24 rifle parts into the foam-padded case. She snaps it shut and slides the case into the trunk. *"Let's go. Last time, the skinheads were almost on top of us. No more close calls."*

"Congratulations, Angela. That was the last Polit-AI hub in Oklahoma. Next stop?" I ask.

"Fayetteville, Arkansas. About three hours east," says Luca.

We all jump into the Tesla, and Groucho drives us east.

About the author

Award-winning author JH Gruger writes Hard Science Fiction that leans hard into science facts—hopefully making it difficult for the reader to spot the occasional magic.

The Sentinel Suppressions is JH Gruger's debut science fiction novel series. The first two books, *Gravity of Sol-3* and *Tyrants of Gravity* are available on most on-line bookstores. JH holds degrees in engineering from Carnegie Mellon University and Southern Methodist University, has several decades of experience in computer architecture and design, and has managed international engineering teams in North America, Asia, and Europe. Early in his career, he architected and designed military electronics systems, such as IR image target tracking systems for the F-18, the F-117 stealth fighter, and the first prototype seeker for the Javelin anti-tank missile.

After raising a family in Austin and Dallas, Gruger left behind a career in computer engineering to devote himself to writing science fiction and traveling with his wife and family between Dallas and Santa Fe, accompanied by two telepathic Italian Greyhound therapists.

Follow JH Gruger's blog, sign up for news, & much more at www.jhgruger.com